SOLDIER OF FORTUNE

Soldier of Fortune

Ernest K. Gann

WILLIAM SLOANE ASSOCIATES, INC., Publishers
NEW YORK

FOR RUDY WITH THANKS FOR SO MUCH

Hong Kong is a pore upon the body of Asia.

Through this minute vent, the immense carcass of China still breathes feebly of the non-Communist world.

From the sea, the region known generally as Hong Kong becomes an archipelago of humps, protruding from the greenish-brown water. And then there is a projection of the Chinese mainland known as the Peninsula, which rumbles away from the sea in a series of near barren hills for almost fifteen miles—until it becomes China. The Peninsula is almost forty miles in length if you count all the islands which in turn surround it, and the British call it the "New Territories." It is populated by Chinese farmers and fishermen and forty thousand British soldiers who sweat until their green uniforms are splotched with black, and swear like all soldiers, and are homesick like all soldiers, and go into Hong Kong to pound the welcome pavement with their hard-heeled boots whenever their meager pay will permit.

At the end of the Peninsula, exactly facing Hong Kong, stands the newer city of Kowloon. It is almost entirely flat and, if it were not bursting with refugees from the mainland, might have remained a drowsy suburb of the city across the harbor. But some place had to be found for over two million people where only six hundred thousand would normally be, and so, many of the refugees discovered themselves in Kowloon. Some of these people came all the way from Peking and were miserably hot and found they were unable to speak Cantonese which was bad for business and worse for face, and since both were the breath of life to any Chinese, they sometimes went back to Peking.

Some came down from Shanghai and if they had been quick enough to get their money out, they built villas on the Hong Kong hills.

People from Shanghai almost never went back to Shanghai.

Those who came down from Canton were on relatively familiar ground. Sometimes, discouraged with the frantic business of trying to live off each other, a few of them went back to Canton.

The interchange was easy. A railway departed from the tip of the Peninsula and proceeded on meticulous schedule to the British Border. After a brief inspection, the railway continued on to Canton and that was all there was to it—except that those who chose to return after a sojourn in the British Colony were seldom, if ever, heard from again.

The forty thousand British troops, the million-odd refugees, the American businessmen and the British businessmen, the hawkers in the streets and the shopkeepers in the shade, the dance-hall girls, the few remaining Pukka-sahibs, the smart police, and the merchant seamen of every nation in the Kowloon Hotel bar, the rag-tag remnants of Chiang's betrayed army, the sprinkling of white Russians, Parsees, Sikhs, French and Dutch, the coolies grunting on the docks, the prostitutes in their sampans on Shanghai-Gai or their rooms off Nathan Road, the Jesuit priests, the child beggars, and the high-necked matrons sipping tea in the Gloucester House, the thieves and pimps and few bewildered tourists, the compradores in the godowns and the amahs in Government House, even the pitiful women who collected night soil, existed on tolerance.

For the might of China brooded always just beyond the mountains and whenever her newest conquerors decided this fingernail hold on the shelf of their continent was no longer expedient or might be interpreted as a loss of face, they could dispossess it in a matter of hours.

Everyone knew this including the British, who could not afford to admit it.

1

The sun was already screaming hatred at the hills when the *Pioneer Mail* slipped through Sulphur Channel and entered the harbor of Hong Kong. Because it was cooler, and because they were convinced they had seen everything in the world, a few of the passengers stood on the north side of the vessel and stared thoughtfully at the submarine net which stretched from Green Island toward the distant blue-iron mountains of China. The passengers on the cooler side were as one person—they leaned against the rail and their bodies assumed almost identical postures of exhaustion. The men wore white suits which were already wrinkled in the same places. They occasionally patted at their brows with the same tired gestures and their women, whose faces were vacant and almost entirely bloodless, smoked continuously.

As the *Pioneer Mail* penetrated further into the main harbor the vibration which had enlivened her all the way from Kobe eased, and the parade of junks past her steel sides began. But the people on the cool side ignored the junks. They looked through and beyond them. When they spoke, which was seldom, the melody of their words was clipped and monotonous and the words were few. It was like a person talking to himself, mercilessly prodding a worn-out mind to final speculation. Anything that might be said had already been said a thousand times and so even the provoking became an amenity, a mere series of sounds which failed to break their mutual trance.

The people who stood on the cool side of the *Pioneer Mail* were the old China hands and they were thinking of the past—for without the past they were dead.

On the hot side the sun stabbed straight along the short promenade deck. The passengers who suffered the sun did so because they were unable to resist the spectacle of Hong Kong. Those who had seen the city before pointed at the steep hills and asked all who would listen if they had ever seen anything so beautiful. There was no setting like Hong Kong's—you might mention Rio or San Francisco or Sydney in the same conversation, but most certainly not in the same breath with Hong Kong. See how the hills surrounding the harbor form a perfect bastion against the sea. Hong Kong was the most efficient port in the world. There was labor and energy and best of all there was stability.

You could thank the British for stability . . . the British knew how to run a colony . . . everyone, even the Chinese sought the protection of the British. Hong Kong might be the last important British colony in the Far East, but it revived the hopes of every Englishman who had lost hope. It was all nonsense about the Empire coming apart at the seams. There had been some frightful bungling, of course, but things would come round. You had only to wait and Asia would regain her senses. The British would muddle through as they had done for centuries if only the Americans would mind their own bloody business.

The *Pioneer Mail's* engine-room telegraph tinkled three times and the vibration ceased entirely. A sampan, sculled furiously by two men, a woman and a little boy, took her mooring line to Buoy A-4 in the Central Fairway. The passengers on the hot side could now watch the heart of the city gasping in the sun and the vision held them tight against the rail in spite of their discomfort. For the city began like a proscenium only a few hundred yards away.

There were first the junks and sampans, so crowded together and intermixed and alive with activity and movement it was difficult to separate them at all; then Connaught Road which passed just beyond the junks as if to hold back their rude bustle from the imposing business buildings which marked the face of the city. Between the buildings there were narrow slashes into which the sun had yet to penetrate and these rose straight up against the hills, twisting off occasionally to reveal themselves as streets solid with people. A pall of smoke from the morning cooking fires hung over the Chinese sections of West Point and Wanchai, but between them, in the area known as Victoria, the air was clear.

About halfway up the hills, the streets and masses of buildings became spotted with vegetation; then very suddenly, as if the city lacked the energy for further ascent, there were only a few scattered villas and apartment buildings. These were perched along the tops of minor hills and in ravines, and from the deck of the *Pioneer Mail* it was impossible to discover how anyone could reach them.

One man stood back from the rail far enough so that the overhanging boat deck protected all of his body except his fat legs from the sun. He wore shorts and matching white stockings which reached nearly to his knees. Tufts of black hair protruded from the open neck of his shirt, but the rest of his keg-like body was entirely free of shadow. He had a scalded look, as a pig ready for slaughter, and his small pale-blue eyes made a perfectly harmonious color combination with the pink of his skin. He was not looking at Hong Kong. His entire attention was fixed upon the woman who stood quietly at the rail. He followed her slightest movement—when she raised her hand to shade her eyes against the sun, his eyes followed the exact arc of her wrist and came to rest simultaneously. He looked at her legs again—powerful legs, peasant-like, yet so well formed that they were without heaviness, and since he considered himself a connoisseur of legs, the rediscovery pleased him so much he found it necessary to wipe the sudden moisture from his lips with a fat finger. Then, after what seemed like a lifetime of waiting, his patience was rewarded.

The woman turned slightly; the brilliant sun sliced through her light dress outlining her figure from the waist down. She held the position only a moment, but he was compelled to wipe his lips again. Watching her now, content for the moment that her back was turned, he relived their first meeting and scolded himself for being overhasty.

From the same position in which he now stood, he had watched her board the *Pioneer Mail* at Kobe and he had thought instantly that the voyage down to Hong Kong was not going to be nearly as dull as he had anticipated. The flash of gold on her left hand he dismissed as a minor annoyance; husbands, unless they were overly muscular, often added spice to what otherwise might become a dull liaison—it was his belief that they had taken the corkage only, that there always remained the clear full-bodied wine for any man who had enterprise to drink it. She gave the name Hoyt to the steward who directed her to stateroom 112. This was surprising since those rare Americans who bothered with a ship like the *Pioneer Mail* always took the best and most expensive cabins. She had financial limitations then, for 112 was practically next to the engine room.

She had almost moved away before he bothered to look at her face. He had expected more glamour. American women, he had found, somehow achieved a unique glow of health, and because they removed cigarettes from their lips when they smoked their teeth were relatively unstained. Judicious use of cosmetics and a fortune spent at the hairdresser's enabled them to appear practically ageless in many cases. But there was no mistaking the age of this Mrs. Hoyt. She was thirty, no more and no less, and he wagered ten quid with himself on the exact figure. She wore lipstick, but he could discover no other indications of make-up. Her lips he found full and pleasing and there was a subtle depression of each corner of her mouth which particularly intrigued him. Her nose was straight enough, but spotted with small freckles, and these extended across her cheeks in a manner which he considered regrettable since they gave her a rather boyish look. Her eyes were wide-spaced, blue and evidently weak. She used glasses to search in her handbag and find her boarding ticket.

The first meeting had been so easy he almost became wary. He had followed her to the boat-deck rail in the late afternoon, choosing the time because he wanted to suggest a few drinks before dinner.

"My name is Stoker," he began. "Excuse—"

"I'm Jane Hoyt. It's nice to know you. You're English?"

"Hong Kong English. A colonial. I was born and brought up there."

"How wonderful! You're just the man I've been wanting to talk to."

She accepted the invitation for drinks—two Martinis. After dinner there were ten laps around the deck, and a final Scotch and soda as a nightcap. He found himself talking almost continuously, until the impossible happened, and he became bored with the sound of his own words. She wanted to know everything about Hong Kong, about the cost of living there, the prominent citizens and what the surrounding Communists meant to the Colony. She wanted to know about Red China, and it required considerable invention to please her because there was no sense in telling her that no one with round eyes knew very much about China these days. She had been warm and almost overfriendly considering the extra time it took for a fat man to ingratiate himself.

Then it happened. She was turning the key in her stateroom door when he spun her around and pressed her tightly against the wall. He held her there, waiting for her to raise her mouth or perhaps put up a show of twisting away, which would have been even better. But she remained absolutely rigid. He bent toward her mouth and she turned her head further away. He cupped her breast in one hand, seeking beneath her blouse. Instantly he felt an excruciating pain in his left foot. She had brought the heel of her shoe down hard on his arch. Before he caught his breath enough to swear, she was gone and he heard the door being locked from the inside. After that first night she barely favored him with a nod as they passed on the deck.

Now, watching her as he had done for six days, Stoker still found this young woman's behavior incomprehensible. She might have been in love with her husband, a proposition which was barely possible though antiquated, but even if this were so, she was an American and according to reputation, of consequent easygoing morals. For a moment he thought about reducing—that might have been the trouble. Then he changed his mind. He hitched up his shorts with a confident gesture and stepped toward the rail.

"Mrs. Hoyt?"

She turned her head only. Her eyes were cool and her lips were pressed together in a way that froze his smile. He pointed over her shoulder toward the shore.

"My office is just there . . . on Ice House Street. You can always mark the place by bearing on those two tall buildings. The one on the right is the Hong Kong and Shanghai Bank. The newer building on the left, which you'll notice is just a shade higher, is the new Bank of China. It was deliberately designed that way. Rather strange to think of Communists running a bank, isn't it?"

For a moment he thought she was going to reply, but the flash of interest in her eyes vanished instantly and she turned away.

"Their chaps keep the place bright and shining, too," he finished lamely. He took a business card from his shirt pocket and slipped it beneath her fingers. "You just might want to keep that, Mrs. Hoyt . . . just might be useful some day. If you're planning to do a bit of shopping I could set you right, or you might need . . . other kind of help. Hong Kong's like any other city. It can become very difficult without friends. I suggest you ring up before you come round. I'm not always there."

"Don't wait, Mr. Stoker." She moved her fingers to the edge of the rail and flipped the card outward. It flashed white in the sunlight and fluttered slowly to the water.

The *Pioneer Mail's* passengers were politely herded into the dining saloon for immigration inspection. It was hot in the saloon despite the whirring fans. The passengers, strangers to each other once more and suddenly self-conscious as their names were called aloud, moved cautiously toward the table which held their passports.

A young British inspector sat behind the table. The silver buttons on his starched drill uniform glistened in the reflected sunlight and he barely glanced at the passengers as he stamped their visas. Occasionally he would ask a question in a voice that was almost inaudible, but he worked swiftly and surely as if he already knew the most intimate details of each person. He brought his stamp down smartly, made a quick notation, returned the passport and went on to the next.

Waiting in the peculiar hush for her name to be called, Jane Hoyt thought how different it was from the last time she had entered a foreign country. That was almost a year ago, into Japan . . . with Louis. And the Japanese immigration inspectors, obsessed with their importance, had hissed and rattled through papers, sucked in their breaths and sighed, and shaken their heads and conferred endlessly among themselves. She remembered counting them while she waited with Louis. He was rubbing his stiff black hair—a sure sign he was losing his temper. There were eight Japanese and they could not accomplish in an hour what this single young man was doing in a few minutes. Maybe the British did know how to run things.

"Jane Hoyt . . . if you please."

He was holding her green passport—the only one on the table. He glanced at her photo and then at her face. He looked cool and well-scrubbed and there was only welcome in his eyes.

"Going to be with us long, Mrs. Hoyt?"

"I hope not. Oh, I didn't really mean that the way it sounded."

He smiled and picked up her white disembarkation card. "Tourist?"

"Not really. I'm hoping to join my husband."

"If you remain in the Colony longer than ninety days would you be good enough to apply for an extension?"

"Certainly."

Still smiling, he stamped the passport and handed it to her. Moving away from the table she was sure she heard him say, "Good luck, Mrs. Hoyt," and for the first time in months she was no longer afraid.

At the gangway, the chief steward hailed a water taxi which he explained was called a walla-walla. "He'll take you to the Kowloon Pier," he said, handing her three small bags down to the launchman.

"Thank you. Thank you very much." She swung easily down into the launch and waved back at the steward. The launch engine obliterated his words, but he was waving his hand and smiling and she was certain the steward had also said, "Good luck." She wondered if there was something in her face that told people about Louis, some indication of the longing and the fear. It must be that—or else the young inspector and the steward were very sensitive men.

The Peninsula Hotel is a massive structure of stone and concrete which faces Hong Kong across the narrowest part of the harbor. The lobby of the Peninsula is enormous and is broken only by great marble columns which support the high neoclassic ceiling. Along the far side of the lobby there are the reception desk, the offices of Thai Airways and Cathay Pacific Airways and the cable office. At one end of the lobby is the bar, which is almost always deserted since the patrons of the Peninsula are in no hurry and prefer to have their drinks served to them at the tables which stretch from the bar to the other end of the lobby. There are many tables and many white-coated waiters to attend them. During moments of·inactivity the waiters vanish magically into the potted palms. The lobby of the Peninsula is a busy place, but the pace is leisurely and the hum of conversation is seldom noticeable above the remote whirring of the overhead fans.

There is a division down the exact center of the great room and though it is invisible, it is there as surely as if it were wrought of steel, for this barrier is a product of custom and expediency, and none of the habitués of the Peninsula lobby would think of violating it.

The division begins at the entrance door and runs straight across to the reception desk, bisecting a wide thoroughfare between the tables.

The right side of the lobby is almost invariably pure British and in the mornings is relatively unpopulated except for a few eccentrics who prefer eating their kippers and reading their *China Mail* in public rather than in the privacy of their rooms. About noon and continuing through the day, the space slowly accumulates life, for here the older and more solidly emplaced China hands meet to transact what crumbs of business there may be left for white men in Asia. Or they simply have a quiet tonic and talk about home. Their ladies, too, frequent this space. At late lunch and teatime they are most evident, sitting like wan pink flowers in bunches of four and five. They almost never join their men and are rarely to be seen after dark. The waiters on this side are all called "boy" regardless of their age and by tacit agreement the Chinese customers who frequent the Peninsula, both male and female, stay entirely away from it.

The tables are the same on the other side of the barrier and the waiters are the same, but the patrons are of another planet. Some of them are seated at their favorite tables by ten o'clock in the morning where they remain all through the day and a large part of the night. These are the regulars and though they live elsewhere, the Peninsula is their true home, their office, their club and their window on the passing world. The Chinese sit on this side of the barrier. The men are sleek and well-groomed, and their women are of breath-taking beauty in their high-necked silk gowns. Those Englishmen who were never commissioned in a regiment or who missed a public school tie also prefer to sit on this side of the barrier. The Australians and the Indians, the Siamese, the French and the Eurasians all maintain outposts here and mix without prejudice or rancor.

The American businessman seldom attends the fair at the Peninsula; he is more at ease shaking poker dice at the air-conditioned American Club in Hong Kong. But there are many other Americans and they sometimes need sleep so badly they doze off in their chairs. They are mostly the crews of airliners which either terminate or pass through Hong Kong. Their uniform when drinking beer on the gayer side of the barrier is the Hula shirt, and they are mostly young men. Sometimes they have their Chinese wives with them and sometimes they are joined by Chinese girls who are not their wives. But in either case their faces are dead and their eyes have a way of wandering to the windows or the high ceiling where they remain transfixed as if upon a remote world, ten million miles beyond the Peninsula.

Marty Gates could easily have been mistaken for one of these Americans except that his eyes were alert and he was drinking Scotch and soda instead of beer. Marty had a hang-over. He could remember very few mornings when he had not had a hang-over, but he knew that if he could suffer through two drinks before noon some of his remorse would disappear. The dreams which he had always dreamed since the Communists had taken over China National Aviation and deprived him of his flying job, would become feasible. Ohio, a vague place in his memory which he had not seen since 1943, was a long way from Hong Kong and he had no intention of returning to it without a fortune. But the fortune seemed to dance away no matter how vigorously he approached it. In the meantime his handsome face had fallen into classic decay and the once firm line of his jaw was hidden beneath sagging jowls. His cheeks were colorless and even his loose-fitting Hula shirt failed to disguise the paunch which he called his child.

Now, only Marty's brown eyes were worth looking at. There were heavy pouches beneath them, but his eyes still held the same life and intelligence he saw in the wartime photos which decorated the room of his cheap Chinese hotel. He looked at the pictures when he was broke and no one would buy him a drink. Studying them amused rather than depressed him. He had come to think of the young man in the photos as a lost companion, rather than a representation of himself. When he looked at the photos he felt very old and sometimes stood before the mildewed mirror several minutes to confirm his belief. Then he would laugh and run his fingers through his thick hair and try to remind himself that he was only twenty-nine years old.

On this morning, Marty looked at his brief case with renewed interest. He always placed it prominently on the table, lest anyone should doubt that he was the most enterprising young man in Hong Kong. For a change there was something in the brief case—proof that if a man kept his ears and eyes open he could always make a dollar. A week before he had provided a Chinese girl for a Scandinavian Airlines pilot. Marty refused to take money from the girl, although when desperate he had done so several times before, but his agile mind recorded a single remark made by the Scandinavian. A small airline based in Copenhagen would have to suspend operations until they could obtain a certain type of spark plug and these were not readily available even in the United States. When he left the girl and the pilot together, Marty went straight to the telephone and spent the last of his available cash on a call to Copenhagen. He could provide the spark plugs—eight cases of them. Immediately. He agreed on a price of one thousand dollars air freight collect. The profit was all clear except for the telephone call. Three years before, when China National was disbanding, he had stolen the plugs and secreted them in a warehouse near the airport. At the time he said he just hated to see things lying around and he had almost forgotten about them. Which proved that you never knew. Now there was a check for a thousand dollars in the brief case and among other things, Marty Gates, of Gates Enterprises, could pay his room rent.

And so he was in an expansive mood this morning and surveyed the people who sat in his vicinity with open approval. He was willing to let bygones be bygones—if a few had snubbed him occasionally, or deliberately turned the other way when he needed a drink, they were now to be forgiven. Financial survival in the Far East was becoming a dog-eat-dog affair, anyway. It took a natural-born big operator, he thought, to ignore the minor slights and finally stand on the throne. You began by obtaining all the information possible on everyone. No detail was too small to be overlooked; even a fragment of gossip pieced together with another fragment could sometimes provide a tremendous advantage. Knowing other people's business was knowing your own, when wits alone met the payroll, and, as in the case of the spark plugs, the most innocent remark could often be turned to profit.

Looking about him, Marty was satisfied that his sensitive receiving apparatus was functioning normally. Two tables away a Portuguese man was sipping lime squash with an Englishman and a Chinese. Their conversation was inaudible, but Marty was certain he knew what they were talking about. He knew the Portuguese made three trips down from Macao a month, and it wasn't because he liked the ferryboat ride. He was an expediter—that is, he arranged for the bulk transfer of certain desirable items to persons beyond the Chinese border. In a way, Marty thought, the embargo was a blessing because otherwise the Portuguese, the Englishman and the Chinese would all have had a much harder time making a living than they did. Marty would have liked to join their enterprise or any one of the countless others he knew about, but he had so far never been invited to participate. Unfortunately, you did not invite yourself to sit around such a lush rice bowl. It was healthier to wait for an invitation.

There were two American Air Force captains drinking beer at the next table. Except for their neat and expensive-looking uniforms, which created a moment of nostalgia in Marty, he took little interest in them. They would be down from Japan on a holiday, as attested by their elaborate photographic equipment. Ordinarily Marty would have approached them, flashed his most ingratiating smile and after a few beers offered to show them around the city he knew so well. Just for old times' sake, of course, because he had also once been an Air Force man. They were certain to want some junk jewelry or worse ivory for their wives, and perhaps a few watches for themselves and their comrades back in Japan. Marty would be glad to introduce them to a friend of his—the only honest merchant in the New Territories. The captains would get a fair deal, not more than twice as much as any local resident would pay, and of course Marty would drop around to see the merchant later for his cut. It was a perfectly legitimate business and the captains would write down his name and address and tell others to contact their old pal Marty. Later, as night fell, they would want women and this was the easiest of all to arrange. Marty would take his cut from the girls, too, when he felt like it.

On this morning he was not going to have any part of the captains. Someone else could shear them. There was a check for a thousand dollars in the brief case.

Two windows away from his own table, also with her back to the light, sat Madame Dupree. Marty was surprised to see her upright and about so early in the day, but he reminded himself that she no longer had any reason to stay awake nights. Madame Dupree's strawberry blond hair looked even more offensive with the light from the window striking directly upon it, and Marty decided to warn her about the matter the next time he felt like talking to her. It was dangerous to feel sorry for anyone, particularly a woman, but Marty was sorry for Madame Dupree. She was a White Russian who claimed to be French and for three years she had lived extremely well as the mistress of a Chinese general. Only recently Chiang, the master, had beckoned from his stronghold in Formosa and the general had departed without so much as a farewell. Madame Dupree still managed to keep her room on the third floor of the Peninsula, but it was simply a matter of time before the management became tired of her excuses. She had tried, poor girl, tried very hard to snare a substitute for the general, but her forty-odd years were an impossible handicap and she should be made to realize it. Madame Dupree would be better off in Marty's own hotel, where rooms were only a dollar a night. She would just have to stop playing the great lady. Even now it was embarrassing to see her sitting there behind a bare table, anxious-eyed, and trying to look as if she were waiting for someone. She *was* waiting, for any of the men who sat in the great lobby to favor her with the slightest smile—but they never did. Marty would not smile either—there was too much else on his mind this morning—but since he was rich, he could at least dress up her façade a little better. You can't do business from an empty wagon, he thought. And so he beckoned to the waiter.

"Hey, Smiley, come here a minute."

"Yes, Missla Gates?"

"Take a bottle of champagne to Madame Dupree and bring me the chit. No . . . hold on a minute. Ask her first if she'd rather have breakfast. Whatever she wants, bring the bill to me, okay?"

"Okay, Missla Gates."

"And bring me another samee-samee."

"Okay." Grinning broadly, the waiter turned away and only after he had done so did Marty realize something was wrong.

"Hey, Smiley, come back here! Let me look at you." When he returned, Marty examined his face carefully. Now what was wrong with this Chinaman? For years his broad smile had been a fixture among the Peninsula tables—it was a beautiful weapon against arrogance and anger—but on this morning something was different. Then suddenly Marty remembered and laughed.

"You rascal!" Smiley allowed a look of mild surprise to cross his face. "Let me see your teeth again."

Smiley opened his mouth and Marty's suspicions were instantly confirmed.

"You've done it again!"

"Gold market go up, Missla Gates. This pair . . . in-between teeth."

"And when the market goes down, you'll buy another set of goldies . . . right?"

The waiter shrugged his shoulders. "Fills rice bowl, Missla Gates."

"You ever sell at the wrong time, Smiley?"

"Never. Maybe some day make mistake."

"I don't think you'll make any mistake. As long as your cousin works at the exchange you'll always stay a little ahead of the market. You must be a rich man, Smiley. Go away from me. I get nervous around really smart people."

Yes indeed, he thought as the waiter turned his back. It was important to keep tab on many, many things, no matter how trivial. The next time he felt like taking a flier in gold, he was going to keep a most careful eye on Smiley's teeth.

Marty's mind had left the gold market and transferred with practiced ease to an evaluation of a customs inspector who was fool enough to be spending too much money openly, when he first saw Jane Hoyt. She came through the main entrance door following the red-haired bellboy toward the reception desk, and Marty almost missed her in his preoccupation with the customs man. This laxity he considered unforgivable, even though she moved quickly. For here was that rarest of creatures—an American girl in Hong Kong.

His brain recorded the pertinent facts with the rapidity of a calculating machine. Good figure . . . healthy . . . intelligent . . . face, nothing to launch ships, but far superior to the average American reject who might be on her vacation from a government job in Japan. Clothes and gear . . . smart, but not costly. Not a wandering heiress, more's the pity. Bags . . . medium-priced and no stickers. She wasn't a tourist then and there was no cruise ship in Hong Kong anyway. First time in Hong Kong . . . obvious the way she looked around as she crossed the lobby. Somebody's wife? She had to be. Single girls who were not rejects or hiding from the police just didn't come to Hong Kong. They should, because they would have a guaranteed ball for themselves. Marty had often pondered on the fact that the proportion could be as high as forty or fifty to one . . . there were so many young, lonely, single men both

British and American, yearning for an evening with a girl of their own race—and no questions asked. But where was the husband? Or if he couldn't be around, why hadn't he sent a trusted friend to meet her? The husband should be more careful. He could not possibly fail to appreciate the local starvation unless he was dead. So . . . she's come over here to take his bones back home. Nothing else made any sense. Come, Martin! You can do better than that. You must.

He reached quickly for the newspaper beside his brief case and opened it to the section covering port arrivals. She had not come by air—he was certain of that. Hong Kong airport was inadequate for night landings and, therefore, all plane arrivals occurred during the day. Whether they came from the north or the south passengers were required to fly all night. Her dress was not wrinkled along the back. She had not slept in it. So— the *President Jefferson* from San Francisco via Manila? No. She wasn't carrying enough baggage. The *Anna Bakke* from Bangkok? General cargo but no passengers. The *Empire Pride* from Bombay? What the hell would she be doing in Bombay? Besides, she didn't have that drained look so characteristic of women who spent any time in the tropics. This girl was very much alive. The *Pioneer Mail* from Kobe? General cargo and twenty-two passengers. That made sense. Quick! Down the list. Back a page. Here . . . Kawasaki . . . Leonard Hardy, Angelica Stone—God, her name *couldn't* be Angelica! Too British—Mr. and Mrs. Chuck Tze . . . Dr. and Mrs. Karl Seversen . . . Lindsay Prout . . . Edward Netland . . . Koyo Sugimura . . . A. Stoker . . . Lee Quong . . . Jan Hoyt . . . Jan? That was a man's name! The bastards must have made a misprint, for it was the only non-Oriental name left on the list. It had to be Jane then. That girl, by powers of deduction, had to be Jane Hoyt. The next step was to prove it.

He waited until she finished at the reception desk and watched carefully as a bellboy escorted her toward the west elevator. No heiress. The cheaper rooms were on that side of the hotel. And good—the west-side room boys were more cooperative. For a single Hong Kong dollar they were always happy to report the exact comings and goings of the guests on their floor—for two dollars they were quite willing to report on the contents of their suitcases, and for five dollars they would trouble themselves to gather the most personal details plus bits of conversation not otherwise available.

Marty finished his drink and made his way without haste to the registration desk. He was perfectly at ease as he leaned on the counter.

"Has Mrs. Hoyt registered yet? She was due this morning."

"Mrs. Hoyt?"

The Chinese clerk looked at him coldly. The fool, Marty thought. He is pretending ignorance or loss of memory in the hope I'll slip him a few dollars for information I already know. When would these slope-heads learn Marty Gates had his own intelligence system?

"Sure . . . Mrs. Hoyt . . . Jane. She wrote me she was coming. She's from my home town."

The Chinese clerk pretended to look in a drawer behind the counter. His brows were puckered in thought.

"You won't find her in that drawer. Did she come in yet?"

"You just missed her."

"I'll phone her. What room is she in?"

"Three-o-seven."

"Thanks."

Marty bothered walking to the house phones only to please the clerk. It would be foolish to call now and risk the chance of a rebuff. Jane Hoyt had given off distinct vibrations which denied she was on the make. Jane Hoyt had a worried, frightened look. She had a great deal more on her mind than accepting a casual date for a drink with a stranger.

Marty was pleased with himself, but there were still a lot of loose ends which would have to be tied off before he swung in for a final approach. And the name Hoyt. What was there about the name Hoyt which prodded at his memory? Hoyt . . . Hoyt. There was a link, an annoying, broken link, in that name somewhere. Hoyt . . . ?

2

The only sound in the room was the murmur of the ceiling fan. Jane tried to ignore the fan because its restless spinning was so like her own thoughts. It was one thing to make decisions in relatively familiar surroundings, in Japan where Louis at least had a few friends to offer encouragement—but here the quiet and the heavy dark furniture were too oppressive. It might have been better to spend a few dollars extra and take a more expensive room—just for morale purposes. If there was only going to be one troop in this army, one person who was willing to fight, then maybe something should be done about her frightened, lonely spirit.

She sat on the bed with the telephone and after what seemed to be an eternity of waiting, the operator answered. She asked for the Pacific Hotel and the sound of her own voice broke the stillness so sharply it startled her. This first step, insignificant as it might be, was somehow terrifying. For an instant she had a wild notion that Louis himself might answer her call.

"I want to speak to the manager of the Pacific Hotel. If he does not speak English . . . would you please tell him I would like to bring an interpreter and talk with him."

"Moment, please." It was a long moment—five minutes by her watch before a man answered, and the connection was a very poor one.

"Matthew Long, here."

"This is Mrs. Louis Hoyt speaking. My husband stayed at your hotel for about three weeks. It was in May and the early part of June. Did you know him?"

"What was name again, please?" The man was shouting.

"Louis Hoyt . . . Hoyt."

"Oh yes, yes . . . Mr. *Hoyt!* Not here now. Leave long time ago."

"I know that. But he must have left some things in his room. There should be some bags and perhaps one or even two cameras. Do you have those things? I can barely hear you!"

"Mr. Hoyt go away. Much trouble. Gone long time now . . . not pay bill. Nobody pay bill. Nobody can find Mr. Hoyt—"

"I know. I will pay his bill tomorrow . . . but do you have his things? His baggage?"

"Everything all go to police . . . everything. Inspector Rodman take everything. I keep receipt paper. You pay bill, yes?"

"Yes. I will come by tomorrow. Give me the inspector's name again so I can write it down."

"Inspector Rodman . . . T-Lands police station."

"T-Lands?"

"Yes . . . yes."

"What time will you be there tomorrow? I want to talk with you."

"All the time here. You want room?"

"No, I have a room, thank you. I'll see you tomorrow. Good-by."

She hung up the telephone and lay back on the bed. She closed her eyes because for a moment she thought she was going to be sick. It was like gathering the possessions of a dead man—asking for the few pitiful things Louis might have left behind. But he was not dead. Louis was just too much a part of the living world to die until he was a very old man—or in a way that was not according to his own formula.

"I am going to die as a result of one of three things," he had said. Repeating his words in her mind now brought him to her very suddenly, as if he had just arrived to stand beside the bed. She could see him again, with his fists jammed down in his pockets and his feet spread wide in the way that he stood whenever he had one too many rums and felt like talking. "I am going to die in your arms, which I would much prefer . . . or eating your food, which is much too good . . . or of a broken neck on a ski slope, which would be the most embarrassing." All of his predictions had some foundation in fact, for Louis was a very enthusiastic man about anything he attempted. As for dying in her arms . . . well? He had once whispered it was a gallant end. "Oh, Louis!"

Living with him was like shooting rapids in a fragile boat. There were rocks and swift currents everywhere, and you never knew just what was around the next turn. It was never secure—but it *was* fun—and Louis always said you could be very secure when you were dead. He was a wild, wonderful, Irish leprechaun who led you across mountains and valleys of enchantment without ever touching the ground. He drank too much, but that was because men enjoyed drinking with Louis and he with them. Men loved Louis—he took them beyond themselves somehow, and they laughed louder and forgot their ambitions and their need to impress each other. They never talked of money when Louis was around because he was not interested in money and they found themselves talking of things far from their ordinary lives and they wondered at their own newly discovered opinions and were proud of them. Men loved Louis because he represented freedom to them—he moved and thought as he pleased and said things which were sometimes shocking but usually true, and which no one else would dare to say. He was a good husband because he wasn't a husband . . . and so the last five years had been like the first five days. "After we're married ten years I'll break down and give you a wedding ring," he said. "It will mean more and give you a bigger kick then."

But it was no good thinking of Louis this way. Remembering was a waste of precious time. *Someone* had to do something about Louis because for the first time in his life he couldn't handle things for himself.

She rose quickly from the bed and went to the mirror. It took only a gesture to smooth her short brown hair into place. She touched up her lips and straightened the seams in her stockings until they were exactly perpendicular. Turning before the mirror she thought again that if there was ever an undistinguished-looking girl, Jane Hoyt was the prize contender. How had she ever managed to hang onto Louis against the competition which always surrounded him? There were far too many girls who appreciated Louis, and a lot of them were not members of the women's mutual protective association—only now the enemy was monstrous.

She made certain her passport was in her handbag; then after a last quick look in the mirror, she closed the door and started down the long hall. She nodded to the room boy, who sprang from behind his desk and pressed the elevator button for her.

"Thank you."

The room boy, who was a gray-haired man of sixty, looked at her with mild disapproval because he was unaccustomed to thanks and there was potential danger in accepting them. Thanks did not fill rice bowls.

When the elevator reached the lobby floor, she set out briskly across the canyon of pillars and eyes. Madame Dupree appraised her shrewdly because every female body, particularly when it was shapely, was a threat to business. If the body lived in the hotel, as this one appeared to do, that was worse because men liked things handy. Marty Gates watched her and if her walk had not been so purposeful he would have found a reason to say, "Hello, Jane Hoyt." The customs man watched her because he was nearly drunk and he was beginning to think it was time to spend some of his bribe money on a woman—a white woman if he could just arrange it. The Portuguese and the Chinese and the Englishman interrupted their quiet negotiations to watch her, and so did the Air Force captains, because they were bored with each other and her swift pace created enough breeze to mold her light dress tightly against her figure. Cuyas, a gambler from Manila, watched her because he watched all women, even the middle-aged, and Jaffe, his companion and bodyguard, watched her for the same reason. Truesdale, a Cathay Airways pilot, watched her avidly because he wanted to start another fight with his Siamese wife, who sat smoldering across the table. General Charles Po-Lin watched her because she might be a tourist and his recently established guide service was foundering. Smiley, the waiter, caught a glimpse of her out of the corner of his eye because that is how he saw all things in his lobby world. Major Leith-Phipps, who tolerated Americans only if they were female, lowered his copy of the *South China Morning Post* just far enough so that he could peer over it, as he might reconnoiter from a trench. Thus, he was able to follow her entire transversal of the lobby and even hold her in his sights as she talked briefly to the doorman without embarrassment to himself or risk of discovery.

On the doorman's advice, she walked to the ferry landing. It was only two blocks, but now the sun was like a gigantic blowtorch and she wondered how the Chinese moving so rapidly along the streets, each one apparently bent on an errand of pressing importance, could show any energy at all.

She paid twenty cents at the turnstile for a first-class passage. Then she joined the slower-moving mass of humanity which oozed through the labyrinth of barriers toward the ferry. It could have been the clicking of turnstiles, a sound she had almost forgotten, or the vacant, waiting look on the faces of the passengers, as they moved obediently toward the boarding ramp, that made her think of Weehawken. She had only to bend her head and she was once more crossing the Hudson River to Manhattan on a summer morning.

She was working as a photographer's retoucher then, and that was how Louis Hoyt established himself as the number-one factor in her life. Part of her job was to fend off the hundreds of free-lance amateurs who thought commercial photography might be an interesting way to make a living. They were always eager and half-starved and it was the policy of the studio to let them tell their story at least. They went away feeling better when their names were on file. It was right after the war when Louis strolled in, hands in his pockets, as usual. He smiled and rubbed his fist through his short hair and said he needed any kind of work.

"What experience have you had?" Usually the question eased them out because if they were any good, they had their own business.

"The army spent lots of money training me."

"Have you had any professional experience?"

"You might call it that." He explained that he had been a combat photographer with the Ninth Air Force and this was his first application for a job since discharge. Even second lieutenants, he said smiling again, had a right to prove they could make a living.

"But this is a portrait studio. We take pictures of babies and brides."

"Does anyone shoot at you?"

"Sometimes the mothers do."

"Then let's forget the whole thing. What are you doing for lunch?"

"I don't go out. I eat a sandwich here."

"I wasn't asking you out because I couldn't afford it. Just curious. How big is the sandwich?"

"Big enough. Why?"

"Let's go out in the park and watch you eat your sandwich. You look pale."

"All right. You look hungry."

It was as simple as that—no frills, no false waltzes of courtship, and no long speeches about eternal devotion. It was as natural and easy to marry Louis a month later as it was to share a sandwich with him in the park, and there had never been any regrets. Two people sometimes came together and understood the needs of the other without ever saying anything about them. They melted into each other without the heat of conquest, and the excitement was in knowing that this was right and bound to be. And the union lasted because the joys of living closely together were many, and the spice was in laughing rather than arguments. The reasons for this, as Louis said, were bounded on the north by mutual respect and on the south by utter lack of interest in who was getting the most out of a marriage. And he also said that in the beginning there would not necessarily be a thing or an emotion called love, but he said it would come along later like a wanderer who would not enter a house until he knew his welcome was assured—and Louis had been right.

But the ferry to Hong Kong was nothing like the ferry from Weehawken. It was spotlessly clean, the people made way for each other on the benches, and the ferry moved across the harbor as part of a stately pageant. There were high-pooped junks with faded lavender and ox-blood sails moving in every direction. There were frail sampans and walla-wallas and patrol boats, lighters and smaller ferries all converging on each other without signal or design, avoiding collision by inches, busily churning up the yellow water until the wavelets met and splashed upward and fell back again in complete confusion. Jane understood now why Louis had written such enthusiastic letters about Hong Kong. In a way its energy matched his own.

She took a taxi to the Hong Kong and Shanghai Bank and paused for a moment to study the enormous bronze lions which guarded the entrance. They were imposing and majestic—British lions. Their massive cold solidity should have reassured her, she thought, but she waited and the feeling would not come. For not so long ago, in this same city, the little Japanese had spit on the power and the glory of the British lion.

On the second floor of the Bank building, she turned down the hallway to the American Consulate offices. She took a deep breath and entered the reception room. A frail young man came out of one of the offices and asked without enthusiasm if there was anything he could do to help her. She had trouble finding her voice. For this was the beginning—it *must* be—of Louis' return.

"I'd like to see the consul."

"Do you have an appointment?"

"No."

"We're in between consuls now. Mr. Stewart is in charge until the new one is appointed. I'm afraid—"

"Then I'd like to see Mr. Stewart."

"What was it in relation to?" The young man played delicately with his tie and his eyes were fixed on the ceiling as if he were listening to distant music. She realized suddenly that he had not really looked at her and she knew instinctively that he had never looked at any woman with natural interest. And she was angry to find him here, where she should have been proud.

"I insist on seeing Mr. Stewart."

"I suggest you telephone for an appointment . . . perhaps later in the week."

"I am going to see Mr. Stewart today." She wanted to slap the young man and was sure she would knock him flat if she did. "You take my name in to him," she said firmly. "It's Mrs. Louis Hoyt." He hesitated and then examined his carefully manicured nails.

"You don't have to be so testy about it. Have a chair."

While she waited, she tried hard to forgive the young man and soothe her resentment.

He returned almost immediately and there was a marked change in his manner.

"Mr. Stewart will be happy to see you, Mrs. Hoyt. Please follow me."

It was a large air-conditioned office and her spirits rose as she took Mr. Stewart's hand. He was also young, about her own age she thought, but she knew at once that he was capable and there was a warmth in his brown eyes which put her quickly at ease. He was built like Louis, stocky and strong. His voice was deep and resonant and the words came quickly when he spoke, as with a man who believed in himself and what he had to say. Jane thought he might appear more at home on the bridge of a ship.

"I hope it's not too cold in here for you, Mrs. Hoyt," he said. "I keep it this way to remind me of my last station, which happened to be Norway . . . and where, quite frankly, I wish I were again."

"It's a relief."

"Hong Kong is always hot before a typhoon. There's one kicking up a fuss off the Philippines now. But it will be up this way. You can almost depend on it." He waited, looking at her while he filled a short, thick pipe. Just before the silence between them became embarrassing, he placed the pipe on his desk without lighting it and began to speak again.

"Hong Kong is a hot place in more ways than one, Mrs. Hoyt. I believe it was explained to you that I'm only the consul in charge. We're standing by for a new appointment. What can I do to help you?"

"That's what I came to find out."

Then she asked the question which had burned in her mind for so long. "Where is my husband?"

"I wish we knew."

"But you *must* know something about him. It's your duty!"

"I'm sorry, Mrs. Hoyt. You're mistaken. It is not the function of the consular service to investigate the whereabouts of American citizens living abroad. We are in sort of an embarrassing middle-man position, and there is really no agency charged with the duty, although I agree that in these times there should be. We ask all arrivals to register with us, but except for convenience in notifying relatives should death occur, I'm not sure myself just why we maintain the formality."

"I believe my husband is still very much alive."

"So do I." He reached into his desk drawer and pulled out a Manila file. "Purely as a personal enterprise, and without either the approval or the disapproval of the consular service, I've gathered such facts as I could about your husband. I'm afraid there isn't very much, but some of these things you may not know. Would you like me to read them to you?"

"Please. Everywhere else I've been I seem to have run into a stone wall. No one seems to care. I've written to the State Department, I've cabled our congressman, I've even written to the newspapers back home. . . ." She pressed her hands against her eyes to hold back the feeling of tears. "I'm trying not to be discouraged. . . . They just do nothing."

"We all care, Mrs. Hoyt. But you must understand there's so little we can do. This is what we have done." He opened the folder and read quickly.

" 'Louis Murray Hoyt . . . passport number . . . et cetera, et cetera—you don't care about that—arrived in Hong Kong via Pan American Airways March 2, 1953. Occupation . . . free-lance photographer . . . age thirty-four . . . et cetera . . . et cetera. . . . Ah . . . here. Registered Pacific Hotel Kowloon March 2 . . . room 405 . . . entry visa applied for—thirty days.' Now . . . Louis Hoyt apparently avoided other Americans resident in Hong Kong or Kowloon with the exception of Tweedie's Place, where he was seen frequently in the company of various unidentified individuals both Oriental and Caucasian. Do you know Tweedie's Place, Mrs. Hoyt?"

"No . . . I'm afraid I don't."

"It's not a bad place at all. They serve rather good food, as a matter of fact. It's sort of a gathering spot for homesick Americans. Now—" He began reading again.

" 'Hoyt is reported to have stated several times during his visits to Tweedie's that if he could obtain pictures inside Red China, however innocent, they would sell for a very high price to American news services and greatly enhance his chance of being hired on a regular status by one of the magazines.' I suppose you know all this, Mrs. Hoyt?"

"We discussed it many times. Louis always sets a very high standard for himself. He knew this wasn't going to be easy. That's why he chose to try it alone."

"Did he ever indicate to you that he might attempt to photograph things of a military nature?"

"No. He simply wanted to do a picture story on life in Red China as it is today. Behind the Bamboo Curtain was to be the general idea."

Stewart placed his pipe carefully between his teeth and took a long time lighting it. He puffed for a moment, then swung around in his chair and stared out the window. His back was to her now, whether deliberately so she could not be sure.

"May I ask you a rather personal question, Mrs. Hoyt?"

"If it will help Louis."

"Was your husband ever a member of, or associated with, any subversive organization in the United States?"

"Certainly not. He was a rock-ribbed Republican. He used to laugh and say that he guessed he was just one degree to the left of slavery. But most of all he believed that a man should make his own way independently and he always had the courage to do it."

"That's too bad. Courageous people can often get themselves into a great deal of trouble. If your husband had more left-wing friends it might be possible to contact one of them and eventually find out where he is. As matters stand . . . well, China is a very big country."

"So are we, Mr. Stewart. Certainly we're big enough to do *something* about American citizens who have been kidnapped by those maniacs."

Stewart swung around in his chair and sighed. His pipe had gone out, but he did not bother to relight it.

"Mrs. Hoyt . . . in your understandable concern for your husband's safety, you have apparently forgotten that we Americans have accomplished a miracle of diplomatic thinking. If what I am about to say goes any further than this office I assure you I will be very promptly drummed out of the foreign service, because I have no right or authorization to discuss such matters with you or anyone else. But I do feel that I must explain our helplessness—to myself as much as to you. Please remember that for the moment we are like the three monkeys . . . you know . . . hear no evil, see no evil, speak no evil. We do not *recognize* the existence of the Red Chinese Government. I do not say this is wrong or right. I only want you to understand that until this is changed, or Chiang returns to the mainland, which I very much doubt he will ever be successful in doing, we diplomatically isolate ourselves from about five hundred million people. That's a lot of people." Stewart clamped down hard on his pipe and shuffled the papers in the Manila folder. "And so we are, in simpler words . . . just not talking to them."

"Good." The word came out involuntarily because in spite of Louis, she found herself remembering Korea.

"Not so good . . . in the case of your husband. I never met him, but my guess is he is pretty much of a hamburger and apple pie American who was simply trying to make a living. He might even have thought that if he got into trouble, he could smile his way out of it, because we are all the most innocent smilers in the world. I wish he had talked to me before his attempt. I just might have been able to change his mind, although he must be rather stubborn since certainly someone in Tweedie's must have tried to discourage him."

"He believed in himself."

"Exactly . . . which is a very old-fashioned way of thinking according to the people just over those mountains." He pointed the end of his pipe at the window over his shoulder and Jane rose a little in her chair to look at the mountains. The peaks were sharply etched against the cloudless blue sky now, and the refraction of brilliant light brought water to her eyes. Or was it water? Louis was beyond those mountains, perhaps *just* beyond them—a few miles only, and yet so unattainable.

"I am going to get my husband back," she said softly.

If he heard her, Stewart gave no sign of it. He began to read again from the Manila folder. " 'On twenty-second March Inspector Rodman, Hong Kong Police, made telephonic inquiry this office as to one Louis Hoyt. He advised that aforesaid was the object of a complaint by Pacific Hotel, Kowloon . . . specifically that he had not occupied his room for a period of eight days, and rent including certain food bills had not been paid. We were unable to give inspector any information since aforesaid Louis Hoyt, who was presumably an American citizen, failed to register upon entry this port.' "

"Mr. Stewart," she said evenly, "I want to know what is being done about my husband."

"I'm coming to that. I apologize for this official language, but I think you may better appreciate the situation if I read directly from such reports as we have." He read on, holding up a new paper.

" 'On second May, 1953, Hong Kong Harbor Police advised that an unidentified Caucasian of medium build, and thought to be an American, attempted to hire a junk in the Yaumati typhoon shelter. He was unsuccessful. Junk owner stated he wanted the junk for transport outside British territorial waters.

" 'On fourth May, 1953, Royal Navy Launch number 1323 on routine patrol in the vicinity of Tai Shan Island apprehended small motor-driven junk running without proper display of navigation lights. Said junk was boarded. Routine search revealed two cameras of American manufacture concealed under floorboards port side aft. Junk owner stated he was returning from Canton empty and was afraid to display lights properly for fear of interception by Communist and/or Nationalist vessels. Junk owner claimed cameras were given to him as passage payment by a Chinese friend. Junk owner, Lim Chau-wu, was fined HK dollars three hundred for proceeding without lights and the cameras held in bond until further proof of ownership could be established.' " Stewart paused and set the paper aside. "It is possible those might have been your husband's cameras, Mrs. Hoyt."

"Where are they now?"

"I assume the British still hold them unless the junk owner has obtained some kind of proof. It was early June before any of this information came to our hands. And about that time the first inquiries came from Washington, which were, I would assume, a result of your own efforts. From then on the record is more precise, if no more encouraging. Here it is. Please listen carefully.

" 'Eighth June, 1953 . . . inquiry made through British Chargé d'Affaires to Chinese government Peiping as to possible knowledge of whereabouts, one Louis Hoyt. No reply transmitted.

" 'Twentieth June, 1953 . . . inquiry made through British Chargé d'Affaires as to original filing, dated eighth June, regarding Louis Hoyt. British advised no reply received from Peiping government.

" 'Thirtieth June, 1953 . . . ditto. Fifteenth July . . . ditto. First August 1953, similar inquiry forwarded to British Chargé d'Affaires, Canton, with further request for any possible information he might have on Louis Hoyt and/or other American citizens presumably held in his area. Reply stated no information of any kind available.

" 'Fifteenth August, 1953. Formal protest lodged with Peiping government through British Chargé d'Affaires insisting on information relative to one Louis Hoyt and immediate re-return to New Territories border if held in custody. No reply received. . . .' and I might add, Mrs. Hoyt, that I would be very much surprised if we *ever* received one."

He closed the folder and placed both hands flat upon it.

"I'm sorry, Mrs. Hoyt . . . very sorry indeed. I suspect that you came to Hong Kong with the intention of learning a great deal more than I've been able to tell you."

"Where can I go to find out more?"

"I couldn't say. I don't think there's any place. You'll just have to wait. I am only guessing, but I would say that your husband is probably not in any immediate danger . . . provided he did not attempt to photograph things which might be considered of a military nature."

"Then why would they hold him?"

"Remember we are not even certain that they are holding him . . . but *if* they are, he is a hostage . . . and along with a great many others, an embarrassment to us. The Chinese are old hands at hostages, since the days of Genghis Khan. They want recognition and they want Chiang removed as a threat . . . among many other things. And time means nothing to them."

"It means a great deal to me . . . and to Louis."

"You'll forgive me if I point out that your husband should have thought of that before he entered their country as an uninvited guest. Please, Mrs. Hoyt—" He winced as he saw her head go down. It was the first time her shoulders had slumped since she entered the room.

"Please . . . I am not trying to be cruel. I am simply trying to point out the utter futility of a one-woman crusade against the whole Chinese race. I admire your determination, but—"

"Surely there's some kind of an underground . . . some way. I have money. Seven thousand dollars. I refuse to believe the Chinese are so dedicated to their new world they won't accept a bribe!" Her head snapped back up and her fists were clenched tightly on her knees.

"Do you know anything about communism, Mrs. Hoyt?"

"No. And I don't want to."

"That's a dangerous mistake so many of us make, because if we don't understand it, we can't fight it successfully. It is not just a redistribution of wealth as is commonly supposed . . . nor is it simply an exchange of power. Either one of these things would eventually fall of its own weight. Communism is a *religion*, Mrs. Hoyt, and those who accept it are as fanatical as the early Christians. In other words, no sacrifice is too great and, if they can find a place as a martyr, so much the better. Believe me, when a Chinese gives up bribes—or squeeze, as it's been called out here for centuries—he's got religion and he's got it bad. I don't think you could bribe your husband out of China for seven *hundred* thousand dollars. If you don't believe me, go talk to the British who are dealing with them almost every day. They'll tell you there's a new face on China. They're out to rebuild Asia in their own way and they just may do it."

She stood up suddenly and looked at the mountains beyond the windows. And she took a moment to hate them, but it did not drive away the feeling of helplessness. When she was empty of fury, she turned to Stewart and tried to smile.

"Your lecture has been very interesting, Mr. Stewart, but it doesn't solve my problem. Isn't there anyone you could suggest I might see?"

"Yes. My wife. Mrs. Stewart and I would be delighted to have you as our guest for dinner tonight. It might help your loneliness if you could talk to her."

"Thank you. You're very kind . . . but I have another engagement."

She started for the door and he followed her, sucking thoughtfully on his pipe.

"We'll give you a raincheck then . . . any time you're in the mood. We live up on the Peak and it's quite pleasant." Then at the door, when she turned to face him, he knew she was not listening. For her lips were set and her eyes were as undefeated as when she first walked into the office.

"You wouldn't be going to Tweedie's tonight, would you?"

"Yes, Mr. Stewart. I would."

She walked slowly toward the ferry landing hardly aware of the hurrying hordes of Chinese who so crowded the sidewalks they sometimes overflowed into the street. Now the sun had softened with the afternoon and a light breeze brushed against her face. A beggar clawed at her dress and near the Gloucester House, where the crowds were most concentrated, two Australian sailors barred her passage and asked if she wanted a beer. They were drunk and they were very young and when she said, "Please—" they smiled and made elaborately formal bows to let her pass. But no other person looked at her and she thought that if she had ever needed the sound of a familiar voice or the sight of a face she had seen before, it was this lonely moment of first defeat.

She turned down a narrow lane toward the harbor and saw that it was named Ice House Street. She looked up at the stone buildings and wondered which one contained the fat body of Austin Stoker. It was so hard to fight entirely alone. Stoker might know someone. Stoker might be willing to help. Then she shivered in spite of the heat. Stoker would be only too glad to see her—but he wasn't giving help away.

3

Tweedie's Place was in Kowloon, almost hidden on a side street which branched off from Nathan Road. A small well-polished brass sign beside the glass door set it apart from the Indian curio shops, Chinese food stores and small hand-factories which gave purpose to the neighborhood. Tweedie's Place catered to sailor men and flying men and so was known all over the world. To some it was home, others cherished it as a place to eat without the risk of dysentery, and for some it was just a place to get drunk under circumstances favorable for survival. For there were no fights in Tweedie's. Those who wanted a fight could go to the Kowloon Hotel bar and beat each other's brains out all they cared to—raising a fist in Tweedie's had long been regarded as a sin. In Tweedie's Place if a man rose once in anger, it was the last time, for then Tweedie would exile him and this was the worst thing that could possibly happen to a sailor man or a flying man who wanted easy companionship in Hong Kong. Tweedie would ostracize such a person as effectively as if he had leprosy—and so there was no fighting in Tweedie's Place. Tweedie was the mother and the father, and some said the Holy Ghost, to all white men who found themselves on the loose in Hong Kong. Tweedie's, as the proprietor liked to point out, always had been and always would be a gentleman's place. He kept a two-by-four behind the bar to make sure it stayed that way.

To his few intimates, Tweedie was the Giraffe—or Gi, for short—and anyone who was not an intimate and called him the Giraffe soon learned better manners.

It was understood that Tweedie hated his name, but he did not like being called the Giraffe either. The name was given him when he was cook in the barque *Penang*. He had jumped ship in 1920 and had been in Hong Kong ever since. He would say, as he spread out his cable-like arms as if to include the world, that at least he came by his nickname honestly, and this was true for he was well over six feet tall and an extraordinary portion of his height was due to his neck.

"The first time they tried to hang me, it stretched," he explained whenever anyone was drunk enough to ask about his neck. "The name is the only thing I ever come by honestly."

The rest of Tweedie's body faithfully carried out the name. His head was long and his ears large. His nose swept down over heavy lips and his eyes were large and mournful. His shoulders sloped steeply from his neck and the rest of his thin frame consisted mostly of legs. The Japanese occupation of Hong Kong was a particularly difficult time for Tweedie, who along with all other white civilians was held prisoner in the compound on Nathan Road. Whenever the Japanese officers wanted to amuse themselves, they made him dig a hole in the ground with his hands and stand in it—so they could curse him eye to eye.

The principal room in Tweedie's Place was large, and the constantly moving overhead fans created the impression that it was cool. The tile floor was clean and there were very few flies. The tables were laid with checkered tablecloths because Tweedie thought these were more homey and their use cut down on the laundry bill. You could spill a lot on a checkered tablecloth without having to change it. The customers in the principal room sat in comfortable wicker chairs which both saved on the insurance and contributed to Tweedie's peace of mind. Years before, when he had first come off the *Penang* and was new to the business, he had furnished his restaurant with heavy Chinese-type chairs of teak and mahogany. He found to his dismay that they became very deadly weapons when used to settle an argument. His investment in those chairs was considerable, but after the third customer expired of brain concussion, he substituted the lightest wicker chairs he could find. No customer had been seriously injured since. It had been a long time since anyone had even bothered to swing one of the wicker chairs.

Toward the rear of the restaurant, there was a smaller, more intimate room. The walls were decorated with photographs of ships and autographed pictures of the famous and the near-famous who at one time or another had patronized Tweedie's Place. The bar was in this room and there was a long bare table beneath the pictures which commanded a view of the principal room. This was Tweedie's personal table and here he held a leisurely court from midafternoon until very late at night. The back room was open to the public, but the long table was open only by invitation. Sometimes a daring customer would attempt to join the group at the long table without proper introduction, but he soon departed, trailing the burning accusation of his mistake behind him. For he was utterly ignored, talked through and around and unheard, no matter how loudly he yelled; he became merely a lump sitting in an insulated cage of silence.

Three men were always to be found at the table. They served as Tweedie's advisers, negotiators, errand boys, purveyors and interpreters of news, strategic committee and sounding board. They were allowed to call Tweedie the Giraffe. Faithful relics of Tweedie's lustier days, they were sad and bewildered at his alarming and ever-growing preference for respectability.

One of these men was known as Gunner, although no one knew why because he had never been a gunner. He claimed to have been first engineer on a freighter and also claimed a wife in Boston, though everyone knew it had to be over twenty years since he had seen her. After a gallon or so of beer he became very sentimental about his wife, speaking of her as —the wife. Gunner was squat and fat with breasts like a woman, and the tattoos which decorated his arms were so faded the designs were difficult to follow. He considered himself an old China hand although he had never been farther into China than the port of Hong Kong.

There was also Big Matt, who had once been a marine guard at the American Legation in Peiping. His enormous hands so encircled a glass of beer it seemed a thimble, and he drank beer all day long and most of the night. He was sixty-two years old and said that he was fifty-two. He was so remarkably preserved that he was almost convincing except that his dates never jibed. The most simple arithmetic made him a marine when he was eight years old. But he spoke two Chinese dialects and he knew China as far as Szechuan.

Icky made no claim to being a China hand although for length of residence he qualified easily. No one, not even Tweedie, had any idea how old Icky might be. Estimates ranged from fifty-five to seventy-five, yet no one could say for certain because Icky did not know himself. He had never been to school. He could read, but he could not write anything except his name and that he seldom wished to do because it was Herman Schultz and he hated his name as much as Tweedie did his. Though he was a small gnarled monkey of a man, room had once been found on his chest to tattoo a full-rigged ship in the traditional fashion. It was the British ship *Talus* gone missing with all hands in 1919, the same vessel which served as his escape from a vaguely remembered childhood in San Francisco. Icky wanted to die in Hong Kong, preferably in Tweedie's Place. It was the only home he had ever known.

These three men lived entirely on Tweedie's bounty and so they were inseparable. He furnished them with a small house near his own, and there, in a sort of land-bound forecastle, they cooked such meals as they bothered to eat, and bathed occasionally, and shaved twice a week, and argued interminably. But unless they were occupied with some special project for Tweedie, such as grinding the valves on his car or butchering a pig or collecting the rent from his three tenant farms, they were always to be found drinking beer at the long table. This had been going on for many years and they loved one another with the need and recalcitrant passion of old men who are very lonely.

It was Tweedie's determination that his place should have a good name, and as his wealth increased he had become more than ever intolerant of a clientele that might jeopardize his reputation. In the old days merchant seamen and sailors from the battleships that came to Hong Kong were his only customers, but since the Japanese had left and the war was finally over he catered to what he considered more stable trade.

He welcomed the airmen, particularly when they brought their wives, and he was immensely pleased when elements of the permanent American Colony in Hong Kong troubled themselves to take the ferry across to Kowloon for an evening at his restaurant. They were also certain to bring their wives because a white man in Hong Kong was too conspicuous to risk bringing anyone else. On such nights Tweedie's Place took on an air of easy respectability. The Chinese were all right, too, since they were far too civilized to be anything but physically well-behaved. And those rare Englishmen who ventured into Tweedie's Place were welcome, except that it distressed him to see them mashing peas on the same fork with a bite of his carefully aged steaks. But one type of customer Tweedie could not abide and since his objection was generally known in both Hong Kong and Kowloon, he was seldom troubled with them. A woman without escort was not welcome in Tweedie's Place.

"All women is whores at heart," Tweedie would say, rubbing his great sad eyes. "I don't care if you tell me a woman is the Queen of Bulgaria or the head of the Girl Scouts, she is a whore at heart. By this I don't mean that there is anything wrong with whores . . . I like them . . . but not in my place, you understand. Because a woman alone is trouble, and two of them alone are twice as much trouble, and three of them alone can start a riot with a smile. It ain't their fault. You take a creature God put on this earth and train her from the time she can think that her only chance for a decent life is to be as attractive as she can and you got yourself a whore. She's only got so much time and she knows it, and if I was a woman I would be a whore, too. Because she knows that she's got maybe forty years at the most to get everything set for the rest of her days. She's got a body and it's only going to last so long before she finds people looking through her instead of at her. If you start trying to separate the respectable whores from the unrespectable whores you'll just drive yourself crazy, under-stand? How can you say one woman is wrong because she takes maybe ten or twenty dollars from a man in cash after a nice pleasant evening and another woman is right when she takes maybe fifty dollars out of her old man's pants to pay the grocery bill? Women have got a common denominator and that's making sure they ain't bounced out on the street. So when a woman comes in here alone she just don't come for the food. She's sizin' up the market, understand? If she's with a pal and they pretend to be only interested in each other, that ain't on the level because women don't know how to be pals and they ain't got time to find out how. I'm sorry for all women and I'm sorry they got to be whores. They got a problem all right, but I don't want them working it out on my front doorstep, because somebody always gets his feelin's hurt."

Tweedie was therefore shocked to look up from his beer and see a lone woman sitting at a table near the door. She was, moreover, white and under forty, a combination he knew was potential dynamite since there were no less than three tables of airmen sitting opposite her along the wall. He saw instantly that they were already neglecting their drinks to gauge their chances with the woman. He turned to Icky, who was mopping the perspiration from his head with a bar towel

"How did that broad get in here?"

Icky put down the towel and squinted to compensate for his failing sight. He clicked his false teeth smartly and said, "I dunno."

"You know her, Matt?"

"No. I never seen her before. She ain't local."

"Gunner?"

"No. But she ain't no ordinary broad."

"Who says?"

"I do. There's no paint on her hull, her fingernails ain't red and her handbag ain't big enough to carry all the stuff a real broad's got to carry—and she's havin' a real drink instead of a phony orange and she ain't payin' no attention to them guys at the tables."

"She's lookin' for *somebody*," Big Matt said.

"I told them waiters a thousand times," Tweedie said, "never to serve no woman who is alone."

"She's got a nerve," grumbled Icky, who was doubly resentful because his bleary old eyes prevented him from seeing any more than a vague shape at the distant table. He washed part of the resentment from his mind with a long drink of beer and clicked his teeth again. "She's got a nerve comin' in here when she knows the Gi don't like it. Toss her out on her ass, I say."

"I guess I got to," Tweedie sighed. "You let one get away with it, then they'll all come in just like they used to."

He rose reluctantly from the comfort of his wicker chair. And he stood a moment, watching her before he left the long table. He told himself that maybe this once it wouldn't do any harm to let the woman stay awhile. She was only trying to make a few dollars. It was, as the Chinese said, always painful to break anyone's rice bowl. Then she could be just a tourist maybe, who was lost, or just didn't know her way around. But that was impossible, he decided, because tourists were never alone. Even so he tried to think of many excuses for the woman as his long legs carried him slowly toward the table.

"Hello, sister."

She looked up at him and Tweedie saw that she was surprised and uncomfortable beneath his examination.

"Kind of in the wrong place, ain't you?"

"I don't . . . think so."

Tweedie tried to keep his voice firm though he took no pleasure in what he had to say.

"Beat it, sister. Now. Forget the drink. It's on the house."

"I'm sorry . . . I don't understand—"

Tweedie rubbed his sad eyes and was about to begin his lecture—the one about how he understood the problems of women these trying days, but this wasn't the place to solve 'em—and please tell the other girls and please leave without kicking up a fuss—when a man moved quickly between them. He reached for her hand and sat down opposite her.

"Hi, Jane. Sorry I'm late. I hope you weren't waiting too long." He looked up at Tweedie and smiled. "Hello, Gi. Have you met my friend, Jane Hoyt?"

"We were just . . . talking," Jane said evenly.

"Double Scotch for me, Gi."

"Yeah . . . sure, Marty. I'll send the waiter." Tweedie permitted a grateful smile to crease his long face, then sighed with relief. "Glad to know you, miss. Any friend of Marty's is always welcome. I'll send the waiter."

Tweedie moved away as slowly as he had come and Jane looked at the young-old man who sat across the table. He was completely relaxed, almost to the point of insolence, she thought. She tried to remember where she might have met him before.

"I don't know whether to thank you or not," she said.

"It depends on how long you wanted to stay here. Unescorted women are poison in Tweedie's Place."

"So I gathered. Who are you?"

"Marty Gates." He reached into his shirt pocket and handed her a card. The printing was in Chinese characters. "Other side. You'll find I'm president of Marty Gates Enterprises."

"Oh." She turned the card over. "How did you know my name?"

"Hong Kong has a lot of people in it, but it's really a very small place."

"But I've only been here since this morning."

"I know. You arrived on the *Pioneer Mail* and you're staying at the Peninsula. Room three-o-seven."

"I think I'd better leave now."

"That would be sort of foolish, wouldn't it?"

"Why?"

"Because you haven't accomplished what you came for."

"How do you know I want to accomplish anything? How did you know I was coming here in the first place?"

He leaned forward and she found it difficult not to like the tired way he shook his head and smiled.

"Look. Let's level. You came to Hong Kong alone. A girl like you doesn't do that these days unless she has to. You've got a lot on your mind . . . I can tell by the way you move . . . the way you look . . . the way you walk. And I like what I see."

"You're so observant. Apparently you forgot to notice my wedding ring."

"A lot of people wear wedding rings."

"This one means something."

"All right. I'll buy that . . . temporarily."

"You're a cynic, Mr. Gates."

"Right. And with reason." The waiter arrived and set the double Scotch before him. He downed it in one long swallow as if it were the purest water. Then he ordered another. He wiped his lips with the back of his hand and lit a cigarette. "I was sort of thirsty," he said easily.

"So I see." She looked at him more closely now and saw the marks of many double Scotches about his face. And she thought it was too bad because there was no real weakness in his eyes and somehow a quality emanated from him that made her reluctant to leave.

"Where's your husband?"

"I don't know."

"That's handy. Will he stay put, I hope?"

"He's a prisoner somewhere in China."

"Oh. . . ." His manner changed instantly and he took a long drink from his glass. "I'm sorry I said what I did." Then suddenly he snapped his fingers as if he were on the verge of a great discovery. "Hoyt! *Now* I got it! Photographer, wasn't he? Stocky guy?"

"Yes. Did you know him?"

"We had a few drinks one night. Right here. There were a lot of people around. I could see he was heading for trouble."

She leaned forward eagerly. Now all her coolness was gone.

"*Why? How* did you know? Anything you could tell me might help."

Marty scratched his sagging jowls and brushed away the cigarette smoke which burned his eyes.

"I don't remember him too well . . . just the name for some reason. It stuck with me and I wondered about it this morning."

"Please try to remember. Where were you sitting?"

"Right over there . . . along the wall. I was drunk. I just made a deal and it paid off and I was drunk. And this fellow—your husband—was there. I know he was there because Fernand Rocha was there, too."

"Who is Fernand Rocha?"

"A no-good Portuguese."

"*Please* help me, Mr. Gates. Tell me everything you can."

Now a silence fell quickly between them and was all the more startling because it descended on the rush of words like a slammed gate. Marty crunched out his cigarette and his eyes were a long time searching the room before they returned to her. He looked at her shrewdly.

"What's it worth to you?"

She took a moment to answer and he saw her surprise turn slowly to cold anger. But when she spoke again her voice was as controlled as his own and she looked directly at him.

"A great deal. . . . Make your own terms."

"You mean that?"

"Yes."

"I'm not talking about dollars."

"I didn't think you were."

"You'd make a blind bargain . . . not knowing whether I've got anything worth telling or not?"

"I'm going to get my husband back."

"Yeah. . . ." Marty sighed heavily. For a moment he squirmed uncomfortably in his chair and examined the tobacco stains on his fingers. He drained his glass, but took no pleasure from the whisky. He forgot to wipe his mouth as he had done each time before and his lips remained half-apart as if they were waiting for a word that would not come. "Thanks. . . ." he said finally.

"Tell me."

"I will . . . what little I know, and for what good it might do. But first I want to thank you for being alive. I guess I've gone Asiatic and maybe it's past time I went home. I didn't think . . . there were any women like you seem to be, left in the world . . . and notice I say *seem* to be, because I still can't believe it. You've got a lot of guts, Jane Hoyt."

She sat motionless, waiting. Marty raised his hand to the waiter, who brought him another drink. He drained it in quick little sips, twirling the glass expertly as he took it from his mouth each time and moving it across the checkered squares on the tablecloth as if he were playing a game.

"If I could believe you entirely, I might start to believe in a lot of things again," he said finally. "I'd like that." He looked at her again and saw that although her interest was with him, her eyes were still cold.

"Forget the bargain," he said. "I haven't been a sucker for a long time. We'll make a new one anyway. Like this. I'll tell you all I know—and it isn't really very much—if you'll let me buy you dinner."

The tightness about her mouth went away and she relaxed slightly.

"You must be a very lonely person."

"I am."

"Ask for the menu then."

"Later. I don't want to upset my system. And I don't think you'll eat very well until you hear what I have to say. Let's have another drink."

"All right."

"You're waiting, aren't you, and I'm tormenting you, and it isn't fair . . . especially when I know so little. The reason I'm doing this is because I've been a heel for so long I don't find it very easy to get out of the habit. I'm always looking for a shadow behind every person I meet, male or female—it's a habit you get into out here—and I put more trust in the shadow than I do in the person. I'd do the same thing if I were you because that's the way things are in Asia. Now don't get that worried look on your face again. I'll shut up about myself right now and get on with what you want to know . . . but you've got to remember that the night I saw your husband I was a lot drunker than I am now. I'm rambling around a little bit trying to remember who was with him besides Fernand Rocha, who would eat his own mother."

"Mr. Rocha doesn't sound like a very stable character."

"Rocha is a very stable character. You can depend on him one hundred per cent to give you a bad time. You can depend on him to lie and cheat and if there's some way he can squirm out of keeping a bargain, he'll go to a lot of trouble to find it. Which was why I hated to see this fellow Hoyt, who obviously didn't know what the score was, get mixed up with him."

"How was he mixed up with him?"

Marty took a long pull at his new drink and looked thoughtfully at the pilots who sat at the nearby tables. Then he looked beyond them to the back room, where the Giraffe sat at the long table, and finally he glanced over his shoulder at the tables near the door. Marty's head was already a little wobbly on his neck, but though his eyes were taking longer to communicate thoughts to his brain, they were still alert.

"The plates have ears in this place," he said. "Always remember that."

"Are you afraid of this man Rocha?"

"He's a tin horn."

"Then—?"

"But sometimes he works with Hank Lee and that's one man I stay clear of . . . strictly."

"Just a minute. You're wandering. Who is Hank Lee?"

"Not so loud!" Marty looked quickly at the other tables. When he saw that no one could possibly have overheard her, he returned to his drink. "I don't even like to talk about Hank Lee because he doesn't like to have anybody talk about him. Anyway, Rocha sometimes does odd jobs for him and you never know . . . you never know."

"Hank Lee sounds like a Chinese."

"Far from it. He's as American as you and I are . . . well, maybe not quite so much so. He's sort of a fallen away American . . . like a Catholic who doesn't go to church any more. He's still got his passport to get into Heaven if and when he has to, but he doesn't drop any tax money in the alms box."

"I'm confused. We started with this man Rocha and now we have Mr. Lee."

"Let's just not mention his name in a public place again, okay? Forget it. I don't see how he could have had anything to do with your husband anyway."

"What about Mr. Rocha then? What happened at that table over there? Please try to remember!"

"I am, but it doesn't come back easy because in the first place I was so drunk and the second place it was a long time ago."

"*How* long ago?"

"It must have been spring or even winter because the girls weren't wearing light silk yet. It must have been April or May because the girls weren't fanning themselves either."

"What girls? How can you remember things like that?"

"I always remember what girls do . . . and what they wear. Sometimes for years. One girl I didn't know. The other one was Maxine Chan."

"Chinese?"

"Yeah. Guess I'm telling tales out of school . . . on your husband. But Maxine's regular . . . one of the best. You wouldn't have to worry about her. She's what they call a family girl out here."

"I long ago gave up worrying about girls and my husband."

"You sure you want that guy back? How about me? I may be getting a little loaded, but I'm pretty."

"You're very pretty, Mr. Gates . . . and I like you. Now what were Louis and this Rocha talking about?"

"Your husband was talking about how he couldn't hire a junk or something like that. Anyone could have told him he wouldn't stand a prayer on a junk unless he went through Hank Lee—"

"There's that man again."

"And Rocha was saying that if you were willing to spend a few dollars there was more than one way to get in and out of China. It made me so sick listening to him I had to leave."

"What was so sickening about it?"

"Rocha is a phony . . . a tin horn, like I said. He was offering to get someone into China, which anyone could do, and standing to make some money on the deal, but he sure as hell couldn't get anyone *out* of China."

"Why didn't you stop him then . . . warn Louis?"

"Because I didn't know your husband from Adam and we're all trying to make a living out here . . . one way or another. It's getting harder all the time."

"But at least you knew he was an American?"

"Yeah . . . but I was too drunk to care."

"You're pretty tight now. Don't you think we should eat?"

"You eat. I like to drink my dinner."

Jane ordered steak, which was almost the cheapest thing on the menu at a dollar and fifteen cents. Marty had three more drinks while she ate it. He told her that the steaks were cheap because they came from Australia and so there was never any sense eating anything else in Hong Kong. He was weaving in his chair now, and there were long moments of silence when his chin fell on his chest and he seemed to doze. But he would brighten again when she spoke of New York City or New Jersey or said anything about the States, and once she thought he was going to weep when she said Ohio in the fall was the most beautiful place she had ever been.

When the waiter came with the check he fumbled in his pockets and brought out a twisted wad of money. But he could not count it and so she separated the large and clumsy Hong Kong bills until the waiter was satisfied. As she sipped the last of her coffee, he slumped down in his chair and fell asleep again, this time more soundly. Then she was conscious that the tall man was standing quietly beside her.

"You'd better take Marty home, sister," Tweedie said. "I wouldn't ordinarily recommend that, but I saw you put his money back in his pocket. You can come in here anytime if you want . . . even alone. You can even sit at the long table with the boys."

"I don't know where he lives."

"The Fountain Hotel with the other bums. Seems peculiar to me a woman like you would get mixed up with Marty."

"What's the matter with him? He's been very kind."

"Sure, Marty don't mean no harm. He's just a bum and I hate to think of takin' care of him ten years from now. But it would seem to me you could do better." The Giraffe placed a hand on Marty's shoulder. He shook him gently without result. He started to move in with more determination when Jane stopped him.

"Wait a minute. You're Mr. Tweedie, aren't you?"

"I be." He frowned at the sound of the name.

"Do you know a young man named Louis Hoyt?"

"What kind of likker does he drink?"

"Rum. He's stocky . . . short black hair."

"Used to recite poetry a lot . . . all the time smilin' bedamned to you fella?"

"Probably."

"Yeah. I knew him. Sometimes he was a inarrestin' problem. He's dead."

Jane caught her breath. She pressed her lips tightly together to hold back any sound until she could be sure of controlling it.

"You must be mistaken," she said slowly. "You must be wrong."

"I ain't wrong very often. You couldn't easy forget that fella and people keep me posted. The Commies nailed him. Some kind of a spy. You'd never know it to hear him talk. I hate to see them Commies get Americans. They is so unreasonable."

"How well did you know Louis Hoyt?"

"He comes and he goes like anybody else . . . but I sure remember his poetry now because it were so pretty and he was awful good at it. Made up some of his own, too. Great hand with the ladies in a sort of reverse way. Let them chase him. Don't know quite how he managed it, but it was truly surprisin' . . . very surprisin'."

"But what makes you think he's . . . dead?"

"I don't think. I know."

"*How* do you know?"

He looked at her suspiciously again and his great sad eyes suddenly became darker as if he were able to deepen their color at will.

"Why so inarrested? You chasin' him for some special reason?"

"I'm Mrs. Hoyt."

"Oh. Too bad." For a moment he stood uncertainly, shifting his weight from one long leg to the other. "Well . . . anyway, you still got a lot of your life ahead of you. And young widows who is clean and white is at a premium out here. Just be careful of the company you keep. Like Marty here . . . he's all right, but he won't do your reputation no good and whatever he says don't believe a word. He's the biggest liar in Hong Kong."

She reached out to catch his arm as he extended it toward Marty again. "How do you *know* my husband is dead? Please . . . tell me exactly how you know. Please. . . ."

There was in her voice a pitiful sound beneath the words which Tweedie had heard before, and he steeled himself to ignore it.

"Wake up, Marty!"

"*Please* tell me!"

"If I was to tell you exactly . . . I'd never learn anythin' else, and that I can't afford to do."

He shook Marty roughly now, turning away from the woman because he could not stand the look in her eyes. "Wake up, Marty! Get the hell out of here! Your friend is takin' you home!"

The endless series of neon lights along Nathan Road flashed through the taxi windows, changing the color of Marty's sleeping face from red to green and back to sickly white again until the taxi turned to the right on Tak Shing Street, where there were very few lights and the black-clad Chinese pedestrians moved dangerously close to the fenders. He sagged heavily against her now with his head on her shoulder, but after the first semiconscious gropings at her legs and breasts, movements which he had made automatically and without heart, he had remained perfectly quiet. Jane was not sure why she had agreed to take him home—except she knew that for a little while at least, she dared not be alone. Even Marty, poor, drunken, harmless Marty, was company. He had known Louis. He had spoken to him. And he had not said that Louis was dead.

The taxi swerved to a stop before a single light which illuminated a large Chinese sign. Below the characters the name Fountain Hotel was spelled out in crudely painted English letters. A beggar child, hardly beyond the toddling stage, reached instantly for the taxi door.

"Marty. You're home."

He opened his eyes just enough to see and pulled himself to the door. "Yeah. Come on up to the room and we'll have a party."

"No, Marty. But tell me where I can find Maxine Chan."

"Maxine? Wha' you wanna see Maxine for?"

"I just want to talk with her."

He stood in the street weaving against the light over the sign and the beggar child clung to his coat sleeves making soft little cries.

"Maxine's good girl. Runs good business."

"Where, Marty? What business?"

"Curio shop . . . Salisbury Road. Right next to the pier. Lotta junk but she sells it. Come on up to the room. I'll show you pretty pictures."

"Thanks, Marty. Good night."

She pulled the door closed and Marty staggered backward with an injured expression on his face. Then he managed to smile and waved his arm loosely.

"Goo-night."

As the taxi pulled away, she looked out the rear window. The beggar child was leading Marty to the hotel entrance.

4

Inspector Merryweather bore the weight of his twenty-five years very heavily. And on this night he became increasingly morose as he considered his age, because it seemed to him that he was expending the best part of his life in the dark. Yes, and in the bloody lonely dark, too—sharing it with seven men who could not possibly comprehend the earth-shaking importance of the recent football defeat suffered by Swansea against West Ham. The tragic news had come over the London wireless just before Merryweather departed for patrol and he had not had a chance to discuss the disaster with anyone. And so he brooded, for Merryweather came from Swansea and he wished he was back in Swansea where the nights were cool instead of wretchedly humid. Yes, back in Swansea there would be a good many chaps willing to explain how West Ham racked up a score of four whilst Swansea managed only one. A whacking good game it must have been, though.

He leaned against the wheelhouse door and stared down at the black water which hissed along the hull of his patrol boat. He calculated that he had watched the water for sixteen nights without relief and he was incredibly bored with it. Normally he would have alternated with Inspector Potts, but Potts was in the hospital with amoebic dysentery and God knew when he would be fit again. There was a shortage of inspectors. There was always a shortage because most chaps when they had finished their schooling at home, did their best to remain with the Metropolitan Police. Only the most junior men were left with the choice of Hong Kong—which made things rum in a way because everyone was about the same age, but it was dull sticking out these duty tours alone with never a chance to drop by the dance halls for sixteen nights.

He looked into the wheelhouse where five of his Chinese crewmen were chattering happily together. The other two would be down in the engine room trying to talk above the noise of the diesel. They were good men, all things considered, and they kept the fifty-foot harbor patrol boat in spotless condition. Even in the dim reflected light from Hong Kong which filtered through the windows, the brass shone, and their white uniforms, which were a hybrid of the Royal Navy, were spotless. They were good men if not companionable, and their devotion to duty was surprising when one remembered that the whole Hong Kong police force was only seven years old. A very few young Englishmen commanded a large number of Chinese policemen both on land and on the water. The problems had multiplied almost beyond belief since the refugees had poured into Hong Kong, but somehow the force had matured and become efficient and Merryweather doubted if the Chinese would turn on their British leaders as the Sikhs had done when the Japanese came. There were no longer any Sikhs on the force—now dependence was placed on the Chinese, who everyone hoped would prove more loyal if the Reds descended on Hong Kong. Loyal up to a point, Merryweather thought. And where that point was, no one knew. It was the business of the British Army to defend Hong Kong and the Territories, but their strength would be bled considerably if the police became a dagger at their backs.

Merryweather glanced at the luminous dial on his wrist watch. Almost three o'clock. Another five hours! This night was going to last forever.

The patrol boat passed a Dutch freighter working cargo from her decks down to a cluster of junks alongside. Merryweather could hear the sound of her winches and the sing-song babble of the junk people, and he thought how they never seemed to sleep and how futile this night patrol was anyway. He was showing the flag, as the saying went, and that was about all.

There were three patrol boats, one a few dark miles to the east around Quarry Bay, another which ranged up through Rambler Channel toward Tsun Wan, and Merryweather's boat which covered the inner harbor. It was his private opinion that they all might as well have remained tied to the dock. Besides keeping normal order in the harbor and along the waterfront, they were supposed to prevent the smuggling of gold, opium, and —within the confines of the harbor—the transfer of strategic materials to China. All of which was like holding back a wind with a newspaper. For who could know, out of the thousands of sampans and junks and miscellaneous vessels which moved constantly through the night which one was guilty and which was not? It was impossible to stop them all.

The chugging of a walla-walla's engine attracted Merryweather's attention. He watched the little boat a moment as it bounded through the harbor chop, then saw that its course was not the usual one from Kowloon to Hong Kong. It was crossing the course at right angles, bound toward the outer part of the harbor. He reached into the pilothouse for his signal lamp.

"Ring down," he said quietly to the coxswain. "We'll just have a look at this fellow."

He flashed the "K" signal and at once the walla-walla turned toward him. Before it was alongside, Merryweather knew almost exactly what he would find. Nothing. It was deadly boring, but again he was showing the flag. Word got about among the water people that the British were on the job and that presumably had some value.

Stepping carefully to avoid soiling his white shorts, Merryweather followed his Chinese sergeant to the deck of the walla-walla. While the three Chinese aboard waited with stony indifference he examined the boat's license. The sergeant pulled up the floorboards and let down the doors beneath the seats. Merryweather poked his flashlight into the compartments. There was nothing of interest in them, of course—there never was—only a few cooking utensils, rice bowls, a dirty collection of spare parts for the engine and a single motheaten life jacket. He was about to return to the patrol boat when the sergeant hauled out two childlike women from the cuddy forward of the engine. Small as they were, Merryweather wondered how they had managed to cramp themselves into such a small space. They stood side by side on the deck now, looking up at him without fear, insolent almost, and he thought, Oh God, what a bloody nuisance and why did the sergeant have to be so diligent? The girls were about sixteen, if indeed they were that old, and their black eyes stared at him out of smooth, round faces which were far from innocent.

"Going to the ships, of course?" Merryweather said in Chinese. "Launchman, you know you are subject to fine?"

The launchman shrugged his shoulders and nodded his head. Of course he knew. So did the girls. So did everyone else, including the sailors who would be waiting on some freighter off in the dark for the girls to be delivered. Sometimes whole boatloads of girls were delivered to the ships. It was standard practice and stopping the traffic was impossible. Prostitution was not illegal in Hong Kong, nor was it legal. It was just ignored as long as the countless thousands of girls who were engaged in the business stayed out of trouble. But going to the ships was another thing, because the girls could bring any kind of contraband from the ships to the shore. And so Merryweather wished he had never stopped the walla-walla because now he would have to write a report the next day when he should be sleeping.

He wrote down the license number of the launch and the name of the skipper. He told him to report to T-Lands police station within twenty-four hours. He ordered the girls aboard the patrol boat and dismissed the launchman.

"Ring up half ahead, Cox'n."

Merryweather hardly glanced at the girls as he stepped inside the pilot-house. They were standing close together, leaning against a bulkhead and chattering softly. Merryweather gently pushed them aside. There was a cabinet underneath the bulkhead and it contained his nightly bottle of milk. He wanted his milk before he did anything else.

"Where do you sleep?"

"Shanghai-Gai."

"Sampan girls?"

"Hai."

Hai—naturally. Well, it was time for a look about there anyway. Check on a few identity cards. Show the flag.

"We'll take you home."

"Nay, yau-sum."

"You're welcome."

Merryweather drained the milk bottle and threw it overboard. He told the coxswain to proceed to the Yaumati typhoon shelter.

No one knew exactly how many junks and sampans crowded the Yaumati shelter and no one would ever know because the population changed constantly. Unlike Aberdeen, which was a natural indentation in the side of Hong Kong island where the fishing junks moored, the Yaumati shelter was man-made. A breakwater had been built against the west side of the Kowloon Peninsula and within its protection a vast city had grown upon the water. There were streets laid out within the city, but the streets were liquid and the life of all the population was as changeable as the tides.

Just inside the breakwater entrance the broader streets began. Here the great ocean-going junks were moored, most of them well over a hundred feet long. They were tied hull to hull, row upon row, and in the dark haze their high galleon-like poops diminished to a vanishing point in such an orderly fashion they might have been there forever.

There were three mile-long streets of ocean-going junks. Sometimes fifty people lived on one of the larger junks and sometimes only twenty or thirty, but it was true that many of the people had never stood on the land for more than a few hours in their life. They were born on the water, they loved and were loved, and ate, and were sick, and laughed and wept, and sweated, and defecated, and died upon the water. Only then, when the mourning was well begun and the white lanterns of death were hung from the poop, did the junk people condescend to go permanently ashore. The funerals, too, were most often held on the junk of the lost one, but the final burial must be on the good land of China. The deceased would be buried in the earth of China and allowed to rot until only the bones remained. Then during the festival of Ching Ming, the bones would be dug up, washed and tenderly arranged in an earthenware jar which preferably stood on a hillside overlooking the sea. As soon as the relatives could afford the land and the stone, a permanent tomb would be built in the shape of a womb. And so the return was complete and all would be well.

The ocean-going junks seldom left Yaumati these days. For trade in the China Sea had dwindled to a fraction of its former activity and everywhere there were hazards worse than the storms. Even the pirates were poor since the Nationalists and the Communists had usurped their trade and, though they came aboard armed with official papers as well as weapons, the junk people found themselves speaking almost nostalgically of the older pirates.

Shoreward of the large junks there were streets of smaller vessels. These were the coastwise junks and though the people who lived on them were of less stature socially, they were in the same tight bind for trade.

Inside the smaller junks there were thousands of sampans tied together so that they formed narrower streets, intersections and alleyways. These stretched in a complicated maze to the putrid shore where the sewers of Kowloon emptied, and only a citizen of Yaumati could find his way through the twisting lanes. The sampan people were better off in a way, though they were the lowest of water-born society. Their boats were seldom more than fifteen feet long, which made a crowded home for as many as five persons, but they performed innumerable small services to the community and so they were able to eat with regularity. The sampans served as taxis through the streets, and their people were vendors of fresh water, vegetables, soda pop, hardware and cloth.

There were wedding barges in Yaumati, and food barges, and restaurants and sampans where men could go and drink beer or rice wine of the first distillation. There was even a street of pleasure among the sampans. Toward it, Merryweather directed his patrol boat.

The larger streets accommodated the patrol boat well enough, but as they penetrated further into the harbor, Merryweather was obliged to commandeer a sampan. The two girls were yawning now and as he directed them to follow his sergeant into the sampan, he thought they were more childlike than ever. He hated to think of the numbers of men who had used their bodies.

The street known as Shanghai-Gai was the pleasure street and the sampan glided to it through cavelike darkness. But the street itself was relatively brilliant. There were more than fifty sampans along each side and a kerosene lantern hung from each rounded canopy. These sampans, Merryweather knew, were owned by a syndicate and in return for her services a girl was allowed one of her own. And so they furnished their floating cribs according to their fancies and kept them astonishingly neat and clean.

Merryweather deposited his girls on their respective sampans and moved on, turning his flashlight occasionally on a sampan that was dark and sometimes surprising a man and a girl who were locked on the matting. But he turned his light away instantly, for this was China—the ponderous living, breathing, dying, copulating monster of a nation that was as difficult for the human mind to comprehend as the distance between stars.

Most of the girls were asleep. Merryweather could see their forms huddled on the matting and he had no wish to awaken them. But near the end of the street he came upon two sampans where the girls were awake and he told the sergeant to check their identity cards. One was very young, like the girls he had taken from the walla-wallas. The other was older and, as Merryweather's sampan slipped toward her own, she greeted him in English.

"Hello . . . police. Go 'way. No trouble here."

"I'll just have a look at your card," Merryweather said.

"What trouble? I do no bad things." She scrambled on her knees to the miniature dresser at the end of the sampan and brought a card from the drawer. Here the light from the lantern better illuminated her face and Merryweather saw that although it was a peasant face it was unusually intelligent—particularly so, he thought, for a sampan girl. He looked at her card, which gave her occupation as nil, like most of the cards along Shanghai-Gai, but her home was given as Canton which was unusual because most of the girls simply gave Hong Kong or the island of Lan Tao. It was easier that way.

"I do no bad thing," the girl said again. "You want make love . . . policeman?"

"No." He was about to return her card when he noticed the pictures which surrounded the small mirror above her dresser. Photos were standard decorations on the sampans, but they were invariably poor, faded snapshots of relatives or movie stars torn from magazines. These pictures were different and he knelt to study them more closely. They were rather remarkable studies of a Chinese girl's face. There were eight poses, some joyous against a sky and others tragic in deep shadow. These are the everlasting face of China, he thought, and they're damned well done.

"Pictures . . . me!" the girl said proudly.

"So I see."

"Good . . . yes? Good picture?"

"Very good. Who took them?"

"'Merican man take pictures. Give me pictures all same money. Very good, yes?"

Merryweather started to leave. He was becoming bored again. You didn't have to think in another language when you talked to a girl in Swansea. But how the hell did an American get down into Yaumati? The pictures were new, or at least they looked new. It didn't make sense.

"You lie," he said. "American men don't come here."

"No . . . no! I no lie! 'Merican man make pictures. He not make love. Just make pictures. Give me. I no steal! Give me pictures in Canton!"

"Now I know you're lying. There aren't any Americans in Canton. These are new pictures."

"Yes . . . yes! New pictures! Take small time ago. I jus' come Hong Kong small time."

The girl was almost in tears now and Merryweather was sorry for her. He would get off her sampan and leave her alone.

"Have it your way. You should have been in the cinema."

The girl brightened and smiled. "Yes. I like cinema!"

"Carry on. Stay out of trouble . . . and stop lying." He gave her a pat on the shoulder and boarded his own sampan. "Let's get out of here, sergeant. It's almost four."

Merryweather did not sign the patrol boat over to Inspector Simpson until 8:32 A.M. The delay angered him because the sun was already well up at eight, and sleeping would be difficult. He spoke sharply to Simpson because he was late and then, regretting it, wished him a good tour. He was another fifteen minutes filling out the report on the walla-walla after he reached T-Lands police station. Then rubbing the beard stubble on his face he walked sleepily toward the quarters he shared with Inspector Rodman.

At T-Lands, a fortress-like building overlooking the harbor, the young British inspectors lived on station, which was fortunate because their pay was so low they could not have lived anywhere else. Beyond the booking desk and the prisoners' holding cage, which were much like any police station, the atmosphere was more military. There was a hall where thirty Chinese constables were receiving their morning briefing as Merryweather passed along it. One end of the hall led to the cells. The other end opened upon a covered porch which ran the length of the entire building and was bordered by a well-kept lawn. Offices opened onto the porch, and beyond them were Merryweather's quarters, which consisted of a sparsely furnished living room and a bedroom.

Merryweather said good morning to his chief inspector, who waved back at him, as he passed one of the offices. He went on to the screen door at the end of the porch. Letting himself in, he yelled to the amah for tea. He threw his cap on the table and himself on the couch. He stared at the revolving ceiling fan while he waited for tea and silently cursed the heat. He had almost dozed off when Inspector Rodman came into the room.

"Good morning!" Rodman said cheerfully. He was a husky young man, square-faced and so dark of complexion he looked more black-Irish than

English. He was very quick of movement, a quality which contrasted strangely with his soft, slow speech, and Merryweather thought that his fresh white shirt and shorts plus his well-rested appearance were almost more than he could bear.

"Good morning, I said."

"Oh, bugger off!" Merryweather rolled over on his side and pulled a cigarette from the tin on the table.

"Some people are pleasant in the morning, and then there are other people," Rodman said. "I worried about you all night. Missed you, as a matter of fact."

"Where were you? The Princess Ballroom, I've no bloody doubt."

"Right. The girls were asking for you. I told them Potts was in horrible shape and would probably die and therefore you wouldn't be dropping around for several months."

"You bastard."

"I particularly enjoyed little Fay Yang . . . the one you fancied . . . quite a dancer . . . remember, the little Peiping girl—?"

"You filthy, rotten bastard."

"Pity you couldn't have been along."

"Why don't you ever get bonged with a night duty?"

"My boy!" Rodman drew back in mock astonishment. "I was up half the night chasing the most desperate criminals from Sham Sui Po to Kap Shek Mi to Ho Mun Tin and back to Sham Sui Po again. I wouldn't be surprised if the chief would hand me out a medal for my efforts. I barely managed my eight hours' sleep and have just this moment opened my baby blue eyes."

Merryweather groaned and rolled to a sitting position on the couch as the amah came in with the tea.

"I'll have a spot with you," Rodman said. "How was your night?"

"Awful."

"You don't say." Rodman filled Merryweather's cup and patted him tenderly on the head. "Swansea was licked . . . or did you know?"

"I know. I don't care to discuss it just now."

"My sympathies anyhow. Do you have the duty tonight, too?"

"Every night until Potts gets better. I'm sick of it. Nothing ever happens. Last week I fished three bodies from the harbor, all of them in loathsome condition. This week I stopped a few walla-wallas just to show the flag."

"Cheer up. Perhaps tonight you'll find a few more bodies." Rodman drained his teacup without taking it from his lips and stood up. "We're playing tennis at five. Care to join us?"

"I haven't the strength." Merryweather yawned and half-closed his eyes.

"One thing I saw last night rather haunts me, though. I keep thinking of it as the face of China."

"You're raving. You do need sleep."

"I checked a few I.D. cards in Shanghai-Gai to pass the time. One of the girls had several photos of herself and they were really splendid."

"In the nude, no doubt?"

"No. Just heads."

"How uninteresting."

"She said some American took them of her in Canton."

"Which was a lie, of course."

"Of course . . . but they were quite remarkable. Art pieces, you might say. I told her she should be in the cinema."

"My exact words to Fay Yang last night."

Rodman's Chinese sergeant knocked politely on the screen door. He wore the customary black silk coat and pants and thus was indistinguishable from the ordinary Chinese in the street except for a small brown spot over his hip where the butt of his revolver rubbed against the silk. He was a pleasant-looking young man with a ready smile, but he came from Kwantung province and Rodman had been grateful on several occasions that he followed the tradition of Kwantung men and was very tough. He was known by his badge number—1303. It never occurred to Rodman or the other British inspectors to call him anything else.

"Come in, One-Three-O-Three."

The sergeant's English was not of the best, but at least it was equivalent to Rodman's Chinese and so they managed to work efficiently together. Rodman went armed only in extreme emergencies. It was a long-established custom with the British inspectors—the theory being that British authority was so absolute, arms were never necessary. Even so, it was comforting at times to know that One-Three-O-Three always stood near and sometimes wore Rodman's own revolver concealed beneath his loose coat.

"American lady come see," said One-Three-O-Three. "Missy Ho-eet. Wait by and by. Booking desk." He waved his arm vaguely behind him.

"See *me*? You sure, One-Three-O-Three?"

"Yes. Sure. Young missy. Sure."

Rodman looked at Merryweather and smiled mischievously.

"I'll come right along then! American heiress, no doubt. Most agreeable way to start the morning!" He turned to Merryweather. "Go to bed. Give your everlasting curiosity a rest."

Rodman walked briskly along the covered porch, waved at his chief through the office window as Merryweather had done, then turned down the hall. He wrinkled his nose at the odor of disinfectant which floated down the hall from the cells, then paused for a moment at the door of the Chinese sergeants' room. It was a spartan dormitory half-filled with double-decker bunks, and those who had been on duty all night were sleeping soundly. Three sergeants were quietly playing cards at a bare table and they smiled when they saw Rodman, which pleased him immensely because their grins were proof that his favorite theory was right and the old Pukka-sahibs were wrong. Ever since he had come to Hong Kong Rodman had practiced what he liked to think of as fraternization. He believed that it was the old Pukka-sahibs, the arrogant, mustachioed, ramrod cold English masters, who had lost Asia to the Empire. Rodman did not believe in the whip or the aloof eye. He had often been criticized by older observers for "lowering himself" because he treated his Chinese aides as equal human beings if not in rank. Rodman didn't care. He knew that the Empire could never be regained, but at least the remnants of it might be held together if only more Englishmen would modernize their ways. He learned Chinese as well as any Englishman could hope to do and next year he was determined to speak Mandarin as well as the Canton dialect. He respected the ways and the customs of his Chinese sergeants and so they came to him whenever they had problems. Yet the best thing of all was the way they smiled now as he stood in the door.

"Card players always die broke," Rodman said in Cantonese.

"When a blind mouse meets a dead rat—there you are," one of the sergeants answered.

It was enough. It was a good morning. Rodman left them and continued toward the booking desk. Just before he turned off the hall he almost collided with a wiry little sergeant known as Two-Five-Hundred. Two-Five-Hundred was the smallest policeman on the force. Two-Five-Hundred was also the clown of the force, and if there was a joke to be played on anyone or elaborate mischief to be planned, Two-Five-Hundred could always be found at the bottom of things. Rodman also knew that the Communists did not consider Two-Five-Hundred a clown. They had openly promised him "fifteen" if they ever got their hands on him—three bursts of five bullets each from a burp gun. This was considerably more than the mere five bullets they had promised Rodman himself and he was well aware that professionally it was a loss of face.

Rodman stepped quickly to one side and caught Two-Five-Hundred's arm. He twisted it back and upward toward his neck and held him struggling and howling in mock pain until the laughter of the thirty constables rattled up and down the hall. But Two-Five-Hundred was really laughing, too, and so was One-Three-O-Three and so was Rodman, and the feeling was good in the hall. Because they all knew it was not easy to catch an agile man like Two-Five-Hundred off balance, and because such horseplay in an Englishman was as rare as an honest Parsee.

"Good morning, you scoundrel," Rodman said releasing him.

"Good morning," Two-Five-Hundred said, still laughing. He rubbed his arm and his eyes were full of affection as Rodman walked away.

She was waiting near the main doorway, wary and nervous. A glance was enough to make Rodman certain she had never been in a police station before. The sunlight came hard through the entrance and splashed her face with light enough for him also to be sure that she was somewhat older than himself, and this was disappointing. But he went directly to her and introduced himself with a slight bow.

"I'm Mrs. Hoyt . . . Jane Hoyt."

"We don't see many Americans here. How can I help you?"

"I'm not sure." She looked about her uncomfortably, at the sergeant who sat behind the high booking desk and the two pickpockets waiting in the bail cage who watched her every movement. "I'd like to talk to you. Isn't there . . . a better place?"

"We could go into my office, but the lawn might be more pleasant. There are some chairs in the shade. Come along, Mrs. Hoyt." Mrs., he thought. Why does she have to be married? She was only a *few* years older and it would be fun to talk to her about America. It would be a relief from the boredom of taking Chinese girls to the cinema.

He led her to the wooden chairs which were placed beneath a tree on the lawn. One-Three-O-Three followed them a little way, and then sat down on the entrance steps to smoke a cigarette.

"Now—?" Rodman said.

"A few months ago you went to the Pacific Hotel on a complaint about a Louis Hoyt. Do you remember?"

"Yes . . . yes, I do." Rodman thought it a pity a ladylike girl should be mixed up with such a chap. Unless his memory failed him, and it seldom did, Rodman was sure the fellow had skipped off without paying his rent. "I'm a bit vague about it now, but I seem to recall his credit isn't of the best there."

"I'm his wife. I paid his rent this morning."

"Oh?"

"The manager claims he left nothing of value in his room when he went away. Is that true?"

"There was a duffel bag, I believe . . . with some clothes in it. There were also some magazines. What does your husband say?"

"I'm fairly certain that he is being held prisoner by the Communists."

"Oh. . . ." Rodman looked down at the grass. The morning had taken a sudden turn for the worse. He was not in the mood for tears, he thought, and he hoped there weren't going to be any. Then as she told him about Louis Hoyt he knew from the firm sound of her voice that there would be no tears.

"I understand your consul's position," he said when she had finished.

"There really isn't anything he can do. Unfortunately we are stuck with the same limitations. Our duties are very definitely laid down."

"Could I see those cameras . . . the ones that were found on the junk?"

"Certainly, if they haven't been redeemed." He waved his hand at One-Three-O-Three and told him to get the cameras if they were still in bond. "Supposing they are your husband's cameras. How would they help?"

"Couldn't you find the captain of the junk and question him? He might know where Louis is."

"We could try, but I wouldn't set too much store by it. There are thousands of junks and they are constantly moving about. Even if we could find him, chances are the chap would never tell us the truth."

"Would you try if my husband were a British subject?"

"We'll *try* even if he's an American. But it will be like looking for a special grain of sand on a beach. It might take months to run across the proper junk fellow. But I'll dig back in the records and send out the poop on him . . . I really will."

"Would you tell me something, Inspector? Who is Hank Lee?"

She said it suddenly and Rodman frowned. If her husband had anything to do with Henry Lee he was determined to retract his offer and get rid of her as soon as possible. Of all the bloody Yanks in the world, Lee was a cinch to be hung. And Rodman would gladly spring the trap.

"You don't know him?"

"No. That's why I ask."

"Did your husband know him?"

"I don't think so. I couldn't be sure."

"Very well then. I'll be quite frank and say that Lee is a disgrace to your country. If we didn't have so much else to do we would long ago have run him out of the Colony. I rather think the Governor is simply biding his time, because the rascal would only move up to Macao and carry on from there. But we'll hang him one day."

"What does he do? Why do you dislike him so?"

"Dislike is a mild word, Mrs. Hoyt. Your Henry Lee is a brigand, a pirate, a smuggler and a traitor. He will do anything to make a dollar and has."

"Then why don't you do something about him?"

"I neglected to say that he is also extraordinarily clever. We can't prove a single one of my accusations, and British law, in case you aren't aware of it, has a peculiar way of favoring the criminal."

"So does American law, Inspector. In the long run, maybe it's a good thing."

"Not for policemen."

"And I'm sure you're a very good one."

Rodman looked at her with renewed interest. There was a forthrightness about this girl which intrigued him. She wasn't at all like the whipped-cream American girls he had seen in the cinema. Whether she knew it or not she was as good as a widow and yet she contrived to appear perfectly at ease now that they were alone. Then Rodman remembered she was the first American girl he had ever talked to for more than a moment, and he decided very suddenly that if they were all like this Mrs. Hoyt he would pass through America on his next leave home and look for a wife. The heat of the day was already coming, he could feel it now pressing even into the shade and yet her vitality remained the same. She sparkles, he thought. Without a movement of her hand or any of the feminine dramatics which might be expected—she sparkles. It would be pleasant to sit with this blue-eyed girl all of the morning and perhaps think of a way to help her. Now wait a moment! Don't go bashing about with blood in your eyes because an American girl, or any other girl, says you are a good policeman! Getting Yanks out of trouble is not the reason Her Majesty pays you eighty pounds a month . . . and behind that sparkle, there is promise of trouble.

"Do you know a Mr. Tweedie?" she asked.

"Indeed I do." Another Yank who would be better off elsewhere, Rodman thought. No, not better off, because he had certainly done well enough in Hong Kong, but just how he made so much money was open to suspicion. Again never proved—but he certainly hadn't made it all running a restaurant.

"Is he reliable?"

"That depends." In spite of the sparkle she wasn't going to be able to quote Rodman too explicitly. A loose tongue could hold up a promotion.

"What I am trying to find out is . . . would his information be reliable? He said my husband was dead."

How can she sit there so calmly then, if Tweedie did say so, he wondered. Tweedie didn't know everything, but there was a great deal he did know.

"He has many sources of information."

"What kind of sources? How could he learn my husband was dead?"

"Wouldn't he tell you?"

"No."

"Did you believe him?"

"No. . . ."

The sparkle vanished and Rodman wished he had never asked the question. He watched her eyes and saw that they were no longer so alive.

"Why not?"

"I know . . . I can't explain it. I just . . . know." She spread her hands apart.

It was a helpless, appealing gesture. Rodman was not surprised, but he was disappointed. Now she was behaving like a woman in trouble and therefore became more like all the others he had seen. The tears would come now, he was certain. In a moment she will be pleading with me to find her husband and she will bawl all over the station and I won't be able to do a bloody thing about it except tell the matron to take her home.

"If he was dead . . . I would know it," she said more firmly.

Nonsense. But if she believed it, why try to change her mind?

"Tweedie is supposed to have connections in China," he said. "What they do, or whether they are reliable, I couldn't say. No one is sure what goes on behind those hills. I very much doubt if the Communists do, really . . . I'll take that back. Your Henry Lee would know."

"Then I must talk to Henry Lee."

"That's not an easy thing to arrange."

"Why? Couldn't you give me a note to him? Would you, *please?*"

"I would be the last person in the world to set you up with Lee. We're doing our best to make life difficult for him here . . . and one day we'll make it impossible. He doesn't fancy policemen."

"How can I meet him then? What does he do that's so wrong?"

Oh hell, Rodman thought. Give her the poop and be rid of her. Whatever he said about Hank Lee could do no harm. He leaned forward in his chair with his elbows on his bare knees, speaking more rapidly than he usually did because he wanted to finish with thinking of the man. It was turning out to be a rotten morning.

"Lee came here right after the war and set himself up as a business-man. It's possible that he started in a legitimate fashion, but he didn't stay that way very long. He calls himself an import-exporter. Before the Communists took over China he confined himself pretty much to drugs and gold. Now he's found a better product . . . strategic materials . . . titanium . . . tool steel . . . aluminum . . . electrical products and just plain arms. He ships them on his junks, mostly motor-driven and quite fast . . . to your friends, and my friends . . . the Communists."

"Why doesn't someone stop him?"

"Who would you suggest?"

"Your navy."

"We are not at war with Communist China. If we fired on every junk we might start one, since Lee's junks sail under the Communist flag. And there are so many others it's impossible to tell which are engaged in authorized trade."

"But how can they? This is British territory."

"A few miles of land . . . yes. But just outside the harbor the waters are Chinese. They can and do stop British vessels when they please. They actually fired on a Royal Navy launch last year. Practically within sight of this police station . . . killed seven fine chaps and wounded all but one of the crew. Protests were made but nothing was done about it. Absolutely nothing."

"I'm sorry to be so stupid . . . but you *do* trade with China?"

"Nonstrategic materials only. We do it to keep alive and we're not very proud of it. Without that trade, Hong Kong would become a ghost city."

"What about Chiang Kai-shek? Can't he stop this Lee man?"

"Chiang spends most of his naval energy pirating British ships. You supply him with the money and the equipment to do it."

A silence fell between them. Rodman rubbed his knees with the palms of his hands and wondered why he had said so much. How could anyone hope to explain the complex problem of Hong Kong to a girl from America who obviously had only one thing on her mind? He looked up gratefully when he saw One-Three-O-Three coming across the lawn with the cameras.

He watched her face as she held the cameras in her hands. Now the tears would come, he thought—if they happen to be the right cameras. He waited while she opened one case and examined the lens carefully. Her fingers were knowing and perfectly steady, as if she were merely considering a purchase. And suddenly Rodman was sick of his profession—for it was not the first time he had turned over a dead man's effects to a new widow. He glanced at One-Three-O-Three, who stood waiting solemnly with his hands folded behind him, and saw him outlined in the sunlight against the mass of the station itself. One-Three-O-Three was authority, and you, Rodman, are even more authority, and so your beautiful mornings are soon ruined by the tears of people who must rely on authority. And it said in the regulations that there were only certain things you could do to relieve the tears. Never make any statement that was not fact. And the regulations were as the laws of Moses. And he was sick of himself in the morning shade because he could not offer this woman any facts which might give her hope. Her face now would haunt him all day— he would think of her sitting there, holding the cameras so quietly. He would think of her all day long.

"These are Louis' cameras," she said and Rodman dared to look at her face again because there was not the slightest indication of hysteria in her voice.

"I was with Louis when he bought them and so I am sure."

Rodman stood up. He looked at the station and admitted to himself that he was a coward. To hell with the regulations—he would give this woman some hope. He would tell her now about Merryweather and what he had discovered in Shanghai-Gai—fact or not.

"One of our inspectors has an insatiable curiosity, Mrs. Hoyt," he said.

"Quite proper, of course, for his work, but it's a fetish with him. Last night he was poking about the sampans in Yaumati . . . purely routine, but he came across a prostitute who claimed an American had recently taken pictures of her in Canton. He said the pictures were extraordinarily good. They move, those girls . . . move about a good bit, but I'll go have a talk with her . . . if she's still there."

"*Recently?*" She leaned forward anxiously.

"It may have been a month ago . . . it may have been only a fortnight . . . or less. I'll find out."

"Thank you, Inspector Rodman," she said quietly. "You *are* a good policeman."

"My chief might not feel the same way. But if your husband is still alive, you possibly won't have much time to waste."

He turned away from the building and studied her eyes for a moment. She was smiling and the morning was better again, but he knew he would curse himself if the hope he had given her was false. His slow speech returned and his voice was almost inaudible when he said, "And because he is the only person who could really help you, I'm also going to tell you how to find Henry Lee."

5

A concrete ramp descended from the elevation of T-Lands police station to Salisbury Road. Jane almost ran down the ramp. I would like to really run, she thought. It took so very little to lift a heart. I would like to run and throw my hat in the air and sing. I would like to do exactly what Inspector Rodman told me not to do—and that is hope too much. For at last there was a crack in the barrier . . . something definite about Louis . . . and who else could it have been but Louis? He was alive only a short time ago—maybe only a few weeks, and that explained so much! If he took the pictures of the girl as long as a month ago, he must have been free then. At least free enough to take pictures even while you were protesting to Washington and everywhere else that he was a prisoner. He couldn't write, of course—that was understandable, if he was hiding out as he had planned to do—but he was alive!

Then why did Tweedie say he was dead? How long ago had he received the information, or was it all a lie to begin with? You must go back to Tweedie's and you must find out. And the cameras? How could Louis take pictures when his cameras were stolen in May? He might have bought a third camera in Hong Kong, but there were only those two when he left Japan.

Her mind spun with the questions, but there was a light in the jungle now, a feeble light true enough—still it might guide the way to many things. Tweedie . . . Marty Gates . . . Inspector Rodman. And now written on a slip of paper in your bag, the address of Henry Lee. Lee must help. Seven thousand dollars would *make* him help if nothing else. Three thousand dollars in traveler's checks and a four-thousand-dollar letter of credit. Seven thousand dollars, saved the hard way. It would be a crime to turn the money over to a man like Henry Lee, but if he could bring Louis back to safety, then that was what the money was intended to do. It was all in the little account book.

She turned to the right on Salisbury Road and her pace slowed as she walked toward the ferry landing. The feeling of dread was coming again; the fear was capsizing the new hope and the more she analyzed what she had learned, the less honest reason there seemed to be for even a moment of exhilaration. And there was time. Inspector Rodman had suggested that time might be very important. How much time, and how could Henry Lee be hurried? There—you are taking it for granted that Henry Lee will do anything at all. Seven thousand dollars might be meaningless to a man like him. But he *must* . . . somehow he must, and he must hurry.

The thought quickened her walk again and she was almost breathless when she arrived before a small curio shop which faced upon the broad square of the ferry landing. The window of the shop was crammed with small ivory statues, cheap silk pajamas, ivory elephants, fans and crudely made models of Chinese junks. Jane hardly glanced at the window. It was the only curio store on the block and that was enough, for here, God willing, she would find Maxine Chan.

She entered the doorway and halted a moment to accustom her eyes to the shade. Out of the gloom at the rear of the store a soft voice welcomed her.

"Good morning. May I help you?" A Chinese girl emerged from the shade and except for the soft rustle of her long Chinese dress she moved silently toward the light.

"I am looking for Maxine Chan."

"I am Maxine."

Jane looked at her and for a moment was lost in admiration of the girl. Oh Louis! You were doing all right! It's a wonder your sense of the exquisite didn't keep you in Hong Kong forever! Her eyes were enormous, deep brown and perfectly set against skin which had the texture and almost the color of gold. And the dress did her no harm either. It was a deep blue-green and the high Chinese neck band made a flawless pedestal for her delicately modeled face.

"I'm so glad you speak English," Jane said uncertainly. How did you tell a strange girl, without frightening her, that you wanted to talk about your husband?

"I should. My family has always spoken English. We still do when we are together . . . and I went to school in the United States."

"Oh? Where?"

"Mills College in Oakland." She looked questioningly at Jane. "Would you like to see some silks, or—"

"I'm just trying . . . I mean if you have a few minutes I'd like to ask you some questions about my husband." Jane held up her hand quickly and smiled. "Oh no . . . no! Don't run away. I'm not a jealous wife looking for revenge." The way she said it must have been right, she thought, for now there was a smile on Maxine's face. "Although I should be jealous, I wouldn't blame him if he never came home to Mama. You're the loveliest thing I've ever seen."

They laughed together, guardedly at first, then Maxine said she was very kind. "Wait a minute! I know you. You're Louis Hoyt's wife! He showed me your picture and the picture was a laughing picture and so now I recognize you." And then their laughter became warmer.

"I . . . I'm glad he did. That's a healthy sign."

"Don't worry about your husband. He's a wonderful guy. He makes everybody who comes anywhere near him feel good. I envy you. Please come in the back of the shop and have some tea."

"All right."

They sat opposite each other at a low table and drank their tea from the thinnest cups Jane had ever seen. And soon a feeling of well-being came to her because it was obvious Maxine had nothing to hide. Louis said you could always tell the bitches. You could tell them a mile away no matter what their nationality. They were so often sweet or coy—those were the worst—or they protested their innocence so continuously they were sickening. But Maxine Chan was far more than a charming creature. Listening to her as she made the tea and talked of her family, and how they had been forced out of China and obliged to make such a living as they could from the little curio store, was good. She was not feeling sorry for herself. She was simply talking to place her guest at ease and she seemed to find more humor than complaint in her situation.

"I am going to wind up an old maid if I don't stop going out with Americans," Maxine said. "Nice Chinese girls simply don't do it. But what can I do? These slant eyes of mine present a lot of problems. They may look pretty to you and for a few hours they are attractive to a Caucasian, but if he's in his right mind he doesn't get very serious. Sure I want to get married. But who? I'm ruined. I went to school in America. I think like an American and I can't help it. If I married a Chinese I think I would die . . . because I'm spoiled. Chinese love for people in my class is mixed with finance. In a few years, if my husband gets a little tired of me, he can take a concubine . . . or two of them, or three . . . or as many as he can afford. And there's nothing I could do about it. Where does that leave Maxine? Home tending babies maybe, which would be all right if there was any security along with it. But if anything happens to my Chinese husband, if he dies . . . he can leave all his money to his concubine or her children, and there's no law to stop him. Don't believe all that talk about a Chinese wife having security. Unless she's very lucky, she has a lot less than you have. I like to have fun . . . but Chinese boys won't take me out—for one thing because I've been seen with Americans. Also they consider it a waste of money because if they take me out more than once or twice, it means they want to marry me. That's custom, because I'm what is known as a family girl—in your language, a nice girl. The Chinese boys stick with the dance-hall girls until their family makes some suitable arrangement for them. So I might as well have fun while I can. I'm the visiting fireman's delight and since I know just about everybody in Hong Kong, or sometimes when I'm having tea at the Peninsula I think I do . . . things keep happening and most nights I have some kind of a party or a date . . . I never have time to brood really."

"Do you know a Fernand Rocha . . . or is it Fernando?"

"Sure. He was with us the night your husband took me to dinner. Fernand plays the mandolin. He can be fun when he wants to be. But never as much fun as your Louis. Your husband always looks things right in the eye. He is not afraid to tell the truth always . . . and he makes it fun—even when the truth is bad."

"Does Fernand Rocha just play the mandolin?"

"He's also a language teacher. He has a small school in Macao, but I don't think he has many pupils."

Then, carefully watching her eyes, Jane told her about Louis and how he had disappeared. And watching her she was satisfied that at last she had found a friend. Because in Maxine's eyes there was a look of genuine surprise, and then anger mixed with fear.

"I know he wanted to go to China," she said. "But I thought he had given up."

"Not Louis. Do you think Rocha might have arranged a one-way ticket for him?"

"He would do anything for money."

"Louis didn't have much. Five hundred dollars or so."

"Fernand would sell his own mother for ten."

"Marty Gates said the same thing."

Maxine raised her eyebrows. "You certainly get around in a hurry."

"I have to hurry. How can I find this man Rocha?"

"In Macao. He spends most of his time there."

"I'm a little vague about Macao. Where is it and how do I get there?"

"Easily. Take a ferryboat. There are two a day and it's only a four-hour ride. It's a very small place . . . entirely surrounded by China."

"Maxine . . . do you know Henry Lee?"

"Sure." Was it the way she spoke the single word or the way her voice had dropped? Maxine's face was expressionless now. She was on guard again.

"What kind of a man is he? What do you think of him?"

Maxine took a cigarette from a cloisonné box on the table. Her long, beautifully formed fingers toyed with the cigarette, turning it end over end. Jane saw a box of matches near the end of the table. She reached for it quickly and as Maxine leaned forward to accept the light, their eyes met.

"I think he is the most wonderful man in the world." Maxine spoke so softly her voice was almost a whisper. And suddenly Jane was fascinated with the look in her eyes, for she was almost certain they were telling far more than her words. In one look, Jane thought, she has given herself away to another woman, and to me at least, she will never be able to deny she is in love with Henry Lee. Be careful. The judgment of a woman in love is as unstable as the wind.

"Some people are not quite as enthusiastic about him," Jane said carefully. Careful. Watch a woman in love. She can turn like a wild thing and destroy even a lifetime friendship. And this relation was less than an hour old. Maxine! Look at me again! I like you and I need you and I understand! But I must know about Henry Lee! Please, Maxine. Look at me and my eyes will only repeat your own! I don't care, Maxine. It's none of my business and I don't want to make it so. It's only instinct that makes me sure you're in love, Maxine. You're Chinese and I'm an American, but it's all the same if you're a woman. Say something, Maxine. Look at me.

"Whatever you've heard about Hank Lee is only a part of him," she said finally.

It's all right, now, Jane thought. It's all right. She is not trying to hide her love from me. She will tell me, if I wait.

"I'm sure it is. All I want to know is, do you think Henry Lee could help me . . . or would he? How can I approach him? How can I make him listen to a total stranger?"

"Are you going to try to make him listen?"

"Yes. No matter what I have to do. He's almost my last hope."

"Then I will tell you one thing. Hank can never resist a stranger. I know, because I was once a stranger to him. He put up the money for this shop. My father came out of China with only the coat on his back. My mother, who had never worked with her hands in her life, got the job doing Hank's household laundry. She was his shirt-amah, as they're called out here. One day she told him about us and how we wanted to start a shop. Hank gave her the money . . . right then . . . without a question or a time limit. It was over a year before I even saw him, and then—well, I saw him." She took a long drag on her cigarette. Now, Jane thought, she knows I know and it's all right with her if I understand there is more than gratitude in the way she speaks of him.

"Hank can never resist a stray," Maxine went on more easily. "You'll see. He's got a great big wonderful heart . . . as big as his body. To me . . . he will always be like the Emperor of China."

"Do you see him very often?"

"No." Jane instantly regretted asking the question. She had intruded too far. Maxine's whole manner had suddenly become distant and cold.

"Is it too early for me to call on him?"

"Hank always gets up early. But he may be out." She hesitated. "I'll phone for you."

She rose and went out into the shop. Jane waited a long time. She could hear her talking on the telephone, but the conversation was all in Chinese and it seemed endless. She was certain, though, that at one point in the conversation the melody of Maxine's voice became more plaintive, as if she were trying to project herself over the wires. Finally there was silence again and Maxine was standing in the doorway. Although her voice was perfectly normal her poise was undone. She has been crying, Jane thought, and she cannot wait to be rid of me. She is asking me to go.

"Be ready at the Peninsula at seven o'clock," Maxine said. "He will send a car for you."

"Could you go along?"

"No. He didn't invite me."

Though she spent most of her waking hours in the lobby of the Peninsula, Madame Dupree was always in her room between the hours of five-thirty and seven. For this was her time of magic. With the door locked, with all of the blind world excluded, the magic time began. Shanghai would come back, and Saigon—the splendid days before the war. There was always a young and pleasantly impatient man waiting in the chair, or by the window, as she swept gracefully about the room. Those little dancing gestures—so well remembered. And the kind of young men who waited and watched as she spun so gaily before the mirror were always the most dashing in the city. The son of a general . . . the son of a minister . . . a handsome attaché at the legation who was so very tall . . . a concert pianist who had come all the way from Munich. Madame Dupree knew them all and permitted them to call her Helene, and sometimes there were two young men waiting at the same time which obliged her to float between them, fluttering her delicate hands and tantalizing them with her superb figure.

"La . . . la!" she would say to the chair, "la . . . la! You must forgive me, darlings! I am exhausted! Such a busy day!"

And turning to the window she would say, "I am so stupid . . . such a foolish girl. I know I am late but I simply cannot keep track of the time. And my maid has not even run the bath. She has not even placed your lovely flowers!" Then she would glide about the room, moving with the sound of music in her heart, and place the flowers on the dresser and beside the bed and on a small table near the door. There were so many flowers there was never room for them all.

The window would say, "Permit me to run your bath . . . permit me!" And the chair would say, "Enchanting!" when she returned from the dressing room, which was large and so filled to brimming with exciting creations it was nearly impossible to choose the right one. But it was always the right one because the chair would say again, "Enchanting." Twirling before the mirror in the thin negligee, so full of joy, she would say to them, laughing, "Cover your eyes!" And they would pretend to do so all smiling, but they would cheat most certainly and see for themselves the exquisitely molded young body and know that the breasts would never sag, or the belly grow fat, or wrinkles plunder the face. La . . . la!

Madame Dupree would sit long in her bath talking to them through the half-open door, shouting to be heard over the sound of splashing water. The bon mots, the très jolies, would fly. When she emerged from the bath, warm and slightly breathless with the rapture of the moment, she would command them to hand her this and that through the door and they would run about seeking the wraithlike clothes with their strong hands and she would tell them they were insane little boys who could never find anything. At last she would return to the room, merry and glowing, to pirouette before the window and the chair and allow them to admire her gown. Finally, she would reluctantly blow them a kiss and the magic time was done.

The magic time could last for an hour or sometimes more. Madame Dupree adjusted it according to her need and she let herself down from it slowly, fading away from it with closed eyes as she might walk through a series of curtains. Motionless at last, not seeing, the voices and the music and the gowns and the young men would go away more easily.

On this night there was still half a bottle of Marty Gates' champagne which she had saved and brought to her room. It was warm and flat but she drank it and wept, for how much longer could even the bath be true?

She took up her station at the window, looking down at the driveway which curved around the hotel entrance. From this vantage point she often scouted her evening. Although the angle of view was nearly vertical she had become expert at identifying a likely prospect as he mounted the steps from the driveway to the lobby. She was particularly interested in older men who walked alone. Yet there were many other things to be seen from the window and sometimes they were helpful when matched with local knowledge. As now, when the American girl came out of the lobby and stood for a moment on the steps talking to the police inspector. Rodman was his name—stuffy British hiding in his shell like an escargot. But equally as interesting. The inspector left her with a smile and a little salute. The American girl stepped into a car waiting in the driveway. A black Bentley. Henry Lee's car—unmistakable. There wasn't another in Hong Kong like it.

When the car pulled away Madame Dupree went quickly to the telephone. She gave the number of Tweedie's Place without hesitation.

"Gunner? Madame Dupree here."

"So? What's on your mind?"

"I'm hungry and I'm broke."

"Lots of people are."

"I have some interesting information. It should be worth something to Tweedie."

"You always say that. What is it this time?"

"A new American girl . . . just arrived yesterday. She's been talking to Inspector Rodman and she just left in Henry Lee's car."

"Wait a minute. . . ."

She made a clumsy arabesque as she held the phone and at the completion of it she found herself facing the door mirror. She turned away from her image instantly, squeezing the phone tightly as if she would press Gunner's voice from it. Then she heard him and the desolation left her face.

"Tweedie says it ain't worth it but come and eat."

The bellboy who stood always ready to open the Peninsula's heavy doors beneath the portico or shoo away ricksha men, watched the black Bentley pull away and turn to the left on Salisbury Road. When it had completely disappeared and the British inspector had definitely turned in the direction of T-Lands station, the bellboy opened the door for himself and entered the lobby. He marched briskly across the vast room, proud of the whiteness of his uniform and the rows of gleaming brass buttons. His uncle, the doorman, had even more brass buttons, which naturally gave him more face, but there were very few Chinese boys of thirteen who had even seen the outside of the Peninsula.

He went to the telephone behind the stairway. Standing on the tips of his toes, he managed to place his lips close to the mouthpiece. He spoke with the Chinese headwaiter at Tweedie's Place and told him of the American woman who had just come to the Peninsula and who had only a moment before been transported away in the car known to be the property of Henry Lee. He gave the exact time of departure and mentioned that the American woman had also talked briefly to Inspector Rodman, although he could not follow their English speech.

He hung up the phone and retraced his path across the lobby. His heels clicked smartly along the marble as he thought how enjoyable it would be to have money for an extra cinema.

6

It seemed to Jane that she had been riding a long time before she recognized the lights of Kai Tak Airport. She was now determined to keep track of the chauffeur's change of direction instead of brooding on what Inspector Rodman had told her. Yes, he had found the girl in the Yaumati junk shelter and her description of the American who had taken the pictures fitted Louis exactly. There could be no question about it now. But Rodman said he had run into a stone mind when he tried to pin down the date. "A short time ago . . . short time," the girl had insisted. "A short time," according to Rodman, could be two weeks or two months in Chinese thinking. Or it might be even more. The girl could not remember, or Rodman thought she *would* not remember because she was in the Colony without proper papers and was afraid she would be sent back to Canton.

So that little hope had died and Louis was as lost as ever.

He had been in Canton and that was all anyone knew.

The car swerved off the broad avenue which bordered the airport and turned into a street barely wide enough to accept it. The street twisted and inclined steeply toward the hills behind Kowloon. It was crowded with people who seemed to regard the car as an antagonist to be defied with suicidal indifference. Although the car brushed their clothing, they were far more intent on the brightly lighted shops which lined each side of the street. The chauffeur honked continuously, but even the blare of his horn was lost in the boisterous anarchy of sound which possessed the street. Radios screeched full volume from most of the shops, tinkers and tradesmen and peddlers beat gongs and sticks upon tin to draw attention and signal their identity, and over all flowed the cries and laughter and accusations of a multitude suffocating for space. Even the smells congealed and became solid—the draperies of dried fish, the baskets of herring, the tubs of rice, the snakes, eels, and animal intestines, the fresh killed goats, ducks, pork, and the lily roots and ginger, and soy bean sprouts, the smell of everything which turned its back to heaven mixed with the mass of people and became a part of them.

The pavement gave way to a dirt road and the region of shops fell away as if it were sinking into the sea. Only a few people stared into the glare of the headlights as the chauffeur slowed to negotiate the tortuous turns. Then there was near darkness for a time on both sides of the car, until a gate appeared at the summit of the road. The chauffeur turned into the gate and stopped before a large Western-style house. A dog barked.

Jane was halfway up the broad steps when a shadow fell across the light from the door and she saw a man descending rapidly toward her. He was a fat man and he was obviously in a great hurry. Jane bent her head and turned her face away. It was Austin Stoker, the man from the *Pioneer Mail*. He had almost passed her when he paused and called her name.

"Mrs Hoyt! How delightful to see you again." He was puffing for breath, like a giant frog, Jane thought, and he nervously mopped his face with a large handkerchief.

"I wish I could say the same, Mr. Stoker."

"And in such an interesting place. You're getting well acquainted in Hong Kong, I see. I must congratulate Henry for succeeding where I failed."

"Is he a friend of yours?"

"We are associates in a business way."

"Oh?" She turned abruptly away from him and continued up the steps. She heard him call after her, but she did not turn around. Those bright little pig eyes were already undressing her.

"Don't forget, Mrs. Hoyt. If you need anything . . . Ice House Street."

A white-coated amah met her at the door with a smile. She said, "Please" and indicated with a wave of her arm that Jane should seat herself on an enormous couch which stood in the middle of the reception room. An Angora cat mewed at one end of the couch and a dog of uncertain heritage came out from behind it to lick at her hand and wag his tail. When she was seated the amah smiled once more and turned away, her slippers hissing softly against the floor. Jane looked at the cat and saw only hostility in the yellow eyes, but the dog pressed against her leg happily. She looked around the room and tried to forget about Austin Stoker.

There was a wide doorway opposite the couch which led into another room and she could see one end of a dining table with a place set at the head. Beyond the table a bank of flowers was arranged on a buffet. The wall curved away from the dining room entrance and became a huge, round Chinese window which faced on a garden. There were shelves stretching the full length of the wall beneath the window which held lines of magnificent stone statues. There were horses and Chinese warriors and maidens and bearded old men. Jane was certain they were worth a great deal of money.

A doorway led to the garden and just beyond it a staircase with a wrought-iron rail curved gracefully to the floor above. The cat mewed and Jane thought again of Austin Stoker. What did he have to do with Henry Lee? She thought of Marty Gates and the way he had spoken of the man, and Rodman, too. Only Maxine gave Henry Lee any qualities. The dog was warm against her leg and now he placed his head beseechingly in her lap, but the cat mewed again and she shivered.

She was looking at an elaborately inlaid Chinese screen beneath the staircase when she knew instinctively that someone was behind it. She heard a footstep and what sounded like the creak of leather. Then she caught her breath as the barrel of a revolver emerged slowly from behind the screen. She was frozen on the couch. She wanted to cry out, but no sound would come from her throat. She closed her eyes hoping her imagination had tricked her. When she opened them again she barely managed to contain her laughter, for her foe was now entirely visible. He wore a complete cowboy outfit and he was all of eight years old.

"Hi, pardner," he growled, taking a step toward her.

"Hi. . . ." Jane sighed with relief and looked into the boy's serious brown eyes. The cowboy outfit was so like home, it was a moment before she realized he was at least half-Chinese. Still holding the cap pistol, he moved a few steps closer.

"I could have clobbered you," he said solemnly.

"I guess you could have."

"But there's no fun in shootin' women."

"Not unless they steal your cattle."

"What's your name, pardner?"

"Jane Hoyt. What's yours, pardner?"

"Billy Lee." He shoved the gun into its holster and extended his hand. "Shake." She took his small hand and shook it once, vigorously. He inspected her with grave interest.

"Where you come from?" For the first time she noticed that although his words were entirely familiar, he spoke with a slight accent—a strange mixture of Chinese tonality and clipped English diction.

"America."

"Killed any Indians?"

"Not lately."

"How many horses do you have?"

"Not any . . . that is . . . right at the moment."

"Ever ride in a stagecoach? My daddy says women always ride in the stagecoaches. It's in the cinema, too."

"Well . . . sort of." Jane thought of a bus trip she had once made with Louis and decided the lie was not too farfetched. And it was strange, she thought suddenly, she had never considered Henry Lee as being married.

"You ever been held up?" Billy asked.

"No. . . ."

"You *sure* you come from America? Your story is kind of phony." He looked at her uncertainly and then smiled as if to reassure himself. "When I go to America I'm going to arrest all the bandits."

"Good."

"Perhaps I'll hang the very bad ones from the trees."

"Hey, Billy!" a heavy voice called from the stairs. "Don't be so blood-thirsty."

Jane looked up and saw a smiling man descending the staircase. His movements were lithe and powerful—his appearance was almost exactly the opposite of what she had expected, but she knew instantly that she was rising to meet Hank Lee. And something rose with her body, accompanying the purely physical movement—as intangible sensation leapt from behind the guarding of years. It came upon her like a swell rolling in from the ocean and she barely had time to recognize it before she heard him saying, "I'm Hank Lee."

He was tall, but the power in him did not come from his height. She thought of a well-built ship—there was an impression of sturdiness rather than mere muscular strength. There was true color in his cheeks, the first she had seen in a man since her arrival in Hong Kong, and his eyes were frank and entirely unafraid. She found herself unexplainably happy about his nose—it was large and had obviously once been badly smashed. His nose saved him from being a pretty man. He was smiling now as he talked, and laughing, and the heavy timbre of his voice echoed through the house. The cat mewed and bounded off the couch to brush against his ankles and the dog barked joyously as he lifted Billy first high above his head, and then settled him on his broad shoulder. At the sound of his laughter another dog, a sort of half-police half-Airedale, Jane thought, came running full tilt out of the dining room and slithered across the polished floor. It barked frantically for attention and Henry Lee put his spare fist in its mouth to satisfy it.

"Excuse the family reunion!" he said above the confusion. "I've been gone most of the day!"

"She says she comes from America!" Billy yelled. "But she never killed an Indian or even a bandit, I bet!"

"I'm going to buy you a space ship so you'll get off the subject!"

"There aren't any Indians on the stars!"

"Okay! Okay . . . then shoot some Martians!"

"How can I when they have no blood?"

Henry Lee looked appealingly at Jane. "You explain to me how kids know such things," he said.

"I've often wondered myself."

"This little guy is nothin'. You should hear his sister. After I listened to her prayers just now she asked me why you couldn't take a big balloon and fill it up with dark night air and then let it out when you wanted to sleep in the daytime."

"That's not a bad idea. How many children do you have, Mr. Lee?"

"Three now. One is going to school in the States and another one I'm going to get rid of right this minute." He swung Billy to the floor and patted his backside. "Git along, pardner. It's way past your bedtime." He kissed him again and shoved him playfully toward the staircase. Billy moved away reluctantly, looking over his shoulder at Jane. She tried to find some resemblance in his face to Henry Lee, but she could find none.

"I bet you never been to America," he said as he slowly mounted the stairs.

"Them's fightin' words, pardner," she called after him. And then she was strangely uncomfortable because she was alone with Henry Lee.

He stood watching her a moment and she knew he sensed her nervousness. He smiled wryly and she thought that even his half-smile was strangely warm and direct.

"You're wondering how I can have a Chinese kid," he said.

"No, I wasn't . . . really."

"No race prejudice?"

"I've always managed to avoid it."

"Then I'll tell you the truth. They're only mine by adoption. The other boy is a Filipino kid. He's pretty much of a genius."

"Proud father."

"You should see his marks at school. But he's older . . . thirteen almost, and I miss him."

He paused and once more as their eyes met, Jane forced herself to look away. What was there about this man which made her feel giddy and unnatural? Something lifted her right out of reality and even the sound of her own voice seemed to come from another person.

"But you didn't come here to talk about kids," he was saying. "Come on in the bar and have a drink."

"I really don't care for—"

"I've got some of the best Spanish sherry you ever tasted. Stole it years ago so the flavor is extra special."

He did not wait for a refusal but took her arm and led her across the garden toward a small pagoda which had been artfully set in the middle of a lily pool. He pointed to a pair of swans gliding across the pool and said he had brought them especially from England. "It was a mistake," he explained. "Swans hate everybody. Worse than camels." The two dogs and the cat led them across the small arched bridge and were waiting for them when they stepped into the pagoda.

"Sometimes this bridge gets to be a problem," he said with a chuckle. "It's pretty and it's built just the way the old Chinese used to have them, but every once in a while somebody gets too much to drink and falls into the pool. I had the rail built higher and they still manage to wind up with the lilies."

The inside of the pagoda was matted with bamboo cane set in intricate designs. An ebony bar reached across one end of the pagoda and the other walls were mostly large windows with comfortable benches beneath them.

"Sherry all right?" Jane nodded her head and he poured her a glass from a bottle wrapped in burlap. He poured a shot of Irish whisky for himself and said that since the Hong Kong water supply was so critical he certainly didn't want to put any added strain on it. He raised his glass and said, "Cheers." And then for a long time they studied each other in absolute silence.

"Would you like to hear Chicago?" he finally said and Jane noticed that his voice had become subdued—almost melancholy.

"Chicago?"

"Sometimes I sit out here alone and just listen to it. I guess it's bad for me, but I can't help it." He stepped behind the bar and switched on a small record-changer. And at once the pagoda was filled with the sounds of diesel buses, police whistles, pneumatic drills, clanging street cars, and calling newspaper boys. When the record was done he switched off the record-changer and downed his drink. His smile was gone now and he stared moodily at the lilies in the pond.

"I had that recording made specially," he said. "They did a pretty good job but they forgot the elevateds."

"I take it Chicago is your home."

"No. Hong Kong is my home."

"You don't seem very cheerful about it."

"You always want what you can't have."

Why couldn't he have what? Jane wanted to ask him a hundred questions, but his easy manner had vanished. She waited, hoping the hard look about his face would go away as quickly as it had come.

"Maxine told me about your husband."

Jane realized with a shock that she had not thought of Louis since the first moment Henry Lee had taken her hand. So it *could* happen! She had not only forgotten Louis, but looking back over the past few minutes she remembered little mannerisms she had affected which supposedly were long forgotten. She recognized a certain inflection in her voice, a strut

to her walk when they came to the pagoda, and knew her eyes had
openly invited flirtation. Under any other circumstances it might have
been funny, but it was not funny now.

Disgusted, she pushed her sherry away. She was amazed to find that
she wanted Henry Lee to see her move the glass. Why should she care
what he thought as long as he would help Louis? Yet she did care—there
was no denying it, and now she could not look away from him. At least,
she thought, I am not guilty of comparing him with Louis. I simply met a
full man when there are so few, and for a moment only, a juvenile, silly
moment . . . forgot myself. Louis, you would be the first one to laugh
. . . I hope!

"Can I talk to you about my husband, Mr. Lee?"

"Hank, please. Sure . . . you can talk about him if it will make you
feel any better. But talk won't get your man back." She liked the way he
said "your man." It sounded as if he understood and believed that such
a relationship could exist and was right and that Louis represented more
than a husband.

"What can I do, Mr. Lee . . . Hank? I can't just go to China and pull
him out by the ears."

He smiled and studied her face and once more the feeling of instability
rose in her.

"I've got sort of a hunch you'd try it if you had half the chance . . .
wouldn't you?"

"It's easy to say, yes."

He shook his head and lit a cigar. He drew in the smoke, then exhaled
slowly and Jane knew she was being judged, for his eyes never left her.
But he was not looking at her body as Austin Stoker had done—he was
looking inside and now, in spite of his examination, she was not uncomfortable. I hate cigars, she thought, trying to outwait him. I have always
hated cigars and the sight of men smoking them . . . and yet this man
somehow manages to make them attractive. Speak to him, talk about
Louis—look away from the strength in his face, and—grow up, Jane Hoyt!
You have a man, a fine one.

"I guess I've been looking for a woman like you all my life," he said.

"You're late. I happen to belong to someone else." There! He was smiling
when he spoke and he obviously meant it only as a compliment, but there
was no sense letting this thing go any further.

"I guess you've heard I never bothered too much about what belonged
to who."

"You have a reputation . . . for helping people in trouble."

"That depends on who you talk to. My main business is helping Hank
Lee. If I didn't think that way I'd still be driving a gravel truck in Chicago
. . . or I'd be dead. You get smart, figure the odds, shove a few people

around, and you're rich and happy. No strain. But if you start letting people get close and work their way inside of you . . . you've had it. That's why I like the Chinese. The only time they get sentimental is when they're drunk on rice wine and they don't get drunk very often."

"Are you trying to discourage me before I start asking for help?"

"Yeah. The only reason I let you come out here is because I got soft once with Maxine and I can't get out of the habit."

"It seems to be a vicious habit with you. How about Billy? Where did he come from? Mars? Where the people have no blood?"

"Billy was a special case. Someone left him lying by the gate when he was only a little brat. I came back here late that night and almost ran over him. Naturally I couldn't leave him there."

"Naturally."

"He would have got pneumonia. The Chinese think all Americans are suckers so in the old days they used to get rid of a lot of extra mouths that way."

"The old days? How long have you been in Hong Kong?"

"Since the war."

"Were you in the service?" It was a moment before Jane realized she had gone too far with Henry Lee. She had asked the question without thinking, to make conversation only, to satisfy her growing curiosity about this strange man.

"Wasn't everybody?"

"My husband was in the Air Force." Why did she say that? Why did she keep pursuing a subject which he obviously didn't care to discuss? You had better get your thinking cap back on, friend Jane. Seven thousand dollars isn't going to mean anything to a person like Hank Lee and he is acquiring that look which only comes to a man when he is thinking of a way to end an interview.

"Good for your husband."

"The little girl," she said quickly, "is she Chinese, too? Forgive me for asking so many questions, but you'll have to admit a bachelor with three children is enough to pique any woman's curiosity."

His smile returned. His eyes came alive again and she knew she was on safer ground.

"No. She's Malayan . . . partly."

He was still looking away. He reached for the police-Airedale's belly and scratched it thoughtfully. But he isn't talking. Quick, Jane! He's gone several thousand miles over the horizon and you must haul him back.

"Landed on your doorstep, too?"

"She was born to a friend of mine in Bangkok. Slight mistake. Her mother used to come to see her whenever she could, but she hasn't been around in a long time. I think she's in Colombo."

"The boy in the States. Where did he come from?"

"Manila. He sort of attached himself to me. He was on the streets right after the war . . . eyes bigger than his stomach, like all the rest. I couldn't get rid of him. Little beggar was always at my heels. It took a long time to check on his parents. They were both dead . . . so. . . ." He spread his big hands helplessly. "What the hell could I do?"

"Are . . . are you planning on having any more children, Mr. Lee, I mean Hank?"

"Lady . . . you're talking to a tired man. Yesterday I spent four hours working on a model plane with Billy. I like to cut off my thumb when the engine finally started and that was just for openers. The plane flew all right . . . too good. It landed on the roof. I went after it, forgetting that the Chinese only set their tiles in mud. A tile gave way and I slid off the roof right on my—well, the only thing that saved me from breaking my back is the lily pond. I landed right there just to the left of the bridge. That pool is deeper than it looks and I hit the bottom hard. After I came up for the third time one of the swans got mad and bit me in the ear. When I finally managed to climb out, Billy was still laughing. Said he was going to get me a parachute. Funny kid, eh?"

He looked at her sadly for a moment and then they both burst into laughter. Jane thought, What a laugh the man has! He tipped back his head and it came roaring from his soul like the lusty joy of a buccaneer.

"And the worst of it is," he said, wiping his eyes, "we start on another plane tomorrow! Having kids is the most dangerous business in the world."

A gong rang in the house. Henry Lee downed his drink and then looked at her thoughtfully.

"What I like about you," he said, "is you're in trouble and you can still laugh. That takes something special. How about some dinner? The cook bawls hell out of me if I'm not right on time."

She hadn't thought of food. It was hard enough trying to remember that every hour might count for Louis. "I hadn't planned . . ."

He took her arm. "Come on. You'll like it. New England boiled dinner tonight. It will take you right back home."

She told herself that she could not really have refused even if she had wanted to, the pressure of his hand on her arm was so strong as he led her across the bridge. And he had a sweeping way, as if all the world must join in his enthusiasm. No wonder the people of Hong Kong spoke guardedly of Henry Lee. He was vitality and force. He was, she thought with a final twinge of conscience—wonderful.

The table was long and the center was lavishly decorated with silver pieces wrought in the shape of peacocks, elephants and tigers. And now Henry Lee became more what she had expected, for he sat at the head of the table as a conqueror, benign for the moment, yet capable of changing instantly if his will was crossed. Here was a leader no matter what anyone said, and here was *the* man, the one man who could bring Louis out of China.

He ate with gusto, urging her to take more on her plate than she could possibly finish. The way he used his knife and fork and tucked the napkin around his neck matched the flow of history which he began and continued throughout the meal. He talked even when his mouth was full of food, pausing in the middle of a sentence to chew and pointing his knife at her to punctuate his thinking. After a time, she was convinced Henry Lee was the loneliest man she had ever known.

"School for Joe—that's the Philippine kid—is important," he was saying. "I know, believe me. Because I never went beyond the sixth grade. So Joe's going to the best school in the United States, and Billy will, too, when he gets a little older. They're going to be gentlemen and not get kicked around like I did. I was lucky, see? And I knew how to fight. You can't make a living in the Orient unless you do . . . or anywhere else for that matter. You burn up inside when you haven't got the things you see other people have . . . you burn up so bad you can feel it singeing your gizzard and you go either of two ways. You let the flame burn out until you're just a cinder or you keep throwing fuel on it until you explode. Sure I move my lips when I read. I know it and I don't have to care. But I live it up pretty good for a gravel-truck driver. And I own the biggest fleet of junks in China."

"What do the junks do?" There was no risk to the question, she thought. He was in a genial, expansive mood—a successful man talking about his business.

"Carry cargo, naturally. No use fooling with fishing junks. They never make any money."

"But your junks do?"

"Plenty." He swallowed a potato almost whole and for a moment it made a lump in his cheek. Then he wiped his face with his napkin, threw it carelessly on the table and pushed back his chair. "Go on . . . *eat*, woman! You're too thin."

"I'm afraid I don't feel much like eating. But it isn't the food. It's delicious."

He stuck a toothpick in his mouth and tipped far back in his chair. She dallied with her food, knowing he was watching her every movement.

"Thinking about that guy again, eh?"

"Yes."

"I could use some of that. I could use a woman who would miss a meal because she was worrying about me."

"I think there might be such a person."

"You're pretty smart."

"Maxine won't keep forever."

"I want a fighter . . . like you." He held up the palm of his hand and laughed. "Don't get scared. I know the only reason you came here is because you thought I would help you."

"Please . . . Hank."

"Why should I? Even if I could do anything?"

"I have seven thousand dollars. I'll pay it to you the minute Louis is over the border."

His eyes narrowed and she was certain she saw a look of disappointment behind them.

"Seven thousand bucks. Is he worth that much?"

"It's all I have."

"Too bad a woman like you has to buy a man when there's so many around for free. Well . . . seven thousand bucks is nothing to me."

"Would it be to a man like Austin Stoker?" Ah! Look at his face now! You said exactly the right thing! You're in there swinging now, Jane! Keep pressing because for a moment he's off base. He is shocked and confused.

"How did you ever know that bum?"

"He came down on the boat with me."

"How many times did he chase you around the deck?"

"I lost count."

"Stay away from him. He's no good. I don't want to see you mixed up with a man like him."

"Why should you care who I get mixed up with?" she said quickly. "How about Fernand Rocha? Or Tweedie? Would they be interested in seven thousand dollars?"

He lowered his chair until all four legs were on the floor. He took a cigar from his shirt pocket and examined it carefully before he placed it between his teeth. Then he sat staring at her in silence for a long time. He has it all now, she thought. I've fired every last bit of ammunition across the table and my aim was good. But if I missed somehow, if I have misjudged this rock of a man, then it's all over.

"Lady . . ." he said slowly with an incredulous shake of his head, "you . . . need a protector."

"Right." She returned his steady gaze although she hardly dared to breathe.

"How in the name of God did you get mixed up with those bums in such a short time? They'd steal you blind."

"I'm not exactly mixed up with them."

"Do you know what Austin Stoker does? He supplies me with faked manifests and arranges for customs inspectors to look the other way. Once in a while Rocha does the same thing for me in Macao when it's necessary. Tweedie is the worst of the lot, with his racket. The Commies have a sure way of getting American dollars by simply putting the bite on Chinese families in the States. Pay up . . . or good-by your relatives. Taxes they call it. But a couple of years ago the U.S. government wised up and made such payoffs illegal. That's when Tweedie moved in with his messenger service. They send the money to Tweedie and he supposedly gets the relatives in China off the hook. Sometimes he does, and sometimes he doesn't. If he finds out the relatives are already liquidated he keeps the money. Whatever happens, he takes his cut. He's a crook and that restaurant is only a blind. Stay away from those guys."

"Isn't the pot calling the kettle black?"

"I'm not that kind of man!" He pounded his big fist on the table angrily. The silver peacocks, the tigers and the elephants shook beneath the force of his blow.

" 'Beware yon Cassius,' " she said very quietly.

"What's that mean?"

"A speech from Shakespeare. 'Beware yon Cassius, he hath a lean and hungry look.' "

"What kind of a racket did this Cassius have?"

"You might say . . . his specialty was stabbing people in the back."

"Well, I've never done that."

"Are you sure?"

"I've always faced up to everybody. If I didn't trade with the Commies somebody else would."

"You seem very anxious to defend yourself."

"I don't have to defend anything. You just hornswoggled me into a position where—" He hesitated and then went on lamely—"where . . . well . . . I'm only trying to show you that I'm not as bad as maybe some people have told you I am."

"Why don't you prove it, then?"

"By helping you?"

"Yes."

"What's the percentage in my risking my neck for some other guy's wife?"

"Do you have to receive a pound of flesh for everything you do?"

"What's this pound of flesh business?"

"That's Shakespeare, too."

"To hell with you and your Shakespeare friend. I'm sending you back to the Peninsula!" He stood up and clamped the cigar firmly between his teeth. "You're too smart for me. Come on."

She took her time folding her napkin, then she stood up slowly and deliberately.

"All right, Mr. Lee. I should have known better. Thank you for dinner anyway." She kept her voice cold and refused to meet his eyes. She stood very straight as she moved toward the reception room and the sound of her heels on the polished floor was so empty of emotion Henry Lee followed after her, anxiously rubbing his smashed nose. He reached for her arm and stopped her in the hallway.

"What do you mean you should have known better?"

She looked up at him and while he waited uncertainly she examined his body with open distaste. Her eyes moved slowly from his shoes to the top of his head.

"For a little while tonight I thought I had met a real man . . . the kind people talk about and read about and love beyond their understanding, because there are so few. But I was wrong. I should have known better. You're a shell, a blowing hard shell, Mr. Lee . . . as weak and rotten inside as the rest. I should have known that any man who would work against his country for his own profit, brag about it even . . . wouldn't have a true bone in his body. You fancy yourself as a soldier of fortune and you partially get away with it because you're in a foreign country. To me, you're just another gangster . . . a bum, in your language. Good-by. I hope you enjoy living with your money and yourself!"

"That was quite a speech. Wow!" He rubbed his nose thoughtfully and after a moment the suggestion of a smile crossed his mouth. "What are you like when you really get mad?"

She turned away from him without answering and walked to the doorway. She stood waiting, looking out at the driveway. She was still breathing hard, but her immediate anger was subsiding enough for reason. She wondered if she could walk back to the hotel. No—that was too far, but she could walk down the hill through the village and perhaps get a taxi on the main road. Anything to get away from Henry Lee. Then she knew he was standing close behind her and when he spoke his voice was different. The braggart was gone.

"I guess I deserved that . . . for a long time. Sometimes it's hard to figure things straight when you're always thinking alone. You risked a lot by telling me off . . . maybe your husband's life. It wasn't very smart. If you're trying to sell a customer, don't get mad at him. But you did and that shows me one thing anyway. You're thinking with your heart instead of your head . . . which is good, because I'm tired of people who think with their heads. For the same reason, you don't realize what you're asking."

She turned to face him. Her anger was almost forgotten and once more, searching his face, she found the strength she had seen before. She said, "I didn't come to you because I thought it would be easy."

"It would be worse than not easy. You can't buy your husband out of

China. No one can. The old war lords who had their hands open for anything are all over on Formosa with Chiang, or living in South America or Paris, counting their money. The people who run China now even tell Moscow to go to hell. So the only way to get your husband out is to pull him out . . . bodily. I don't know who could do that or even how anybody could go about it."

"When you first came to Hong Kong did you ask yourself how a thing could be done so many times?"

"No, I didn't. But I was younger then, and hungrier, and this is different."

"You're still hungry. You're starved for a little self-respect. Never mind. I don't need you. I'll get him out myself . . . somehow."

"God help the Chinese," he laughed. Then he reached down and took her face in his big hands. He studied her eyes and sighed heavily. "Look. I've got round eyes and fairly white skin. People like me are not only very conspicuous in China . . . they're unpopular as hell. What's more you don't even know where your man is, or if he's alive or dead. But I'll tell you what I'll do. I'll find out . . . it will take me a while, maybe several days, so don't get discouraged. Then we'll see what the situation is. If they haven't got him way up in Peiping or back somewhere in Szechwan, maybe we can work something out. I won't make any guarantees . . . but I'll *try* to at least find out about him. Okay?" He continued to hold her face in his hands while he waited for her answer. But she made no sound. Instead her eyes began to fill with tears and in his embarrassment he bent down and suddenly kissed her on the forehead.

"I'll call the car. You've had a big day. It's time you went to bed."

"Hurry," she whispered. "I know you must hurry!"

7

The typhoon struck the Hong Kong area just before dawn. It spiraled up from the South China Sea, spewed its bellyful of wind and rain at the outer islands and then moved inland to drench the hills and fill the streets of the city with rushing water. The heavy clouds delayed the light of day for almost an hour and otherwise bedeviled the life of the Colony. Wise men stayed in bed. Rheumatics complained. The Kowloon-Hong Kong ferries remained tied to their piers. The harbor was empty of movement except for the freighters and the great warships which frothed at the bows and strained their moorings. The red double-deck buses were not running—a seventy-knot wind might capsize them. The few hardy people forced by circumstance to leave the shelter of their dwellings scurried through the streets like subterranean creatures. The observatory on Signal Hill displayed a red-green-red light series and hoisted a signal-ten black cross. On the weather charts, the radio, and in the newspapers, where the progress of the tempest had been plotted for several days, the typhoon was identified as Rita.

Hank Lee remembered a girl named Rita. As he shaved in the gloomy morning light and listened to the rain hiss against his bathroom window, he reminded himself that Rita had caused him to do a great many things —at least she was the basic cause if the twists of fortune were traced backward some ten years. He thought that naming typhoons after women was a good idea. They were both unreliable and could change course on a whim—as did Rita, who was probably still living in San Diego.

Rita was a schoolteacher and there was a long time when she was going to be Mrs. Hank Lee. She came to the petty officers' dance in 1943. She was being patriotic . . . October, it was. Rita didn't smoke and she didn't drink. It was hard to believe she had ever heard the word "damn"—let alone use it. She taught kids during the day and after the dance she started teaching Hank Lee in the evenings. She carefully removed the "ain'ts" and put the "comes" where they ought to be instead of where they had been ever since a man could remember. Without being a nuisance about it she saw that your words ending in "ing" didn't just forget about the "g." It was quite an education . . . in more ways than one. She put you on to the right books and almost how to read them. Look at the stack beside the bed right now—those were all on account of Rita. She taught you to write without wetting the end of a pencil and so somebody else could read it. She kept you sober and out of fights and worked out a program where you could save a lot, even on Navy pay. There was going to be a little house out Chula Vista way and a trucking business of your own. Right after the war was over. And after a while some kids.

Then came the second part of Hank Lee's education. The diploma—which proved you could never be sure about a woman no matter what her exterior was like. Same as typhoons. First there was the Marshall Islands campaign and a chunk of shrapnel in the hip. It still hurt, dammit . . . especially on low-pressure mornings like this. Not a bad wound—just enough to get back to San Diego, and after the hospital there were those four months strutting around Stateside sporting a purple heart. Rita was already heading for trouble then, although you never recognized it until it was too late. It happened to a lot of women in San Diego. There were too many sailors. Some of the good women got tarnished and some of the bad ones got worse. Rita started out too good. She was supposed to look after your combined savings—and she sure did. Looking back it was easy to remember that she had suddenly discovered make-up and seemed to like a little drink once in a while. Looking back it was easy, but right then, waiting around for BuNav to make up its mind what to do with Hank Lee, it wasn't so plain.

The leave couldn't last forever. The new minesweeper was a fine packet, but she wasn't near as nice as Rita's farewell at the pier. She bawled like you were the only man in the world—like she could hardly live until you got back. She must have kept right on bawling after the YMS 34 disappeared past Point Loma. Apparently the only time she stopped bawling was when she took some sailor home and climbed into the alfalfa with him. That was bad enough, but she showed up loaded at the school one morning and was fired. From then on she started her private USO—operating on your money. The sailors in San Diego never had it so good. Free food, free booze, free bed. There must have been a line a mile long. The only guy who ever got thrown out was the smart guy she discovered was selling her telephone number.

So ended Rita, but not the damage she caused. Or was it good? That was something still worth figuring out. Supposing there never was a Rita. Go back to Balabac Strait again . . . 1945 and the war almost over. Just a few weeks more, everybody said. A normal sweep that night . . . the same old thing except the Japs had strung the mines closer to shore than usual. You were standing by the galley door drinking coffee and brooding about Rita. The letter from her lawyer was folded up in the pocket of your windbreaker. It said Rita was in jail again—charges drunk and disorderly, resisting arrest, and unless bail was sent immediately she was going to the women's prison at Tehachapi. How about that for a school-teacher?

Then there was that granddaddy of all carr-umphs! Everything went white and black and whamo—you were in the water . . . still holding the coffeecup for some reason or other except now it was full of oil instead of coffee. Everybody was yelling and swearing and trying to swim in those damn life jackets, which was nearly impossible. There was plenty of light. The whole foredeck of YMS 34 was a torch to the waterline and the PT rescue escorts were right on the job with their searchlights. Nobody worried about the Japs any more—they had all run home to Japan leaving their dead and a few thousand odd mines behind them—including this particular one. All the guys in the water were trying to bunch up except Hank Lee, who saw the shore not very far away and suddenly had other ideas. Why sweat out the Navy any longer where the chances for an uneducated thirty-five-year-old man were practically nil—especially in peace-time? Why go back to Chicago and a gravel truck? In San Diego there was only Rita. It was easy to be a hero. No one was within fifty yards of you. Just take off the damn lifejacket and start swimming. Missing in action.

That night was the beginning of the new Hank Lee and you might say it was all because of Rita.

There was a slight hitch. It wasn't a coastal shore, but an island, and later you found out there were almost seven thousand islands in the Philippine archipelago. This one was inhabited by Igorots who were nearly starving to death, but they shared what they had and the only thing you got out of it was a lot of time to think, and ringworm. You thought while you were scratching the ringworm and building the boat—five months of trying to build something seaworthy out of nothing, and thinking. How long did a man live? Not so long as he should, maybe. The arithmetic was wrong. He grew up until he was twenty or so and if he came from a poor family he didn't have nothing. Like Hank Lee. From twenty to thirty he didn't have nothing either, usually. He was struggling, but for some reason he never seemed to get very far. People still wouldn't give him any responsibilities and so no breaks. All right. From thirty to forty something ought to start happening, but if there was a war right about that time in a man's life, or if he didn't have much education and so was slow to catch on to things, then there always seemed to be a delay. Like Hank Lee. Unless something drastic was done about it.

Say a man got to be forty-five and there was still nothing substantial under his feet? Who was winning—time or the man? He might have a house, a wife and some kids. That was something, but the chances were the job he had would just about make ends meet. And so for the next fifteen years he sort of skated along the edge of a cliff all the time wondering when he might fall over it. No wonder he was tired when he got to be sixty-five. Damn tired. And he was already figuring up his chances of living to eighty. Maybe there would be fifteen years of his whole life when he could sit back and relax. The Igorots on the island didn't worry about such things because they seldom lived beyond fifty anyway. But they lived one hell of a life while they were at it. They hunted and scratched and fished and scratched and fought and wondered where anybody got the energy to build a boat. They didn't care if time was slipping by and they never worried about falling over any cliffs. They didn't realize something drastic had to be done or Hank Lee would wind up as always, having nothing.

That first boat was only eighteen feet long and she barely stayed afloat long enough to reach Manila. But she was the real beginning of a fleet. She was named the *Chicago* and now there was a hundred-and-ten-foot diesel-driven junk with the same name translated phonetically into Chinese—just for old times' sake. Finally there were a lot of others. So Hank Lee didn't have to worry any more. Hong Kong did all right by the forty-fifty span of life. It sure wouldn't have worked out the same in the States. Not for Hank Lee. And it was a lot more convenient to stay missing in action than face a charge of desertion. Get smart and stay smart. Remember Rita.

He cut himself with the razor. Although he had always used a straight-edge, it had been a very long time since he had cut himself. And he knew the reason. He was thinking about Jane Hoyt.

He took a shower and afterward when he was drying himself he saw in the mirror how the water had sopped his head, laying the hair down flat so the signs of baldness became uncomfortably apparent. And he thought, Am I too old for Jane Hoyt? Forty-five, and she's thirty at the most— maybe not that old. No, the age spread was considerable, but it was all right. But a blow-hard shell, huh?

Ruffling his hair with the towel he saw that the muscles in his arms were as big and hard as ever. He was lean around the waist and there was no flabbiness anywhere. Forty-five wasn't so bad when you were in good condition—and rich. Walking along a very safe distance from the edge of the cliff made a difference, too. A soldier of fortune, huh? Right—except it was a sailor of fortune, and why not? Counting the junk families at least five hundred people managed to stay away from the edge of the cliff because Hank Lee had guts enough to run a few risks. Profiting at the expense of your own country, she said. What did the United States ever do for Hank Lee except let him drive a gravel truck? And while you were being shot at there were plenty of smart guys sitting home and making a profit out of their country. Now there wasn't even a war on. The woman had spunk, though, wrong or right. She was one hell of a woman. How could a husband be dumb enough to leave her behind and go to a place like China? Those bastards played for keeps—just like Hank Lee. They were leery of the cliff, too.

He would ask her about that. He would ask her how maybe she was mixed up on who was a soldier of fortune.

He brushed his teeth vigorously as if the ceremony would drive away any more thoughts of the cliff. When he was finished he spurned the glass on the shelf above the basin. Instead he bent down to the tap automatically, distorting his mouth so it would fill with water in the manner of a man who was accustomed to drinking from streams or hoses or any handy open faucet which might quench his thirst. It was habit, he knew—one habit formed at the edge of the cliff during the days when glasses were superfluous—or just plain unavailable. He would not break this habit. Water never tasted quite the same out of a glass.

And he would show the Hoyt woman Hank Lee kept his word, no matter how many names she called him. He would find out about her husband, but he would be damned if he would do anything about him. That would be heading straight back for the edge of the cliff. The Commies were good customers. They paid. Why slap them in the face? Smart people didn't cut their own throat—or, he thought, looking at what the razor had done to his neck—did they?

Inspector Rodman watched Merryweather through the screen door. He was trudging along beneath the overhanging porch, head bent and arms dangling, his usually neat cap a squashed mess, his uniform a sopping collection of wrinkles. Rodman opened the door for him, and stood back to avoid the spray of rain whipping around the corner of the building. He chuckled.

"You're quite a lovely vision," he said when Merryweather passed into their room without raising his eyes.

"Oh God. . . . Oh God. . . ." Merryweather groaned. He went straight to the sideboard, poured himself half a glass of whiskey, swallowed it and then said, "Oh God" again. Water dripped off his shorts and away from his shoes forming small pools upon the floor.

"Did you have to bring the harbor in with you? What did you do . . . fall overboard? On snap judgment I should say you're a disgrace to the force. Should be written up."

Merryweather regarded him coldly from beneath the dripping brim of his cap. "I suppose you are hardly aware that it's raining," he said.

"Is it really?" Rodman went to the window and pretended to examine the weather with new interest.

"Or that since zero three hours this morning a slight typhoon has been in progress."

"Really. I never would have known. It's so quiet in the bedroom. One sleeps so soundly."

"The wind," Merryweather said, slicing off each word as if he wanted it to stand alone, "has occasionally reached seventy knots."

"You don't say."

"I do say. Do you have any idea what it is like to bounce around Hong Kong harbor in a fifty-foot boat when the wind is blowing seventy knots?"

"A bit uncomfortable and rather damp, I should imagine."

"Oh God . . . sweet God, when will Potts get well so I can live like a human being again!" Merryweather massaged his red eyes and sank into a chair. His bony knees were wide apart and he stared at them disconsolately. "I have been in and out of the filthy harbor water like a seal playing the Palladium. We rescued eleven coolies, four sampan people and a drunk Finn sailor who socked me one on the jaw after I hauled him aboard."

"Good show. Merryweather serves humanity. I trust you socked him back."

"I hit him with the cox'n's billy. He was quiet for several hours."

"How long will this little storm last?" Rodman knew as well as anyone else how long it would last, but he wanted to pretend as much innocence as he could before his roommate. The contest was part of their life together, a constant depreciation of the other's work, and yet they both knew there were very few safe and easy jobs for young Englishmen left in the world.

They were both vaguely aware that they were victims of a benign senility which through no one's fault but time, had gradually choked off opportunity for all young Englishmen. The war and austerity only hastened the accumulation of verdigris on British enterprise. It had happened to other nations and it would, in the future, happen to still others as they rose and fell with power and time. It was not a sickness, the kind which came to France and a hysterical Germany, but rather the beginning of exhaustion which Merryweather and Rodman and so many other young Englishmen sensed but rarely believed. There was nothing they or anyone else could do about it anyway and so they comforted themselves in the lonely truth that their Britain was far ahead of the rest of the world in a very few things like the development of high speed aircraft—and they were proud. Secretly they knew that a young man in England rarely had more than two choices—he could stay home and wrap the social protectorate around him, sinking his roots deeper and deeper into the familiar, or he could become a colonial. There was Canada and there was Australia. There were still a few bits of Africa and the dubious outpost of Hong Kong. As a consequence young Britons who left home spoke to each other with abnormal vigor, as if to reassure themselves. They were also recklessly courageous and made almost a fetish of slighting their accomplishments.

"It won't last long," Merryweather was saying. "Possibly another four or five hours. It's moving off to the northeast, but it will only take a part of Hong Kong with it."

"Pity the Princess Ballroom is such a flimsy structure," Rodman said at the window. "Like as not you'll never see it again."

But Merryweather had lost interest. He yawned and said, "I'm going to bed."

"Do that. And you might try a bath, chum. I dislike mentioning it, but you exude a not exactly subtle odor. Parfum de harbor de Hong Kong."

Merryweather pushed himself to his feet and staggered toward the bedroom door. "You're a witty fellow," he said sourly.

"Oh . . . one thing," Rodman called after him. "I suppose all the junks will be in during this blow?"

"Those that aren't sunk. What do you care with your landside cinch?"

"I don't especially. But there's one chap I've been looking for so I thought I might just poke round a bit. I think he swiped some cameras."

"If he's junk people, this is the kind of day to find him."

With One-Three-O-Three sitting silently beside him, Rodman drove slowly through the heavy rain to the Sham Sui Po police station. Sham Sui Po was near the Yaumati shelter and quartered Chinese detectives who knew the harbor and its people well. It was just a hunch, and he had to go to Sham Sui Po anyway.

The Sham Sui Po station was much like T-Lands except that it was larger and busier because it was located near Shek Kip Hei village and the tenement district around Pei Ho Street. Normally the Chinese citizen was the most law-abiding in the world, but this region of Kowloon was overflowing with refugees from all over China. Their lives were so compressed and their temperaments so different it was remarkable there were not more thievings or crimes of passion, but there was enough to keep a large constabulary force always on the alert.

Entering the station, Rodman passed through a long hallway lined with rows of heavy leather riot shields. He approached the booking desk and as he took off his raincoat a man called to him from the holding cage.

"Top of the morning, you crazy Limey!"

Rodman turned around in surprise and saw Marty Gates smiling behind the wires of the cage. It was a moment before Rodman recognized him. His pants and white shirt were dirty and torn. There was a cut on his lip and one across his cheek, and both of his eyes were ringed with deep purple.

"Well . . . !" Rodman walked slowly toward the cage and placed his thumbs in his belt. "I didn't know we had an earthquake as well as a typhoon. Did a building fall on you, Mr. Gates?" Rodman glanced up at the booking desk. "What is our friend charged with this time, Sergeant?"

"Disturbing the peace, sir."

"Again? You must have made a spot of money lately, Gates. Every time you get a wad you wind up in trouble."

"I can lick any Limey in the world," Marty said, still smiling.

"Come now. In your position you should be contrite."

"I was just sitting there quietly when the Aussies jumped me."

"Sitting where?"

"The Kowloon bar."

"And out of a clear sky they jumped you?"

"It was a rainy sky."

"Who were the Aussies, Sergeant?"

"Air Force men, sir."

"And why did they jump you, Marty? What were the preliminaries?"

"There was a brief discussion about who won the war."

"You're getting a little old for this sort of thing. Why don't you go home to America and forget about who won the war?"

Marty ran his fingers down the wire. "I've got to get out of here first."

"You're a problem child." Rodman took his thumbs from his belt and made a small circle in front of the cage, moving with his catlike grace. He liked Marty Gates—he was one of those Yanks with a great deal of charm. He was probably dishonest when he could find anything dishonest to do, but basically he was harmless. He was just a bad boy, or had been taught that mischief was somehow admirable by his own wild and woolly army. He had never grown out of it, and there was a rumor that for an American he had seen a very tough war. There were a lot of such men still drifting through the Orient. Rodman wished they would all go home. Fraternization was good, and the Pukka-sahibs were wrong about not indulging it, but they were right about one thing. A white man beaten, a white man fighting with another white man, scrambling and clawing and hitting like an animal, lost face for the whole race. It was worse if they wound up in jail. Yes, the Pukka-sahibs were right about face.

Suddenly Rodman stepped closer to the cage. He carefully examined Marty's injuries, then returned his smile. He had found the excuse he had instinctively tried to create.

"Release this man to my custody, Sergeant."

When the door clanged shut behind him, Rodman took Marty to an office at the back of the station. There was a case of orange squash in the corner of the room and he opened two bottles. He handed one to Marty and then stood looking at the gray sky through the barred window.

"That was damned decent of you," Marty said. "It just proves even Limeys can be reasonable."

"What was . . . ?" Rodman's voice was far away and preoccupied.

"Getting me out."

"I'll see that all charges are dropped if you'll do something for me."

"Name it."

Rodman turned to face him. "You're in pretty bum condition. You and a typhoon sort of complement each other. I like those black eyes, and the cuts will help, too. A bandage around your head, close in by your cheeks . . . maybe a spot of adhesive tape here and there . . . ought to do if you aren't sitting in too much light."

"You've lost me."

"There's a junk master named Lim Chau-wu. With any luck we might pick him up today for a bit of questioning about various and sundry. But I've a notion he won't do any talking unless we can put some quite firm pressure on him. If he's as smart as I think he is, he won't cooperate unless he thinks we have him cold. All I want you to do is let him see you and hear your American voice. Then I want you to testify in front of him—it won't be under oath—that your name is Louis Hoyt and that he was the junk master who took you to China. How about it?"

"Sure thing. It's a small world."

"I've got a hunch it just might work."

According to his custom, Hank took breakfast with Billy and his daughter Lucy. As with most healthy men this was his favorite time of any day, for his body was rested and the dents which might have been punched in his mind the day before were automatically smoothed. He was always vastly hungry in the mornings and his great voice boomed through the hallways and the rooms of the house, shaking it alive, and the kind of person who crept suspiciously and uncertainly into a morning, hating their departure from unconsciousness, frowning at the light, and insisting that the world stand back from them until they had consumed their quota of coffee, would have despised Hank Lee in the morning. For normally he began each day as if the one before it had never existed . . . and in this habit all children were in complete harmony with him.

There was a sense of adventure when breakfast began in the house of Henry Lee. Lucy would sit on his left, her bright black eyes sparkling with anticipation as she chattered half in Chinese and half in English about the dragon who had invaded her dreams, and Billy would sit on his father's right, sometimes claiming that the dragon Lucy had seen was barely a snail compared to the one which had picked up his bed and pushed it against the ceiling, or other mornings, already wandering in the marvelously intricate forests of his eight-year-old imagination, he would take careful aim with his porridge spoon, which was really a Winchester, at the painted warriors hiding among the silver peacocks, elephants and tigers.

Yet on this morning, with the rain drumming at the windows and the prospect of an entire day inside, Lucy and Billy were subdued. They were lost in their own quietness and their detachment was shared by the two dogs and the cat that waited motionless beside their chairs while they toyed with their food. Lucy and Billy instinctively keyed their mood to the great person who sat at the head of the table, the god of all things except those indefinable things supervised by the real big God with the white beard and a light around the back of his head who lived somewhere beyond the clouds. On this morning the great one at the head of the table was not laughing and the clatter of his knife and fork against the plate, a sound never before worthy of attention, was intriguing. He must have dreamed of a dragon, for his eyes were remote and he was not with them.

Hank finished his breakfast quickly. He rose without waiting to light a cigar and kissed first Lucy and then Billy. He told them, with this new and faraway tone in his voice, that the rain was bad and because there was wind too there would certainly not be any school on this already hopeless day. As their faces fell, and the beginning of a tear touched the corner of Lucy's eye, he reached out suddenly and took them in his arms. His voice rang out once more and he laughed. He would be gone for several hours, he said, but when he returned most of the rain would be gone, too. And if it was, and if they did as the amah told them to do, and if they ate a big lunch and rested afterward, he would take them to a cinema. And since he had never before failed them in a promise their trust was absolute. So they seized his tremendous hands, which were unbelievably warm, and rejoicing, led him to the door. Billy handed him his raincoat and Lucy held out his straw hat, saying that the rain would surely spoil it.

As he went down the steps, head bent against the rain, he turned to see them still standing in the doorway with the dogs and the cat fawning about their legs, and he saw them wave through the curtain of water. He raised his hand, cursing himself for being so preoccupied with thinking of the woman, and then climbed quickly into the back seat of the car. He told the chauffeur to go directly to the market on Pei Ho Street. It was too early for that son-of-a-bitch Tweedie. He would start things moving by paying a call on old Dak Lai. It had been a long time since he had seen either one of them.

As the car pulled out of the gate he did not look back, for he knew as certainly as he knew it was raining that the old pattern was beginning to form, and he hated the invisible and yet so certain signs of it. He lit his cigar and sat back against the soft and comfortable seat, trying to gather his thinking. His hand caressed the soft and expensive upholstery and he remembered the hard, cracked leather which once covered the seat of his gravel truck. In the not so long ago.

He thought, Here am I, Hank Lee, sitting on my tail with a fine cigar and being driven as I please by my own chauffeur in one of the most expensive cars in the world. I have a house to keep the rain off my head and the house is filled with treasures few other men in the world possess. There is Lucy, and Billy, and Joe in the States, who love me. There is enough money in the bank to live for a long time—sitting like this so soft. There is a business, if it could be called that, which almost runs itself. My fingernails are clean and there is not a callus on my hands. I will not eat lunch out of a tin box sitting on the running board of a truck and I do not have to cheat on my time sheet at the end of the day. How did this happen? How can an ignoramus from Chicago become a king in Hong Kong? Yes, there is even a small crown inlaid in the wood which trims the rear side of the front seat. It happened because I had guts, more guts than the other bone-headed gravel-truck drivers who were still pushing the same trucks for the same construction company—with time and a half for Saturday mornings. I risked my neck to make the difference between Hank Lee and those other bums. I stole a lot of things. I almost drowned in Formosa Strait trying to deliver glygnite to Foochow in that first worm-eaten junk which wasn't even paid for. Chiang's crazy navy shot at me and they would still shoot at me if they had the chance—on land or sea. The Commies shot at me because they shot at everything, even businessmen who were trying to arrange it so they could keep shooting. For a fairly reasonable fee.

He smiled and puffed his cigar with increasing satisfaction. That was one thing. The Commies paid through the nose for every item delivered by Hank Lee. They were suckers—anxious suckers who paid in advance in gold. They hate me and the feeling is mutual, but they are stuck with me and their money has made me a king.

He tried to remember how long it had been since he had been to the godowns or even near the junks. Six months . . . maybe more. Stoker, that overfat hog, took care of those things now. For Hank Lee, there were only occasional decisions to make . . . big stuff . . . policy. Growth. Some day, he thought, I am going to punch Stoker in the belly and watch him explode. I used to punch a lot of people because usually they were standing in the way. But when you had power and money that kind of punching wasn't necessary any more. It was a standard beginning out here if you had to come up from nothing. Look at the Jardine empire. They owned shipping and wharves and godowns and buildings until hell wouldn't have it. Now they were legitimate and as respectable as the Bank of England. But they didn't start out that way. They started with sailing ships and the only cargo they made a penny out of was mud. Mud was opium and they finally sold so much of it they wound up owning a very fat chunk of the Far East. What was wrong with Hank Lee doing the same thing?

Some day there would be a Lee Building in Hong Kong with polished brass plates on each side of the entrance engraved with the words "Lee Company Limited," or "Henry Lee and Company Limited." A bank would be a sideline, to occupy the first floor, and the ships which sailed under the Lee flag would not be junks but great ocean-going freighters and they would call at ports all over the world. Their sailings would be announced in the newspapers and their cargoes would be rice and farm machinery and automobiles and soy bean and camphor and maybe, just for old times' sake, a few gravel trucks now and then.

Joe would run the Lee Company then, and he would run it well and be invited to make speeches at public gatherings because he was smart and rich and respectable and had an education even the British couldn't beat. A kid who had been a beggar on the fly-blown stinking streets of Manila would be as big a shot as any of the Pukka-sahibs who lived on the hills of Hong Kong. Then there would be Billy, or William Lee, as they would call him then, who would be Joe's assistant, or better yet, run one of the various divisions of the Lee Company—the shipping line if he took to it. Billy, whose real milk name would never be known because whoever left him at the gate never bothered to pin a name on him. Billy, whom nobody wanted—like in the beginning nobody wanted Hank Lee. And Lucy, who just happened to exist because somebody was drunk or got careless one night, wouldn't have to settle for some slant-eyed gravel-truck driver in Bangkok because there was some doubt about her name. Lucy would speak a couple of languages all with the right accent . . . she could go to school in Switzerland for a while . . . and she would have plenty of money so people wouldn't spend too much time wondering how come she looked so all Oriental and was still supposed to be the daughter of old Henry Lee.

There would be a special office on top of the Lee Building—with a view of the harbor—so a man could look down at the junks if they were still around. It would be good to remember when you stood on the decks of a lot of them and worried about what was under those decks.

The office would be paneled with teak. There would be thick carpets on the floor and it would be air-conditioned, of course. It would be known as old Captain Lee's office, and because there was so much formality and money around nobody would ever remember that the only ship the old man ever captained was a lousy junk. Things would be respectable and legitimate all around.

All of this was definitely in the cards, he thought, if only I keep off the reefs. Most of the risks were over. It was clear sailing and the compass was steady as a rock. All right then, why am I deliberately heading off course, steering in a direction where I know there is going to be risk? I can blow the whole thing, just when it's well started. I can lose the whole business or I can even get killed because the wounds made on a lot of people when Hank Lee was on the way up are still fresh enough to hurt. There are a lot of people who would be very happy to attend my funeral. They would be more than glad to pay for the firecrackers. So why?

Wiping the steam from the window at his side, he knew there was only one explanation. It was all a part of the pattern and this was one more risk that had to be taken.

The Empire, the beginning Lee Empire, lacked one very important element. It was like trying to sail without a mast and the lack had disturbed him for a long time. He needed a woman—not just any woman who would, with softness, or with concern for herself, weaken the pattern. Hank Lee needed a woman who was more than a decoration, although she must be attractive enough to win friends in the new social world which was about to come. She had to be a lady. She must also like kids because for the next several years Billy and Lucy were going to need a mother. But most of all she must have courage, real nerve to stick with a man who intended to be more than a two-bit king. And he thought, The only woman I have ever met who seems to have all of these things is another man's wife. She will never be taken, as I might capture a junk. She has to be won.

On normal days it would have been impossible for the car to penetrate the sprawling market near Pei Ho Street. It was always, from the first light of dawn until late at night, a crowded place, where the people swarming over the square and spilling into the streets moved in a solid mass, flowing backward and forward like mercury in an enormous tray. It was also the most vivacious and hustling place in Kowloon. For every Chinese is a passionate gourmet and the business of eating brings his other endeavors to a halt five times a day. And this is said to be bad by many who have seen the ways of the rest of the world, because it leads to waste, which in itself is an unforgivable sin, and the food taken so frequently can never be properly digested. But most Chinese do not care. They are more concerned with the flavor of the rice in their bowl, or the freshness of a fish which they much prefer to buy alive from a tank, or the succulence of green vegetables which must not be more than a few hours torn from the nourishing earth. A housewife then, or an amah, or a coolie who feeds himself, is therefore much in the market, purchasing the ingredients of each meal as short a time as possible before its con-sumption. There is no haste in these vital transactions, though twenty customers may gather about a pile of muskmelons or argue about the quality of young pea leaves in a wicker basket set upon the ground.

Yet on this day the rain and the wind had devastated the market, for Chinese hate getting wet almost as much as they abhor passing money to strangers. No one sat at the tea stalls and the proprietors huddled discon-solately behind their counters and tried to keep their canvas roofs from flapping away on the wind. The individual peasant merchants who some-times trotted half the night, balancing their wicker baskets on a bamboo pole, so they might be the first to set up shop, were not squatting in their usual places along the curbings. The fish tanks were empty and not a sound came from the crates of chickens stacked alongside the public la-trine. Even the beggars had found a place to hide from the morning.

And so the chauffeur had no difficulty in driving directly across the market to a large tenement-like building which faced on the square. Hank Lee jumped across the gutter which ran deep with water. In three long strides he stood before a wooden door plastered with soggy red paper. He pushed open the door and stepped quickly inside.

He waited a moment just inside the door until his eyes could become accustomed to the gloom. Breathing the pungent smell of burning joss sticks he heard the familiar and monotonous pounding on small gongs be-fore the candle-lit altar. Then he saw Dak Lai sitting at her fortune table in the dark corner. She was smoking a cigarette and thoughtfully caressing her completely bald head. "Good morning, you ancient fraud," he said in Cantonese.

She looked up, squinting through the shadows, and, recognizing him, said in a voice that sounded like the rattling of tin, "Welcome, Brother Predominant." It was his milk name, given to him by Dak Lai when he first came to Hong Kong, and he smiled at the memory of it. It had been a long time, he thought, since he had been in a Buddhist temple. They had always amused him with their easy, almost impudent approach to religion. A temple might be a few small rooms in a tenement like this one, or it might be an elaborate red-pillared structure dating back for centuries. It made no difference. The atmosphere was always the same and as de-pendable as the custom of burning joss three sticks at a time or candles in groups of two. His years on the China Coast had convinced Hank that Buddhism was the most easygoing religion in the world. People who came to stand before the lacquer and gold altars did so not in fear of the many gods, or even of Buddha himself. They relaxed and thought—giving away their earthly fears to the images behind the altar and nursing their hopes against the comforting monotony of the gongs. The attendants in any temple were equally at ease.

Now, as he crossed the room toward Dak Lai, the two neophyte nuns glanced at him curiously, yet barely paused in their rhythmic beating. Behind them, just beside the altar, two very small children, with mucus running from their noses, played happily on the floor.

Dak Lai was a full priestess and thus her head was shaved until it was impossible to tell whether she was a woman or a man. She was very old and slightly hard of hearing. Hank liked her. She was, he thought, two things. She was the smartest woman he had ever known regardless of race. It was Dak Lai who first suggested that he might become a king. He had some knowledge of the sea, and he would do well, she said, because he was not afraid. A Chinese girl had brought him here to have his fortune told. Hank could not even remember the girl's name now, there was only that one night with her—but he would always remember old Dak Lai. After he had stood before the altar and shaken three fortune sticks from the wooden tube according to ritual, Dak Lai examined the characters on the ends of the sticks and began to write on a long strip of bright red paper. And as her brush deftly inscribed the characters she spoke slowly so the girl could translate as she went along. She said that Hank Lee had for too long been like a god who walked as a pigeon and she said that this was wrong for he had the body and the heart of an eagle. He must release himself from the captivity of meekness and throw aside the belief that the world held his betters simply because they were richer, or had education, or visible power. From that time on, he began to think differently, and for years he stopped often to talk with Dak Lai. But one thing above all he valued. It was the second thing about Dak Lai. She had become the only person in China he could trust.

He took the withered hand she offered and sat down opposite her. He placed a carton of American cigarettes on the table and because she saw instantly that they were genuine and not the cheap imitations made in China, she threw her cigarette on the floor and opened the box.

"How goes business?" he asked. She peered at him intently while he lit her new cigarette. "What are you charging for a good fortune these days?"

"The same. Where have you been?"

"Counting my money."

"Is there so much that it takes so long? I am older by almost a year." He thought, Has it been that long since I've been here, and he knew that she was right. The accusation in her black lacquer eyes made him suddenly ashamed and he resolved that whatever happened he would come to see Dak Lai more often. She was a mother, a confessor and a firecracker beneath the spirit of Hank Lee, all in one; and somehow she was good luck, too. Her fortunes, of course, were a lot of malarkey—the telling of them was a concession in all temples—but Dak Lai had a special way of making her predictions seem convincing. A part of her deep wisdom flowed from her as she set the characters down on the red paper and she seemed to believe in them herself.

"You look younger," he said.

Her laughter was a metallic cackle and the smoke caught in her throat added a fit of coughing. "You are learning," she said when she at last recovered her breath. "The stone of you is wearing smooth."

"My thanks to you."

"You did not come out in the rain for cleansing," she said.

"I need help."

"Ah?"

"I have to find a man in China . . . an American."

"Ah?"

"He may be dead."

"Then he should be easy to find because he will not move."

"Not so easy."

"Ah!"

Hank thought that he had never been able to use the Chinese "ah" in just the right way. It was the most versatile sound in the world, an exhalation of breath that became both punctuation and a signal of understanding. It was as if two people in a conversation had individual radios. The one receiving would send out a flow of "ah's" saying, "I am listening . . . I still hear you . . . we have not lost communication . . . continue sending." The "ah" was more of a staccato grunt than a word. It leaped quickly from the lips when properly done and had infinite variations of tone and emphasis.

"The Communists hold him as a prisoner."

"Ah. He is your friend?"

"No."

"Ah." This time her "ah" signaled complete lack of understanding. She frowned until the wrinkles climbed high on her glistening head, and she sucked heavily on her cigarette. He was certain Dak Lai would have to know everything before she would do anything, but how was he going to explain Jane Hoyt to her? How was he going to explain Jane Hoyt to himself?

"She . . . he, is the husband of a woman," he said lamely, seeking through his Chinese vocabulary for phrases which would make sense.

"You sound like a fool. The rain has wet your brain."

"She is a wonderful woman."

"Ah."

"I want her."

"E-e-eh!" Dak Lai made a sound that bore no relation to her "ah's." She sounds like a billy goat, Hank thought. Damn her! Why was it so hard to explain this business about Jane Hoyt?

"I have needed a woman."

"Ah." She nodded her head. "Then find one before it is too late."

"I am trying to tell you that I have found one . . . or at least I think I have."

"Ah."

"I want you to send inquiries to your temples on the mainland. Your priests and nuns are supposed to know everything. Find out where this American is . . . then I'll try to think of some way to get him out."

"It is not the same these days. There is much talk against the temples. The young people are sick in their brains."

"Will you try for me? He has round eyes, so he shouldn't be too hard to find."

"You ask, so I will try. How old is he?"

"Probably in his thirties . . . I'm not sure."

"His name?"

"Louis Hoyt. He is a maker of pictures."

"Ah."

"He would not speak any dialect of Chinese."

"Ah."

"He entered China sometime in June or late May by our calendar. That's all I know."

Her face almost disappeared behind a thick cloud of cigarette smoke. When it cleared he saw that she was still far from satisfied. She glanced at the neophytes before the altar and made a signal with her clawlike hand. They stopped their beating and walked silently to an electric plate at the end of the altar on which a teapot was steaming. And though the sound of the gongs had never been loud, the sudden quiet was oppressive. There was only the liquid noise of the rain as it dribbled to the cement beneath the ill-fitting street door and the occasional whisper of a candle as the wind squeezed its way under the door and puffed across the room. Dak Lai vanished behind another cloud of smoke and from behind it she said, "Brother Predominant, I will do what is possible. But if you want the woman, I do not understand why you want the husband. It is twisted thinking."

"It's a crazy American way of thinking, but I know it has to be done."

"You are becoming a sheep again. You will lose all you have won."

"Is that an opinion or a fortune?"

"It is an opinion. In Yunnan they say it is reasonable to buy one teapot and many teacups, but who ever heard of buying one cup and many teapots."

"Meaning I should settle down and live like a Chinese with a houseful of women?"

"Ah . . . why not?"

"No thanks. I am too much of a sheep for that."

"So you would risk everything for one woman?"

"That seems to be the way things are."

He stood up and she rose with him. They walked to the door together and once again he was conscious of her size and frailness. Her black gown hung loosely on her scrawny frame and the top of her head barely reached his chest. He reached out gently and was surprised to discover that the breadth of his hand covered her entire shoulder.

"Think about this," she said solemnly. "Think with reason."

"I haven't thought about anything else since I first saw her."

"Bring her to see me. Only a woman can truly penetrate another woman."

"I'll try. When will you have some news?"

"Allow me ten days."

"That's too long."

"Five days then . . . but the cost will be more."

Hank smiled. He had been waiting for the inevitable. He reached into his pocket and brought out a wad of bills. He peeled off a bright-pink Hong Kong five-hundred-dollar note and pressed it into her hand.

"Don't waste any time, little mother."

He jerked down the brim of his hat and went out into the rain.

8

The typhoon had an indirect yet shocking effect upon Tweedie's Place. It swept across the harbor from Hong Kong and arrived at the door in full belligerence just as Tweedie decided closing time had come. But the occupants took one look outside the door and decided unanimously that it would be the height of foolishness to venture a step further. They retreated immediately to the long table which they had left only a moment before, and announced that they were going to get drunk. In the history of man, they agreed, there had never been a more favorable time to get drunk. They seemed entirely unaware that they were already stony-eyed long before reaching their decision, and began afresh, as if they had recessed for sleep and a cold shower in the short interval between going to the door and returning to the long table. And so, gathering strength and enthusiasm from hidden reservoirs, their voices rising and falling from shouts to confidential whispers, sitting and standing and sometimes collapsing in temporarily quiet bundles—they drank.

Tweedie was there, and Icky. Big Matt and Gunner were there and so were the two American Air Force captains, who maintained it would be crazy to risk their lives walking three blocks back to the Peninsula Hotel. Major Leith-Phipps was there and had been since early in the evening when he persuaded himself that a spot of Yank food might add spice and variety to his life. He also might chance upon the American girl whom he had observed in the Peninsula lobby only the day before. Madame Dupree was there, remaining in Tweedie's after her free meal only by grace of the typhoon, and it could have been her electrifying presence that gave an unorthodox twist to the whole affair. For neither Tweedie, nor Icky, nor Matt, nor Gunner, nor the two Air Force captains had ever seen a woman who could drink so much without falling flat on her face. Even Icky, who clacked his false teeth and complained openly when the long table was sullied by a woman—"and especially an old bag like you," as he kept saying to Madame Dupree—was finally won over. The climax came when Madame Dupree began to sing lustily in Russian, finishing her performance by dancing a Kazachek on the long table. Icky fell in love with Madame Dupree then, and when her dance was completed he rose gallantly to help her to the floor. He asked her to marry him and she accepted with becoming reticence, protesting only that he must never call her an old bag again.

It was arranged that Tweedie should give the bride away, Gunner would be best man, and Big Matt would sing *Lohengrin*. The Air Force captains were enlisted as supernumeraries with roving functions. They tried to get a priest on the telephone, but either the wires were down or the phone was out of order from the rain, and so for a time they forgot about the wedding. Later, Major Leith-Phipps rose uncertainly from his wicker chair and brushed the remnants of Yankee food from his mustachios with the edge of a beer stein.

"I have a confession to make," he said. "I was not, as some might presume, a Sandhurst man—"

"Aw stow it!" Gunner yelled, not knowing or caring what the Englishman had to say.

"So go hire a hall," said Big Matt.

"The point is . . . just before the war, I was defrocked."

"Don't use them words in here!" Gunner said quickly. "The Gi don't like it!"

"Besides they's ladies present," Icky said, suddenly remembering Madame Dupree and putting a protective arm around her.

"But my dear chaps, you don't know what this means!"

"You Limeys got a way of twisting everything around when it comes to words and meanings," Tweedie hollered.

Then all of them began to yell their particular views on the English language as spoken by Englishmen, and it was some time before Major Phipps could again rise above the noise.

"No . . . no! I was *defrocked!* I was a Methodist minister and they jolly well stripped me of my vestments."

Big Matt, a new light in his eyes, pounded his stein heavily on the table for order. The beer splashed over the tattoos on his arm and they glistened as he waved his hand.

"Wait a minute! Wait *just* a *minute*, you smart guys! I *git* the major . . . I *git* what he's trying to say even if he does talk with a mouthful of hot potatoes. The major is sayin' that he stood a court-martial and they yanked off all his decorations. He done somethin' he shouldn't of . . . so he got himself defrocked which is just the opposite of what you're thinking, see? He was a minister and they took off all his clothes and said go to hell out in the world and never come near us again because ministers ain't supposed to do this sort of thing. Is that correct, Major?"

"Precisely."

Big Matt swept his great arm over the assemblage as if he would press them to his bosom. "So the major is sayin' he can perform this here wedding we all been talking about. He's got the word. Correct, Major?"

"A brilliant analysis!"

"You remember the right words?" Tweedie asked suspiciously. "I don't want nothin' happening here that ain't legal."

"They are engraved on my memory forever."

"Then what we waitin' for?" Big Matt yelled. "Icky, go comb that fuzz on the top of your dome so you'll be pretty, and, Helene, go fix up your lipstick and see if you can wipe some of the beer off the front of you. We got to do this thing right!"

Major Leith-Phipps threw himself promptly into his role. The wicker chairs were shoved into two lines so that they formed an aisle stretching from the street window to the back room and the piano. It was thought that the long walk down the aisle would do Icky and Madame Dupree a tremendous amount of good by way of sobering them. One of the Air Force captains volunteered to play the wedding march, but in spite of his best efforts he could not always remember the middle portion. The beginning and the end he rendered faultlessly, if a trifle on the syncopated side, but the middle part invariably became "Oh Susanna." This departure from form made Big Matt extremely angry and he took away the captain's beer.

It was well on toward seven in the morning and the typhoon had reached the peak of its force before Icky and Madame Dupree actually started down the aisle between the wicker chairs.

Then the unforeseen occurred. No one had counted on the final impact of the preparations, nor had anything like this ever happened before in Tweedie's place.

When everything had been done that anyone could think of, when Tweedie stood waiting near the street door and Madame Dupree had placed her hand delicately on his arm, when Icky was ready and waiting with a mixture of astonishment and sudden shyness before the long table, a hush fell on Tweedie's Place. There was only the muffled drumming of the wind outside and the rain fizzing against the street window. It may have been the half-light in which Madame Dupree was standing that somehow transformed her, or it could have been the oceans of beer, but it was so that she appeared young and quite beautiful. The bags beneath her eyes miraculously disappeared and the wrinkles which creased the flesh beneath her neck could no longer be seen. Her strawberry hair took on a golden look, and she stood so straight and radiantly expectant that the paunch which had long caused her to resemble an eggplant, was hardly noticeable.

Icky, too, was altered magically. Though he swayed perceptibly, as if he were balancing himself once more against the heaving deck of the old *Talus*, his eyes were as bright as a sailing cadet's and the whole of his small gnarled body seemed revitalized. He had borrowed a razor from one of the Chinese waiters, perfumed himself with the scent of a joss stick, and forced back his shoulders so the magnificent tattoo across his chest could better be displayed. All were agreed that Icky did not look a day over sixty and they pounded him continuously with congratulatory swats on the back. Consequently, no one perceived the true power of their preparations until Big Matt signaled to the Air Force captain for the opening chords. There was a tense moment when he struck entirely the wrong notes, then paused, and began again. He struck out boldly. Recklessly inspired, he played out the march as if he had done so every day of his life. Not a note was wrong or missing and as Tweedie started down the aisle, head held high on his giraffe neck and Madame Dupree keeping perfect halt-step beside him, everyone in Tweedie's including the Chinese waiters began to cry.

Gunner wept so uncontrollably he was forced to set down his beer. Big Matt blew his nose fiercely in a napkin from one of the tables and blubbered that he didn't see how he was ever going to sing *Lohengrin* when the time came. The Air Force pianist fought through his tears to see the keys. Tweedie's Adam's apple cavorted up and down his neck as he swallowed to relieve his new-found paternal emotions and Madame Dupree arrived at the side of her groom with tributaries of mascara streaking her face. Even Major Leith-Phipps, who stood ramrod straight as long as the table was behind him, discovered cracks in his British reserve. When he said, "And do you, Herman Schultz, take this woman," his voice choked and it was several moments until he could continue, for he had been told Icky hated the mention of his true name and yet now he heard it spoken without wincing and smiled at the major courageously when he said, "I sure do . . . by golly!"

Afterward, when the major assured everyone that all had gone according to the Gospel and the kisses were exchanged, Big Matt said it would be impossible for him to sing *Lohengrin* because there had been enough crying and he couldn't stand to see any more.

"I'll sing 'On the Road to Mandalay,'" he yelled, "and you can all join in!" Which they did.

Fragments of the wedding celebration were still in evidence when Hank Lee strode into Tweedie's Place. The bride and groom had gone to Madame Dupree's room at the Peninsula to consummate their union. The Air Force captains had also departed when the wind eased. Gunner and

Big Matt had each arranged lines of chairs to accommodate their bodies and were sound asleep on top of them. Major Leith-Phipps was also resting, but he was on the floor in a corner and somehow as a last gesture to British prestige had managed to cover himself with a tablecloth so that he looked quite respectable. Beer bottles, glasses and cigarette stubs littered the room. The overhead fans were still stirring a veil of smoke against the ceiling.

Tweedie was taking his fourth aspirin when he saw Hank come through the door and he wondered for a moment if the pills had affected his eyesight. Hank Lee had only been in his place once before, he remembered with displeasure, and that was when he was on his way up. He was a harbor thug then, and only a thug in Tweedie's opinion. He had called on a matter of business to say that if Tweedie didn't keep his goddamned spies away from his godown he was going to kill one of them. The informant in question happened to be Big Matt, who was tall and square enough to stand eye to eye with Hank Lee. And he did so for approximately three minutes during which time Hank Lee gave Matt the beating of his life. Damage to the restaurant amounted to three thousand dollars Hong Kong, as the two slugged their way among the tables. That was bad enough, but worse was the lost opportunity of joining Hank unofficially in what would become a promising business. No one, not even Big Matt, could be persuaded to go near Hank's godown again and without exact information which might be used as a lever, Tweedie had been helpless ever since. Even the Chinese, who would risk anything for a decent reward, were afraid of him. So, Tweedie thought ruefully, am I. Hank Lee was one of those men better left alone.

He walked toward him warily, threading his way through the disarray of tables and trying to estimate the expression on Hank's face before he approached too closely. But the light came from the street window, which was behind him, and the brim of his straw hat partially covered his eyes, so Tweedie stopped several arm lengths away from him and said as calmly as he could manage, "Hello, Hank."

"Hi."

"It's a little damp outside, I guess."

"Yeah." Hank looked around him and saw Matt sleeping on the chairs beside Gunner, then glanced at the major in the corner. But his hands remained jammed down inside his raincoat and there was still no indication of his mood. "What struck this place?"

"We had a little celebration, Hank. Icky got himself married."

"Yeah?" Again he surveyed the room, as if it was the only thing he had come to see. "What for?"

"He was lonesome, I guess. A lot of people get that way."

Hank brought a cigarette from his pocket and lit it. He blew the smoke

directly at Tweedie's eyes, yet his manner of doing so left doubt in Tweedie's mind whether the act had been deliberate or not. I wish he would say
something, Tweedie thought. I wish he would get to talking so I can
know which direction things are heading. At least he looks a little older,
so maybe he's not so damn strong. But he's richer and in a way that's just
as bad.

"We ain't been near a one of your godowns, Hank," Tweedie said finally.

"I know that."

"Then . . . how come you happened to drop by?"

"I might want you to do me a favor."

Tweedie took a moment to recover from his shock. Hank Lee asking
me to do him a *favor*? And he looked sober, too. Maybe too much money
had made him take up drinking for real . . . or he had a monkey on
his back, maybe.

"Why sure, Hank. Christ's sake! Anything you say. I always did think
we ought to understand each other better. Siddown. Have a drink."

"No. I don't want to sit down and I don't want a drink. Are you still
swiping money?"

"I dunno what you're talking about, Hank."

"The U.S. dollars that are supposed to go to the mainland for some
poor relation."

"You got it wrong, Hank. I'm doin' those people a favor. It's the only
way they can get the money in there now. You know that. Sure, I take a
little commission . . . I got to maintain a lot of contacts. But I don't
swipe nothing. In a way you might say I'm just being humane."

"Yeah. You're humane, all right. It's those contacts I came to see you
about. You know a man named Louis Hoyt?"

Tweedie was about to say he had never heard the name in his life when
the training of years flashed a light in his brain. And the light burned
with such sudden intensity it even penetrated the viscous mud of his hang-
over. Acting as adrenaline upon his soggy intelligence, it told him to
mouth words with extreme care and illuminated certain recesses of his
brain wherein he had cached tidbits of information which at the time of
absorption appeared utterly worthless. Not only did he remember Louis
Hoyt, but he remembered that his wife had come to make inquiries.
That fact was easy to analyze and uninteresting, but when pieced together
with Madame Dupree's observation—the wife was seen to leave the Peninsula in Hank Lee's car—it not only became interesting, but worth much
more than a free meal plus the expense of a wedding party. And what
was Hank Lee doing with the wife? Oh yes . . . and there was the con-
firming report of the bellboy. Alert now, Tweedie decided he at last had

his hands on the long-sought lever. Just which way to pull it was still a question for research.

"The name sure sounds familiar," he said.

"You're damn right it sounds familiar. You told his wife he was dead."

So? He had been talking with the wife. How did those two ever get together? What else did they talk about?

"Now that I think back . . . maybe I did."

"How come you told her that?"

Watch out now! That question was loaded, Tweedie thought. He resolved to stick as close to the truth as he could without saying too much. Hank Lee wasn't swinging his weight around this morning. He was asking, and until there was some certain indication of his mind there was no use making things any easier for him than could be helped.

"I thought she might as well know the facts. I felt sorry for her."

"You never felt sorry for anybody. What makes you think he's dead?"

"I got some information. Why you so inarrested, Hank? The man a friend of yours or something?"

"Yeah. And I sure wouldn't want anything to happen to him."

"I didn't have nothing to do with him."

"Then how come you got the word he was dead?"

"I get all kinds of information. This is a public place. People come and go. I got ears—"

Tweedie had no time to move back before Hank's hand shot from the pocket of his coat and seized his shirt. His fingers clutched the shirt until it cut into Tweedie's armpits as he was lifted two inches off the floor. Hank held him aloft and shook him until his eyes popped.

"Listen, you lying son of a bitch! You're talking to Hank Lee."

"Lemme down, Hank!" But he shook him again as his face gradually turned purple.

"Tell me where and how you got the word or by God I'll use you for a shillelagh and really wreck this place!"

"All right!" Tweedie choked. "Lemme down!"

Hank slammed him to the floor so hard the shock ran up his body from his feet to his teeth. It was a moment before he could even see through the red curtain which swam in front of his eyes.

"Now," Hank said. "I'm listening."

"He come in here last spring," Tweedie said, anxiously massaging his long throat. "He come in several times and said he was all hot to go to China. I told him it was a damn fool thing to do, but he kept pesterin' me. He weren't makin' any progress with anybody else so finally I decided to help him."

"How much did he pay you?"

"A thousand bucks."

"U.S. or Hong Kong?"

"Hong Kong. It was reasonable considering what I had to do."

"Keep talking."

"I set him up with a contact of mine and that's all I done. Nothing else . . . and that's a fact."

"Who did you set him up with?"

"Lim Chau-wu."

"Who's he?"

"He's got a junk. He makes trips up to Canton now and again. He takes money up for me once in a while."

"Did you guarantee Hoyt he'd get out of China?"

"No. I never done that."

"If you're lying, start writing your will."

"I ain't lyin' . . . well, maybe I did sort of suggest we could make arrangements about getting out later. Given time I could of arranged it, too . . . but he was eager . . . awful eager."

"Who told you he was dead?"

"Lim Chau-wu."

"How do you know he isn't lying?"

"I don't."

"Find out. I'll give you two days."

"How the hell can I find out?"

"That's your problem. You're always bragging about all the contacts you have. I want proof he's dead and how he died, every last detail, where and how . . . or if he's alive I want to know where he is . . . *exactly*, understand? This is Tuesday. You phone me Thursday morning or make a reservation at the morgue."

Watching Hank's cold eyes Tweedie knew that he was not talking simply to make a noise. And he thought, the lever has broke off in my hand, but it is better to have a broken lever than a broken head. He was relieved when Hank put his hands back in his coat and looked away from him at the room again. He sighed heavily when Hank suddenly turned his back and walked toward the street door. He called after him.

"This is going to cost a lot of money, Hank."

"Use the dollars you got from Louis Hoyt!"

When he was gone Tweedie stood looking after him for a moment. He rubbed his neck and turned his mournful eyes toward the ceiling fans, thinking about Hank Lee. People, he decided, could say all they wanted. They could say Hank Lee was a dumb thug who made his way up because he had a strong arm, which he certainly had. They could say he didn't have a friend in the world, which was probably true unless Louis Hoyt was really a friend, which probably wasn't so, but might just as well be so if Hank Lee wanted it that way. They could say he was a killer and maybe they would be right, although they would have one hell of a time proving it. They could say he was selling out his country for his own benefit and they were sure as hell right. But one thing they didn't say, because he kept so much to himself and asked nothing of the rest of the world— and consequently nobody knew what he was really like. Except a smart giraffe. Hank Lee, by God, was one hell of a man.

Thinking so, Tweedie walked slowly toward the groups of chairs which served as havens of repose for Gunner and Big Matt. He looked down at them for a long time, studying their collapsed, smashed-pie faces. These were not Hank Lees, he mused. Far from it. They were as big and nearly as strong perhaps, but they were rotten potatoes. Snoring now, they looked like a pair of yams. They had never been and would never be competition for anybody—and competition, Tweedie decided, was the only thing left in life that was thoroughly enjoyable. Hank Lee had broken off the lever where it hurt the most, but the broken piece had a jagged edge. It could possibly be used to skewer Hank Lee if applied by an imaginative and well-informed man.

Tweedie drew back one long leg and stood for a moment poised like a stork. Then he kicked Big Matt soundly in the rump. He turned easily in a sort of tango step, and without losing rhythm brought his foot hard against Gunner in exactly the same place.

"Wake up, you free-loadin' tanks! Go over the Peninsula and get Icky out from his bride! We got a lot to do!"

During the morning the typhoon swung away from Hong Kong territory and plunged northwestward in the direction of the Chinese mainland where the irregularities of the earth punctured it so frequently it became a mere storm. By early afternoon the cities of Hong Kong and Kowloon were once again linked by ferry, the buses ran, the streets became active, and the rain became a light drizzle. It was relatively cool, for the cloud overcast was still scowling and acted as a solid shield against the sun. Watching the progress of the day from the window of his cheap hotel on Peiping Road, General Charles Po-Lin concluded the time had come for his constitutional. For years, ever since he could remember, he had walked at least one hour every day, swinging his Malacca cane for tempo, striding out smartly on his long, muscular legs.

General Po-Lin was seventy-one years old and he had seen the face of China change far more than his own. He was by birth a Manchu, and thus considerably taller than any southern Chinese. He had been born in Kalgan, the dry dusty city where the camel caravans still made up for the crossing of Mongolia, and he was inordinately proud of the fact that the Lin family could accurately trace their genteel ancestors for two thousand years. Some of this pride was evident in his own carriage as he performed the ritual of his walks. His back was straight, he moved with dignity and assurance though entirely devoid of arrogance, and always his head was high. He credited his devotion to exercise with his remarkable state of preservation. His skin was smooth and there were only a few wrinkles about his eyes. His teeth were good and his elimination, when these days there was anything to eliminate, was perfect. His mind was active and still capable of guiding his lips through every known Chinese dialect in addition to French, Portuguese and nearly faultless English. The only concession he had made to age was heavy bifocal glasses and these so disguised his eyes that he could, when observed from a distance, easily be mistaken for a lightly tanned Caucasian.

The general was, he knew, old school in many ways—placing value on education and manner—but he tried not to look back. Looking backward brought memories and with the memories came hunger—a far more despairing hunger than gnawed at his stomach now. There was Sun Yat-sen to remember and Peking before it became Peiping, and then Peking again. There was Nanking when it was the capital of China and Chungking when it was the capital of China. There was a vast assortment of warlords, both minor and great. There were the Japanese. There was the personally honest though ignorant peasant, transformed by far shrewder minds into a Frankensteinian general, who had taken the name Chiang Kai-shek.

There were also more personal memories which sometimes, when he lay on the sagging bed in the night and stared sleep-starved at the window, made a banquet of his loneliness. There was his wife, Glory—now exactly eleven years in the earth of China. There were the three houses, one in Peiping, one in Shanghai and the third, a summer place in Hankow. There was Glory alone, presiding over the servants and the children, for there were never any concubines in the house of Po-Lin. It was all gone. The honors, the friends who came and prodded the intellect and sometimes composed poems over wine of the third distillation, the respect, the ease and reason, the sense of achievement in serving China, the order of things set by ritual and custom, and yes, sometimes by force—were all gone. General Charles Po-Lin was abandoned by time and Chiang, as both had abandoned so many other people. He lived in suspension, somewhere between the new China, which he could not recognize, and the exiled poltroons on Formosa, who still polished their bayonets in a hopeless charade and could not afford to recognize him. They wanted younger men, much younger, and even they must be fit, for all the hills around Hong Kong and Kowloon were filled with young soldiers who had fought for Chiang. They dwelt in shacks made of bent tin fuel cans and packing boxes. They clothed their scrawny bodies in the remnants of their uniforms and rags, and on this problem they could often save, because almost invariably there was an arm or a leg which was not there to be clothed. They eked out an existence making wicker basketware, or when they had two hands they put them to work on embroidery, for which they received a few coppers every day. The British did not want them, although Christian charity compelled them to tolerate and help as they could all refugees. Chiang did not want them, even if the United States furnished both the bayonets and the polish. Only New China wanted them—for target practice. In this status of desirability they were in exactly the same position as General Po-Lin. Their vacuum-like days were passed in a colony which was itself suspended for an unpredictable time and which was neither British nor Chinese, Caucasian nor Oriental, nor the like of anything else human beings had ever seen before.

Now standing at his window, Po-Lin debated the question of his walk. It was not the drizzle which deterred him, for he still had a fine umbrella. But a walk would take energy which would sharpen his appetite and a man who was starving had to be very careful about his appetite. Until something turned up, he thought for the thousandth time. Until some tourist desired the services of a former general, which could be had at a most reasonable price; until some European or preferably an American was willing to pay a few dollars for an intelligently conducted tour of the city. A general, even a former general, could not make basketware or work at embroidery. There the common soldier had a distinct advantage. A Lin kept face or he perished. Face—the true emperor of all Orientals. The trouble was, these days there were very few tourists who were inclined to pay money so an ex-general could maintain face.

He decided in favor of the walk. It might enable him to forget the letter which was in his pocket, the letter from his last living son, who was no longer a son—the letter which so far could not be forgotten.

He took from the table beside his bed the copy of the *China Mail* of the day before which he had carefully saved. He folded the sheets of newspaper meticulously in two foot-length pieces. He inserted them along the worn soles of his shoes so that he would have at least some protection against the wet pavement. After he was satisfied there were no wrinkles to cause him unneeded discomfort, he placed his straw hat squarely on his head. He tried to disregard the frayed edges of his shirt collar and concentrated on the fact that both his shirt and his shorts were freshly laundered. He adjusted his long tan stockings until they were exactly level at a point just beneath his knees. He placed a clean white handkerchief in the same breast pocket which held the letter he intended to forget, and arranged the handkerchief in a neat triangle. Finally he took up his umbrella and Malacca cane. He closed the door to his room without locking it, squared his shoulders, elevated his jaw a trifle higher than he normally carried it, and went down the narrow hotel steps to the street. He was still thinking about the letter. It would not leave his mind.

Walking briskly along Peking Road he tried to ignore the displays of moon-cakes in the confectioners' store windows. It was not easy, for the moon-cakes represented far more than a powerful reminder of his hunger. As gifts they were packed in boxes of four according to custom, and the prices varied from two dollars and twenty cents per catty for those made of simple bean paste and sugar to more than seven dollars per catty for those made of fried chicken and filled with chopped duck's eggs.

It was neither the contents nor the price of the moon-cakes which tantalized Po-Lin. This month was the festival of the moon and the presentation of cakes was a vital part of the old China he knew so well and could not seem to forget. Now, glancing at a window in spite of himself, he was relieved to see that the moon-cakes were piled in pyramids of thirteen, corresponding to the maximum number of months, which could only fall in an intercalary year. It was good to see people keep the customs, for there was stability in customs and it showed they were still mindful of the legends behind them. They would know, even the young people, that the cakes signified more than a festival in honor of the moon. They would know of the final overthrow of the Mongol troops and the restoration of the first native Chinese dynasty since the magnificent Hans. They would know that for reasons of economy and security the Mongols billeted their troops on the population. In every humble cottage there was at least one soldier who made his demands not only upon their food supply but upon their women, until their presence became intolerable. They would know that the signal for a general rebellion against the Mongols was given by the distribution of moon-cakes, with the fateful hour of rising pasted on the bottom. And so at midnight, according to legend, every family took the kitchen chopper to its unwelcome guest and slew him—thus overnight vanquishing the whole army of occupation.

They would know all of these things and even the young people would not write letters such as the one in his pocket.

"Father—" it began. Not honorable father, or esteemed, or respected, or even dear father. What was it the English said? No serpent hath the bite of a son? Only "Father." It was like a kick in the stomach. A kick in the stomach from Canton.

Father—

I have recently obtained your address from representatives of the People's Government in Hong Kong. I now write to you not as a kin, because the childish institution of family is no longer a stone around the neck of China, but only because I have news which should interest you and perhaps directly benefit our struggle. I have recently the honor to be appointed to the Director's Office—Intelligence and Communications of the

People's Government. I presently serve as liaison officer with special assignment, Canton.

We are in need of experienced engineers, particularly with telephone long-wire and radio-telephone experience. Your record in supervising such installations for the military in the past is well known. I am instructed to say that if you will present yourself to this office in the immediate future, an opportunity to serve People's China may be forthcoming.

I am also obliged to say that your past political affiliations and bourgeois inclinations are also well known. However, if you have come to your senses and are willing to recognize the empirical ambitions of the so-called democracies, and their degenerate puppets, I believe I can successfully intercede for you with my superiors.

Even under the inspired leadership of Mao, our task is great. We are besieged on every hand, not only by gangster armies, but by paid spies who seek to destroy our liberation from within. For example, we now detain almost a hundred Americans who deny military status yet admit to crimes against the People's Government. I will show you these miserable and misguided persons as part of your own enlightenment.

You have lived a falsehood long enough. The truth is here. The masses have been enlightened and our duty is clear. The People's Government is not vindictive and will forgive your ignorance if you are willing to serve the future of New China.

Lin

Lin! It was not even his milk-name! They would be wearing queues next! They would do anything Mao told them to do, including step on the faces of their fathers. Vomit. It was a letter from a stranger.

Po-Lin cleared his throat and spat as if the action would relieve his disgust. Chiang, my general, rotting on Formosa! China, my mother, bewitched until my son sucks only poison from her breasts! The nurse becomes a brute and I, Po-Lin, am castrated. He spit again, seeking to be rid of the fungus taste which plagued his mouth.

He turned the corner at Ashley Road, which was hardly more than an alley, and walked north, still thinking of the letter. Holding his umbrella high to avoid collision with those protecting other pedestrians, he continued resolutely, breathing deeply of the rain-cleaned air to soothe his passion. Near the corner of Haiphong Road, where the passage became so narrow it was necessary to squeeze between two buildings, he came upon a group of men huddling and squatting about a storyteller. Some held umbrellas. Others had only pieces of newspaper to protect their heads, but they were all enrapt with the voice of the narrator who stood gesturing in their midst. Po-Lin stopped to listen, for this was the old China again— the good, sound, reliable China.

The storyteller, he saw at once, was a good one. He waved his arms and turned skilfully so that no section of his audience would be long neglected, and his voice rose and fell from shouts to whispers as he emphasized the more dramatic moments of his tale. He had not, as yet, launched his main story. That would come later, after this opening bid for attention. He was preparing his audience now, whetting their appetites with a prelude. When it was done, he would attempt to sell the packets of razors on the small portable stand which he had so placed that his listeners must see it to watch him. If they bought sufficiently during the pause after the opening story, then he would commence the main story, breaking it three times at the moments of greatest suspense so their reluctance to spend money for razors would be overcome by their desire to hear him out. Thus he made his living, and so his predecessors had filled their rice bowls for thousands of years. No book, no cinema, no play upon the stage, Po-Lin thought, could replace a good storyteller. And though he knew the story almost by heart, he stood fascinated as the man spoke in a soft Kwangsi accent and so captured his audience that even their eyes became hypnotized and were motionless.

"Hitherto," he was saying, "the Tatars were the only interruption of peace in a thousand years. And so in China there was wealth . . . indeed even the peasants were rich, and the scholars were as kings, while of soldiers there were none. And the Emperor then was a man who walked alone upon feast days, walked among the like of you and you and you and you, wearing his golden trappings without fear though he brushed against the multitudes. There was in this world, only China and Chinese of any consequence.

"Now the Emperor had a daughter whose name was Glamorous Gold and she was easily the most beautiful woman in the land. Her cheeks were of the texture of ivory and her lips were like the promise of a lotus yet to ripen. And her feet were of this size . . . yes!" he said, cupping his hand, "her feet were of no greater size than this . . . delicate as teacups. The Emperor and everyone in the land was in love with the Princess.

"Now it came to pass that a hundred evils were heaped upon the Princess. And it came to be in this way. I ask you to remember that in the nine provinces there was no more beautiful or virtuous woman. Therefore—" The storyteller allowed his voice to fall almost to a whisper as he circled the stand which held the razor blades. He made a pattern suggesting a wall and raised his hand as if to follow the branches of a tree.

"Therefore on the day of tragedy the Princess was walking in her garden. The sun was brilliant and yet she was spared its heat by the superb vegetation surrounding the wall . . . as here, a tree, and here a bounty of bush, and here an explosion of flowers."

Po-Lin forced himself to watch the other listeners for a moment. Now the storyteller had carefully erected the scenery. His audience had each created his own garden and they stood smelling the fragrance of their particular flowers and not feeling the heat of the imaginary sun or the sogginess of the very real rain.

"Hitherto, the Princess had always been carefully guarded, for such was her beauty even the most impotent of men felt a stirring in their loins as they observed her. But remember that the day was warm, the breeze was soft, and even the insects moved without energy. And so the guards were asleep, dreaming of times before their castration, and nothing could rouse them.

"Now there was an enormous acacia tree near the wall of the garden . . . just outside, mind you, yet its branches reached over the wall offering both beauty and shade. It was while walking beneath this tree that tragedy came to the Princess whose name was Glamorous Gold. Ha! Yes!"

The storyteller paused dramatically and the only sound was the light patter of rain on the newspapers and umbrellas.

"Yes! Watch carefully and see the monkey swing down from the acacia tree! Before the Princess can cry out, the monkey is upon her. He rapes her. He scampers back over the wall. Yet this is only the first of evils. Not even the power of the Emperor can undo what has been done. Before the leaves have fallen, when the winds of winter have yet to come, the Princess can no longer conceal the fact that she is with child. You, who have understanding, can appreciate her disgrace. What can she do? Where can she go . . . this flower, who was broken on the lance of a monkey? I will tell you what she did!"

There were murmurs of anticipation from the audience. Of course, Po-Lin thought, they know the story as well as I do, but they want their knowledge confirmed. It would be even more satisfying than surprise. They were poised for the laughter which all of them knew must come.

"I will tell you what the Princess did!" the storyteller said, his voice rising to a shout. "In her disgrace the Princess had no other choice! And so she fled to an uninhabited island off the coast of China! And there she finally gave birth to the Japanese race!"

The instant laughter bounced off the wet walls of the surrounding buildings. As he waited for it to diminish the storyteller circled his stand with his arms outspread and his head cocked smugly to one side. He held up a packet of razors, his eyes sparkling with the promise of his main story, and Po-Lin knew it was time to leave. He had no money for new razors and he would lose face if he listened without buying.

He passed along the fringe of the audience as inconspicuously as he could and emerged from the alleyway into Haiphong Road. He turned east, and after he had gone some distance he reached into his breast pocket and brought out the letter. He crunched it in his fist without looking at it and threw it into the gutter. I will not disgrace myself, he thought, quickening his pace. I will collect night soil if need be. I will work beside the lowest coolie. But I will not feed upon the scum of my son.

At Nathan Road he turned south in the direction of the Peninsula Hotel. He lengthened his strides as he passed the rows of shops, and the Indian merchants stared curiously at a Chinese who was so tall and erect and who was apparently in such a hurry. There wasn't the slightest reason for hurry, he knew, but it drove away the despair if he could pretend his presence was required at a certain time. It was ten minutes until three o'clock. At three o'clock, he told himself, I must be there. They will be impatient. I am needed. It is important.

By slowing his progress slightly he contrived to arrive at the Peninsula's front entrance exactly at three o'clock. He mounted the stairs two at a time and nodded at the freckle-faced bellboy who swung back the heavy metal door. He placed his Malacca cane over his arm as he crossed the lobby, eyes straight ahead. Right on time. Important to be prompt. Face.

He turned past the registration desk and approached the familiar counter over which a blue neon sign spelled out "Tours." He stopped before it, took off his glasses and wiped the steam from them with his white handkerchief. He said good afternoon to the fat-faced young Indonesian who looked up at him from a jungle of travel posters.

"Hello, General," the fat-face said in English, and Po-Lin's confidence melted instantly. It would be the same now, the same as every day. No one wanted a guide. A shrug from the fat shoulders. No one could explain why the tourists were so few and there wouldn't be another cruise ship for—"I've been trying to catch up with you," the fat-face was saying. "I sent a boy over to your room but you weren't there." Fantasy? Hunger was said to cause hallucinations.

"I . . . I've been extremely busy."

"So? Then maybe you wouldn't be interested. We finally got a job for you . . . a couple of days anyway." The smile on the fat-face was cruel and knowing. He was enjoying taking his time.

"A few days . . . ?"

"Yeah. There's an American woman wants a reliable man to take her to Macao. I said there was no reason she couldn't go by herself, but it seems she wants someone along who can speak any dialect. I figured you would be just the man."

"Thank you."

"She's pretty smart. Set her own price. Fifty dollars Hong Kong per day and pay your own expenses."

"That isn't very much. Couldn't you—?"

"No. Take it or leave it, she said. Maybe I ought to get someone else."

"I could arrange my affairs . . . make myself available. When would she want to leave?"

"Tomorrow if the boat is running. You'd better telephone her. Mrs. Hoyt . . . room three-o-seven."

"Very well."

"There will be our usual commission. You understand that?"

"I understand."

9

Jane paced her room making patterns of diamonds, quadrangles, squares and triangles. She would maintain one design in her pacing for a while and then shift abruptly as her thoughts changed. When she passed the full-length door mirror, she would occasionally catch a glimpse of herself and think, I am moving like a lioness caged. I even feel like one, yet I am also a very scared lioness and unless the keeper comes to pet me soon I will crawl into the corner of my cage and never find the courage to come out again. Oh, it was a fine show so far—a noble, dedicated female you are, Jane. An actress—tearing up the Hong Kong scenery—suffering without a tear. The trouble was, any real actress could have played the part better and accomplished just as much, which was nothing. Louis was no nearer safety than the day he went to China. Some lioness. The nerve of a mouse.

Stewart, the consul—nothing. Marty Gates—nothing. Tweedie—he *had* to be wrong. Inspector Rodman—a vague interest, nothing more. Hank Lee—a vague promise.

Hank Lee. How many times in her life did a woman meet a Hank Lee? Once. It was to be hoped only once. Louis said it would happen—he sort of threw it away one night when he was feeling mellow on rum. He had just eyed a little brunette with more than passing interest and you were giving him a bad time about it—joking really, but underneath you both knew the joking leapt off a springboard of insecurity. Louis wasn't mad; he never seemed capable of petty anger. He just leaned back nursing his rum in his hand and smiled thoughtfully.

"Listen, Jano," he said, using Jano instead of Jane as he always did when he was in one of his speculative, half-mischievous moods. "Listen, Jano . . . one of these days you are going to get a big surprise and you're going to have to work your own way out of it because it would only complicate matters if I tried to help. So I just cast a sheep's eye at that little brunette?

Let me tell you that I'm going to cast a lotta sheep's eyes in our life and you should be glad of it, because when I stop I'll be dead. Quite dead, Jano. But this not so uncommon sport is expected of men by most people . . . we established the tradition a long time ago and nobody much is surprised, except at a man who never casts sheep's eyes and he has trouble making himself understood. It's sort of like a badminton game and just about as dangerous so long as none of the players try to change the rules. In other words, men are expected to cast an eye here and there and the only ones who get huffy about it are those who never get to play the game. That's why a man can stumble off a curbstone when he's been at the game and the cop will pick him up and brush him off with sympathy. It's the basis for one billion international jokes . . . always has been, and always will be. But it's not the surprise I'm talking about which sometimes doesn't turn out to be such a joke.

"It's a shame in a way . . . really," he said, and remember he took a long pull at his rum just then. "Because, in the open at least, it's a one-sided game. Women are not invited to play . . . they do . . . all of them who've got any red corpuscles . . . but they're not supposed to. Except in Italy, it isn't understood and it isn't accepted for women to go around casting sheep's eyes; so usually, unless they just don't give a damn for anything . . . they hide their feelings. It was easier when they had fans, but they don't even have those any more. Which is why they get caught sometimes and which is why other women call other women bitches even though they have just done, or will do, the same thing themselves. It's safe to sigh over a movie star or some guy on the stage a hundred feet away, or get that faraway look over a singer's voice on the radio . . . nobody minds. But just try the same thing on the poor little bald-headed guy who lives next door and all hell breaks loose. It isn't fair or honest even, but that's the way it is . . . all of which you know. What you may not know is the surprise that's bound to come and God bless you when it does. Because you are a human being and not exactly suffering from an overdose of ugly pills yourself. Here it is . . . and the only way to look at it is as sort of nature's way of balancing the so-called single standard.

"You married me with the intention of being a true and faithful wife. That's more or less customary. Remarkably few women marry with the idea they are going to whoop it up as soon as the ceremony is over. By now you love me, fortunately . . . and you're smart enough to give at least the outward appearance of never looking at another man with any particular interest. So very few other women consider you a bitch, I'd lay ten to one. Now I may be sort of a funny-looking guy, but by great luck I manage a surface charm, an adroitness of the spirit in a way, which continues to fool you . . . so if I just don't beat you up very often and remember anniversaries and halfway behave myself and provide a decent living, the chances are you'll stick around without too much feeling of self-sacrifice. No one on this earth sees me quite as you do, thank God . . . we've been together long enough for you to overlook my faults, and our chances of staying together, then, are pretty good. There isn't a hell of a lot of competition around anyway. But one of these days the law of averages is going to assert itself and you'll meet a man who will represent all the stifled yearnings I couldn't fulfill even if I tried. I'm on the short side . . . he's going to be tall. I'm dark . . . he's going to be light. I'm easygoing and I'll never amount to much . . . he's going to be rough, tough and plenty ambitious. He's going to like kids. Maybe I never will be ready for them because much as I hate to admit it I'm basically irresponsible and I'll always be barely solvent. He'll be the kind to take the world on his shoulders and he'll be rich. This character will come along when you least expect it and you're going to be surprised in more ways than one. You'll go for him . . . how far you go will depend on circumstances at the moment . . . and not on you, the way you think it will. Sure, you're true blue . . . I can see you saying to yourself now that it never could happen because you're in love with me and ladies never let such things enter their heads. Nuts. You might not like the feeling and you may even fight it hard . . . it may, in the end, amount to only an exchange of sheep's eyes . . . but, little girl, he'll come along as sure as you've got blood circulating in your veins. Just remember one thing . . . I never *did* want our marriage to become a prison . . . either for you or for me."

Oh Louis, you smart rascal! How, five years ago, could you know there would ever be a Hank Lee? How could you analyze then how I would feel now . . . thousands of miles away from where either one of us thought we would ever be? But you're wrong about one thing. Jano is all yours. True-blue Jano.

She stopped suddenly before the mirror and frowned at her image. "You're a liar," she said aloud. As if in reply the phone rang. She went to it quickly. It would be Inspector Rodman . . . it must be! Or Hank?

"Hello."

"Good afternoon. Is this Mrs. Hoyt?"

"Yes."

"General Po-Lin here."

"General . . . ? I'm—"

"You inquired at the tourist office for a guide to Macao?"

"Oh. Oh yes!"

"I am at your service."

"Do you know Macao?"

"Very well. I lived there some years ago. I speak Portuguese and all Chinese dialects."

"Good. Did they explain what I am willing to pay?"

"Yes. It will be acceptable."

"Can you leave tomorrow?"

"My time is yours, madame."

"The boat leaves at noon, doesn't it?"

"No. The schedule has been changed. It sails at one o'clock. The S.S. *Fat Shan*. She is quite comfortable and I think you will find the trip most interesting. There are many antiquities in Macao, madame. I am experienced in the operation of most cameras and if you wish I will take such pictures as you may desire."

"Where will I meet you?"

"I recommend we leave the hotel an hour before sailing. If it is satisfactory to you I will await you in the lobby at noon just by the tour desk."

"What was your name again?"

"Po-Lin. General Charles Po-Lin."

"All right, General," she said wondering at the title. "I'll meet you at noon."

"Good afternoon, madame."

"Good-by."

She hung up and the phone tinkled immediately. The operator said, "I have another call waiting for you." A click and then a woman's voice, distant and distorted.

"Hello-hello!"

"Hello . . . ?" It sounded, she thought, like the call was coming from Mars.

"Mrs. Hoyt?"

"Yes. Speak louder, please."

"Maxine Chan here."

"Oh . . . oh yes, Maxine! How are you? I am so happy you called. I've been trying to reach you, but your shop doesn't answer."

"I close always when there is a typhoon. There is no business from the rain. I called because I thought you might be lonesome and it is now such a gloomy day."

"I am lonesome . . . plenty. But I refuse to be depressed." She turned to the mirror and called herself a liar again.

"Any news about Louis?"

"Nothing new . . . nothing I believe. I saw Hank Lee—"

"Ah?"

There was that plaintive quality in her voice again. Jane half-wished she had not mentioned Hank. I want Maxine on my side, she thought . . . I want her on my side very much.

"He was very nice. I see what you mean."

"Ah?" A pause. There was a frying noise in the phone. For the rest of my life, Jane thought, I will appreciate the American telephone system. "Will he help you?" Maxine called from afar.

"I think so. Won't you come to the hotel and we can have tea . . . or something?"

"My father is sick. This weather is bad for his rheumatism. Perhaps I could come tomorrow."

"Tomorrow I'm going to Macao. I want to see that Rocha man. He might know something and I'm getting a little desperate."

"Ah? Rocha. Don't trust him."

"I won't. But what's his address? I forgot to get it from you."

"He has a small office on Rua da Felicidade. It is called Lingua Casa. The taxi driver will know. But must you go there alone?"

"I've hired a guide. Some general . . . he says. Wait a minute . . . here's his name. Charles Po-Lin. Have you ever heard of him? He was recommended by the tour office."

"Uncle Charlie!" She heard Maxine laugh. "Sure I know him! Since I was a little baby!"

"Is he your uncle?"

"Not really . . . not like you say. He is just an old friend of my family and all Chinese girls call old man family friends "uncle." He's sort of honorary uncle, see? He's a very fine old gentleman. I'm happy he will go."

"He isn't too old to make the trip, is he?"

"Uncle Charlie?" She laughed again. "Don't you worry about him. Uncle Charlie will wear you out. You can depend on him."

"I'm glad I can depend on someone. Thank you, Maxine. I'll see you when I return."

"Yes. Please do." She hesitated and for a moment Jane thought she had hung up. "And . . . and if you should talk to Hank again . . . tell him Maxine said . . . hello."

"I will, Maxine. You can depend on that."

"Good luck. Remember to be careful with Rocha. See him only in his office and do not warn him before you go. Offer him money if you think what he has to say is worth it, but don't give him any. Keep Uncle Charlie with you all the time no matter what Rocha says. Even if he offers to just show you a cathedral . . . don't go."

"Thanks."

" 'By now."

"Good-by, Maxine."

She hung up and walked slowly toward the window, not daring now to look at the mirror. It was days like this, she decided, looking down at the rain-swept street, black days with a black sky and a heaviness in the air, that revealed things about Jane Hoyt—that Jane Hoyt didn't like. The specifications called for a Jane Hoyt who was more or less one-dimensional, alert, well-educated major in English literature, matter of fact, sense of humor, American society pigeonhole number sixteen, which was located a little below the junior league pigeonhole and a little above the shopgirl pigeonhole. In other words she took her fashions from V*ogue* instead of the movie magazines and she honestly preferred long-hair music to jive. There were a vast number of Jane Hoyts in American society which was why the pigeonhole had to be especially large to accommodate them. But were the others so two-dimensional? Did the others, on black days like this, discover in themselves a sort of winsome beast—that was a black-day combination if there ever was one—a beast which coyly said, "Hey look! Your pattern of behavior was set by other people of dubious understanding and, though most of the things you do come more or less naturally, there are a lot of things which don't."

The beast had a point. There was no allowance in the pattern for healthy girls, regardless of pigeonhole, who still had a renegade ghost of savage underlying their well-groomed exterior. It wasn't sex; that was a separate and relatively well-disciplined department. It was something else—a primitive hang-over from the days when women sat on the skin of a mastodon and suckled their young in a cave. It was a sense of survival combined with an animal-like desire to dominate the cave over all other women, an intoxication with the odor and vibrations of men who were not necessarily their own, a battling, hair-pulling instinct which could cause no end of trouble when released, a mysterious urging in the second dimension which evidenced itself on black afternoons in blackhearted girls like Jane Hoyt.

She laughed suddenly, trying to invite some relief into the strange and lonely room before she wept. Jano! You maudlin, self-pitying coward! You frightened cream puff! You intellectual, emotional fraud! Winsome beast, indeed. Get the hell out of here! Your man is in trouble and you spend half a day brooding about yourself. If he were around he would throw you out of the cave right on your ass where you belonged and he would be so right. Oh, Louis . . . you *were* so right!

There was a sharp knock on the door and she spun from the window as if she had been caught naked.

"Open up!" a voice called gruffly, "in the name of the law!"

She went quickly to the door. Any visitor, any interruption on this black afternoon, would be welcome. "Who is it?"

"Her Majesty's finest!" She wondered how anyone had passed the room boy, who announced everyone including the laundry amah; then she remembered the voice of Inspector Rodman. She opened the door and saw him standing in the hall beside a tall, pink-cheeked young man.

"I hope I didn't frighten you, Mrs. Hoyt," Rodman said as they both removed their dripping caps. "Sometimes our British humor gets a bit dim."

"Not at all, Inspector." She laughed. "I'm very glad to see you. Please come in."

They walked past her shyly, as if they already regretted their intrusion, and for a moment they stood uncomfortably, holding their dripping caps in their hands.

"May I present Inspector Merryweather," Rodman said. "Mrs. Hoyt—" He left the name up in the air as if he was so embarrassed he could not manage further sound.

"How do you do," Jane said.

". . . do," Merryweather said, swallowing heavily. He blushed crimson as Jane smiled and took his half-extended hand.

"Merryweather's my pal," Rodman said, feeling his way as a man might explore a hall of mirrors. "We just thought it wouldn't bother you too much if we dropped in rather than ringing up."

"It's wonderful. I was very lonely with the rain. Won't you sit down?"

They looked at the one chair and then nervously at the bed.

"Thank you. We're quite all right. I—" Rodman hesitated. "I hope you don't mind—"

"Mind what?"

"He means," Merryweather said, "that he hopes you don't mind that I came along. It is nervy of me, but Rod said he was certain you'd be sporting about it even if there's no reason for my being here at all."

Jane tilted her head to one side and smiled uncertainly. They were so young and they stood so straight like wooden soldiers, and they certainly looked less like policemen than any men she had ever seen before.

"You boys have me a little confused," she said easily.

"It's a difficult dig, all right," Rodman said.

"Where did you learn that word?"

"Merryweather heard it at the cinema. We're not exactly certain we use it correctly but it's most expressive."

"I dig you. You're doing very well."

"Mine's a social call," Merryweather said bravely. "Rod's is more or less official. What he was about to say is that I've never seen an American girl . . . a real one, that is, and we hoped you wouldn't mind." He twirled his cap and laughed apologetically.

It was a moment before Jane could find an answer. Why had Rodman come and why did the British always approach everything by the most indirect route? Then looking into Merryweather's frankly curious eyes she knew that she actually *was* the first American girl he had ever seen. Woman . . . not girl. She'd better straighten him out on that.

"I wish your first impression could have been more exhilarating, Inspector. I never have been the Miss America type and right now I'm a little beat. If you weren't warned you should have been."

"I'm sorry about your husband, Mrs. Hoyt," Merryweather said. "Perhaps—" He broke off his speech and looked shyly at the floor.

What were they trying to say? A terrible fear stabbed through her mind. It seemed to drain the blood from her head all at once. Had they come to tell her that Louis was really dead—Rodman bringing his friend because he couldn't face a new widow alone? Ridiculous. Rodman was still smiling though his eyes were serious.

"I've been able to dig up a few more bits of information on your husband," Rodman said, "so I thought I'd just pop in and tell you about them."

"Oh . . . yes, please!"

"Nothing too recent, but we did have a bit of luck. We bagged the chap who took him to China. He admitted it, rather reluctantly, about an hour ago."

"How did you *ever*—! Oh God bless you, Inspector Rodman and Inspector Merryweather and all of Her Majesty's forces wherever they may serve on land or sea!" She wanted to throw her arms around them and kiss them, buy them champagne—whatever they wanted in the whole wide world! It wasn't raining. There wasn't any black sky any more! But Rodman was holding up his hand, cautioning.

"Now just a moment, ma'am," he was saying. "It's still a bit early for rejoicing. But I think it would be safe to guess that Tweedie was misinformed when he said your husband was dead."

"I knew it! I *knew* it! No one can ever tell me there isn't something to a woman's intuition!"

"Tweedie hired a junk master named Lim Chau-wu to transport your husband to Canton. He paid him two hundred dollars which apparently did not satisfy our friend Mr. Lim . . . not when he had a crew of eight and your husband was the only passenger. Fortunately, Lim has been in trouble before and has a healthy respect for us. So he avoided physical violence when temptation got the better of him. There's a Chinese incense called luan. It's entirely odorless and has the remarkable property of putting even the lightest sleeper into such a deep slumber he will not waken for several hours. A few breaths are sufficient, the victim has absolutely no hang-over when he awakens and it might be quite a contribution to medicine if anyone could ever discover the formula. But even Lim doesn't know it."

"I hope you put him in your jail," Jane said.

"I'm afraid not. If I had, we'd never have found out anything."

Rodman reached into his pocket and brought out a roll of money. Handing it to her, he said, "I had to make a bargain with Lim because we really didn't have a thing on him. Here's the two hundred dollars Tweedie paid him. The cameras are yours, of course, whenever you care to pick them up.

But what Lim told us finally might be of much greater value. He informed Tweedie your husband was dead because he did not carry out their bargain. It was the best way to avoid any trouble with Tweedie in the future. Also, if he went to Canton and was caught with a Caucasian on board, the Commies might twist things around and make life extremely difficult for him, and Tweedie's contacts in Canton would so advise him if his junk never showed up. So Lim used the luan. He put your husband in a small sampan and dumped him on the beach close to the village of Luk Ti where he was sure he would be found in the morning. He left him one small camera to incriminate him. If he was found he got away somehow, because the dates now match up with the pictures of the girl our inquisitive Mr. Merryweather saw in Yaumati. Lim sailed on to Canton, picked up a few barrels of tung oil and came back. I'm quite sure he finally told us the truth."

"Is that all he said? I don't see—?"

"Don't look so disappointed. You started out with an extraordinarily large haystack. It's much smaller now. Two days ago we didn't know where your husband might have entered China and it's a very big country. Now I'd stake a few quid on his being in Canton."

"I can't thank you enough, Inspector."

"You might also thank your Yank friend, Marty Gates. He was most convincing as your husband."

"How in the world—?"

"A few bandages helped. He looked quite aggrieved. Lim will never forgive himself if he ever finds out the truth."

"What can I do? I can't just let Louis rot in Canton."

"Did you meet Hank Lee?"

"Yes. He promised he would help . . . sort of."

"Then most unofficially, I suggest he is the only person who *can* help further. Don't tell him how you found it out, but advise him your husband is very likely in Canton. He'll know what to do about it better than anyone."

"I was going to see Fernand Rocha in Macao tomorrow. Do you think it's worth the trip?"

"Possibly. I know the man only by reputation since he stays out of our way. But the village of Luk Ti isn't far from Macao. He might have heard something. Have you a Portuguese visa?"

"No."

"You jolly well better have it. Macao is a Portuguese colony, ma'am."

"I wish you'd call me Jane . . . it's an old Yank custom."

Rodman glanced quickly at his wrist watch. "You've just time to make the consulate before it closes. Come along. We'll see you to the ferry."

". . . Jane."

Rodman smiled, looked at Merryweather as if seeking his approval and said, "Come along then, Jane. Quickly."

The ferry to Hong Kong was nearly deserted and the few passengers sat as far from the storm awnings as they could for the rain swept across the benches and drummed hard on the wind-tight awnings.

On the Hong Kong side, Jane approached the first policeman she saw. She handed him the slip of paper on which Rodman had written instructions in Chinese. He saluted her after he had read the characters, beckoned to a ricksha and helped her inside. He spoke briefly to the ricksha man, who stood half-naked in the pouring rain, buttoned the protective flap across the ricksha top until only Jane's eyes were visible, then waved him away. The ricksha boy padded up Ice House Street, his enormous feet smacking softly at the wet pavement. After a few minutes he stopped before an office building. Jane entered the Portuguese consulate just as they were closing for the day.

The Portuguese consular representative stamped her passport and took fifteen Hong Kong dollars with a minimum of formality. Ten minutes later she was standing beneath the portico of the office building. Of one thing she was certain—she was not going back to her room again until night. Black days and empty, silent rooms were a miserable combination anywhere. In a friendless city, so many thousands of miles from anything familiar, they were unbearable.

There was a movie theater across the street. She bent her head against the rain and walked quickly toward it. A ricksha almost knocked her down. She spun off the wheel and a taxi horn blared in her face. She ran the rest of the way to the ticket window, paid her admission and entered the theater without even considering what the picture might be. "I am not," she said grimly to herself as she passed into the darkness, "in the least critical mood. Just let me forget for a little time."

It was an American picture, something about a circus which seemed to be having trouble keeping the sheriff from taking all the animals—she wasn't sure, and she didn't care. It was enough to see the American countryside and hear the flow of American voices. Whatever the actors were saying made little difference when the only reminder that she was anywhere but home was the Chinese characters flashing along the bottom of the screen. After a while she managed to ignore them and slipped happily into the notion that she was really at home and that Louis was beside her. Then long before she was willing, the picture was over and the house lights flashed on. She walked wearily up the aisle, wishing that Chinese movie theaters would run continuously so that she could stay longer.

She made her way slowly through the lobby and passed on to the street. It was dark now and the rain had ceased. She stood for a moment, undecided whether to walk back to the ferry and have something to eat in her room, or attempt to find a restaurant in Hong Kong. Then she felt a tugging on her sleeve and a thin voice said, "Hi there!" She turned to see Billy Lee. He was holding one of Hank's big hands and a little girl held the other.

"Well . . . Hi! Pardner," she said looking first at Billy and then at Hank Lee. "Hi, everybody!" she said again as the night suddenly became worth living.

"You haven't met Lucy," Hank smiled. "Lucy, this lady is Mrs. Hoyt. She's a real live genuine American." Lucy looked up, a thousand questions behind her sparkling black eyes. She reached out with one small hand as if she would touch a star and Jane felt the unbelievable softness of her skin.

"Your daughter?"

"Yes. I'm going to give her a new name, though. Good-as-Gold . . . they're always both good as gold when I promise to take them to a movie."

"Did you like it?"

"The animals were good, but there weren't any cowboys," Billy stated flatly.

"You can't have cowboys in every movie," Hank said.

"Why not?" Jane said.

"You're a big help." Hank laughed and once more she thought of a buccaneer. "Can we drop you someplace?"

"I was going back to Kowloon."

"So are we. Let's all put to sea together . . . and a fine crew we'll make, too."

"Thank you. If I had your number I would have phoned you tonight. I have some new information on Louis."

"Save it." He placed his hand on her shoulder and for a moment Jane thought she could easily identify herself with Billy and Lucy. There was such strength and great security in the solid pressure of his hand. "We'll have a chance to talk sooner than you think."

The ferry ride back to Kowloon was like a wild episode in a dream—the kind of dream Jane invariably had when she had eaten too many spareribs and too much sauerkraut in that German restaurant back in New York. All of the elements were present, she thought, jangled and opposed in a cuckoo fantasy which made just enough sense to be lucid. She was on a ferry crossing an Oriental harbor. Now that the rain had stopped, the junks and sampans were crossing and recrossing the water, dark ancient shapes against the lights from the ferry. She was surrounded by people reading newspapers, presumably catching up on the latest typhoon news, but the headlines were all in hieroglyphics and the people reading them did not look in the least like commuters from Weehawken. Their mannerisms were orthodox, but their eyes had a marked tendency to slant and their skins were the color of ocher. Beside her sat a man who was anything but standard commuter. He was a pirate—an American pirate. And he looked like one, smashed nose and all, with overtones, perhaps, of a quiet forest ranger. And beside him sat two children, one all Chinese and the other at least half-Oriental, and these were the children of the forest ranger who was playing pirate on a ferryboat. Dream? The conversation clinched it. The children were chattering happily about a movie concerning a bankrupt circus and asking the pirate about cowboys, and the pirate was patiently trying to answer them just as nine jillion commuting fathers had always done. And Jane Hoyt was right in the middle of it offering an occasional observation on cowboys herself. Please pass the Benzedrine. I cannot seem to wake up.

The Bentley was waiting on the Kowloon side. Hank led Lucy and Billy to the back seat and then turned to Jane.

"Are you busy for dinner?"

"No."

"Have it with me?"

"Yes."

He studied her eyes a moment. "I sure like the way you make decisions."

"What about Lucy and Billy?"

"They eat breakfast with me . . . dinner with their amah. Besides it's getting close to bedtime." He leaned into the car. "Will you two monkeys be sure to say your prayers?"

"Sure," Billy yawned.

"All right. Sleep tight." He leaned into the car and kissed Lucy, then took Billy's hand and shook it solemnly. Jane said good-by to them as he spoke briefly in Chinese to the chauffeur. The Bentley pulled away and he took her arm.

"Do you mind walking? It's only a few blocks."

"No. I've been inside all day."

"There's a place called the Peacock if you like Chinese chow."

"I don't think I've ever had the real thing."

"Then you haven't lived, girl."

They walked in silence along Salisbury Road. They passed Maxine's shop and Jane hoped he would say something about it. He ignored it. Farther along the Road three men staggered out of the shadows and spread across the sidewalk blocking their way. They were scrawny, very young and obviously drunk. They wore their pants high about their waists in the manner of English soldiers who occasionally try to change the monotony of garrison by wearing civilian clothes. Their faces were bright red, even in the dim street light, and their cocky, belligerent smiles reeked of stale beer.

"Well now, 'ere's a proper-sized bloke," their leader said. "Out for a stroll, mate . . . breathin' up the bloody Chinee air?" He could not have been more than eighteen or nineteen and he thrust his pinched face forward pugnaciously, as if inviting Hank to strike him. "Now, ain't this nice?" he said, doubling his fists. "Such a nice size ye are fer entertainin' the troops."

"Get out of the way," Hank said quietly.

"I don't see why we should . . . all ye 'ave to do is go round us, mate."

" 'e's a *Yank!*" one of the young men said in a voice which broke from falsetto. "A mother-bloody Yank! I can tell by the wai he talks!"

"Now, ain't that marveloos!" The leader grinned and pulled back his fist. "All Yanks is rich. Ye wouldn't mind settin' us up for beer for three, would ye, mate? Sort of a levy . . . unnerstand?"

"Get out of the way before you get hurt, son." There was no anger in Hank's voice. He remained motionless and his hands hung loosely at his sides. The leader looked back uncertainly at his comrades, then craftily moved a step closer. "Jane. . . ." Hank said softly. "Take a step to your left . . . just in case."

"Time's gettin' on, mate. My hand's itchin'." The leader made a suggestive pass at his own chin with his fist. "I don't min' tellin' ye we like a fight."

Hank sighed. He looked down at the leader, whose head was barely level with his shoulder, and then he looked at the others who stood poised behind him like underfed cocks. He reached into his pocket and slowly withdrew a roll of bills. He peeled off a red hundred-dollar bill and handed it to the leader.

"All right, fellows. Go have yourselves a ball." Instantly he caught the leader's nose between his bent fingers and tweaked it sharply. "Don't try this levy business on your next pass, though. It might not work." He took Jane's arm firmly and moved quickly between them as the leader rubbed his nose and stared in amazement at the bill.

"Blimey!" he said, all the fight gone out of him. "Blimey . . . thanks, mate! Yer a swell."

They had turned into Ashley Road before Jane knew exactly what she wanted to say. He had released her arm as soon as they were well past the soldiers and now he walked almost leisurely, as if the encounter had never occurred.

"Mr. Henry Lee . . . I salute you, sir."

"Why?"

"Because you paid the toll. Because you didn't have to soothe your male ego by fighting with those men."

"They aren't men. They're kids . . . poor, miserable kids . . . a long way from home. I really shouldn't have given them money . . . it will make it tough for someone else the next time they load up on beer. I just should have spanked them."

"Which you obviously could have done without mussing your tie."

"Maybe . . . maybe not. I wouldn't want to. They're just soldiers and a British soldier never has it very easy."

"Did you ever read any Kipling?"

"Who's he?"

"He wrote stories about British soldiers a long time ago."

"Yeah? I'd like to try reading stuff like that some time. But I don't think he could have written about soldiers like these because these aren't really soldiers, if you get what I mean. Only the officers are professionals and a lot of them aren't either. These kids have been drafted like ours and the big majority of them don't know what it's like to get shot at. I hope they never do know. But it's hard to be a good soldier when the only thing you have to prove you're in an army is a lot of hard work, a uniform which doesn't fit very well if you're in the ranks, and poor pay. Let's forget it."

"Before we do . . . I'd like to ask you if being shot at gives you a special sort of understanding. Louis once said it gives you a new sense of values."

He looked at her quizzically and a little smile played around his mouth. "I wouldn't know," he said, and then he was silent again until they came to a brightly lighted area which stood out like an oasis of noise in the night.

There were plaster arches along both curbs of the street which covered the sidewalks and supported the overhanging floors of the buildings above. Beneath the arches a series of cubbyholes appeared to have been tunneled in the base of the buildings and these were crowded with sweating, laughing, murmuring men in T-shirts and black silk coats. They were huddled about Mah Jong tables so compactly they became almost a single mass, and the clatter of the ivory playing pieces rose and fell like the sound of a distant surf.

"One thing you always have to remember about a Chinese," Hank said as he took her arm once more and guided her through clusters of spectators who overflowed the cubbyholes until they poured across the sidewalk. "There's just one thing they'd rather do than eat . . . and that's gamble."

"Do you like to gamble?"

"Not with money."

"Louis loves it."

Again the quizzical look. "How is his luck?"

"Very bad."

"Ever try to stop him?"

"I've never tried to stop him from doing anything. I married him for what he was . . . not for what I might have had some vague idea he should be. Why should I want to change the man who attracted me in the first place?"

"It seems to be more or less customary. You should have talked him out of going to China."

"Should I? I suppose that would be customary, too. But if I succeeded I think I would have created a much greater danger. He would have a perfect right to brood about the inconvenient weight of a ball and chain. And after a while I would try to talk him out of something else and then again something else . . . until finally I might rob him of himself entirely. If I was clever I might reduce him little by little, and every time it would be easier . . . until finally I would have manufactured a man I could barely recognize . . . a lump of worthless wax and certainly I could never change him back again. I make a lot of mistakes, but that's one woman's mistake I refuse to make."

"He wears the pants then?"

"I've always thought women looked ridiculous in pants . . . ridiculous and secretly unhappy."

"That's kind of an old-fashioned idea, isn't it?"

"Yes. But I believe in it. I never have understood why a woman should necessarily lose either her pride or her identity just because she elects to chew on a man's moccasins. Maybe I'm just a squaw at heart, but I think it's fun in the wigwam."

Even the blast of noise from a Chinese band on one of the balconies above the street could not smother Hank's laughter. He took her hand and clutched it tightly. His laughter echoed under the arches and ricocheted off the Mah Jong players until even they paused momentarily and looked up from their games. Then still chuckling and holding her hand as if he were afraid she might escape him, he stopped before a brightly lighted staircase and said, "This is the Peacock. I hope you worked up an appetite."

"I did. You haven't got the shortest legs in the world. Walking with you is sort of a track meet."

"Poor little girl. I suppose I'll have to carry you up the stairs?"

"I'll bet you'd try it at that."

He looked at her questioningly. Then before she knew exactly how he accomplished it, he was holding her lightly in his arms. She gasped and tried to look disapproving.

"If you stumble," she said slowly, "you're going to look mighty silly."

Instead of answering her, he bent his head slowly until their lips met. For an instant her body became rigid. But the pressure of his mouth was very light and he broke away before she was entirely certain she had not imagined his kiss. It wasn't a real kiss anyway, she told herself.

With a strange detachment, as if her hand belonged to someone else, she saw it move slowly around the back of his neck. "I wish you hadn't done that," she said.

"Why?"

"Because I've been wanting you to do it. It can't happen again, do you understand . . . because Louis isn't around to defend himself."

"In a lot of ways, I wish he was." He hesitated but did not set her down. He made sure there was no anger or further invitation in her eyes and then he smiled. "We're supposed to be hungry. Here we go."

He started up the long flight of stairs carrying her easily. And the Chinese who stood in the street and even those across the street who looked up from their Mah Jong watched their ascent with unbelief. For a man who would so exert himself as to carry a mere woman up a long flight of stairs was unquestionably mad—particularly when there were so many singsong girls waiting in the Peacock who were more than willing to climb a mountain if you paid them enough. One of the Mah Jong players was inclined to be tolerant and said that beyond a doubt the woman was an invalid. Another said no, that he had observed her walking beneath the arches and that such behavior was simply the way of all Fahn Quaie Low, or foreign devils, and therefore automatically incomprehensible to any civilized man.

The other players emitted a fusillade of "ha's" since this certainly settled the matter, and returned to their games.

10

In Kowloon the Peacock was a favorite rendezvous for many of the wealthier Chinese because it offered all of the ingredients so dear to their souls. The food, ever the primary consideration, was Cantonese and superb. There was light, a vast amount of light, brilliant enough not only for a man to see what he was eating but enough to illuminate fully the visual qualities of the food and thus contribute to its delight. The light splayed across the white tablecloths, making of each an island of interest, and the decorations which were traditional, and therefore comforting both to the stomach and the mind, could easily be appreciated. Two lines of bright-red pillars crisscrossed the restaurant, and the dragon heads which served as their capitals gleamed with gold paint. There were curtained booths along one side of the large room for those who required privacy, and the other side was elevated three steps, forming a long platform on which stood four small pavilions. These were complete with roofs and windows and so became houses within a house. The pavilions were normally occupied by older men who ate with gusto and applied themselves to Mah Jong as soon as their meal was done.

There was noise in the Peacock, enough noise to please the most boisterous Chinese, and this approached pandemonium. A jukebox clashed and cymbaled full volume near the entrance. The cashier who sat behind an elevated podium rang his bell relentlessly as he directed the attention of seemingly innumerable waitresses, towel girls, tea pourers, clean-up boys, and singsong girls to this table and that table and to the booth where the squeals of delight were becoming a little too loud even for the Peacock. The constant *click-click* of the cashier's abacus somehow managed to tip-toe beneath the sound of the jukebox and agreeably shared the owner's prosperity with all who were present. It mixed with the clacking of the Mah Jong pieces from the pavilions and penetrated even through the constant bang and clash of dishes which bounced off the ceiling and was returned instantly to the ceiling by the tile floor. Customers were not supposed to think in the Peacock. It was a well-managed playground for their physical senses.

Hank ordered the dinner and they ate with chopsticks because the chemical action of metal would have been an insult to the food. They had shark-fin soup, steamed shrimps served in lacquer bowls which held a fine grill so the meat would not become overmoist, pork with a succulent gravy, chicken, bamboo shoots, mushrooms, wine of the second distillation, and rice as only the Chinese could fry it. They talked very little as the serving girls moved in relays between their table and the doors to the kitchen. It was important, Hank explained, that during the business of eating they hold conversation to a minimum. For the Chinese gourmet would not tolerate the slightest delay between the kitchen pot and his mouth lest a nuance of flavor be absorbed by the air. And so the dishes were brought one by one fresh from the stoves and replenished the moment they showed the slightest signs of depletion.

Two distinct classes of girls hovered about the table. There were the dish girls who carried the food and maintained a smiling silence. They wore plain white gowns and seemed obsessed with the idea Jane was not eating enough. And there were two hostesses who confined themselves to refilling the teacups. They were beautiful girls, and their skin-tight turquoise and amber gowns, with the skirt split seductively to a point just the right distance above their knees, greatly enhanced their figures. They made no attempt to hide their interest in Jane, staring at her as if she had just come from the moon and barely managing to keep their distance as they examined and commented upon every detail of her clothing.

"I have a strong suspicion your girl friends are talking about me," Jane said a little nervously.

"You're right. They're talking about the low neckline of your dress and comparing it with their own high collars and split skirts. They think it's pretty funny the way American girls dress their bodies down while Chinese dress it up."

"Pretty funny, all right. I wish they weren't so darned attractive. I feel like the ugly duckling."

"Don't mind them. They don't get to see American girls very often."

"Are they singsong girls?"

"No. That's another department. Right now they are wondering how much your dress cost."

"Tell them twenty-five dollars."

"Then you would be a disappointment to them. They would expect it to be much more expensive. Now they're trying to figure out why you don't wear more make-up. I've sort of wondered about that myself."

"Do Chinese ever have freckles?"

"There is a freckled bellboy at the Peninsula Hotel, but he's the only one I've ever seen and I'm sure he's half-Irish or something."

"Then the Chinese can't realize that freckles and make-up just won't go together. If you've got them, you're stuck with them."

"I like them." And I sure as hell do, he thought.

He placed his chopsticks crosswise on his rice bowl to indicate that he was finished eating, but as host, he would await the further pleasure of his guest. He took a thin cigar from his pocket and rolled it reflectively between his big fingers. Why, of all the women he had ever met—and there had been a lot of them since Rita—why did Jane Hoyt seem so valuable? There was the future and the Lee Empire—sure. There would have to be someone for that. But the Empire took a secondary position somehow when Jane was present. The old drive melted away and was replaced by a feeling of tenderness, almost like she was one of the kids and had to be looked after accordingly. Come on—get smart. She is playing on her helplessness and she knows you are the biggest sucker in the world. So either get rid of her or admit you're in love with those freckles across the nose, the blue eyes beneath those naturally heavy eyebrows, and a hell of a lot of other things you can't separate or define, like her mouth on which she does wear lipstick. Maybe there's a touch of it on your own lips now.

"In fact I like everything about you," he said solemnly. He leaned back in his chair, studying her and gently patting his stomach. Then he belched with open satisfaction.

"Excuse you," Jane said.

"Why?"

"Where I come from you don't do that."

"You aren't where you came from. If you don't burp after a Chinese dinner you'll hurt everybody's feelings. The cook might commit suicide."

"Oh." She sucked in her breath experimentally. Then she shook her head. "I've just never been able to do it."

"You'd better learn if you ever want to become a social success in China."

"Why should I ever want to be a social success in China? I have trouble enough minding my manners at home."

"You may . . . some day. I got some ideas about you."

"If you can correct me, I can correct you. It's I *have* some ideas . . . never, I got."

He smiled. "You sound like Rita."

"Who is she?"

"A girl who tried to make a silk purse out of a sow's ear."

"If you let that little scene on the stairs influence your ideas, forget them. As soon as I get Louis back I'm returning to the land of the free, and beer on Saturday nights. Incidentally, when are you going home?"

He lit his cigar and looked away from her. Then just as he seemed ready to answer, the hostesses placed small wicker baskets containing hot towels before them. Hank wiped his mouth and fingers. She copied his gestures and the girls took the baskets away. They returned almost immediately to pour more tea and resumed their study of Jane.

"I'm beginning to feel like a fish in a bowl."

"Want me to send them away?"

"Why should I spoil their fun? I asked you a question a while ago. You didn't answer."

"I told you once before . . . Hong Kong is my home."

"Nonsense. You're an American. Have you got a mad on about your country?"

"I send my boy to school there . . . and the others will go."

"So?"

"Maybe America might have a mad on about me."

"Aren't you making yourself overly important? They have a lot of things to think about back home besides what Henry Lee might have been up to."

"I have no desire to be shot or at the least spend a few years at hard labor. It doesn't fit in with my plans."

"I'm talking about going back to America, not Russia. Or did you murder someone?"

"Yes. Myself. Officially, I'm dead."

"How did you manage that . . . or am I asking too many questions?"

"You'll have to know some day. I went missing in action just at the end of the war. The Navy would call it desertion."

There, it was out. He watched her carefully and saw the disappointment come to her eyes. Well . . . what the hell could you expect? It had never made any difference to you before, but with Jane it did make a difference . . . a big one. She was looking away and through you. All of the warmth that had flowed from her was gone.

"It seems to me," she said hesitantly, "I remember reading . . . somewhere . . . didn't the President grant an amnesty to men like you . . . or something like that . . ." She kept her eyes on her teacup, turning it around and around.

"Only to those who were convicted of desertion. I would still have to stand a court-martial."

"So you'd rather stay a man without a country?"

"What did America ever do for me but let me drive a gravel truck? To hell with it. This is a tough world and you better take your chances as they come."

"Thinking about you—and I confess I have thought about you a lot—one thing never occurred to me, Henry Lee. I never thought you were a coward. It looks like I was wrong."

"You really haven't got much use for me now, have you? All of a sudden . . . just because I won't let the world walk all over me?"

"It isn't that . . . I'm just sorry for you. Very sorry. I wanted to tell you something tonight that might change the world for me. I wanted to tell you that I know where my husband is and I hoped you would be the one man on earth who would have the courage to bring him back. I was going to ask you . . . beg you, if I had to . . . promise anything if you would see him safely out of China . . . but it looks like I chose a twisted-thinking boy to do a man's job. Maybe we'd better go now."

She stood up quickly. He did not move from his chair. Instead he took a long pull on his cigar and looked up at her thoughtfully. Jesus, what a woman! Like carrying around a stick of dynamite!

"You'd hurt your husband's chances just for patriotic reasons, right?"

"I don't think he'd appreciate your help."

"Well, he better have *some* help. Now dammit, sit down! Every time I see you, you go off like a pinwheel and bawl me out. I didn't invite you to louse up my life. I was a lot happier before you came. Sit down, woman. I got a lot to tell you and some of the things are the facts of life. *Sit* . . . down!"

He pointed the end of his cigar at her chair. She sank slowly into it, her eyes still angry and her back stiff. The noise of the Peacock seemed louder than ever as he sat watching her in silence for a long time. Then haltingly, as if he was speaking of another person, he began to talk. He told her about Rita, the YMS 34, Manila, the gravel truck and Chicago. Finally he told her about Dak Lai and Tweedie.

"I don't think you realize what a hell of a jam your husband is in. I doubt if even he realizes it. This is not like trying to get a man off the hook for a speeding ticket. It would be easier and a lot safer to try springing him out of a place like Sing Sing. I don't have any real friends in China. No one does . . . not so long as your skin is white and your eyes are round. The Chinese are just finding out how much steam they can let off by hating, and the easiest way for them to forget their own troubles is to start off every morning hating Americans. It's getting to be an international relief valve but the Orientals are playing for keeps and your husband is in China for keeps unless somebody passes a miracle.

"And there's another thing you might as well know right now," he said, looking at her steadily. "I may be a roughneck. I may not have a country. I may not be very good to look at because I got a busted nose. Maybe I been lonesome too long . . . but I want you to know I'm in love with you. If you were free I would ask you to marry me tonight. I want your husband out of China worse than you do, and I'm going to do everything in my power to get him out of there. I wish he was sitting right here now . . . so I could stand a fair chance with you. Any questions?"

"No. . . ." Her voice was almost inaudible against the sounds of the Peacock. She avoided his eyes and he saw that her hands were trembling. "Yes . . . one thing. Does what you have said include risking all that you have . . . even your life?"

"It does."

"I . . . I'm sorry, Hank. Forgive me. I'm half-crazy with fear. Maybe I just didn't *want* to realize what I've been asking, but I've turned every which way and there's been so little. Louis is probably in Canton if he's alive . . . I don't know anything for sure. I was even going to Macao tomorrow to see your friend Rocha . . . hoping— You can't know what it's like to be without hope."

"Why should Rocha know anything?"

"He was with Louis a few nights before he went to China. Also Louis was put ashore near the village of Luk Ti. It's not far from Macao and Rocha just might have heard something. I'm taking a guide with me . . . a General Po-Lin. He's an old friend of Maxine's."

"Remind me to always tell you the truth. I don't think I could get away with a lie. And I would sure hate to try hiding from you."

"Will you go with me, Hank? Please. . . ."

"I can't. I don't have a passport. Remember me . . . stateless person? I'm all right in Hong Kong, but wherever else I go, has to be through the back door."

"You've been in the back door before. I thought—"

"Sure. And maybe I'll have to go again. When I do, I want to make sure it won't be half-cocked. You go on to Macao. Keep the general with you . . . the closer the better. If there's anything to find out there, you'll do it easier than I can. But don't tell anyone what you're after or that you even know me. It might backfire. Get back as soon as you can and call me."

"Then?"

"Then we'll see. There's a lot of details to be worked out in the meantime. You'll just have to believe in me. When I go after anything . . . I go in to win. That includes you."

"Can we just forget that for a while?"

"I won't forget it. But now that you know . . . we'll let it ride."

He extended his hand across the table, offering it palm open in the gesture of a handshake. He smiled. And after a moment she took his hand. She pressed it tightly and raised it slowly to her lips.

The S.S. *Fat Shan* was a modern ocean-going ferry of six hundred tons burthen. She was painted a gleaming white and carried the British ensign prominently on both sides of her hull. Her bridge was isolated from the rest of the ship by heavy steel bars which not only prevented entrance from the decks, but extended overboard so that no one could climb around the railings. The barrier was supposed to discourage pirates from taking over the ship, as they had done often in the past to other ships simply by joining the throngs of third-class passengers on the lower decks and making their attack after the vessel was well at sea.

Neither the steel barricades nor the British ensign prevented the Communists from stopping the *Fat Shan* and boarding her whenever they desired. Normally the *Fat Shan* was allowed to pass unmolested over the four-hour stretch of yellow muddy water which separated the ports of Hong Kong and Portuguese Macao. But occasionally, as if to remind the whole of the Orient and the world at large that New China was an authority to be reckoned with, a Communist gunboat would stop the *Fat Shan*. They chose the return voyage from Macao and usually took off a Chinese whose papers failed to satisfy them. No one was surprised if the passenger involved always happened to be a rich Chinese, and everyone knew that he would never be seen again.

When this legalized piracy was completed, the *Fat Shan* proceeded meekly on her way. If some of the passengers stared thoughtfully at her British ensign and finally shrugged their shoulders in disbelief, there was nothing anyone could do to smooth their pride short of starting a war, except to go into the teak-paneled bar and have another drink and shake their heads and say they didn't know what things were coming to when a band of brigands could kick the British ensign around on what technically should be the high seas. More realistic heads said they were surprised the Communists allowed the *Fat Shan* or her sister ferry to operate at all. Wasn't the larger porportion of her voyage within rifleshot of Chinese islands? And what about crossing the mouth of the Pearl River, which flowed out like a vast excretion from the natural and geographical buttocks of the Chinese mainland? And the Caucasians thought, and sometimes said, "What was another Chinese more or less anyway?"

The decks of the *Fat Shan* were spotless. There were white-coated stewards and deck chairs in the first class. Excellent European-style food was served in her spacious main saloon. General Charles Po-Lin was enjoying this food as he had never enjoyed a meal before. The day was bright with a particularly clear blue sky after the typhoon. Yet the fresh sea breeze which came through the open saloon windows minimized the heat. He had money in his pocket, a novelty which he had almost forgotten; a most agreeable young lady sat opposite him and since their departure from Hong Kong she had been openly intrigued with his descriptions and tales of the China that was. It was true that at times her attention wandered and she closed her eyes momentarily as if she were recalling scenes in her own homeland, but her questions about Chinese temperament, philosophy and history were intelligent and stimulating. It had been a long time since he had found an opportunity to display his rather unusual and intimate knowledge of cloisonné. And now she appeared equally interested in what he had to say about Macao.

"I am no longer young, Madame Hoyt," he said as he delicately speared the last bit of yam on his plate. "You will forgive me, then, if I become garrulous, for it is the curse of all old men that they talk too much when their spirit is mellowed with food . . . and other times, too, I might say. The reasons for this social blunder are numerous and rather worth contemplating. You have perhaps observed children also talk too much. In my opinion the relation is exact and represents two periods in the cycle of emerging from, and returning to, the womb. A child talks because he feels he has a great deal to say and it is also a secondary method of gaining attention. Old men talk for precisely the same reasons. Both fear lack of attention, because without it they are easily convinced the world has forgotten them. Also a child, knowing very little, has something to say about everything. It is only the wisest of old men who are courageous enough to admit they also know very little, and so, knowing much, most old men also have something to say about everything. Unfortunately for you, Madame Hoyt, I am not one of the wiser old men."

"I could listen to you talk for days, General Lin. You are fascinating."

He bowed slightly and a wry smile crossed his mouth. He took a sip of coffee from his demitasse and patted his lips with his napkin. " 'Music's golden tongue flatter'd to tears this aged man and poor' . . . Madame."

"Isn't that Shelley? Or wait, I always get him mixed up with—"

"Keats. I once attempted to translate him into Mandarin. There were days when we had leisure for such things. Unfortunately, even with leisure my attempt was a dismal failure. Chinese poetry can be translated into English and retain a remarkable amount of its original flavor. The reverse is not true, sadly enough."

She reached for the coffee pot. "More coffee, General?"

"If you would be so kind. This has turned out to be an extraordinarily happy day for me. The thought of showing you about Macao has charged me with a sense of adventure. There is one cathedral, of which only the façade still stands—"

"I don't think we'll have too much time for cathedrals. I am very anxious to talk with a man named Rocha."

"I am at your service whatever you wish. But you will be agreeably surprised with Macao. Time rather stands still there . . . as it has done for centuries. If you can manage to ignore the population you will forget you are in Asia. Macao is a little bit of Portugal. It was settled about the same time Drake defeated the Armada. It's a very small place really, more or less run by a man named Lobo. You'll find the climate more agreeable than Hong Kong. A feeling of tranquility always comes over me when I am in Macao."

"Who is Lobo?"

"A gambler. He's a complete autocrat, yet he's done a great deal for the colony. I suggest we visit his principal establishment. It's all quite open and legal. A young woman such as yourself should see all sides during your tour. There is also a very old Buddhist temple and perhaps you'd like to shop around a bit. Their gold filigree work—" Po-Lin stopped talking as if someone had suddenly cut his vocal cords. He looked at the table, around the saloon, and then at Jane. He placed his hand very carefully on the table and held it there while he cocked his head slightly to one side. The color left his face.

"What's the matter, General? Are you ill?"

He glanced out the window, then looked down at his hand again. For a long moment his whole body was rigid and absolutely motionless.

"I believe the engines have stopped," he said quietly. "The vibration is gone."

"Now that you mention it . . . I do notice it. We can't be there so soon, can we?"

"We're not. I wonder . . . ?" He folded his napkin with great care and rose slowly from his chair. "Would you excuse me? I would like a breath of air. I'll just step out on deck a moment." He bowed, picked up his hat and Malacca cane and walked toward the saloon door. His back was very straight, yet Jane thought he suddenly moved like a very old man.

She waited and felt the breeze die from the windows. There had only been a few people in the saloon, but now even the waiters had vanished. She heard a shout and then a babble of conversation on deck. There was still no vibration. She picked up her purse, tucked it under her arm and walked uncertainly to the saloon window.

The *Fat Shan* had stopped off the rocky point of a barren island. Hundreds of fishing junks dotted a vast area of yellow water beyond the island, their sails breaking the horizon as though they had been cut out of cardboard and pasted against the sky. She looked down and saw that a long gray boat had attached herself to the *Fat Shan's* high steel sides. The boat carried a heavy-caliber gun on her foredeck. Her engine exhausts snorted angrily against the muddy water as if she were a terrier gnawing at the *Fat Shan's* vitals.

Then, in a sudden, sickening flash, she knew why the *Fat Shan* had stopped. A flag licked at the soft, hot breeze like a red tongue. There was a gold star on the flag—the emblem of Communist China.

She left the window and went at once to the main promenade deck. A steward stopped her just as she reached the door.

"Please . . . please," he said, pushing her back, and she saw that he was very much afraid. "You all right. Better you stay here. No trouble for you. No worry. Please."

He led her to a small alcove just off the bar, where the other first-class passengers had gathered. They were all Caucasians except for one bearded Indian and his wife. A squat Chinese in a white sailor cap and T-shirt stood barefooted in the door which led to the deck. He wore a bandoleer across his shoulders and held a submachine gun loosely in the crook of his arm. A cigarette drooped from his lips and he occasionally stared at the little group of passengers as if it were the first time he had noticed their existence.

"The buggers," an English voice said. "The filthy, rotten buggers have a cheek. Stopping a British ship!"

"They won't dare do anything to us," the woman who was with him said. "This is British territory."

"They'd jolly well better not."

"I hope your confidence is well placed," a man said in a heavy Scandinavian accent.

"Obviously they don't care about us," another passenger said. He was quite fat, swarthy and rumpled in his white linen suit. Jane was certain he was Portuguese. Then there was silence as they were drawn involuntarily to the window where they could watch the subdued tableaux on deck.

Several Chinese sailors carrying submachine guns lined the rail. Their faces were expressionless as they pushed a line of passengers toward an officer who sat stiffly behind a card table. Jane recognized a few of them as Chinese who had been in the saloon or sitting in the deck chairs when they left Hong Kong. There was almost no conversation as the officer examined their passports. He would glance at their black books, many of them British passports, then toss them contemptuously aside. A sailor would return their passports and push the Chinese farther down the deck.

Then Jane saw General Charles Po-Lin. He was standing before the card table, looking over and beyond the officer's head, scorning him. The Malacca cane was crooked over his arm and he held it against his side in the manner of a swagger stick. He was casual, entirely at ease, as the officer questioned him. Only the contemptuous curl of his lower lip told Jane he had transformed himself from the man she had just begun to know. The cultivated, aesthetic scholar, the man who knew so much about cloisonné and the poetry of all the world, the genial, philosophic old gentleman who could smile at himself without losing pride was gone.

The officer did not return Po-Lin's passport as he had all the others but one. He made a quick gesture with his thumb. A sailor shoved Po-Lin hard against the rail, away from the other passengers. He shoved him roughly along the rail until he stood beside another Chinese who was half his size and shuddering with fear. Po-Lin stared straight ahead, his long, lean body erect, his eyes not moving.

"What are they doing to those people?" Jane asked aloud.

"Nothing, I suppose . . . to those," the Englishman said, pointing to the men and women who were huddled nervously by the steel bridge barricade. "Those poor chaps . . ." he said, aiming his thumb at Po-Lin and his companion, "are apparently considered fair game. I shouldn't care to trade places with them."

"But we ought to stop them! Isn't there an English crew on this boat?"

"My dear lady. Only the officers are English. Even they are not so foolish as to aggravate that stupid-looking chap by the door. He's just waiting for a chance to shoot off his new toy."

The *Fat Shan* had hardly been stopped for fifteen minutes before the officer rose from behind the card table and marched to the accommodation ladder. He ignored the people in the windows. The sailors followed him without a backward glance. The last four were preceded by Po-Lin and his now utterly distraught companion. Po-Lin paused by the window and looked at Jane.

"I apologize for this inconvenience. Enjoy Macao, madame. Take your time. It is a slow, untroubled place. Remember your friend Po-Lin and do not think all Chinese are barbarians. . . ."

A sailor rammed the butt of his gun into the small of Po-Lin's back. He grunted with pain as the blow propelled him toward the accommodation ladder. Then just as he started his descent, he turned to look once more at Jane. There was the wry smile again. He raised his Malacca cane and touched his hat. Then he was gone.

Almost at once the *Fat Shan's* engines sent a shudder through the ship. As the vibration became steady the passengers left the alcove and ran to the deck. Jane was the first to reach the rail. She looked down and saw the long gray boat pulling away. Her engines roared and the red flag straightened in the wind.

Far below, Jane saw the now doll-like figure of Po-Lin standing on the deck beside a sailor. Then suddenly, as if activated by puppet strings, she saw the doll raise his arm. The Malacca cane flashed in the sunlight as the arm whipped it against the sailor's face. The doll began to run for the gray boat's stern—toward the red flag. There was a quick burst of firing, like the roll of a snare drum. The doll bent impossibly backward, broken in the middle, but the legs kept running. His straw hat blew off. Then, jerked by the invisible strings, the doll plunged into the yellow water. The sharp angry spasms of firing continued, relentlessly making lacelike patterns around the doll's head. A touch of crimson came to the yellow water, spreading through the lace. The head turned, mouth open toward the sun, and then vanished. Jane covered her eyes.

She remained at the rail, clutching it tightly, as the *Fat Shan* gathered speed and swung on course for Macao.

From his office Austin Stoker could see a patch of blue sky between the tall buildings which lined both sides of Ice House Street. He watched a flight of RAF Vampires cross the patch of sky and he thought of them lazily, as it was his habit to think of anything during the sensual period of the day which always overcame him after tiffin. He had enjoyed his repast thoroughly, taking two helpings of kidney pie, and now he lolled back pleasantly muffling his brain and occasionally stirring the air about his red face with a paper fan. It was time for what he called his matinee. So he scratched at the tufts of hair on his pink chest and, leaving the patch of sky for more intriguing things, raised the skin above one eye where a brow should have been.

His small blue eyes were half-hidden in the folds of his fat face and he was almost asleep, but he could see enough of his two clerks to satisfy him. They were Eurasian girls—he had never cared for pure Orientals—and Stoker had chosen them himself. It was one thing Hank Lee never had a hand in. Ho-ho! he thought lazily . . . hand in, indeed. As a matter of fact, Hank Lee did not know his right hand from his left these days. He had chosen to become the great gentleman . . . which was most convenient for Austin Stoker. He had not been near the office in six months. Consequently the girls were of dual interest during this matinee. The subtle movements of their young bodies were easily observed beneath their thin silk Chinese gowns. As they turned and bent over their papers, looking so cool in spite of the heat, certain lines of their breasts and the flowing formation where their legs made union with their bodies tantalized his imagination. It was a pity. They would never know what an artist and connoisseur their employer happened to be. They would never know, either, that the manifests which they were checking had been cunningly altered so that the profits they presumed to represent no longer went to Henry Lee. They went to Austin Stoker, who did all the work . . . in good, solid English pounds. Which was as it should be. If Hank wished to play the fool and never go near the godowns, if he wished to spend his time wiping the faces of a pair of sniveling Chinese kids—that was his folly. Ho-ho and righto! Look at the cute little ass on that little rascal as she leans against the counter. Should get a higher counter so she would have to stand on a stool. He reached out mentally, across his desk and across the long room, and pinched her hard on the bottom. He closed his eyes to increase the reality of the sensation, picturing many things, and the result was so vivid that small bumps rose on his hairless arms.

Stoker was almost asleep when a voice that he knew too well smashed his dreaming.

"Wake up, you hog!"

It was Hank Lee and Stoker rolled his head toward the voice trying to tell himself that he must be enmeshed in a nightmare—what could Hank want here? He took his feet off the desk quickly and his blue eyes opened so wide the pupils were completely surrounded by white.

"Hank. . . . Oh! Well . . . well?" He shuffled some odd papers on his desk trying to look businesslike. "Well . . . well," he said uncertainly as Hank sat on the edge of his desk. "Well, well. . . ."

"Stop saying well, well, and listen to me."

"I am listening, Hank. It's a bit of a shock, you know . . . seeing you here. It's been some time."

"I come around when I please."

"Sure, Hank. It's your business."

"Don't ever forget it. Are you awake?"

"Bright as a coronation shilling."

"I wish you were. Where's the *Chicago?*"

"In Aberdeen. Laying up with the fishing junks. I thought it best to keep her there, more or less out of the way, until we had a good cargo. Things have been slow, Hank . . . like I told you the other evening . . . very slow. Also I considered it advantageous—"

"Never mind that. Is she in good shape? Ready to sail?"

Stoker took a moment to estimate Hank's mood. Outwardly he seemed relaxed, the bastard—and yet somewhere beneath the easy way he lounged on the desk, there was an undertone of nervousness—almost anxiety. It would bear probing. Now what did he want with the *Chicago?*

"Why certainly, Hank. She's all shipshape and Bristol fashion. Part of my job, you know."

"I want her ready to sail . . . full tanks on the diesel . . . crew aboard and provisions . . . ready by tomorrow noon."

"Righto . . . that will take a bit of doing, but I can manage. Mind if I ask why?"

"I'm planning a yachting trip. I need sea air."

"West or east?"

"East. I'll want some cargo, too. The more the better."

"The only thing we have is some electrical conduit in number-three godown. You aren't going to be foolish and take it over the line yourself?"

"Why not?"

Indeed why not? Go to China, you silly bastard. Work out your own deals. Go and never come back. Most interesting. Something is gnawing at you, my charming guttersnipe of a gentleman, and the something could be the—

"No reason at all why you shouldn't go, Hank. I was just speculating. Things have changed over the line, you know. They don't love us any more. Not since we insisted on gold payments. I should say your yachting trip might prove a bit risky even." What the hell? Tell him. He was obviously determined to go anyway. That seventeen-pound chin of his was out. He was stalking around the office now, like a caged orangutan—not even seeing the girls. Might as well get credit for a warning, just in case.

"What's the name of that character we deal with in Canton?" Hank asked. "That Pole . . . ?" He snapped his fingers twice. "What's his address and what's his phone number if he's got one? I'll want all that."

"His name was Keim, but he isn't there any more."

"Well, why not?"

"How should I know why not? Maybe he got smart. What makes you so jumpy, Hank?"

"I'm not jumpy about anything. Who do we deal with now? Who's been handling the stuff we send up there?"

"Rajos Adrapura."

"What the hell kind of a name is that?"

"He's an Indian. It was the best I could do, Hank."

"No wonder we haven't been making any money lately."

All right. If he wanted to blame it on Adrapura, so much the better.

"Write me out a note to him. I want it all standing."

"Sure, Hank."

"Get me a couple of million of those no-good Chinese dollars and about two thousand American. Is the Bofors still on the afterdeck? How about shells for it?"

"There's plenty on board, or if there isn't I'll see there is. The wireless is out. I'm still waiting for parts."

"I won't need it. Tell Ying Fai to leave his family in port this time. I don't want kids and a woman around."

"Righto."

"How's the river now?"

"Flood."

"Good. Get me some tide tables and some current tables if you can. Also a weather report for the next three or four days. If there's another typhoon on the way, so much the better. How about the flags?"

"Same as always. We have Nationalist, Commie, British and Philippine. Take your pick."

"Get me Thailand, too."

Stoker pretended to make a note. "You *are* on an expedition. Do you want me to try setting up a return cargo?"

"No."

"You'll be light. If it blows you'll make a rotten trip of it."

"I want to be light. After I've sailed, see if you can have a drink with some of your Navy friends in the Coastal Patrol. Give them the *Chicago's* number and full description. Tell them when I come back we may be flying any kind of a flag but we'll sure be going like hell. It may be day or night and we'll want to keep right on coming. We'll heave to and explain as soon as we're inside Sulphur Channel, so tell them not to get trigger-happy."

"That's not so easy, Hank. Frankly the chaps over at Navy don't think too much of me since—"

"Well, buy them a lot of drinks and they'll think different. Now get off your fat ass and get busy. I want everything stowed and ready to go by noon tomorrow. You meet me in Aberdeen and have a sampan waiting, understand?"

"I understand. We'll load the conduit tonight. Everything will be taken care of."

"See you in Aberdeen."

Without breaking the rhythm of his pacing, Hank turned his back on Stoker and walked toward the door. As he passed the counter he nodded to the girl clerks, smiled and said, "Hello." He was gone before they could reply and as the door slammed after him Stoker took a small pearl-handled knife from the pocket of his shorts. He pulled out a blade and thoughtfully began to pare his nails. He returned his feet to the desk and puckered his thick lips until they became a miniature rose.

All things, he thought, come to men who wait. And stupid people eventually hanged themselves no matter how much power luck had given them originally. So Hank Lee was planning a yachting trip to Canton. Going himself. Perhaps it was nostalgia for the old days. Whatever his reasons they were unimportant. The important thing was, vital to Austin Stoker and so pathetically easy to arrange—was that he never return.

11

It was evening before the *Fat Shan* rounded Barra Point. She turned slowly, her propeller roiling up the silted mud, and ghosted along a hundred yards off the Rua Almirante Sergio, passing lines of junks and sampans until she nudged against the principal wharf.

All along the harbor entrance, the plaster buildings of Macao were sharply etched in the yellow light. The buildings melted gradually toward the northern end of the city into a great blue shadow cast by the Communist-held island which the Portuguese still called Patera. A small crowd waited on the wharf in the blue shadow. They were mostly Chinese, the men in black and the women in spotless white high-necked blouses. They occasionally waved handkerchiefs in the general direction of the *Fat Shan*. A handful of customs officials stood with their hands folded in front of them while the shouting coolies hauled on the mooring lines which darted like snakes from the *Fat Shan's* lower decks. Several Portuguese soldiers in mustard uniforms and French-type helmets leaned idly on their rifles and blinked at the last light of the sun. The blue shadows became deeper as the *Fat Shan* eased against the pilings and the gangplank was run out. All vibration ceased. The coolies became quiet. The only sound was an occasional cry of greeting from the crowd, punctuated by the tinkle of bicycle bells in the street beyond the wharf building. Trying to forget Po-Lin, Jane moved into the main saloon where the immigration inspectors were already waiting.

The formalities were as simple as they had been at the consulate in Hong Kong. In a very few minutes she was walking down the gangplank carrying her small wicker bag. She passed through the arch of the wharf building and emerged into the street. She was besieged by taxi drivers who waved their arms and shouted to her in Portuguese, English and

Chinese. She chose the most substantial-looking taxi, an ancient Plymouth, and told the driver to take her to the Riviera Hotel.

Po-Lin was right. Macao was not Asia. There was no bustling to the city. Flowers tumbled off the walls which lined the streets, and wrought-iron gates only partly obscured the gardens which offered themselves before the houses. There was peace on the surface at least, and if somewhere beneath the city's exterior there bubbled the awesome strength of Asia, then it was still hidden from her. Oh, Po-Lin . . . fine old general! To see and appreciate this place with you under different circumstances. You would know how to lay a hand on this lush and fragrant air and touch the breath of peace.

The taxi turned into a tree-lined street and stopped before the Riviera Hotel. As she paid the driver, bells from a cathedral tolled vespers. Po-Lin!

Her room was enormous. She took a bath and afterward stood on the covered balcony which overlooked a park. There was a large banyan tree in the middle of the street below. Several ricksha boys had gathered beneath it. They sat on the traces of their vehicles and chattered continuously as darkness came. The street was otherwise deserted for long periods. As she waited for her courage to return, a Portuguese soldier strolled by on the sidewalk opposite, his arm around a Chinese girl. A European rode beneath the balcony on his bicycle, his bell tinkling at nothing. The street light came on and still the courage she needed could not be captured. She was weak, and yet the thought of eating revolted her. Again and again she saw the yellow water with the spreading coverlet of red. You are right, Hank. They do play for keeps. All of the propaganda, all of the vacillations and excuses contrived by people who would be tolerant of them, were idealistic fantasies. They will never make me forget this afternoon. Saviors of the workers! Power-crazy murderers and beasts. It didn't make any difference what country they were in. She reminded herself to tell off a few acquaintances when she returned home—if she ever did. She would have a few things to say to those avant-garde intellectuals who thought Harry Bridges and company were persecuted martyrs. But it would probably be a waste of breath. They wouldn't believe what had happened aboard the *Fat Shan* in the full sun of a lovely afternoon. They would rather believe the idiot who killed Po-Lin was a muscled toiler with his chin held high as he bayoneted a diamond-studded banker in one of Rivera's childish murals.

Gradually, as a soft breeze filled the balcony and the evening gave away entirely to night, her anger subsided. Her strength began to return as she thought of Hank Lee. She was not alone any longer. And she was not in Macao to appreciate the climate or brood on misguided liberals. She was here to help Louis and it was getting late.

She walked rapidly down the hotel stairs and went into the lobby. It was as deserted as the street. Wondering if she was the only guest, she went into the dining room and ordered a cup of coffee. It was Portuguese coffee—very black and very strong. She finally ordered a sandwich to cut the heavy taste of chicory. She munched slowly on the sandwich, looking at the empty dining room and the vacant lobby, where she could see a young Eurasian dozing behind the reception desk. Yes, she finally decided, she must be the only guest. Macao was more than peaceful. It appeared to linger on the edge of death, and without seeing beyond the brightly lit dining room and the lobby, she at last sensed the power of China which entirely surrounded the city. Macao was like a single flower blooming on a gigantic and alien bush. Now it received no nourishment and was withering in the sun.

She went into the lobby and asked the clerk for directions to Rua da Felicidade.

"It is but a short way," he answered in a voice that was as languorous as the night. "Senhora may walk there in a few minutes."

"Is it safe . . . to walk alone?"

He smiled. "Oh yes, senhora. Quite safe."

He gave her the directions, which were simple enough—turn to the left out of the hotel, then to the left again after reaching the second street.

She passed a few rickshas on the way, their small kerosene lamps dancing mechanically in rhythm with the hauler's energy. At the intersection of the first street a half-track clanked by, but the helmeted soldiers in it ignored her. She turned down the second street, which was cobbled and much narrower. It was dimly lit and inclined slightly. The doors of the houses were closed, but occasionally the sound of voices from the upper rooms dispelled the notion that she was walking in a dream. There was no other sound except her own heels against the cobbles. As she sought unsuccessfully for a number on the doorways a half-moon slid out from behind a cloud and revealed a large, crudely printed sign hanging at right angles to the street. LINGUA CASA. The shutters on the windows were tightly closed. There was no sign of light within. But as she raised her hand tentatively, she heard the thin sound of a mandolin. The player was beginning a flamenco. She looked up at the moon, took a deep breath and knocked smartly on the door.

The plucking on the mandolin hesitated, then more slowly, as if the player were reluctant to leave each note, the opening phrases of the flamenco were completed. Afterward there was a heavy silence, broken only by the trickle of water in the gutter which ran between her feet and the door. She heard a fumbling at the latch and a man was saying, "Bon noite."

"Excuse me. I'm looking for Mr. Rocha."

"Are you alone?"

"Yes."

In the moon shadow she had an impression of a very thin man as he made a gesture with the mandolin and invited her in English to step through the doorway.

"Your search is ended," he said, moving aside. "Forgive my simple place."

An acetylene lamp hissed on a plain oak desk which stood almost in the center of the large room. Its garish light cast huge shadows in fantastic designs on the closed shutters and on the walls, which were covered with posters in French, English, Portuguese and Spanish. Moving across the path of the lamp she saw herself become ten feet high on the wall. The floor was bare. There was an opening in the back wall with a dirty curtain across it. In the corner there was a large couch. As her own body threw it in shadow, it was a moment before she realized a Chinese girl sat on the couch. She was smoking a cigarette and one hand moved to smooth her gown.

"You wish to inquire about lessons?" Rocha asked. His voice was high and thin, as if it had through constant association absorbed the tone of the mandolin. He shuffled toward the desk in carpet slippers and put down the instrument. Now, in the light, his face was cadaverous and his sunken cheeks were sprinkled with pockmarks. He placed a pair of horn-rimmed glasses on his long nose and clasped his bony fingers before him in the manner of a teacher. He looked at her solemnly. Behind the glasses his eyes became mere black cavities slashed in his skull.

Jane glanced uncomfortably at the Chinese girl. "I am sorry to disturb you. I should have waited until morning—"

"Eagerness for knowledge is admirable at any time. Since English is obviously your mother tongue I assume you are interested in Portuguese . . . or would it be Chinese?"

"I wanted to ask you some questions. . . ." She looked at the Chinese girl, who remained motionless, as if she were a part of the couch. "Could we—?"

"My fees are quite reasonable."

"Could we talk alone for a moment? I am Louis Hoyt's wife."

"Ah? My great pleasure, senhora. Please—" His long hand waved at a chair beside the desk. The cavities of his eyes narrowed slightly and then became only open holes again. "There is no reason to be concerned about my guest. She does not understand a word of English. I find it more relaxing not to teach her any."

"I am trying to find out where my husband is."

"Is that difficult?"

"It seems to be."

"Why do you come to me?"

"You were with him in Hong Kong before he left there. I thought he might have said something. He was last seen near the village of Luk Ti. I hoped you might have heard some rumor . . . even a rumor would help me."

He stared at the mandolin on the desk as if it were the only object in the room. Then he reached out and made a minute adjustment to the acetylene lamp.

"You have come to the right person. I know exactly where he is."

Jane tried to remain still. She must not show her elation. Remember Maxine . . . and Marty Gates. Remember what they said about Fernand Rocha. Yet there was no hint of uncertainty in Rocha's voice or manner. He was entirely at ease. He was nodding his head and somehow managed to give the impression that it was surprising she had asked about Louis.

"Where, Mr. Rocha?" she asked, trying desperately to match his calm.

"In China."

"Where in China?"

Rocha hesitated. Then he pulled open a drawer of the desk and brought out several small yellow cans. He placed them before her, arranging them with his long fingers like soldiers, in a straight line.

"Do you recognize these, Mrs. Hoyt?"

"They're cans of film."

"Exposed or unexposed?"

She picked up two of the cans. She knew instinctively that Louis had touched these cans; they were his kind of film. Again the feeling of being a widow, examining the forgotten belongings of a dead man. Louis—why did you have to get mixed up with such people? There must have been some other way.

"They seem to be both. This can is still sealed."

"Precisely. Your husband and I were the best of friends. It was arranged that I become his message center, in a manner of speaking, since he wished to travel as lightly as possible. As he used film, he sent it to me . . . you are aware that we in Portuguese Macao enjoy a more or less open border with China? In turn, I would send him new film as he requested it. Our arrangement worked perfectly."

"May I have them?"

"Why not? They are meaningless to me. I am a language teacher and have kept them merely to accommodate a friend. I am very fond of your husband, Mrs. Hoyt. He has an indefinable charm . . . young, like a mischievous boy. The French would say—très sympathique."

"Is he well?"

"The last time I communicated with him he was apparently in high spirits. Of course, now—"

"Where is he?"

"In Canton." Rocha said it with as little concern as if he were saying Louis was in New Rochelle.

He crossed the room to an old wooden filing cabinet. He bent to open the bottom drawer and pulled out a bottle of wine. He set the bottle on top of the cabinet, carefully, as if it were his only concern in the world, then disappeared for a moment behind the curtained doorway. Jane turned slightly in her chair and glanced over her shoulder at the Chinese girl. Their eyes met briefly. Jane tried to smile. She turned her back again when she found there was not the slightest change in the girl's face. Rocha returned with two glasses. He set them on the filing cabinet and raised the bottle.

"Will you join me in a glass of wine? We have excellent Portuguese wine here in Macao. Rather a blessing."

"No, thank you."

"Too bad. Then I'm forced to enjoy it alone."

"What about—?"

"She doesn't drink." He left the cabinet and moved toward the desk, his carpet slippers slapping on the bare floor. Now, balancing the wine glass expertly, he smiled, and Jane thought that under any other conditions he might have been just a devoted scholar trying to ease the nervousness of a student before his lecture began.

"If those films turn out well your husband will be amply rewarded, won't he?"

"There's a much bigger problem now."

"Oh?"

"Mr. Rocha. You act as if Louis were free to leave China as he pleases."

"Why shouldn't he?"

"But . . . ?" Rocha's whole manner was fantastic! He certainly could not think that Louis was his own master. "But if he could, I would have heard from him. He would have left China long ago. I have presumed all along that he's held as a prisoner."

"A few moments ago you said you didn't even know where he is . . . and so you'll forgive me if I say you have been assuming a great deal. However, that is beside the point. Louis is a guest of the Chinese government."

"A guest in a cell?"

"No. He is in a house and quite comfortable. Certain restrictions have been placed on his movements, but if his friends want him out of China it is really a very simple matter. Fortunately, I am in a position where I might act as an intermediary. This I would be happy to undertake."

"What do you mean by that?"

"I could arrange to transfer a sum of money to the proper authorities. They would see him safely to the border."

"And you would take a commission, Mr. Rocha?"

He looked at her and the corners of his mouth turned down as if he had been deeply hurt. The caverns of his eyes closed slightly and he sipped at his glass in a way that suggested wine might restore his faith in human nature.

"I wouldn't think of it. Louis is my friend."

"How much money, Mr. Rocha?"

"It would be in the nature of a fine probably . . . for crossing the border illegally. Perhaps a hundred thousand U. S. dollars would facilitate matters. There would be several individuals I would have to approach. Their national fervor would have to be soothed, and that's not as easy as it used to be."

Jane thought of Maxine again. Remember what she said—promise Rocha anything, but give him nothing. But did Maxine simply have a personal grudge against Rocha? He seemed so sure of himself. He was quietly making sense, even if the amount he mentioned was out of the question. Nothing could be lost now in a vague promise.

"If the money were paid, what guarantee would we have that Louis would ever reach the border?"

"An excellent question. I would never permit you to pay the whole sum in advance. I would suggest a token payment and you could leave the later details to me."

"Where is the house?"

"In the outskirts of Canton."

"That's a rather vague description."

"Canton is a difficult city unless you know it well. I don't believe you trust me, Mrs. Hoyt. I can only say that Louis' best interests are mine."

She studied Rocha carefully, not wanting to trust him and yet already half-convinced he had spoken the truth. She must draw him out a little more—see if his words could be turned into action.

"Supposing I gave you a check for five hundred dollars. When could you start?"

"A check? I'm afraid—"

"A traveler's check. American Express."

"Five hundred would be nothing, of course, but I could begin by making a few telephone calls to Canton. I could cash an American Express check at the Central Hotel . . . the gambling tables are open all night. Then I could go to the main exchange and telephone from there. I might even have some favorable word for you by morning."

"Supposing I just paid for the calls? They can't cost five hundred."

"They would pay no attention to me unless I telegraphed a substantial sum. I will make the call, send the money as proof of our sincerity, and then call again later. It will take most of the night . . . but I don't mind missing a little sleep for Louis."

Po-Lin, she thought. You should be here. You would know whether all this was even remotely possible. She opened her handbag. There just didn't seem to be any way out of it except to risk five hundred dollars for a look at Rocha's hand. Whatever he had to say might help Hank Lee. She opened the leather check folder and searched in the bag for her pen.

"Please," Rocha said holding out a wooden pen.

"I'd rather use my own."

"Of course." He smiled. "Pens are very personal things."

"So is this money."

On a five-hundred-dollar check, she wrote Rocha as the payee. Then she signed her name on the line at the bottom. It was all over in a moment and she was tearing off the check when she saw Rocha raise one long finger and heard a muffled sound behind her. She turned quickly and saw the face of the Chinese girl. She was holding the wine bottle, her upraised arm making a gigantic shadow against the wall. The arm moved down and the bottle flashed once in the light. She gasped and tried to swing off the chair. But in an instant the acetylene lamp became a thousand spinning screaming lamps. Her head exploded. There was no light or sound.

"She was a long time getting here," the Chinese girl said.

"There is considerable doubt in my mind if you would show the same concern for me." Rocha picked up the checkbook and began counting the denominations.

"How much?"

"Three thousand. Better than nothing. And her signature is as simple as her mind. Clean her up and lock her in your room."

He eased off the desk and shuffled toward the door.

"Where are you going?"

"To the telephone exchange."

"Why? You don't really know anyone to call."

"Of course not. But—"

He placed the checkbook in his pants pocket. "There is no reason to be satisfied with a pearl when you can have the ocean."

A man walked with confidence when he carried three thousand dollars U. S. in his pocket. Rocha was inspired to whistle as he floated over the cobblestones in the moonlight. He thought of many things, all pleasant, and in particular the exceedingly favorable rate of exchange more or less set by Lobo for American currency. An express check—duly signed, of course—was more than welcome at Lobo's gaming tables. The cashiers would not be too particular, the way things were going these days. Rocha visualized the stacks of money before him as he sat at the long dice table, and in his mind he could hear the careless cry of the girl croupier who shook the lacquer pot containing the dice. He could see it all minutes before he actually reached the Central Hotel. Fernand Rocha at last was on his way to becoming a rich man.

The brilliant blue neon lights obliterated the moonlight in front of the Central Hotel. It was the tallest and busiest building in Macao. Before the Korean War it made a great deal of money for the Lobo family, yet now it was said to lose money because it was a vast and complicated institution requiring a large personnel. There was a lobby on the first floor and a restaurant on the mezzanine. The next two floors accommodated gaming rooms for the more impecunious. Here the workers of Macao could play fan-tan or bird-cage, or sit at the long dice tables which lacked only a wheel to duplicate the roulette tables Rocha remembered in Estoril. The poor could play on the second and third floors of the Central for less than a Macao dollar, a few cents even, and the area smelled of sweat, cheap wine and anxiety. Rocha had no intention of going near it. Lobo could be made to lose more money on the next two floors, where the basic limits of a wager corresponded with the altitude. The hotel rooms were on the next three floors, but they were not intended for the casual lodger. The rooms sheltered girls, often very young girls, and Rocha intended to visit them after he had satisfied himself at the dice table. The top floor of the Central held a night club. There was a Chinese band which limped noisily through American jazz, a bar, a seedy floor show and an overabundance of hostesses who besieged any male who ventured through the plush-curtained doorway. Rocha had no interest in it. He would shortly be in a position to buy his own night club.

He stood for a time in the blue neon light, annoyed at the child beggars who pressed upon him like grimy swallows fluttering out of the darkness, but such was his sense of well-being that he scattered a handful of coppers among them. All the world would one day know Fernand Rocha, who had acquired a considerable stake of the most desirable currency in the world. They would know him because he would soon acquire far more.

He left the whines of the child beggars and strode into the lobby. He took the elevator to the fifth floor.

It was morning before he came down again.

12

Standing naked and thoughtful in the cool early-morning breeze, Ying Fai looked at the crowded harbor of Aberdeen and relieved his bladder. He remembered when the harbor was not so busy or so crowded, when a man could perform his morning functions standing before the new day unashamed on the high poop, arching his urine to the northwest away from the prevailing wind and not having to half-conceal himself behind the bulwark. For there was a time when Aberdeen was exclusively a refuge for fishing junks and he had known every person in it and they had known him. Ying Fai remembered those days well enough and he looked back upon them with a mixture of distaste and pleasure. For Ying Fai was a Haka, and the Haka people had been fishermen since the beginning of time. Long before the foreign devils had come to Hong Kong Island, Hakas, who were the true seafolk of China, sailed their junks out of the harbor which was now called Aberdeen. They were a separate and different people from those purely commercial mariners who now moored their junks in Yaumati; much poorer, sometimes scraping only a bare existence from the sea, yet for reasons no one could understand, a happier people, too. It was said that a Haka laughed even when he was starving. It was also admitted the length of the China Coast that when it came to maneuvering the smaller junks, the Hakas were the finest sailors in the world.

Ying Fai mused on the periods of near-starvation as the involuntary, yet expected shiver passed through his body when his bladder was emptied. He squinted at the rising sun, which had just topped Aplichau Island to seaward, and walked to the mainmast. He reached automatically for his tongue scraper, which he kept hanging near the main halyard winch. He scraped his tongue methodically, removing the accumulation of night taste from his mouth with the steel band and remembering, as if it might have been another life, the days before Captain Hank, who was like a monument in a man's life—a typhoon of a foreign devil. It was so. And the wind of Captain Hank had blown most favorably though it had caused Ying Fai to leave the normal course of a Haka far and away. It was so. Regard this tongue scraper. Ying Fai was not certain why he still used it, for as soon as he had finished he carefully hung it beside the winch again and took up a bright red toothbrush. He squeezed a dab of paste on the bristles and massaged his teeth for several minutes while he looked at the sun. He preferred the brush and the paste to the scraper. It was a foreign-devil habit, but it was better, even though the paste stung his mouth. It was so. Ying Fai had never seen a toothbrush before Captain Hank—nor had any of his family. It was part of the new life which now seemed the true way of things; the life where the price of fish was only of conversational interest, as was the spirit-breaking cunning of nature which invariably threw storms at the Hakas when there were many fish, and fine sailing weather when there were no fish. It was so.

Captain Hank had bought the *Narcissus* and changed her name to the *Chicago*, which was easy enough to pronounce since it really sounded Chinese, but the junk which had been Ying Fai's home and life for twenty years would always be the *Narcissus*. Captain Hank had changed many things, as he had done for so many other junk people, but certain things could never be changed. In the beginning he laughed at the burning joss sticks which Ying Fai placed on the bow before every sailing. And he said that the bright red streamers hanging from the bow, and the gold-painted ball atop the foremast, would have little effect on the dragon gods of the sea. He ordered them removed—long ago. They were still there and they would always be there—the brass ball glistening even now in the sun. One order forgotten and forgotten and forgotten until it was never given again. And wasn't the *Narcissus* as sound as the day her teak first came out of Burma? Or had she ever been dismasted or capsized or even threatened to broach to, in all of the violent seas which had slipped beneath her high poop? Never. It was so.

Ying Fai washed his face and then his whole body in the pan which he kept on a nail at the break of the poop. He scrubbed carefully, for all Hakas were scrupulously clean. Afterward he put on tan shorts and a white T-shirt and laughed with his family as they prepared the first food of the day. His wife Silver, whose name was repeated in the traditional Haka silver band which graced her jet-black hair, squatted over a sand tub which held the charcoal fire. She was preparing congee, and it would be no ordinary rice soup, for she was certain to add slices of fresh fish which she had received as gifts from the neighboring junks. Later, at the mid-morning meal, there would be Yaw Tiu—the long strips of fried dough which were hollow inside—and a tasty Wo Tau Go made of taro root with perhaps an addition of fresh shrimp if she had time to scull the sampan to market. There would be no meat at any time, but only because they were Buddhists. All of this plenty, Ying Fai reflected, was due to Captain Hank. And so was the happy, unworried look on Silver's face. The health bloomed beneath her shining amber skin and her cheeks were bronze red. Her vitality was mirrored in the children who waited expectantly as she nursed the fire, using out of habit every last fragment of charcoal. There was Heroine and there was Beautiful Moon, daughters perhaps, but much loved even so. There were All Goodness, Addition and Wealth—no finer sons had ever been born to a Haka.

Ying Fai thought, I am forty. I am strong and soon my belly will be full. And all of this is mine. I may not remove the joss which is really a small thing, but I would give of my blood and the blood of my spirit for Captain Hank Lee.

As soon as the meal was finished every living being on the *Chicago*, from Heroine, who was only five, to Wealth, who was a solemn thirteen, automatically began to work. Heroine assisted her mother in cleaning the galley. Beautiful Moon rolled up the seven sleeping pallets in the small, cramped cuddy on the starboard side and polished the deck of the room until the planks shone brightly. All Goodness, who was nine, and Addition, who was eleven, set out the mortar and pestle for there was caulking to be done. They mashed and ground a mixture of tung oil, oyster shells, and bamboo shavings until it took on the consistency of fine putty. Wealth, the eldest son, and consequently almost a sailor in his own right, climbed the main shrouds proudly, pulling himself aloft hand over hand on the steel cable. For his father had spoken. He was going to sea and he wanted a halyard block changed. If he had asked, Wealth would have hung the block on the moon.

Ying Fai entered Captain Hank's personal cabin, which was midships on the high poop, between his own sleeping cuddy and the galley. It had been a long time since Captain Hank had occupied the cabin or even been aboard the *Chicago* to see it, which was regrettable. For it was always kept ready for the master. Ying Fai and all of his family took great pride in this cabin, allowing their seaborne friends to admire its magnificence through the doorway on certain occasions, but never permitting anyone actually to step within it.

Now, in the light which reflected from the water outside the stern windows and danced across the carved ceiling beams, Ying Fai reassured himself that everything was in order. The wide bunk on the starboard side, large enough to accommodate the bulk of Captain Hank, was made up with clean sheets and the coverlet was devoid of wrinkles. The smaller bunk on the port side was ready for a guest. Captain Hank's Westley-Richards, the master's favorite weapon, hung beside the bunk. Ying Fai had seen him bring down many flying fish with the rifle, a feat he would formerly have considered impossible. Near it, a peg supported a full bandoleer of ammunition. Ying Fai had polished the brass of each shell.

A wide frieze of carved teak bordered three sides of the cabin just beneath the ceiling. It depicted a wedding procession and Ying Fai knew that it had cost a great deal of money. There were times when he had come to the cabin alone, only to sit for hours and admire the intricate workmanship. He raised his hand now, to touch the paneling and make certain it had been cleaned with the soft rag Silver kept for the carving alone. In the same way, he caressed the long teak table which stretched almost the full width of the cabin and served as Captain Hank's dining table.

When he was satisfied all was in order, Ying Fai pulled back a corner of the elaborately woven carpet. The carpet came from Shanshi Province, which he could vaguely locate in his mind as being somewhere in the north of China, but what stood beneath it came from a region called Sweden, which he could not place at all. He pulled at a brass ring and lifted a hatch just wide enough to admit his body. Then he lowered himself into the dark compartment which had always remained a well-guarded secret. The British permitted two rifles per junk and no more, although they smiled and looked the other way at the ancient, red-painted muzzle-loaders which many junks still carried on deck in the hope of discouraging pirates through sound and sight, if not accuracy. Captain Hank had more progressive ideas and they had proved themselves on more than one occasion.

Using the rudder post as a guide, Ying Fai ran his hand up its circumference until he felt an electric light switch. Except for the engine room it was the only one on the *Chicago*. All other illumination was by kerosene. The overhead light, protected in a steel cage, dazzled him for a moment; then inhaling a faint odor of cosmoline he looked upon the thing which no other junk in China possessed. A Bofors forty-millimeter automatic cannon stood soundly mounted on steel plates just to port of the rudder post. He had removed its canvas cover only the night before and now its long barrel glistened in the light. Ying Fai was very proud of the Bofors, although its great weight aft, which had to be compensated for by stone ballast in the bow, sometimes caused the *Chicago* to maneuver slower than he liked. He did not understand the Bofors, but he was deeply impressed with its enormous fire power and the destruction contained in the lines of shells which were neatly racked on each side of the compartment.

The installation of the Bofors was ingenious and had been planned with an eye to complete deception by Captain Hank himself. The compartment in which Ying Fai stood had once been open-ended. After the fashion of ocean-going junks it was a part of the stern beneath the high poop. The decking of the compartment was normally perforated, as was the rudder, to permit the easy passage of water. And so in most junks, the compartment acted automatically as a stabilizer when the seas ran heavily. As the bow rose to meet a wave, the compartment filled with water since the stern side was open. Then, as the bow descended a wave and the stern rose correspondingly, the water rushed out through the perforations in the deck at just the proper rate to give the *Narcissus* a relatively easy motion, regardless of the height of the seas. With the stern partially sunk in a following wave, the danger of broaching to was also much lessened. All of this had been conceived by Chinese shipwrights even before they discovered that a bit of metal suspended on a pinpoint would continuously seek the north and so allow the mariner to find his way across the oceans.

The stern of the compartment was covered with bronze-hinged doors at the same time the *Narcissus* became the *Chicago*. She became a junk without a stern ballast compartment; yet seen from a distance there was nothing unusual in her profile. It took but a moment to pull in the doors and the concealed Bofors was ready to fire on any pursuer. The compartment was lined with half-inch steel armor plate, and there was a bronze-jacketed slot in her rudder post which permitted steering from the room. Ying Fai half-hoped to see the Bofors fire again on this voyage although he had no idea of the *Chicago's* destination. But he was already content. It was enough that Captain Hank would be in command again.

He opened a small door in the forward bulkhead of the compartment and descended a short ladder to the engine room. He switched on the light and stood looking at the powerful Lister-Blackstone diesel with contempt. When there was no wind the engine drove the *Chicago* faster than she could go with a fine wind, but it made no difference to Ying Fai. The engine stank. It stank like a dying beast and the odor of its oil filtered through the whole junk. It had truly made the *Narcissus* into the *Chicago*. Though many a junkman would have traded a leg for any engine, let alone such a fine and reliable piece of machinery, Ying Fai hated it. For he was a Haka and a Haka was a sailor.

Now looking at the engine he placed his hands on his hips and deliberately broke wind. And, he thought, the smell of myself is abominable, but it is not as bad as this devil's invention. Then stooping, he turned down the grease cups one by one, which was why he had come to the room, and having done so made his way as quickly as he could through the stern compartment and the after cabin to the deck.

He breathed deeply of the clean salt air and studied the activity along the shore. After a time he observed a sampan scull away from the dock and make toward the *Chicago*. The fat Englishman, whom Ying Fai detested and whose meat-tainted breath stank worse than the diesel, lolled perspiring beneath the sampan's awning. There were four Chinese with him and each carried a small wicker basket. They would be the crew which the Englishman had said must substitute for Ying Fai's family on this voyage. As the sampan came closer he examined each face with increasing anxiety. He thought he knew every sailor's face in Hong Kong Harbor, at least by sight, for the water people were clannish and did not clutter their minds with the multitude of faces on shore. Yet as the sampan came nearer he was certain he had never seen any of the men before and his sailor's instinct warned him to be wary. They were not Hakas.

At breakfast Hank told Lucy and Billy that he would be gone for several days. He was going over their school and play program with the amah when the downstairs boy came and said that master was wanted on the telephone. As he walked into the reception room Hank glanced at his watch. Nine o'clock. This was going to be a full day.

"Hullo, Hank? Tweedie here."

"Yeah?"

"It's Thursday morning."

"I know that."

"I'm right on the dot . . . like you asked."

"You better be."

"Now, Hank . . . be reasonable. We got a lot in common, me and you."

"We got nothing in common. What do you know?"

"You didn't give me much time, Hank."

"Cut it out. What do you know?"

"Nothin' about the Hoyt fellow. I put everybody on the job since I seen you and the result is nothin'. I wouldn't want to make up a story and maybe steer you wrong."

"Not if you want to see Friday."

"But listen, Hank. I come by some other information which will inarrest you more."

"Yeah? What?"

"Will you go your way and let me go mine?"

"I'm not in a bargaining mood."

"I just heard it this morning, Hank. A friend of mine come down on the night boat from Macao. It pays to have friends, Hank. You ain't never learned that." Tweedie's voice was easy and assured. Hank thought it was a bad sign.

"Well, give. I'm not going to stand here all day."

"Will you mind your own business?"

"If it suits me. Now what's so interesting?"

"I guess you got kind of a partial for Mrs. Hoyt . . . right, Hank?"

He squeezed the telephone. That sonofabitch Tweedie knew everything except what he was supposed to know. He clenched his fist, then his anger was replaced by worry. Tweedie said the friend had just come from Macao.

"Well—?"

"I like the tone of your voice better now, Hank. I like the way you said that."

"What is it, dammit! What do you know?"

"This friend of mine is in the Central Hotel last night sharing the wealth . . . and he's having quite a time for himself."

"Get to the point."

"But he ain't having as good a time as a sucker named Rocha. I think you know of him, Hank."

"I do and I don't care what he does."

"The inarrestin' part is that Rocha is shootin' a lot of money over the table, Hank. He's got a pile of signed American Express checks which he is throwin' around. This friend of mine gets curious, as who wouldn't. He takes a look at the signature on the checks." Tweedie paused and Hank knew before he spoke again what he was going to say.

"The checks were signed Jane Hoyt, Hank. I just thought you'd like to know."

Hank was silent for a long time. He was suddenly sick of Hong Kong— sick of the whole Far East. What kind of a life was it when you couldn't trust or believe a single person? Through the hallway he could see Lucy and Billy still sitting at the dining-room table. No matter how much money they had, what kind of a life was it going to be for them? People went off their nut in the Orient somehow, and the contest against them, which had been a challenge for so long, was suddenly souring. That sonofabitch Rocha.

"You hear what I said, Hank?"

"Yeah. I heard you. Are you sure?"

"Why should I make up such a story?"

"All right. Thanks. You're off the hook, Tweedie."

He slammed down the phone and stood cursing himself for being a fool. He should have known better than to let Jane go anywhere near Rocha. But she had a reliable man with her. What was he doing all the time? How the hell did Rocha ever talk her out of the money and why did she carry it with her? Was she coming back to Hong Kong or was she still in Macao? He should go to Macao at once. Charter a plane and get up there quick for a few words with Mr. Rocha. Macao Airways flew there every day. No good. No good without a passport. It was getting to be damned inconvenient without a passport. A citizen of the world couldn't move around the world as he pleased. The *Chicago* then. Run like hell and go ashore at night. In the back door. Like always.

He picked up the phone and placed a call to the Riviera Hotel in Macao. Mrs. Louis Hoyt. He asked the operator not to take forever and began pacing the full length of the room. He had crossed the room only twice when the phone rang. He picked it up eagerly. This was service for a change!

"Hello!"

"Hank. Maxine here."

"Oh . . ." He thought he heard her crying. "Hello, Maxine."

"I'm sorry to bother you, Hank, but I had to talk, I had to tell—" She broke off a moment. "Oh, Hank . . . couldn't you come by the shop to see me for a few minutes? I would feel so much better if I could see you."

"I can't now, Maxine. I can't for a few days. What's the trouble?"

"They killed Uncle Charlie. They took him off the boat and murdered him! He didn't stand a chance, Hank . . . the best friend I ever had . . . it's all in the *Morning Post*. Hank . . . I need you . . . please!" He heard her sobbing.

"Wait a minute . . . take it easy. Wasn't your Uncle Charlie with Mrs. Hoyt?"

"Yes. But she's all right. They only took off two Chinese. I don't know how I'm going to tell my father. Please come, Hank."

"I would. But you'll have to get hold of yourself. I think Mrs. Hoyt needs me more right now."

"Why? Have you heard anything?"

"Yes. And I don't like the sound of it. I'm sorry about your uncle, Maxine. But I'm going to Macao as soon as I can. You'll just have to stand by until I get back."

"Will you come see me then?"

"Yeah . . . for sure. I'm in a hurry now but I won't be when I get back. Remember this is one guy who thinks a lot of you. . . . Wait a minute—" He paused, not liking what he had just said. In too big a hurry for Maxine when she really had something to cry about? "Listen. I have to be in Aberdeen before noon. I have one stop to make on the way to the ferry, then I'll come see you. I'll be there in less than an hour. Okay?"

"Thanks, Hank. Even a few minutes will help. I'll be waiting."

"Keep your chin up."

He lit a cigar and paced the room for ten minutes until the Macao call came through. Mrs. Hoyt was registered at the Riviera Hotel, but she could not be located. He talked to the reception clerk. She was not in her room. She had not signed for breakfast. She was not in the lobby. Was there a Rocha listed in the Macao telephone book? No. Did he know a Fernand Rocha? No. Thanks. Good-by.

He shouted for the downstairs boy, who came running over the polished floor of the hallway, wondering at the urgency in the master's voice. Hank told him to have the Bentley brought around immediately, then went in to see Lucy and Billy. He kissed them tenderly and they ran beside him to the front door. As the car pulled away he waved back at them through the open window. He wondered how long it would be before he kissed them again.

The sun was hot and the market near Pei Ho Street was jammed with people. There was no passage across the square for even the smallest car, and so Hank left the Bentley to make his way through the noisy, laughing, arguing, gossiping, gesticulating multitude, on foot. The door to Dak Lai's temple stood open and the sunlight shafted across the altar lighting up the gold and red lacquer-painted images as if they were incandescent. Dak Lai was sitting at her table curiously turning the pages of a well-thumbed American fashion magazine. She looked up, peering at Hank over her gold-rimmed glasses.

"Leader of Brothers. You are troubled."

"Some day I'm going to buy you a Ouija board."

"The woman?"

"Yes."

"She has rejected you?"

"She hasn't had a chance. What about the man? I know it hasn't been five days but—"

"Calm yourself. I was going to send a boy for you this morning. We know where he is. But if you wish to see him alive, do not waste time."

"I'm not going to. Tell me, little mother."

"There will be great risk bringing him away. Is it so important to you?"

"Right now it's the most important thing in my life."

"You may lose your life. I would be sad. The people who guard him are beasts and there are many of them. Be sensible. If you leave him, the woman would be yours in time."

"Not the way I want her . . . and there's a new reason I can't explain even to myself. Now where is he?"

"In Canton. . . . Near the place where the second gate stood in the old city there is a Jesuit mission. The Christian images have been torn down and it is now a prison."

"Is he fit? Can he walk or maybe even run?"

"Yes. They have fed him, hoping for information . . . but that time has come to an end. He has been stubborn . . . so perhaps he is worth saving."

"I'm afraid he is." Hank started for the door. "Good-by, little mother. I will come to see you when I get back."

She waved her withered hand and her prune face cracked into a smile.

"Do. Ha! I won't be here forever."

"Yes, you will."

At the door he turned and answered her smile. "How did you find out about him? I don't doubt you . . . just curious."

"My friend Father Xavier has just come from Canton. He is one of the last missionaries to leave China. We had many fine words about religion."

Hank said, "Ah!" and for once he thought he had hit the intonation exactly right. "That's a combination I would like to have seen. So long."

He crossed the market, shouldering his way through the press of humanity with one hand on his hip pocket. His wallet was full of money he had ordered from Stoker, and every market contained its quota of clever fingers. He was going to need all the money and a great deal of luck, too. Yet in spite of his concern, his step grew lighter as he approached the waiting Bentley. He tried to tell himself, this was more like the old days. And he managed to laugh at the burning sun. Maybe Jane was right. Maybe he was only a soldier of fortune as she called it . . . which, in less polite language, was only a lonely, wandering bum.

Ten minutes later the Bentley approached the ferry landing and Hank saw Maxine waiting in the door of her shop. He jumped out, dismissed the chauffeur and walked toward her. He took her two extended hands, and suddenly the feeling which had revitalized him as he crossed the market became even more powerful. There was a sense of belonging again —of knowing the way. He saw it in the face of Maxine and he thought the feeling was like being reborn. This is me. It has to be. This I know and understand.

"You do not look the same . . . so much younger," she said in Cantonese, tilting her head far back so she could look up into his eyes. And then in English she said, "It's been almost three months. Thank you for coming."

"I'm sorry about your uncle." He had forgotten how small she was. Standing before him, she was like a child. "He must have known he was taking a chance when he got on the *Fat Shan*."

"He had to go. He was so proud. It was no use to say that he shouldn't go."

"Walk over to the ferry with me. I haven't much time."

"All right. It is enough to see you for only a few minutes. I feel better."

Holding her hand, he led her through the confusion of buses, taxis, freight carts and rickshas which cluttered the water-front end of Salisbury Road. His strides were so long she half-ran beside him.

"You're going after her?"

"Yes. And him."

"How long will you be gone?"

"I don't know."

She was silent as they passed beneath the long, covered ferry building. At the ticket window she said, "Must you go?"

"Yes."

"Be careful."

"I will."

"Why do you do this for strangers? Why do you always take care of the strays?"

"I don't know. I slip a cog somewhere inside. Maybe it's because I've always been a stranger myself. You know what it's like."

"Yes . . . I do, Hank."

"Maybe some day we'll get lucky and feel like we belong."

He dropped her hand and bought a ticket. She followed him to the turnstile. On the other side he turned to look back at her.

"Do me a favor, will you, Maxine? Go out to the house and check up on the kids if you have time. Make sure they're eating enough."

"I'll go tonight."

"Thanks."

"Be careful of yourself, Hank."

"Don't worry about this old joker. I was born to be hung."

He waved his hand and, smiling, turned away. For a time she watched the back of his head standing above the others. Then the crowd pressed around her and though she stood on the tips of her toes, she could no longer see him.

13

Merryweather had been all the morning checking junks moored in Aberdeen. It was beastly hot, he thought, but after all he didn't really care. Potts, at last, had recovered from his dysentery and now he could take the night patrol. Once more Merryweather would know what it was like to get about the job during the day and, by God, he was going to the Princess Ballroom tonight. It had been so long he would have to reintroduce himself, but this first night was going to be a smasher and Rodman had promised to come along to supervise his reorientation. He found himself looking frequently at his watch as he boarded junk after junk to examine their papers. In another four hours he would be free to live as other humans instead of trying to catch some sleep in the day. And so he smiled, even when the junk masters' papers were atrociously out of order, and even when he found half a load of brand-new truck tires on a junk which was licensed solely for fishing. He was in no mood for trouble on this beautiful, hot, exhilarating, stinking day.

To conserve his energy for the coming night, and he intended to dance until he dropped, Merryweather had split his small force. The patrol boat was at one end of the harbor with instructions to examine the papers and crew identification cards of eight junks which had reportedly moved their base of operations from Lan Tao Island to Aberdeen. For reasons of their own, Merryweather presumed, and he held not the slightest hope that the men on the patrol boat would ever find out the true reason. He had sent off his sergeant and a constable to the other end of the harbor in search of one Go-Shan family who had run their junk into the mine barrier outside Sulphur Channel, staved a hole in the bow, and were screaming for recompense from Her Majesty's government.

Merryweather stood on shore in a small, cluttered shipyard. A new junk had just been launched, her wooden hull still glistening with tung oil and varnish. Now as she lay high in the water and the explosion of fire-crackers assured her success, a Buddhist priest beat on a tin gong and chanted the litany which would protect the new vessel from the sea gods' displeasure. The priest knelt in the bow over plates of fish, rice and red-dyed chicken. The meal was intended as further appeasement to the gods, but Merryweather knew that as soon as the ceremony was ended and the last firecracker set off, the priest and the family, who stood solemnly behind him, would eat the food. Merryweather's only official concern was witnessing the crisp new ship's papers. Tonnage and length of a new junk were invariably cut down to minimize taxes, but in this case the difference between the papers and the real junk was only two Chinese feet so Merryweather signed them without comment. The Chinese shipwright and the new owner were delighted with his geniality, and Merryweather thought how odd it was that anticipation of the Princess Ballroom could spread as far as Aberdeen Harbor.

They offered him food and tea, but he refused. No, with many thanks, but if they just had a spare sampan about and someone to scull him out to the harbor for a few minutes, he would greatly appreciate it. For Merryweather had seen something which interested him far more than the new junk, her papers or the fly which he had just flicked off the end of his long nose. Over the heads of his new admirers he watched a sampan making swiftly for the large, well-kept junk moored in the center of the harbor. The junk was the *Chicago* and Merryweather knew it belonged to Henry Lee. More interesting was the white man who now left the sampan and clambered aboard. Merryweather had seen a picture of him. Henry Lee . . . the Hank Lee, that extraordinary Yank who was suspected of everything and yet had never once been caught in the slightest misdemeanor. He had become a celebrity by a reverse process—staying out of everyone's way, particularly the British. It would be something to meet Henry Lee. No other inspector at T-Lands had ever done so. It would be something to brag about to Rodman and tonight at the Princess Ballroom. Even the Chinese girls at least knew of him. So? When would there be a more opportune time? Make it a purely official call. Have a look at his fine junk's papers. Routine, of course, but if Henry Lee offered a spot of lunch . . . ? There was always something intriguing about Yank food, even though it was a trifle on the rich side.

The sampan was alongside the *Chicago* in a few minutes. Merryweather looked up, saw a Chinese peering over the bulwark and asked permission to board. He was determined to be formal and correct. Show the flag. Might impress Henry Lee, and there was no sense antagonizing him by acting the bloody pirate. The Chinese nodded. Merryweather straightened his cap until it was exactly level and mounted the accommodation ladder.

"Good day."

"Good day, Inspector," Ying Fai said.

Merryweather looked about the deck. Four Chinese were eating and talking in low tones by the foremast. There was no sign of Henry Lee.

"I'll have a look at your papers, if you please."

"A moment." Ying Fai smiled and left him, walking aft until he reached the break in the poop. He ducked down a companionway and while he was gone Merryweather took the time to watch his patrol boat moving about at the far end of the harbor. He bent to brush a smudge of dust off his highly polished black shoes.

"Please, Inspector."

Ying Fai was calling to him from the companionway. He motioned him to the door. Good. Now he would jolly well meet Henry Lee unless he had somehow jumped overboard.

Trying to adjust his eyes to the muted light, Merryweather descended into the large after cabin. It was cool here and he wished he was not on an official call and could take off his cap. He stood very erect, taking in the luxury of the cabin and waiting for the man who had his head buried in a T-shirt to emerge. He's a powerful devil, Merryweather thought. Look at those arms. Then the man's head came out of the shirt and he was smiling. The smile rather surprised Merryweather.

"Sorry to trouble you, sir."

"Perfectly okay. Just changing my gear. I was all wet. By God, it's hot!"

"It is that, sir." Henry Lee was much younger than he had expected. Fortyish, maybe. Somehow he had visualized a much older, less agreeable man. It was of course playing the fool to look at the *Chicago's* papers. Henry Lee was the kind who would have them in perfect order. "I'm Inspector Merryweather."

"Good to know you, Inspector." He held out his hand and smiled again. "Harbor Patrol, aren't you? Welcome aboard." Merryweather winced at the force of his grip.

"Wait a second until I get on some pants. By golly, it's a pleasure to be in bare feet again. I never took much to wearing shoes on board." As he pulled on a pair of black silk Chinese pants he waved at the chair before the teak table. "Sit down, Inspector. Relax. How about a drink?"

"I might do with a spot of whisky."

"Scotch or bourbon?"

"Why . . . I believe I'd like to try bourbon. I've never had any."

"I'm not sure whether that's a blessing or a crime. Those two decanters by the window. They're marked. Pour me one too, will you?"

"A pleasure."

"Sorry there's no ice."

"Quite all right. I'm not accustomed to it." Merryweather poured their drinks and after he had handed Hank a glass he took off his cap. You couldn't drink a man's whisky with your cap on. It would be just bloody rude.

Hank sat down and put his bare feet on the teak table. "You want to see the *Chicago's* papers?"

"Purely routine. We're just mucking about the harbor this morning."

"And you got a bit curious?" Hank said smiling.

"Frankly, yes. I might as well admit it."

Hank raised his glass and laughed. "Your Queen."

They drank and Hank was still chuckling when he set his glass down. Merryweather knew he was being judged, yet strangely he was not in the least uncomfortable. Regardless of other rumors, Henry Lee was certainly a generous host. He was saying, "Tell your friends to drop around more often. Always a pleasure to see any of you."

"Thank you."

"Keeping pretty busy?"

"Not too. It's quite dull, really. The Navy has most of the sport. They're outside, of course."

"When do you go home?"

"I've another year. But I might stay on. There's nothing very much left for me back in Swansea. Of course I'd rather like to see England again . . . but frankly I'd like to have a look in on America."

"So would I."

"I suppose the cinema has propagandized me," Merryweather laughed. "Judy Garland now . . . she's smashing. I must admit I'm shamelessly fond of your flicks."

"Don't believe everything you see in them." Hank paused while he reached behind him for the decanter and poured Merryweather another drink.

"Oh, I really should be going."

"Another won't hurt you. This is good bourbon."

"I should say it is. Well . . . cheers."

"Cheers."

Merryweather told himself that what he was doing could be considered as line of duty without stretching the point too far. He was getting acquainted with Henry Lee, wasn't he? The man might be a notorious brigand, but he had never done anything against the Crown, had he? An acquaintanceship thus formed might lead to some bits of interesting information, for if anyone knew what went on along the China Coast these days, it was Henry Lee. And furthermore, this Yank drink, bourbon, was most invigorating. Not up to Scotch, of course, but . . .

He took another sip of the musty liquid and, looking beyond Hank through the stern windows, began to doubt his reason. Was it the heat or the whisky? He looked again and confirmed the impression that the water was moving. There was very little current in Aberdeen Harbor—certainly not so much. Then he saw that Hank Lee was strangely preoccupied with wiggling his toes.

"I say! We seem to be moving!"

"Correct, Inspector."

Merryweather set down his glass and reached for his cap. He stood up and saw that the water was moving with ever-increasing speed. He felt the deck tilt slightly beneath his feet.

"What the devil? Are you—?"

"Sit down, Inspector. Make yourself comfortable. Finish your drink. We'll have some lunch by and by."

"If this is an example of Yank humor I must say I don't care much for it. I order you to stop this vessel." As if he were certain compliance would be automatic, Merryweather started for the door.

"Sit down, Inspector. I give the orders here."

Over his shoulder Merryweather saw that Hank still held his glass in one hand, but now, in the other, there was an automatic. He returned slowly to his chair and sat down without removing his cap.

"Do you realize what you're doing?"

"Sure."

"You are holding a Crown officer against his will."

"Among other things. Also threatening with a deadly weapon . . . which happens to be unlicensed." Still holding the automatic casually, Hank lit a cigar with his free hand. He offered one to Merryweather.

"No, thank you."

"They're damn fine cigars."

"I don't smoke. You're likely to spend some time in the jug for this. Put down that gun."

"How do I know you're a British inspector? You boarded my vessel alone and I have yet to see any credentials except your uniform, which anyone could steal. How do I know you're not a Commie agent, a Swiss, or a Pole, or—"

"Oh, come off it!"

Hank laughed. He set the gun down on the table within easy reach of his hand. "Inspector, you're a sight for sore eyes! I can't tell you how relieved I am to have you as a guest for a few days."

"A few days!"

"As soon as we clear the harbor I want you to make yourself perfectly at home. Move around as you please. Eat all you want and drink all you want . . . we have plenty of both. That bunk over there is yours. Ying Fai will fix you up with some sheets after a while and you'll find it quite comfortable. Enjoy the sea air and consider yourself a valued guest on a yachting cruise."

"If you don't set me ashore at once, the whole British Navy will be after you."

"I certainly hope so. We might need them."

"What do you mean by that?"

"Everything in time, Inspector. I trust you're not pro-Communist?"

"Certainly not."

"Good. We may have been short-handed in gunnery but not in the mess. Ying Fai is not only a fine sailor, he's a damn fine cook. Let's have another drink and then some lunch. I'm hungry."

By nightfall, Rodman had attended to every detail, moving through the formalities in a kind of unbelieving daze. He was not sure whether he should laugh or compose a solicitous letter to Merryweather's parents back in Swansea. The sergeant of the patrol boat had come back to T-Lands with this preposterous yarn—his inspector had vanished and was last seen by a sampan woman boarding Henry Lee's junk in Aberdeen Harbor. The junk had sailed away—over the horizon. Where? No one had the slightest idea. Presumably Merryweather, Junior Inspector Hong Kong Water Police, had not been thrown or fallen overboard—therefore hardly any need to drag the harbor. As yet anyway. But the alternative was inconceivable and after three long and perspiring conferences with the chief inspector, the words inconceivable, incredible and impossible had been worn very thin. People just didn't go about kidnapping British police officers—not even Hank Lee. What possible good could Merryweather do him? It was most embarrassing and it was a lot more embarrassing when the Royal Navy had to be notified. They had listened with unbending grandeur and then asked where the junk might be going. No one knew. Then they laughed their heads off. They volunteered to keep a sharp lookout, but what else could they do? The story was already a delicious hors d'oeuvre in the Royal Navy mess. Haw! Fancy! The newspapers would have it by morning.

Rodman checked personally on Hank Lee. He was gone, of course—no one knew for how long or where. He had One-Three-O-Three question the patrol boat sergeant so there would be no possibility of a misunderstanding in translation. The sergeant stuck by his story in every detail. On a chance Rodman telephoned Tweedie, half-hoping. He omitted any mention of a missing police inspector—Tweedie would have been too overjoyed. But if he knew where Hank Lee was, he wasn't saying. Tweedie said he hadn't seen Lee for a long time and had almost forgotten there was such a man. There was nothing on the books for stealing a police inspector, Rodman thought ruefully. Resisting arrest was the nearest thing to it—at most it paid four days in jail. Four days was a fine book to throw at Hank Lee . . . if, indeed, anyone ever saw him again. It was funny, and it was not so funny. It was a joke and it was an insult which the citizenry of Hong Kong would not soon forget—let alone those who were stuck with trying to do something about it. Merryweather, you bastard! May God forgive your overcurious soul!

Rodman changed into a fresh suit of whites and walked the short distance from the T-Lands station to the Peninsula Hotel. With Merryweather on his own bloody sabbatical their room was lonely, and furthermore Rodman was tired of listening to the other inspectors, each of whom had his pet theory on Merryweather's fate. They all predicted, and quite correctly, that the lad was in for a pot of trouble. The chief inspector was sore as a Tartar and Merryweather would have plenty of explaining to do. There was even a chance he might be cashiered. There ought to be a law, an amendment to the immigration code, barring Yanks from Hong Kong. All Yanks.

But there were Yanks in the Peninsula—a whole loud talking army of them. A cruise ship was in and the tourists filled the lobby to overflowing. They were laden with cameras and packages wrapped in brightly colored paper, and on most of the tables there was at least one wicker workbasket crammed with junk the Indian merchants imported from Japan. The male tourists looked flushed and were already a little drunk. They were leering at the prim, ladylike Chinese girls who sat with their families, and Rodman knew they would never look at their own daughters in the same way. It made him a little sick. Their women companions, very few of whom Rodman judged could be younger than fifty, sagged with exhaustion and sat with mouths half-open as if they were stunned at the accumulated results of their buying sprees.

Rodman discovered the last free table in the lobby and sat down. He ordered gin and bitters, but for a long time it remained untouched before him. He watched a group of BOAC air crewmen who still had that indefinable fresh-out-of-England look about them. They were about his own age and for a moment he considered trying to join them. Then he changed his mind, for they would certainly have very little in common. They would talk of flying almost exclusively, which he did not understand, and if they talked of England the events and personages would be of so recent interest they would be equally foreign. It was also doubtful if they would be very much interested in so microscopic a bit of geography as Hong Kong. For all of the world, yes for all except a handful of semitransplanted Caucasians, Hong Kong was merely a way station.

Rodman watched a woman with strawberry-colored hair piled high on her head. He knew her vaguely as a resident of the hotel, a Madame Dutroit—no, Dupree. She was sitting alone, also watching the crowd, but her vigil was more of a search and she eagerly examined each new face as it came through the doorway. After a while a small wiry man joined her. Though he was freshly shaved and his whites obviously just laundered, he looked unkempt and frowsled, as if he had just emerged from the waters of the harbor. He had short, cropped white hair and there were tattoos on the backs of his gnarled hands. A trident would become him, Rodman thought. But whoever he was, he pleased the lady with the strawberry hair. She beamed and took his hands in her own and soon they were sitting as close as they could move their chairs and the sight of them made Rodman doubly lonely.

Then he saw Marty Gates twisting his way between the crowded tables. He was carrying his inevitable brief case and the bruises on his face were still prominent. When he saw Rodman, he waved his hand and sauntered to the table.

"Hello, flatfoot."

"Have a drink?"

"I have a fine thirst." Marty hesitated and shifted his weight from one foot to another. "But . . . ah . . ." He stood making sounds which were not words. "Um-m . . . ahm. . . ."

"Stony?"

"Shall we say fortune has not smiled upon me?"

"I'll buy. Sit down," Rodman said as the loneliness left him.

Under foresail, main and mizzen, the *Chicago* crossed the mouth of Pearl River in the late afternoon. The wind was fine from the north. Without power the *Chicago* was indistinguishable from the hundreds of fishing junks which spread over the vast delta, their oxblood-dipped sails making sharp brown splotches against the sky.

As evening came the *Chicago* joined a flotilla of six junks making for Macao with their burdens of fish. When the light failed she maneuvered in closer to the other junks, inconspicuously, a few yards at a time, letting sheets go when it appeared she would outpace the dirtier hulls, keeping just to the stern of the group and slightly to leeward, where she was least likely to attract attention. It was dark when she slid past Coloane Island and then the Island of Taipa. Off the Porto Exterior, a considerable distance from the lights on shore, she came about and left her companions. For a time she proceeded, close-hauled on a northeast tack.

Now in the shelter of the Macao Peninsula, she ghosted along, the water burbling softly against her sleek hull, until she was brought up into the wind just off the breakwater. She displayed no lights. The anchor was lowered slowly until it was well in the water; then it was allowed to run free. There was no sound except the occasional creak of a gaff and the whisper of tide running past the anchor chain.

In the after cabin, the blinds were drawn over the stern windows. Hank checked the cartridge clip of his automatic, reinserted it and placed the gun in the pocket of his linen coat. He looked at Merryweather, who stared sullenly at the single kerosene lamp, and said, "Why are there so many sonsabitches in this world?"

"I'm hardly in a position to answer that," Merryweather said, transferring his attention from the lamp to Hank's face.

"Aw, come on. Cheer up, mate. You had a good dinner, didn't you? The liquor seemed to suit you."

"I am not objecting to the cuisine."

"Then what have you got to beef about?" Hank finished lacing his shoes, then opened a drawer beneath his bunk and brought out a pair of brass knuckles. He stuffed them into the coat pocket opposite the gun and clinched his belt tightly.

"You're sagging with all that armament," Merryweather said. "Are you contemplating a war, by any chance?"

"I'm just making sure somebody doesn't declare war on me. It's an old Yankee custom. You can't always be sure of people. They take advantage of you. Sometimes they're just plain obstinate and refuse to act like gentlemen. I found that out a long time ago . . . the hard way."

"Look here, Lee. I demand—"

"Ah-ah . . . !" Hank held up a cautioning finger.

"Very well . . . I *request* that you put me ashore at once."

"Take it easy. Relax. I've got a shore party all planned for you. You said things had been dull, didn't you? We're going to fix all that. Just don't be so impatient."

"I know it's of no interest to you, but if I don't report to my superiors very shortly I shall very likely be bucked off the force."

"When you get back to Hong Kong your superiors will give you a medal. And, believe me, you will have earned it. Now there's some good books over there and some magazines. Might even be a picture of Judy Garland. Put your feet up and improve your mind while I'm gone. I should be back in a couple of hours." He put on his straw hat and started for the door.

"Why can't I go with you?"

"This is a one-man show. Tomorrow night I'll welcome your company." He opened the door and placed a fresh cigar between his teeth. He turned smiling, and winked. "Oh, one thing, Merryweather . . . I wouldn't try going on deck. You know how Chinese are . . . no imagination. Ying Fai might mistake you for a boarder in the dark." He took the cigar from his teeth and pointed the end of it at his head. "It might hurt. And those stern windows. Forget it. We're too far off shore unless you're an Olympic swimmer, and the tide's flooding hard. Just stay down here and . . . relax." He put the cigar back in his mouth and went up the companionway steps.

Ying Fai waited, smoking a cigarette and leaning against the bulwark. In one hand he held the painter of the *Chicago's* small skiff, which he had lowered to the water. He would have much preferred to go along, but Captain Hank had said he wanted to scull himself ashore. Now as he swung his leg over the caprail, Ying Fai placed his hand on Hank's shoulder. He spoke softly and slowly in Mandarin, which was unfamiliar to him, but more so to the four men who squatted on the foredeck, their cigarettes glowing in the dark.

"Captain Hank. Why did you choose those men?"

"I didn't. Stoker found them."

"They are strangers to me. They are not Hakas."

"They are seamen, aren't they?"

"Yes. But they are not good people."

"Are you afraid of them?"

"No. But we should not trust them."

"All right. We won't."

"They can make trouble."

"We're going to have plenty of that, anyway." He descended a step on the Jacob's ladder. "Keep your eye on things."

"Of course."

Hank lowered himself down the ladder and sought the bow of the skiff with the toe of his foot. "Be careful, Captain," Ying Fai called softly to him. "You will soil your clothes."

Hank looked up and smiled. "You are getting old, Ying Fai. Older than an old woman."

He stepped down to the skiff and took up the long oar. He placed it on the pin, inserted the end in a loop of line which ran from the thwart sampan-fashion, and with great easy, rolling, figure-eight strokes, began to scull. In a moment there was only a thin trail of phosphorescence where he had been.

14

In the small open courtyard behind his office and lodgings, Fernand Rocha stood before the mildewed mirror which hung askew over the washbasin. He combed his black hair with rapt attention. The single bare bulb hanging just above his head revealed a bald spot when he tipped his head downward and this displeased him so much that the plans he had contemplated the whole day through became momentarily less exciting. But as he rubbed additional grease into his hair and finally perfumed himself under his arms and about his neck with cologne, he decided that a man of substance could afford to ignore a bald spot. So, too, under the circumstances, could the girls at the Central Hotel. It was money that counted regardless of race or age, and there was still some two thousand dollars in signed traveler's checks, solid as gold, waiting in his back pocket. The power of money was miraculous. It could make a short man tall, a fat man thin and a balding man seem like a sheep dog in the eyes of certain tittering creatures who dwelt in the Central Hotel—or anywhere else for that matter.

The night before had been disastrous. No—unfortunate was a better word. The moon was too full or it could have been that he was too reckless at Lobo's tables. Tonight things would be different. He would be more cautious and he would not spend the entire night gaming. He would vary his pleasures and devote a considerable time to the higher floors of the Central Hotel. He would take not one girl, which anyone could do, but two or possibly three at the same time, arranging and rearranging them according to the enticing visions which had come to him during his siesta. He would experiment with certain ceremonies of passion which he had once seen on a Chinese scroll. Recollection of the scroll had come to him, during his siesta. The scroll was long, about fifteen feet, he remembered, and the painting on the silk was expertly done and delicately colored.

The scene depicted an emperor's night of joy with innumerable concubines —which was exactly what this night was going to be. A work of art. It would be amusing to have the scroll to refer to, but it had long since been bought by a rich Dutchman from Batavia.

He was deliciously lost in memories of the scroll when he saw the face of the Chinese girl in the mirror. She was standing behind him—The bitch moves about like a cat, he thought—and she was angry.

"Fernand. What are you doing?"

"Combing my hair, obviously."

"You are not going back to the Central."

"I am," he said, plastering down the last stray hair.

"You are a fool. You will lose everything."

"Stop snorting. Whoever said that Chinese girls were emotionless stoics was the fool. And I must say anger does not become your yellow skin any better than it does white."

He leaned forward to the mirror and bared his teeth. Studying them, he ignored her as he tipped his head from side to side. Suddenly she reached out and, seizing the arm of his shirt, pulled him around until he faced her.

"You will go with the women!"

"Nor does the fire of jealousy become your slant eyes. Take your hand away."

"I'll kill you if you leave me here!"

"Your English is atrocious. I thought I had taught you better. You have just made an impossible statement in both fact and theory. If I leave you I won't be here . . . therefore it would be physically out of the question for you to do me bodily harm of any kind. Now I suggest you calm down and drive all murderous thought from your heart. It's getting to be a habit with you. You almost killed Mrs. Hoyt. By the way, how is she?"

"Sleeping."

"What did the doctor say?"

"He said it didn't look like an accident. He gave her some pills."

"Good. If she wakes up, give her some more."

"What are you going to do with her?"

"I don't know yet. Right now I'm more concerned about what to do with her money. Investment problems are never easy. If you'll just step out of my way—"

"If you go with the women I'll tell the police!" She clutched both his arms. Her nails dug in deeply as she tore at his shirt. Enraged with pain, Rocha twisted away and slapped her with all his strength. She spun off the washstand and fell to the ground.

"You'll do nothing of the kind! You forget who hit her!"

Through the long hallway which led past the sleeping room and the kitchen to the office, he heard someone pounding on the street door.

"Get up and answer the door. I am not here."

Because she rose so slowly he reached down and yanked her to her feet. She stood looking at him, rubbing her face in the bare light, and seeing her paleness and her quivering lips, he thought of the sudden pleasant sensation which had flowed throughout his body when he struck her. If she does not move in an instant, I will strike her again, harder this time and I will feel my hand sink into her soft flesh, and perhaps I will hit her again and again, and when she is down and screaming I will kick her until she is still.

"Go . . . quickly," he said, raising his hand.

She moved away from him soundlessly—Like a cat, he thought again. But she was still looking at him and he saw that the expression in her eyes was different from any he had seen before. Exactly like a cat, he thought again. Like a cat she hates me at last, and hatred is the most exciting companion of love. For a moment he forgot about the women at the Central and extended his arm toward her. She took a step backward.

"If you catch disease . . . I will sing," she said. Then she turned into the hallway and he thought, I must no longer trust her—not now. But when I return from the Central and beat her until she is senseless, then in the morning I may trust her again.

He returned to the mirror and thought how remarkable it was that money could also make a man look younger and, yes, even more virile. Then without actually turning to see her, he knew that she was standing in the doorway again.

"Well? Who was it?" She was silent as he continued to examine himself in the mirror. "Speak up. Where did you say I had gone?"

"I said you were here."

He turned quickly, feeling the anger rise in him. This night he would not share with anyone.

"Hello, Rocha." Then he saw Hank Lee standing behind her in the shadow of the hallway. Lee pushed her aside gently and stepped into the courtyard. "You're pretty exclusive these days."

Rocha managed a smile, though his mind became a turmoil. He thought of the razor above the washbasin and his hand moved involuntarily toward it. Then he thought, How foolish, I have had nothing to do with the man for a long time. His eyes are cold, but they were always that way. But what was he doing in Macao? If there was money involved—and with Hank Lee it was very possible—welcome.

"I didn't know it was you, Hank."

"You do now." He advanced a step until he stood in the full glare of the light. His fists were doubled on his hips and Rocha suddenly became less sure of himself. He tried to see the girl, but her face was hidden behind Hank's bulk. "Where is Mrs. Hoyt?"

"Who is she?"

"You cashed her checks at the Central last night."

"Not me, Hank. You've been misinformed." He moved toward the washbasin. The razor. "Is she a friend of yours?"

"She is on the couch in the sleeping room," the girl said evenly.

"You slut! Now wait a minute, Hank! The woman is rich . . . there could be a lot in this for both of us. Now listen to me . . . stay where you are . . . I didn't know she was a friend of yours . . . keep your hands off me . . . stay where you are, Hank!" His hand closed over the razor. His finger pushed frantically at the blade. "Hank!"

The first blow broke his arm. Hank brought the edge of one hand down and Rocha heard the bone snap. The razor clattered to the ground and his arm dangled uselessly at his side. "Hank! Please!" Then Hank's knee caught him in the groin. He gasped with pain, wanting to scream, but no sound would come. As he bent over, clutching his stomach, Hank's elbow swept out of the light and caught him across the side of the head. It sent him sprawling into the open urinal beside the basin. There was the warm metallic taste of blood in his mouth. He flattened his body, instinctively trying to hide in the ammonia-stinking trough, but a hand clutched his hair and jerked him to his feet again. A thumb jabbed his throat, forcing him to raise his head. Instantly a hand that was now like the blade of a fan slapped mechanically at each side of his face until his brain joggled in rhythm with the blows. A fist shot out, crunching his nose. He fell back whimpering and slid foolishly down the courtyard wall. For a moment he remained in a sitting position, his hands jerking in spasms. Then he fell over face down and wet the ground with his blood.

"Where's the money?"

"In his back pocket," the girl said.

Hank stooped over Rocha and took the checkbook from his pants. He flipped through the checks as the girl slowly approached Rocha's body.

"Is this all?"

"Yes. He lost much last night." She knelt beside Rocha, looking down at the grotesque mask that only a moment before had been his face.

"Is Mrs. Hoyt all right?"

"She has a cut on her head," she said, not looking at him. "It is not serious . . . but she has taken a sleeping pill."

"Which room?"

"To the right in the hall." She was still looking at Rocha, staring down at him as if she had never seen him before.

"He is breathing," she said. "I thought you had killed him."

"I should have. After I go, you better get an ambulance."

"Yes. . . ." Her hand moved slowly toward Rocha's head, uncertainly, as if the movement was not a command of her will. Then it descended to his hair and she began to stroke it tenderly. "I will clean him," she said.

Watching them, Hank thought that it had been a very long time since he had worked a man over. The old brutal knowledge was still there, the tricks learned the hard way, but now the sense of power was lost. For a moment, he thought he was going to be sick. People were right. I am a thing, a dumb dock-walloper who knows how to half-kill a man in fifteen seconds and knows nothing else. Then, straightening his coat, he saw that the girl was crying and he was sure that among many other things, he would never understand women.

There was no light in the sleeping room, but enough of the moon filtered through the half-closed shutters for Hank to see her face. She lay on her side, and her short hair was tousled down over her forehead so that in the shadow her eyes were hidden. He touched her eyelids gently, but she did not move.

"Jane. . . ." he whispered, for the moment not really wanting to wake her. His lips formed the name a second time, but he made no sound. He sat down on the couch beside her, and while he waited in the moonlight the mellow tolling of the cathedral bells came to him through the shutters. He placed his hand gently on her shoulder and bent to kiss her. As his lips brushed her cheek she stirred slightly and he wondered if she would be angry if she knew. Why was it that of all the things a man could buy, this alone could easily escape him? He thought again of the Chinese girl outside with Rocha. She didn't want his money, or even him to have it. Some deep, mysterious force compelled her to say, "I will clean him," and whatever the force was, it was not for sale. The same urge had driven this woman who lay sleeping in the moonlight ten thousand miles from the security which was supposed to be the most precious thing to all women. Why? Why was one man not as good as another? What did Louis Hoyt have, or Rocha even, that could not be found in Hank Lee? What good did it do to scheme and fight for a place in the world if the place was empty and lonely when you got there?

"Jane. . . ." He kissed her mouth and her lips were warm, and for a moment in the moonlight some of the aching loneliness left him. Then as he drew back he knew, though her eyes were still hidden in shadow, that she was watching him.

"It's me . . . Hank," he said uncertainly.

"I know. I was sure you would come."

"How is your head?"

"All right. I think I was dreaming about you . . . you kissed me."

"That wasn't a dream."

"Then do it again. I'm not afraid any longer. I can pretend I'm still asleep." His arms went around her and he covered her mouth with his own. And for a time, in the moonlight, there was no sound. Then suddenly she turned her head away.

"Please, Hank. I *am* afraid . . . of this more than anything else. Take me away from here."

"Can you walk?"

"I think so. Where will we go?"

"I'd like to take you to a lot of places. Right now. Anywhere where we could be together for a long time."

"Would you want the thought of Louis to go along with us? . . . always be with us? It would be a poor beginning—"

"I guess you're right. Maybe we better settle for the hotel. You can take the boat back to Hong Kong tomorrow."

"Where are you going?"

"After your husband."

With their arms linked, he led her slowly along the narrow Rua da Felicidade. Their bodies were close together and they sometimes looked up at the moon, but they said nothing of it. Instead he told her about Rocha. He said that he had been a fool for ever letting her come to Macao. "And I was dumber yet to hit him. It didn't accomplish anything except get back some of your money. I'm kind of getting the idea through my ape brain that you can't change a man inside just by changing the way he looks."

"You can't take on everyone's problems, Hank. You've got a handful already. I half-tricked you into this. I used everything I had . . . sometimes not realizing it, and sometimes I did realize it. I'm a little ashamed. And I've failed Louis in more ways than one. You've seen it, and it should be enough to discourage you. Later on, if we were foolish enough to make anything of this . . . I could fail you . . . and you would never know when it might happen."

"I'd take my chances. You haven't done anything wrong."

"Yes, I have. And I'm still wrong." She hesitated and they walked on in silence, probing their way over the cobbles. "I'm wrong because I'm so terribly close to being in love with you . . . when I should only be thinking of him."

"I guess that kind of qualifies you as a genuine human being."

"Maybe."

"It's probably not the first time it's happened in this world."

"That doesn't make me like myself any better."

"If I deliver Louis to you in one solid piece, will you go back to the States with him?"

"Yes."

"Right away?"

"Yes. Right away."

"Can you think of any good reason why I should stick my neck out to get him?"

"No. Except . . . perhaps, because you said you love me."

"Still tricking?"

She looked at him and saw in the moonlight that he was not smiling. She remained silent as they turned into the wider Avenida Ribeiro and were at once approached by several rickshas. The haulers laid the traces at their feet, begging their patronage in voices subdued to match the night.

"Maybe we'd better ride," Hank said, still holding her.

"It's only a little way. I'm all right. My head doesn't hurt any more. I'd like the air."

So they continued walking in silence, arms entwined yet guarding themselves, looking at the sky, the lighted shops and the strolling Portuguese soldiers, avoiding a meeting of their own eyes. They stopped on the sidewalk when they came to the steps of the Riviera Hotel. As if hearing a mutual signal they looked up at the row of balconies overhanging the entrance. Here, except for the ricksha boys who squatted under the banyan tree and seemed not to care if either the man or the woman were prospective customers, the street was deserted. A warm breeze flowed from the darkness of the outer harbor and as it crossed the park it caught up the scent of hibiscus and oleander, and the one street light swaying slightly in the breeze was weak against the moon.

"That is my room."

He turned her to him and held her closely, pressing his lips in her hair. She laid her head against his shoulder and he knew from the feeling of her body that she was afraid to look at him. She said, "I sat on that balcony a long time . . . thinking. There were some beautiful thoughts . . . and some very ugly ones, and once I cried like a baby because I was so lonely and afraid. I'm not sure I want to go up there again."

"Do you want me to come with you?"

"Yes . . . but I'm not sure. God help me, I'm not sure of anything now!"

"If I go to your room, I won't leave until morning."

"I know."

"Make up your mind. . . ."

She raised her head and looked directly into his eyes.

"Yes. . . ." Her hands moved up to each side of his face caressing him. "I will . . . I have made up my mind. I can't deny the way I feel forever. After Louis is safe I'll go with you wherever you want . . . for as long as you want."

"You're bargaining now."

"But I'm not tricking . . . either you or myself."

He gently pulled down her hands and kissed them. He studied her face, turning her slightly so the moon would light her eyes. But the pale light would not show him what he wanted so much to see. He sighed and let her hands fall. And he found to his astonishment that he was looking at her without really seeing her. She was standing before him more as a vision than as a person, and he wondered if it had become habit to think of her so, or if it was a trick of the moon.

"The first place I want you to go," he said thoughtfully, "won't take very long. There's somebody I want you to meet."

"In Hong Kong?"

"In Kowloon. Her name is Dak Lai." He handed her the checkbook. "Can I trust you to hang onto this?"

"Yes."

"Take the first boat in the morning. Go to the Peninsula and stay there. The next time I see you we may not be alone. Now you'd better go to bed."

He kissed her quickly and turned away. He crossed the street, passing into the shadow beneath the banyan tree, and then she saw the flutter of his white coat as he moved across the park. He did not look back.

The park was bordered by a low sea wall and beyond it the breakwater extended into the outer harbor. Hank quickened his pace as he moved along it, breathing deeply and gratefully of the sea air. And he thought that this night was a fit companion to another—the night in Balabac Strait, when in a very little time the whole pattern of his life had changed. There were, it seemed, certain peaks in the life of any man; he might plow along for years on the same old course, and then very suddenly, as if a hidden current swerved his rudder, the man could take off in an entirely new direction. It was an influence without logic or explanation. It caused a businessman who for all of his career had been the rock of honesty suddenly to embezzle his company's funds. It caused a model husband and father of many years' standing to wake up one morning and find that he had somehow exchanged all that was dear and familiar to him for a young chippie he could hardly recognize. It caused a drunkard to like the taste of milk and a meek clerk to develop a passion for champagne. Hank decided that it happened at least once to all men—and it usually happened very fast. Now he could feel it for the second time, in the night around him and in himself, and again there was no true explanation. He was about to risk his life for a man he had never known and Jane was only a part of the cause. The real reasons, he thought, were as deep and mysterious as the sea.

He had moored the sampan at the end of the breakwater. He stood for a moment looking down at it, watching its dancelike movements as it swung restlessly back and forth on the end of its painter. Because of its motion he saw it almost as a living thing—dissatisfied and very alone in the moonlight. He thought, The moment I step into the sampan and release it from the stone, then we will complete each other. Because then we will both have joined our natural element—for the sampan movement across the water, and for me movement into the unknown. Which was a lot of malarkey. The truth was that here at the end of a stone wall, pushing out like a rejecting finger from a country which does not want me any more than any other country wants me, I stand alone with a sampan—at the age of forty-five. And I have arranged this of my own choosing. If I liked it that would be one thing, and I might for a time feel sorry for myself and blame the rest of the world. But I do not like it. I have been a fool. I thought that I could make my own world, beat it together with my fists and take what I pleased. But I am standing alone on the end of a breakwater and unless I change my thinking I will be standing so for the rest of my life. Yes—this night is another Balabac Strait and I have been dead for almost ten years. That's long enough—even for a fool.

He bent down quickly and untied the painter. He leaped into the sampan and took up the long oar. He shoved off the breakwater, took a last look at the lights on shore and began to scull rapidly for the *Chicago*.

15

Ying Fai was waiting for him, his T-shirt a white blob in the moonlight. Hank threw the sampan's painter to his waiting hand and climbed the Jacob's ladder.

"All quiet?"

"All quiet, Captain."

"Make sail."

"The wind is favorable."

"We're not going to Hong Kong. We'll set a course for Canton."

Ying Fai sucked in his breath audibly. He shook his head. In Cantonese he said, "We will make the harbor in daylight if we leave now."

"No. We'll run with sail and diesel until dawn. That should put us somewhere off Kiow Island. I think the light is still burning there. If it isn't, the hell with it. We'll sail the rest of the way, which should put us in the harbor just after dark. I'll stay below and so will Merryweather . . . all day. You fly their damn flag and take your time."

"Yes, Captain."

Ying Fai padded forward and roused the crew, who were stretched out beneath the foredeck awning. As they hauled the sampan aboard, complaining of its weight, Ying Fai ran aft and raised the mizzen himself. Hank stood by the purchase on the long tiller. When the sampan was secured, the crew turned to on the mainsail halyard winch. The task required the four of them. The double halyard was rove through blocks on deck and bent to a large drum set thwartships, just forward of the mast. Two men faced each other on either end of the drum and, using both hands and feet alternately, pulled down the long spindles. As the drum turned the great sail creaked up the mast and the heavy bamboo battens rose one after another into the moonlight. Ying Fai leaped to the poop and assured himself the multiple sheets which ran to each batten were free. The *Chicago* swung slightly away from the tide.

When the mainsail was chock-a-block and peaked high, the halyard winch drum was secured with a loop of heavy line and the crew moved forward to raise the foresail. The fore winch required only two men and while the others hauled manually on the anchor chain, Ying Fai lighted the ends of several joss sticks and placed them carefully in the bow. Their musky odor drifted aft and Hank smiled as he raised his fist to signal up anchor. When the chain stood straight up and down, Ying Fai led it to a third winch and once more the crew turned hard with their hands and feet. They grunted at their work and as the strain became greater they began to chant in muted tones. Ying Fai silenced them almost at once and finally the bow fell away from the wind. The mainsail swung over slowly, obscuring the moon. Hank hauled on the tiller purchase. Ying Fai brought home the sheets. The *Chicago* heeled with the breeze and quickly gathered way.

"Get some sleep now," Hank said. "Leave me one man and I'll wake you at dawn."

Ying Fai nodded and wiped the anchor mud from his hands. "I will sleep on deck, Captain. Just there," he said, pointing to the lee bulwark. "Near you. Remember this crew. They are worthless men."

"Slip below and ask the inspector to come on deck. He might want some fresh air."

"Yes, Captain." Ying Fai started for the companionway.

Hank reached out and caught his arm. He spoke in Cantonese. "Ying Fai! How long have you been with me now?"

"Eight years."

"How is your family?"

"All in good health. Our rice bowls are full."

"Is that enough?"

"Most people do not have so much."

"If the *Chicago* was your own, what would you do with her?"

"She is not mine, Captain."

"Supposing she was? What would you do with her?"

"I am a Haka. I would fish her."

"Who would help you?"

"My wife and my sons and their sons when time passed."

"Would you run cargo to the Commies? Why not . . . the profit is more."

"I would rather sit on the poop and pull my beard and give advice to my sons. I would be content to beat the fish drum and listen through a bamboo stick and tell my sons where there are fish as my own father did. In this way I would be complete."

"You are a smart man, Ying Fai. I envy you."

"If an emperor envies a coolie then his throne is rotten."

"Did you think that out yourself?"

"No. All Hakas know it is so. Our mothers teach us this with their milk. And so we are happy and can laugh at many things."

"I see. . . ." Ying Fai started for the companionway again. "Ying Fai! When we return from Canton—if we do—the *Chicago* is yours."

"How could such a thing be?"

"Because I will give her to you."

"Now you are the person laughing, Captain. You drink too much."

"I mean it. . . . And I haven't had a drink. The *Chicago* is yours."

Ying Fai stood in the moonlight rubbing the back of his neck. He looked at Hank and then he looked away. He walked slowly to the lee bulwark and spit into the sea, then returned. His eyes, deep black in the moon, searched Hank's face and he worked his mouth nervously as if it were unable to form the words he wanted to say.

"You have sons," he said finally. "What of them? What if you die?"

"I have been dead . . . long enough. And my sons won't need junks in America. I'm going home, Ying Fai. I'm going to start living again. Do you understand the meaning of home?"

"Yes. It is here."

Hank looked off to the east where the moon made a hard black horizon along the limits of the sea. "Mine is there," he said quietly.

They stood in silence for a moment and the only sound was the brush of water tumbling before the bow and the cry of a cormorant crisscrossing the radiant ladder of wavelets which led partway to the moon.

"I will call the inspector," Ying Fai said in English. And Hank knew it was the look on his face, not his words, which said that at last he understood.

The exhaust of the diesel broke the peace of the night. Hank gestured to the crewmen to haul in the sheets. Taut now, the *Chicago* heeled well over and gathered another two knots of speed. With the tiller purchase Hank brought her bow around until she held steady on a broad reach. He leaned against the bulwark, feeling the wind freshen against his cheek, and looked up at the stars. Despite the brilliance of the moon, they stood out sharply, glistening as if they had somehow risen wet from the sea. Castor and Pollux, Regulus, Procyon . . . Antares . . . Betelgeuse and the grape-like stem of the Pleiades—they were friends in the night to a man who had no true friends, and they were not cold as some thought, but warm and reassuring, and in the last few years it had been a mistake not to stand beneath them more often. These were the empire, and any kingdom a man conceived was ridiculous and puny beneath them. They laughed at a man who thought he could build an empire from a gravel truck, but the good thing about it was, they laughed equally as hard at a man who began high and sought to increase his power. How could any man be proud and look at the stars?

"I hardly suspected you of being the romantic," Merryweather said, and Hank wondered how long he had been standing behind him.

"I was just checking our course."

"If you want me to believe that, I am quite willing to pretend. Are we bound back to Hong Kong?"

"No."

"I suppose it would be presumptuous if I asked where we are going?"

"Canton."

Merryweather lit a cigarette and looked thoughtfully at the water. For a time he was silent and then he said, "I must confess I like your American cigarettes. Bit on the strong side, though . . . like your whisky."

"We'll make a Yank out of you yet."

"I'm quite content as I am, thank you. We have a Chargé d'Affaires in Canton. Any possibility of your putting me with him?"

"No. I might need you."

"Oh? Why?"

"The Commies are holding an American friend of mine. I'm going to get him out and back to Hong Kong."

"That should take a bit of doing."

"I know where he is, so the first part may not be too hard . . . just getting him on board. It's a long run home down the river, though. This is a fast junk, but she won't leave a gunboat."

"I shouldn't think so."

"We may be able to sneak away without any trouble. . . . Still . . . I wouldn't bet on it."

"Neither would I."

"Under the afterdeck there's a Bofors. It takes three men to get any real firepower out of it . . . two for aiming and one to feed the shells. It helps if they are good men . . . and I've always thought a great deal of Limeys when it comes to a pinch."

"I'm a policeman, not a gunner. You should have kidnapped the Royal Navy."

"They weren't available. You'll do, unless you've changed your mind about Commies."

"They bore me."

"They may have the opposite effect, but keep the thought. One more little thing. Ying Fai is reliable. I'd stake my life on him. The rest of the crew are new men. Ying Fai doesn't trust them, so I don't either." Hank looked up at the stars. "Fine way to make a living, huh?"

Merryweather did not reply. Instead he strolled forward along the deck, balancing himself against the degree of heel. Hank watched him carefully, half-wondering if he had made a mistake in telling him so much now. Merryweather could as easily tell him to go to the devil as not. Personally, he would be much better off if he looked away from the whole operation. There had not been the slightest change on his face or in his voice. They could have been still talking about a yachting trip. But Merryweather was British—he would keep his thoughts to himself, if he was like the others. It all depended on what he really thought of the Red Chinese.

Now he was talking to the crew on the foredeck, standing over them straight as a mast, his white shirt and shorts clear-cut in the moonlight. Finally he strolled back, smoking his cigarette and taking his time. He climbed to the quarter-deck and leaned easily on the long tiller beside Hank.

"Ying Fai is right," Merryweather said quietly. "One of those chaps I know. He's a pimp from the Yaumati shelter. He's been in the jug several times . . . smuggling among other things. I don't know the others, but they are all old friends and that's all I need to know."

"I'd toss them overboard now if we didn't need them to sail when the light comes."

Merryweather smiled. "You are speaking of homicide, Mr. Lee . . . in the presence of a British police officer."

"We just passed into Chinese waters. From here on the police that count wear a different kind of uniform."

"You're very anxious to get this Hoyt chap out of their jug. Right?"

Surprised, Hank looked down from the stars. "How did you know his name was Hoyt?"

"The police who really count know a lot of things. Charming wife. . . ."

Their eyes met and seeing Hank's frown, Merryweather began to chuckle.

"What's so funny?"

"Your face. It makes me think of the way Rodman's going to look the next time I see him. Any objection if I come along during the first part of this little show? I'd hate to miss anything."

"You might not come back."

"I'll chance that."

Hank reached across the tiller, and still smiling, Merryweather took his hand.

"I'd enjoy your company."

"Good-o. Now I'll slip down and have a better look at your pop gun."

"Pull up the hatch under the rug in the—"

"I know where it is. I looked everything over while you were ashore.

I'm a very curious sort, Mr. Lee. Rodman says it's a pity . . . but I can't help it."

They laughed together and as Merryweather descended the companion-way, the sound of their laughter drifted away on the wind.

The gigantic Si Kiang Delta, which was the final effort of the Pearl River, became narrower in the dawn. As the *Chicago* passed between the islands of Lintin and Kiow the distant hills of Nam Tau floated on a veil of vapor above the mudflats. Long before the sun inflamed the yellow water, the river came to life, for the Si Kiang was more than the effusion of a single river. It was the mud of all the great rivers and inconsequential streams of South China, mixing their putrid silt, swirling and stinking over the shallows, giving life to the land, slobbering over the rocks where the cormorant fishermen stood, and, finally exhausted, dissolving meekly into the sea. The wind had softened with the light, and junks of every size dotted the twenty-mile width of the river. They tacked back and forth in a timeless, strangely formalized quadrille. The *Chicago* eased along with them, appearing in the day like a stodgy old woman engaged in the lei-surely exploration of her garden. At times she sailed quite alone, her low bow seeming to sniff for a stronger breeze, and at other times she became a part of the fleets of fishing junks, sampans under a lone sail, and cargo junks bound in from Indo-China, from Hainan Island, Malaya and the Sulu Sea.

As the delta narrowed and became the Canton River the traffic in-creased. Both shores were half-submerged, as if sinking beneath the weight of the most heavily populated land in the world. And so precious was the earth here, many people lived in small sampans on the water lest their very bodies needlessly occupy an extra inch of land. This was China and, looking upon it in the searing sun, Ying Fai knew it would never change. Here was the mother, the womb and the tomb; and all of the emperors, and all of the war lords, and all of the invaders and conquerors and exper-imenters could not change it in ten thousand years. They were only as rip-ples on the water of the Si Kiang. Leaning against the bulwark, the tiller purchase held lightly in his callused hand, cool beneath the shelter of his broad-brimmed fisherman's hat, Ying Fai knew that it was so.

By late afternoon, Ying Fai had worked the *Chicago* as far as Whampoa Island. Here he came about to the southwest for a time and entered Blen-heim Pass. The breeze freshened, making a last effort for the day, and it smelled of the land.

Now, as Ying Fai followed the channel's turn to the west, a haze mercifully dimmed the sun. And in the twilight the *Chicago* passed along the Back Reach of Honam Island, where the American-financed Lingnan University had once offered free knowledge to the Cantonese. Moving easily up the channel, sailing almost on a level keel, she passed the wharves and godowns of Butterfield and Swire, Jardine and Mathesen, and the Japanese Nisshin Kisen Kaisha. Ying Fai knew these names as the old names, once mighty, and as solid as western trade with China. But now the wharves and godowns were silent and deserted. The *Chicago* attracted no curiosity from either the water traffic or the shore.

The channel traffic became very heavy and Ying Fai stood warily by the tiller as the lights of the city pricked holes in the haze. He smelled the cooking fires, and the still-hot streets, and the night soil, and the fumes of living created by a multitude of people. There were so many. But no one had ever been able to say with certainty how many people lived in Canton.

The *Chicago* dropped anchor in two fathoms of water, just off the former International Settlement of Sha-Mien Island. She swung slowly with the current and from her decks Ying Fai could hear people talking along the Bund. In the light from the city sampans swarmed hopefully about the *Chicago's* hull, their owners crying plaintively of their wares—vegetables, fruit and the purest of water. Ying Fai waved them away, holding only one to serve as transportation. Then he went below and told Hank Lee that all had been done as he had directed. For a time, with a single kerosene lantern hanging on her foremast, the *Chicago* was simply another junk among the hundreds moored in the harbor of Canton.

While Ying Fai went ashore in the sampan, Hank and Merryweather remained in the after cabin. They each drank a glass of whisky and shared a tin of sardines, for the heat in the cabin was stifling and they were not hungry.

"I don't like to eat much when I have a full night ahead of me," Hank said.

"Nor do I," Merryweather said, delicately lifting a sardine to his mouth. "But those boxes are going to smell like merry hell. I shouldn't blame Hoyt if he refused to come with us."

"White faces and round eyes aren't popular in Canton. You can still back out."

"Damn you if I will."

An hour later, they heard the door to the companionway slide open and then close again. Ying Fai slipped down the stairs and stood sweating before them.

"All things are ready, Captain."

"What about the lighter?"

"One is alongside now. It cost five thousand dollars, but there was not time to bargain."

"Where is Adrapura?"

"Waiting on shore. It is not a good lorry. Very old, and he cannot leave the engine or it will stop. The fuel is bad here."

"Did he ask many questions?"

"No. He is a stupid man."

"Does he have sense enough to find the mission?"

"Yes. He knows where it is. And I will ride beside him."

Hank pulled open the drawer beneath his bunk. He handed Merry-weather an automatic and a pair of brass knuckles.

"I suppose this is unlicensed, too?" Merryweather said, hefting the gun.

Hank smiled. "I can't understand how it got aboard."

"Most irregular."

"Let's go."

They followed Ying Fai down through the deck hatch into the compartment which held the Bofors. Then they went through the engine room and opened the door which led to the hold. They climbed over the coils of conduit wire and Ying Fai held up a lantern as they opened two of the three large boxes marked—CIRCUIT BREAKERS and LEAD PANELS.

Merryweather lay down in one box and folded his hands over his chest. "I must say this gives me a strangely queasy feeling. Fits a bit too snug for a chap who's still breathing."

Ying Fai gently let down the cover and latched it.

Hank lay down in the box marked LEAD PANELS and looked up at Ying Fai's solemn face. "Remember . . . whatever happens, the *Chicago* is yours."

"Yes, Captain."

"Tell them to lower away gently. Load the wire beneath us in the truck."

"Yes, Captain." He tried to smile as he closed down the lid.

Louis Hoyt sat down in the familiar chair and waited for the customary opening of his ninetieth interview with the stiff young man he called the Needle. He thought of him as the Needle because that was his way. He shone all over and his thinking was quick and sharp. Now in the dank heat, his smooth forehead glistened with moisture and his high cheekbones seemed to have been polished against stone. Was it the ninetieth interview? Something like that. It was hard to keep track when the Needle kept prodding constantly. And during the past week his manner had changed. Now when he smiled there was not even a pretense of warmth. His smile was only a display of teeth.

"Any complaints?" The Needle was beginning in the same old way.

"No. Except the bugs. They are getting bigger and fatter."

"Eating well?"

"The bugs or me?"

"You."

"What difference does it make?"

"Have you been fair enough to read the new literature I sent you?"

"Yeah. I read it. I was lonesome and there wasn't anything else to do. Who writes your stuff? Harriet Beecher Stowe?"

"How did it impress you?"

"It's a lot of crap. Not a laugh in it."

"Building a new nation is not a laughing matter. You are making things very difficult for me, Mr. Hoyt."

"That's mutual."

"We can't continue your education forever. Wouldn't you say we've been extremely tolerant so far?"

"That depends on how you look at it."

"What would happen to a Chinese who entered your country and photographed military installations?"

There it was. The same old question, twisted around a little, but still loaded. And the Needle was still waiting for the wrong answer. There was nothing to fear—he had said so many times. Hadn't he spent two years at Columbia University and didn't he know what it was like to take the subway and eat hot dogs at Coney Island? He knew Americans. He *liked* them . . . even if their thinking was warped. Powerful interests had turned the people against themselves, but the time would come when they would awaken if only more voices could be heard. Louis might be one of those voices. He had only to open his mind and look about him and see the happiness and integrity of People's China. "We want you to understand us," had been the underlying theme of all the Needle's explanation. So far. Everything would be forgiven if Louis would only sign the paper.

"I never have, nor did I ever have, any intention of photographing anything of a military nature," Louis said automatically. And as usual, his answer was ignored.

"If you will sign the paper tonight, I can make immediate arrangements for your return to Hong Kong. You must only admit that you were sent here by the United States government to photograph military installations. It's very simple and you will soon be with your wife. You will not find our People's Government vindictive."

"I've told you a thousand times I came here on my own hook."

"Which is, as I must tell you for the last time . . . ridiculous."

"It sure was. I wish I'd never thought of it."

"You have admitted you are an officer in the American Army."

"I *was* . . . a long time ago. Stop twisting my rank and seniority around. I was a shavetail lieutenant and the Army was glad to get rid of me."

The Needle sighed and ruffled through the pile of papers on his desk. "We are tired of your lies, Mr. Hoyt. Here is a telegram from Peiping. I regret you cannot read Chinese because it might clarify your thinking.

Unless you confess your lies tonight, I am authorized to dispose of you in any way I see fit."

"How would you see fit?"

"Ammunition is cheap."

"You haven't got the guts." Louis tried very hard to sound as if he believed it. This was a new turn. He tried to assume the face which had won him so many hands at poker, but it wasn't easy. The Needle was holding all the cards and he knew it. "You'd get in a hell of a lot of trouble. Besides I still don't see how my signing a piece of paper, which would be a lie, could be worth anything to you."

"I will explain again as I would to a child, Lieutenant Hoyt."

"Stop calling me lieutenant!"

"We want recognition of our government and admittance to the U.N. Visualize such a paper as a wedge . . . one of many . . . a complaint. It would help us to show the world why we must protect ourselves against imperialistic powers. You have been exploited. We sympathize with you and only wish to reveal the true intention of your superiors. We can easily forgive you because as a person you are unimportant."

"My wife might not agree with you."

"Exactly. I suggest you think of her in connection with this paper."

"I've been thinking plenty about her."

"Her name is Jane, isn't it?"

"No. It's Matilda."

The Needle placed the tips of his long, pointed fingers together and examined the ceiling. He reached for a bamboo fan and waved it slowly back and forth beneath his chin. There were huge cracks in the plaster ceiling. Louis knew the meanderings of the cracks by heart for there always came a time in every interview when they examined the cracks together. It happened when the Needle started talking about Jane. He was now too smart a man to bother with physical torture. He had tried it just once, at the end of the first week in the old mission. During the beating, which exhausted two sets of tormentors, Louis had not said a word.

Now the Needle's voice took on a purring quality. Louis braced himself against the back of the chair and held tightly to the seat. He tried to close his ears, for he knew what was coming. Oh, the Needle knew his job.

"Your Jane is an attractive woman, Lieutenant. Where is she tonight?"

"How should I know?"

"We are better informed. She is in Hong Kong with a man named Henry Lee. He is a very handsome man . . . big . . . very strong. You'll certainly agree women are universally attracted to very tall men, Lieutenant. And you have been away from her a considerable time. She thinks you are dead."

"When are you going to turn the record over on the other side?"

For a moment the Needle said nothing as he continued to fan himself. Then twisting slightly in his chair, he reached out and pulled a photograph from the pile of papers. He slid the photograph across his desk so that it faced Louis. He returned to his communion with the ceiling.

"Interesting, isn't it, Lieutenant? The identity of the woman should be obvious to you. The man is Henry Lee. The photograph was taken by the cashier at the Peacock restaurant in Hong Kong four nights ago. You will notice that Mrs. Hoyt is not exactly grieving at your absence. They are both laughing."

"She always liked jokes."

"Notice their hands. She is reaching across the table and holding his . . . offering, one might say. Even my limited knowledge of Americans assures me that it is not customary to hold hands during the telling of a joke."

"You're wasting your time and mine."

"I have a great deal of time, but you have very little. Another hour or so before you deliberately make that woman a widow. Visualize her . . . say a month from now . . . or even sooner. She is lying on a bed . . . her skin white and soft . . . her whole body welcoming the hands of that man. You see what he looks like . . . you can even see his hands and know what they would be like as they pressed her flesh. Think about it, Lieutenant! Then see him throw himself hard against her . . . burying her body beneath his! Listen to their quick breathing and have the courage to admit that in her ecstasy she will forget you ever existed. And afterward, when they are spent, he will caress her as he pleases . . . letting his hands and lips wander . . . or he might even beat her. There are some men, you know, who find it deeply satisfying . . . and some women. I wonder . . ."

"The acoustics are terrible in this place. I can't hear a goddamned word you say." Louis gritted his teeth and closed his eyes. He was so tired. Oh God, he was tired of this! But why was Jane laughing?

The Needle slammed down his fan. His mouth became a thin line and the purring left his voice.

"Very well, Lieutenant! I'll give you two hours more to improve your hearing. You have committed a crime against the People's Government of China and your stupid lies have deceived no one! If you will sign the paper you may return to your wife. You will also be contributing in a small but very certain way to world peace. I envy you that chance. Take it while you're alive. In two hours you will go to the garden."

"Stop calling me lieutenant," Louis said dully

Louis knew about the garden. He sat on his cot in the small room which had once been a Jesuit's place of meditation, and pictured the garden in his mind. It was on the back side of the H-shaped mission between the kitchen and the room where the guards slept. It wasn't a very big garden, but it was big enough for one man to stand against the wall and two other men to stand at the opposite end holding burp guns. It had been used twice since Louis came to the mission, both times at night. The Needle was very sparing with ammunition—two short bursts and it was all over. After the ripping sound the mission seemed quieter than ever and remained so until the crockery factory, which bordered one side of the mission, began work just after dawn.

The old refectory and the Needle's office were on the side of the mission next to the factory. What had been the former church occupied the center of the H, and pieces of the altar were still standing. The garden was behind the altar, then a high wall, and then Louis didn't know. The whole mission was floored in clay brick. A wooden staircase spiraled to the belfry on the opposite side of the H, but Louis had never been up to the belfry. A landing halfway up the staircase led off to a balcony along which there were seven small rooms. The rooms, he had decided, must have sheltered the original Jesuits and such traveling missionaries as came down from the provinces seeking spiritual encouragement. His own room was on the corner just beneath the bell tower. From it he could see a small graveyard which contained the remains of former missionaries. There were six graves, Louis had counted them many times. They had sunk into the ground slightly, and were littered with trash and cigarette butts which the guards tossed out their window. For some unexplained reason no one had bothered to remove the small crosses.

A long mud wall extended from the graveyard, and beyond it there was a street which Louis could not see. But in the hours before daybreak, when he lay on his cot staring at the faint outline of a crucifix which dust and time had left on his wall, he could hear sounds from the street and they comforted him almost as much as the mark on the wall. He had learned to identify the flute of the fish peddler, the clacking of two hollow bamboo boxes which announced the seller of water, and the intermittent tinkling of a small bell accompanied by a hoarse cry which told the people of the street that firewood was for sale. Louis enjoyed these sounds in the night. They gave him a sense of still being a part of the living world, and they were something to think about besides the Needle.

The top of the wall was heavily impregnated with broken glass set in cement. Beyond the graveyard there was a volleyball court used every evening by the guards, and then the wall turned at right angles as it met a wider street which Louis could see from the elevation of his room. The wall ran along in front of the mission until it joined with the crockery factory. There was a wrought-iron gate in the wall and a newly painted sentry box stood just outside it, facing the street. The sentries always wore the same uniform regardless of the weather—crumpled cap, olive-brown uniform, wrap-around puttees and tennis shoes. When he first came to the mission Louis sometimes yelled at the sentries, just to make a sound. But they looked up at him uncomprehendingly and seldom left their box. Only one had pointed his burp gun at Louis, but he soon grew bored with the long-distance argument which neither of them could understand and returned to his box.

Inside the gate, a dusty driveway encircled a small plot of palm trees, and on windy nights Louis could hear their blades slithering together. He would watch the palm trees for hours hoping to see a bird and when he did he felt better for the rest of the day. He could also see people enter the gate and study them as the sentry examined their passes. But once they passed beneath the palm trees, presumably to enter the original entrance to the mission, they passed out of his line of sight.

There were no bars on his two windows. But he estimated it was a thirty-foot drop to the ground. And the wall was at least twelve feet high. And there was but the one gate. He had studied and restudied the design of the mission. He was convinced he knew every small activity which occurred within its walls during the day and the night. He had reached only one certain conclusion. Escape was impossible. The Needle was a good organizer.

Now thinking of the Needle and the garden he moved to the window and stood looking down at the tops of the palms. It was hot. There was no wind and the street light beyond the gate made a triangle of light in the thin fog. He wanted to write a note, but he had never been furnished with either paper or pencil. He might scratch it on the wall with his razor, which they had left him, but what he wanted to say would take a month of scratching. And the Needle was being tough with his time.

"Well, Jane," he wanted to say, "this looks like it. I want you to know why I didn't sign the paper. In the first place I don't think it would do the least bit of good for me. Because I'm human and happen to enjoy life very much I would probably have signed it if I thought it would mean everything would turn out all right. I don't think it would—not on those terms. These people have turned themselves into wild animals and when wild animals are afraid, they kill whether it is necessary or not. These people are wandering around in an unfamiliar jungle and they are scared stiff because they are not a bit sure what they are doing, or that what they are trying to do makes any sense at all. And so they are not only afraid of each other, but even of a little guy like me. They are afraid of what I might see or say. I've lost about a pound of patriotism a day in this place. I'll admit it. They knocked some of it out of me and they bled the rest talking about you and showing me that picture. I think it would happen to any man and so I'm not refusing to sign the paper because I fancy myself a hero. It takes a real hero to be a hero when you're alone . . . and I'm not the type. But there's an ounce of patriotism left somehow, and this is from a guy who always ran like hell to get inside some building so he wouldn't have to salute the flag when the bugler played retreat . . . there's enough to tell you and anybody else who's interested that these people hate us as individuals and as a nation. They'll kill us separately or together, if they get the chance, and you have to be this close to them to realize how damn sure a thing this is. Don't give them the chance. . . ."

It would take a lot of scratching on the wall and so it wasn't even worth beginning.

He was looking out the window, thinking he should have started the scratching when he first came to the mission, if only to pass the time, when he saw a truck stop opposite the gate. The engine sounded as if it had stalled. He watched a Chinese climb out of the cab and open the hood. He saw him examining the engine with a flashlight, probing hopelessly, and he made a bet with himself the Chinese would never succeed in fixing it. Bet ten thousand dollars—what the hell, money wasn't going to count much longer, and a Chinese couldn't fix anything. So after all it wasn't a very interesting bet.

As the Chinese continued to tinker with the engine another man got out of the cab and joined him. Then Louis saw something which he considered would make a really interesting wager. If only there was someone around to match his money! He would give fifteen-to-one odds . . . hell, fifty to one! The sentry had stepped out of his box. He was watching the men working over the engine. Louis wanted to bet that within the space of one minute his curiosity would get the better of him. He was a Chinese, wasn't he? And so it followed that he would never be able to resist getting in on the know. Hell . . . make it a hundred to one!

Fascinated, counting the payoff instinctively with the tips of his fingers, Louis watched the sentry. Go, you bastard! Move! Go see what the hell gives! Be a real Chinaman. Give me this last satisfaction and get your nose in things! This beats the mile at Belmont Park! Louis raised his fists and shook them as if he were in a grandstand. Then he stifled a yell of triumph. The sentry was strolling over to the truck. He stood uncertainly behind the others a moment. There was a brief conversation. Then he bent over, joining the other two men as they examined the engine.

Louis was about to turn away from the window when he saw something which caused him to rub his eyes. One of the men from the cab raised his hand over the head of the sentry. A wrench flashed in the street light. The man brought the wrench down and the sentry slumped to the ground. At once they hoisted him into the cab. There was a brief wait while Louis cursed the fact he could not see through the top of the cab—then the engine started. The truck drove through the gate, turned on the driveway and vanished beneath the palms. Now what the hell went on? The Needle wasn't going to like that.

Louis leaned as far as he could out of the window, but he could not see the truck. It was going to be a shame to go to the garden without knowing the answer to that one. Maybe the Needle would grant a last request and tell. But there wouldn't be time to scratch the answer on the wall.

". . . One more thing, Jane. Maybe I should have stayed home and photographed babies or the graduating class at the high school. But that wasn't for me. Some men get shot out of cannons to make a living. Some drive race cars and on the surface it may not seem like they've got good sense. I can't explain it and I don't think anyone else can . . . why we do these things. You get started, you get proud, and you can't stop because you want to be the tops. . . . So part of this was for me inside, and part for you because I never wanted you to look at me and wonder whatever happened to the guy you married. I've got a hunch you'll get lucky next time and find a guy who is more—"

The door was kicked open and Louis turned quickly. The Needle was early. The guard stood a moment looking at him, holding his burp gun.

"You're in an awful hurry."

"Yes," Ying Fai said. "Quick, please."

Louis followed him down the spiral staircase. They ran across the nave and came to the main entrance to the mission. The two guards who normally stood there were sprawled face-down on the bricks. Louis saw two armed white men standing over them. Louis recognized the heavier man. He had a smashed nose.

"Welcome."

"Hoyt?"

"Yeah."

"Come on." The man seized Louis' arm and half-dragged him out the door. He pushed him up to the back of the truck and pointed to an open box. "Get in there. Quick!"

Louis lay down in the box and the lid was slammed shut. In a moment he felt the truck begin to move.

16

The truck turned to the right along the canal which embraced Sha-Mien Island, then cut across behind the customhouse tower and swerved into the Bund. It passed through a mile of heavy traffic until it stopped before the old French hospital. Here the Bund was relatively deserted. Ying Fai told Adrapura to keep the coils of wire and sell them for what he could get. He ordered him to back the truck until the tail gate projected over the water. He slipped out of the cab and hired a sampan manned by two strong girls. Then he climbed back into the truck and opened the boxes. Gratefully inhaling the night air, Hank, Louis and Merryweather slipped silently off the tail gate and landed directly in the sampan.

The sight of their white passengers worried the girls. They chattered excitedly, but at Ying Fai's command they lay hard on their long oars. The sampan gathered speed and the shore line dissolved into the fog.

"Thanks," Louis said looking at Hank.

"Don't thank me yet. Ying Fai! What the hell are we doing in this sampan? Where's the lighter?"

"We go first to lighter, Captain. It gone. Crew gone, too. Not safe at that wharf if they see your faces."

The plan had been to return to the lighter and Ying Fai would supervise reloading the boxes. To the people along the wharf they would simply be outgoing cargo—to the crew, rejected cargo, and it would be placed back in the hold of the *Chicago*. The boxes were to be opened after they were again under way, by Ying Fai alone.

"How about these girls?" Hank said. "They aren't blind."

Ying Fai shrugged his shoulders. His face was expressionless when he said, "They are strong but stupid. They are Hakas. They will not talk to land people until morning."

"I hope you're right. How far is the *Chicago?*"

"Perhaps one mile."

A mile! Twenty minutes in a sampan. Twenty precious minutes with Adrapura and that crew loose on the town and God knows what happening at the mission. He thought, Changing plans at the last minute has hung better men than us. He turned to Louis.

"How often do they change the guards at the mission?"

"Every two hours."

"Is there much activity there . . . many people wandering around? When do you think they'll find those guards?"

"Usually it's quiet at this time. But tonight they had a special event planned. I couldn't say."

Hank cursed the fog, for it meant no wind. They would have to start the diesel and the sound of it running down the harbor would attract attention—or they might run aground in the shallow river and that would be the end of things. But the fog was concealment.

He watched the sampan girls. They stood barefoot on the small, highly polished afterdeck with the oars forming a constantly moving X across their chests. They faced forward, their feet moving in a confined yet rhythmical dance as they threw their full weight against the oars. They whispered softly in the language of the Haka.

"Tell them to scull faster," Hank said to Ying Fai.

"Maybe we can help," Louis said.

"No. That's an art. We'd only slow them down."

"They learn it from childhood," Merryweather said.

It was the first time Louis had heard him speak. "You're a Limey," he said, not trying to hide his surprise.

"Why not?"

"I thought you got along with these people."

"A zoo keeper has to do business with a gorilla but he doesn't lie down beside him and go to sleep."

"Thanks," Louis said simply. "Why did you come? Why did either one of you come?"

Hank and Merryweather looked at each other. For a moment they were lost for an exact answer and then, even in the dim light beneath the sampan canopy, they could see each other's smile.

"You know," Merryweather said slowly, "I've been asking myself that same question."

"You've got a fine wife," Hank said.

"Is she all right?"

Hank hesitated and when he spoke again his voice was barely audible. "Yeah . . . she's all right."

They lit cigarettes and smoked in silence for a time. Hank tried to study Louis' face, but it was difficult in the dim light and when their eyes met, he turned away. I want to know what kind of a man you are, he thought, and he knew instinctively that Louis was thinking the same thing. But why was he so quiet? Didn't he appreciate the risk they were all taking? Then as a black mass loomed up in the fog, Hank decided Louis had said all there was to say. And he liked Louis for his silence.

The black mass enlarged and became the dripping hull of the *Chicago*. Ying Fai paid off the sampan girls, and the men climbed quickly aboard. The decks were deserted.

"Ying Fai. Where do you think the crew is?"

"Ashore. Talking to the police. Impossible to heave anchor without them."

"Cut it free. I'll buy you a new one. Hoyt . . . can you follow a compass?"

"I can read an aircraft compass."

"On a ship it's just backward . . . but you'll get on to it. Stand here by the tiller. Steer the courses I give you. Ying Fai . . . light your damn joss stick and stay up in the bow with a lead line. Sing out in Cantonese when you mark less than two fathoms. Keep your mouth shut otherwise. Inspector . . . you know that Bofors pretty well by now?"

"Rather. I'm itching to give it a pop or two."

"You may get the chance. Go below now. Get the clips laid out and everything ready."

"Right."

Hank pressed a button on the bulkhead beside the companionway door. The diesel started and the noise of its exhaust reverberated through the fog. He lowered his arm. Ying Fai brought a machete down on the anchor line. The *Chicago* gathered way. Shielding his flashlight with his fingers, Hank spread the Canton River chart on the deck of the poop.

"Ever walk a tightrope, Hoyt?"

"I've been on one for over three months."

"You're on another one . . . and it's damn thin. Steer the courses I give you and sing out when you're on." Hank worked quickly with dividers and protractor. "Now steer one hundred and sixty degrees."

In a moment Louis said, "One hundred and sixty degrees it is."

The *Chicago's* movement through the fog brought droplets of moisture spattering down from the masts and rigging. Their faces became wet and soon their shirts were soaked. Now it was cool on the water. They shivered occasionally. Louis wiped a pool of water from the compass glass.

He said, "God, it's good to breathe free air again!"

"It isn't free yet. Don't kid yourself. This is their air and will be for a long ways. We're like a blindman trying to thread a needle."

"I'd just as soon not talk about needles."

"They give you a rough time?"

"Let's say they aren't tourist-conscious."

"Keep your eye on that compass and do your breathing later. This is a narrow river. It winds all over hell and gone and nobody in his right mind would try going down it at night . . . including a Chinese, which is our only hope. There are mud shoals and rocks on both sides . . . mostly unmarked. I don't know what the tide or the current really is, and this chart was made by the Japs in 1938. When the fog's like this the Chinese anchor right in midchannel, or anywhere else they happen to feel like. If we don't hit one of them we're just plain lucky."

"I'm the luckiest guy in the world."

"I agree with you. But we'll see. Frankly I'm getting old for this sort of thing. Now let her come five degrees to the left."

"Five degrees left."

The lights of the city, which had given substance to the fog, faded gradually. Now the *Chicago* was enclosed in a dank, impenetrable blackness, and the only assurance that she was moving at all was the breeze on their faces. Ying Fai had long since been swallowed in the gloom. Even the mainmast, a few yards beyond the fore end of the tiller, was invisible.

"You're a good navigator," Louis said, his voice almost secretive in the fog.

"So far . . . for a guy who never went to school."

"Your name's Henry Lee, right?"

"How did you know?"

"They showed me a picture of you with Jane."

"Oh. . . ."

"They don't miss many tricks. It wasn't easy to look at." Louis kept his eyes on the compass. Occasionally he moved the tiller slightly and for a time it seemed his only concern was the course.

From where he stood by the break of the poop Hank could see only the back of his head and sometimes a quarter of his face. Louis was shorter than he had pictured him—and he was heavier. There was strength in his shoulders and even now there was a defiant look in the way he held his head, despite the fact that it was tipped down. If he had never steered a boat in his life, there was no indication of uncertainty. He was doing a nearly perfect job. Louis Hoyt was a good man to have around, he thought. He was the kind who would try anything—and usually succeed. In a way, Hank wished it could have been otherwise.

"This compass must have belonged to Marco Polo," Louis said.

"Ying Fai prefers it. They don't like change."

"Is this his junk?"

"No. She's mine."

"Why don't you fix her up? At least buy a new compass."

"I haven't been aboard in a long time . . . I sort of lost interest in junks and all that goes with them."

"So? What interests you now? Don't mind my questions. It's just that I haven't talked to a real human being in a long time."

"If I had my way I'd settle for a place to live in peace . . . and a flock of kids. You get that way after a while."

"Not me."

"What stops you?"

"It beats me. The same reason I went to China, I guess. The same reason people climb mountains. They want to get to the top and look around."

"If you get out of this . . . what are you going to do?"

"Climb another mountain . . . somewhere."

"Now steer one hundred and fifty degrees. We ought to be working around Haddington Island."

"One hundred and fifty."

A light rain began to fall. The rain was cold and it washed out to fog until the figure of Ying Fai reappeared standing in the bow. He was swinging his lead line regularly. Once he called out two fathoms and Hank changed course ten degrees to the right. Merryweather came on deck and stood for a time with the rain dripping off the end of his long nose. He climbed to the poop and stood by the taffrail watching what he could see of the *Chicago's* wake. He listened carefully and then told Hank that if any vessel was following them, it must be a long way back. "And I think I'm catching a bloody cold," he sniffed.

"Go below and try to get some sleep. We might need a sharp eye on the Bofors in the morning."

"Call me when you want some relief."

"I will."

The rain beat down harder as they entered what Hank's calculations told him must be Blenheim Pass. He changed the course to forty degrees and slipped below for a cigar. He stuck it in his mouth unlighted and then returned to the deck carrying two large fisherman hats. He placed one on Louis' head. The rain made a drumming sound on the varnished straw.

"It may drive you crazy but it will keep your head dry," he said.

"Thanks. Thanks for a lot of things . . . my life especially."

"Don't mention it. Just watch that compass. In about an hour we should be in the Canton River. It's wider there."

"I've been thinking," Louis said. "I've been thinking about that picture. Is Jane in love with you?"

"What makes you ask a question like that?" Hank bent over the chart and switched on his flashlight. He tried to concentrate on the fathom marks and the dotted areas which vaguely indicated the innumerable shoals. According to time they must be abreast of Wampoa Island and the course must be changed again. And suddenly the meanderings of the channel infuriated him. First Bar Island, Junk Pass . . . Escape Creek . . . then Tseki Creek . . . stay to the eastern side of the channel then, where the current had a better swipe at the land. Then hope some more. By dawn the hills on Anung Island should be abeam with Tai Kok Tau to the west. Narrow in there . . . an armed launch or a gunboat would have it easy picking up the *Chicago* . . . but after that the Si Kiang Delta and lots of room. . . .

"I asked you a question," Louis said.

"I heard you the first time."

"She is then?"

"Why don't you keep your mind on the compass?"

"My eyes are taking care of that. They saw something else because they were trained to see. You know my business?"

"You take pictures. The only trouble is you take them in the wrong places. Now why don't you—"

"I was trained to take pictures and to look at them . . . carefully. We learn to see a lot of things in a photograph the ordinary person never notices . . . little things. It's part of the racket. During the war we could spot a German ammunition dump on an aerial shot from twenty-five thousand feet and figure out when they last used it. That picture of you and Jane was easy. I know her expressions pretty well and it was a good photograph. There must have been a lot of light in the place. It showed her eyes. Now will you answer my question?"

"Why don't you ask her?"

"I don't think I'll have to."

A heavy overcast delayed the day, and the *Chicago* was abeam a wrecked steamer in Chuen Pi Channel before Ying Fai walked aft, moving stiff-legged along the deck and holding the coiled lead line in his hand. Beyond the bow the whole Si Kiang Delta spread like a rusted steel plate beneath the brooding sky. Ying Fai glanced at the sails furled along the booms and Hank nodded, for he was achingly tired and even speech was an effort. He awakened Merryweather, who sneezed, but rolled quickly out of his bunk, and the three of them labored at the main halyard winch while Louis remained at the tiller. It took a long time, but they set main, fore and mizzen. The *Chicago* took a bone in her teeth and, gathering speed, heeled well over in the freshening breeze.

Merryweather relieved Louis at the tiller. Ying Fai crawled into his cuddy and was at once asleep. Hank and Louis descended to the cabin.

"Want something to eat?"

"No. I'm saving up for a steak at Tweedie's."

"You'd go right back there?"

"Sure. He may be a crook, but he serves the best food in Hong Kong."

"I hope you get it."

They crawled into the bunks without another word. In spite of his weariness, Hank could not sleep. He looked across the cabin at Louis, wondering how he could already be breathing so regularly. He could not understand him. There lay a man who had deliberately stood on the edge of the cliff, even leaned over—and it seemed not to have affected him in the least. Less than twelve hours ago he was as good as dead. He had very little money if any. And he stood to lose a wonderful wife. Yet he slept. He slept without apparent concern when he had been told at least ten times they were still a long way from being out of the woods. Either you have no brains or no nerves, Hank thought. No . . . it isn't lack of brains. God takes care of people like you . . . and if He's busy somebody else does. Damn fools like Hank Lee. Hoyt, you're quite a guy. I could have used a man like you when I first came out here. But not now. I've had it . . . and I've got a hunch your wife has, too.

After a long time, listening to the muffled sound of the diesel, Hank fell asleep.

The wind increased and by early afternoon the Si Kiang Delta was flecked to the horizon with whitecaps. The sky became an even heavier gray and the intermittent rain squalls formed solid marching pillars connecting the sky with the water. In the manner of his race, Ying Fai slept only a few hours and then came on deck appearing entirely refreshed. He insisted on taking the tiller and now, standing on the poop, Merryweather had to look down at Ying Fai to convince himself he was not in the North Sea. For he shivered and sneezed almost continuously. It was inconceivable that he could be so cold in China in September, and yet there was no argument with the chart.

An hour before the *Chicago* had passed Lintin Island. Some ten miles ahead Merryweather could make out the heavy shadow of Lan Tao, severed in places by rain squalls. He was pleased with the way the *Chicago* boiled through the water under both sail and diesel, although she shuddered with energy from bow to stern as the heavier gusts struck her sails, and she heeled far over until her scuppers foamed with swift running water. Busy at the tiller purchase, Ying Fai glanced nervously at the straining sheets. He wanted to lower a batten or two, and so take a reef, but Merryweather insisted they hang on. For he had been looking aft ever since Lintin Island melted into the horizon and what he had seen caused him to forget his cold. At first uncertain, he could no longer persuade himself that the single object astern of the *Chicago* was simply another junk going in the opposite direction. Each time it vanished in a rain squall and then reappeared, it became larger, and it imitated the *Chicago's* course as if they were connected with a long string. The *Chicago*, he thought, must be making a good ten knots, possibly more—and still the object closed the distance. Balancing himself against the heel of the deck, Merryweather swung down to the companionway and went below. He shook Hank Lee to wakefulness.

"I think there's a bloody motor gunboat hounding us!"

Hank sat up and rubbed his eyes. He turned to look out the stern windows. "It doesn't surprise me. How close?"

"Four miles, perhaps. But he's coming up quite fast. I should imagine we're for it."

Hank swung his feet to the deck and pulled on his pants.

"What's the penalty for murdering an Englishman in Hong Kong? Burning at the stake?"

"In certain cases I think they might let you off rather lightly."

"This bastard's name is Stoker. Maybe I'll just kick him in the belly. Wake up our friend. He might be interested."

Merryweather shook Louis. He opened one eye and frowned.

"Sorry, old boy. It appears there may be some skeet shooting after a bit."

Louis rolled over and buried his face in the pillow. He mumbled an unintelligible protest and Merryweather shook him again.

"How would you like to sink the Communist Navy?"

Louis turned at once and raised himself on one elbow. "Where are they?"

"Right on our doorstep. Step lively."

Hank knelt on the bench beneath the stern windows. Without taking his eyes from the view he reached behind him and his fingers sought a cigar from the table humidor. He clamped it between his teeth and studied the horizon carefully.

"She's an MTB. She'll do twenty knots if her injectors are clean, which, from the looks of the smoke she's making, isn't so. Where are we?"

"Coming up on Lan Tao," Merryweather said.

"How far off?"

"Six miles . . . perhaps five now. We're bucking right along."

"Two hours . . . maybe two hours and a half to British water. He'll close the gap. We'll have to fight." Hank looked at the end of his cigar and sighed. "Son of a bitch!"

"You're a sad-looking man," Louis said. "Is it that bad?"

"It isn't good. We can't slug it out with him. He carries six machine guns and a four-incher on deck. Let's just hope he hasn't had much practice lately." Hank turned his back to the windows and for a moment he sat looking at his big hands thoughtfully, frowning as if the strength in them repelled him. There was no enthusiasm in his manner when at last he stood up and said, "He's about in range. We might as well get in the first punch."

Merryweather pulled back the rug and Hank lifted the hatch in the deck. They descended to the Bofors.

"I told Ying Fai to hold straight for Lan Tao," Merryweather said.

"Good. We'll drop a few in front of their bow. Maybe they'll get discouraged."

They pulled open the stern doors and latched them fast. There were two metal seats on each side of the Bofors. Hank sat down in the left seat and placed his feet on the trigger pedals. Merryweather sat down in the right seat.

"Well, I'll be damned," Louis said.

"I picked this little gadget up cheap," Hank said, rotating the elevation crank until the grill sight descended on the gunboat. "See those clips over there . . . four shells in each. You stand just behind Merryweather and drop a clip in the loader guide after we use this one. Use the clips painted yellow until I tell you different. I haven't done this in a long time and I need tracers. . . ."

Without taking his hands from the Bofors, Hank worked his cigar thoughtfully from one side of his mouth to the other. "Now give me about five degrees left traverse, Merryweather. If we miss deliberately we'll at least know on which side we're missing."

Merryweather turned the traverse crank and Hank pulled the firing selector lever off "SAFE."

"I think we'll just take this first one very easy," Hank said, so quietly he seemed to be talking to himself. He moved the firing selector lever from "AUTO FIRE" to "SINGLE FIRE." "This could go on a long time and we haven't got all the ammunition in the world . . . had a hell of a time buying it, and it's plenty expensive. We can get fancy after we get good."

The *Chicago* heeled under a gust and the gunboat moved out of the sight. Hank waited patiently. "We could use a deck that would stay level," he said. "However—" He leaned forward slightly, his eyes still on the sight. The gunboat was rapidly growing larger.

"This should be a rude shock to him," Merryweather said.

"Jesus, I'm tired," Hank sighed. Then he depressed the firing pedal.

The Bofors roared and the compartment filled with smoke and the smell of cordite. But in a moment the smoke was sucked out the stern doors and they watched the gunboat anxiously. An incandescent streak of light cut across the gray sky. They saw it penetrate the water a considerable distance in front of the gunboat.

"We're a little hasty. He's not close enough. I should have waited."

"He's changing course!" Merryweather yelled.

"Now he's going to be rude. But if he keeps evading he'll never close in."

A plume of water exploded a hundred yards behind the *Chicago* and far to windward.

"He's a bum shot," Louis said.

"He'll improve."

As the gunboat swung back on course, Hank pressed the trigger pedal again. The streak of light passed directly across the gunboat's bow.

"You hit him!"

"No. But we're getting closer."

The gunboat began to swerve and Hank pressed the trigger pedal twice. Louis dropped in a new clip of shells. They waited. Suddenly a fountain exploded directly astern of the *Chicago*. They were drenched with water. Merryweather wiped his eyes and tried to follow the swerving gunboat with his traverse crank. "Close," he said.

"I think the time has come to get fancy." Hank moved the selector lever to "AUTO FIRE." He pressed the trigger pedal and held it down. The Bofors barked four times in rapid succession. Before the smoke was gone Louis placed another clip in the loader. A shell exploded just off the *Chicago*'s stern. Simultaneously a sharp rattling sound shook the whole vessel.

"Is there a first-aid kit on this junk?" Louis asked.

"One more like that and we'll need more than a Band-Aid!" Hank pressed the trigger pedal again. "Load faster, Hoyt!"

They lost count of the clips, and the shells made almost a steady stream as they clanked into the ejector trough and slid overboard into the sea. Then suddenly the gunboat became lost in a rain squall. Hank sat back in the metal seat and for the first time lit his cigar. He blew out the smoke with a sound that was audible even above the thrashing propeller and looked unhappily at Louis.

"You're one hell of a lot of trouble."

"How many times do you want me to say thanks?"

Hank was about to look away in disgust when he saw Louis move his left hand behind him. There was a large splotch of blood on the deck. "What's the matter with your hand?"

"It's leaking a little."

Hank swung off the seat and reached for Louis' arm. From the elbow down it was covered with blood.

"Why didn't you say something?"

"I did. You were busy."

"Christ. How could you load with that?"

"You can do anything if you're interested and I was."

"Sit down before you fall down. Inspector. Bulkhead . . . foot of my bunk . . . there's an aid kit. He took a chunk of steel right across the artery. Hand the kit down, then see if Ying Fai's all right. Sing out when the MTB comes out of the squall."

"Right."

Merryweather climbed through the hatch to the cabin and handed down a large metal aid kit. Kneeling beside Louis, Hank quickly applied a tourniquet, then poured sulfa powder on the open gash. "It isn't too bad . . . but I think it cut the muscle."

Louis smiled weakly. All of the color had gone from his face. "Thanks, Doctor. Like you say . . . I'm a hell of a lot of trouble. Why don't you just shove me out the stern? No one would ever know the difference."

"I'm getting you back to Jane . . . in one piece . . . if it's the last thing I ever do."

"It may be. About this taking me back to Jane. You aren't a very smart guy."

"That's an understatement." Hank carefully laid an antiseptic pack on the wound.

"You don't know much about people . . . especially women."

Hank tore off three strips of adhesive and bound the pack.

"Yes, indeed."

"I do. I made sort of a hobby of them. You think you can just deliver me to Jane and everything will be the same?"

"Why not? And remember, we aren't there yet."

"It wouldn't be the same because Jane isn't the nursemaid kind. A woman like Jane puts one man on a pedestal and sticks with him. If he falls off, she loses interest. She can't help it. It's a quality, not a fault. No matter how I said it, I could never convince her the best thing would be sticking with me. Not now. I'm not that good a liar."

"Try some of your fancy poems."

"I will . . . and a lot of other things. But the hitch is she's heard most of them."

"Make up some new ones."

"I'll do that, too. But I don't think it will do much good because I can't make up a new Louis Hoyt."

"Does the arm hurt now?"

"Damn right."

"Here's a pain pill. Swallow it."

"Nuts. It'll make me dopey and we have a lot to do. Let me change places with Merryweather. I can work that traverse crank with my right hand."

"We'll see how you feel. Take it easy."

Merryweather's feet appeared in the hatch, then he slid down the ladder.

"Squall's clearing."

Hank helped Louis to his feet, but he made his way unaided to the right-hand seat of the Bofors.

"You load," Hank said to Merryweather.

They waited quietly. The only sound was the muffled slopping of the propeller just beneath their feet and the steady pounding of the Lister-Blackstone in the engine room. Hank's cigar had gone out while he dressed Louis' arm. Now he relit it and they looked at each other across the still-hot barrel of the Bofors. Louis smiled, but Hank found he could not meet his eyes. He tried to concentrate on the sights. The MTB would come charging out of the rain when it cleared a little more—and she would be much closer. Close enough probably to use their machine guns. That could be it. If they used incendiaries the wooden *Chicago* would be a bonfire in a few minutes. Hank wished that he could get mad—as he had done with Fernand Rocha. But it was hard to get mad at an impersonal thing which lurked behind a curtain of rain. Soldier of fortune, huh, Jane? I think the guy you're talking about is just on the other side of this barrel. He isn't scared. I am. I hate this. Especially the waiting.

"How is Ying Fai?" Hank asked, not taking his eyes from the sights.

"Wet . . ." Merryweather said, "but grinning. He's a comical chap. Damned if he hasn't run up your Yank flag. I didn't think you'd mind if I hung the Union Jack beside it."

"I don't mind at all."

They waited silently. The rain began to clear just as the *Chicago* rounded the tip of Lan Tao. First the rocks at the end of the island became visible and then slowly the diagonal shaft of rain withdrew to the west, carried on the strong wind. As the horizon became clearer the muzzle of the Bofors followed the edge of the rain . . . seeking its target.

"Where the hell is he?" Louis said.

"Watch it," Hank said. "He'll be close. Load fast. Those blue shells . . . they're HE. If we're quick enough we can blow him out of the water. Otherwise . . ."

But they could not find the gunboat. There was nothing on the sea except a shaggy patch of rain far to the west.

"He *can't* be behind the island," Hank said.

"Maybe he's abeam or passed on ahead of us."

"He better not be. No . . . Ying Fai would have turned."

"Look!" Merryweather was pointing at the patch of rain. As it slid along the horizon it left a brown smudge where it had been. A small dark object remained at one end of the smudge.

"It's him! We hit him way back there! He's got a fire!"

"I think that's smoke all right," Hank said, climbing out of his seat. "It looks like oil smoke. The wind is keeping it down."

"I wish we had some binoculars."

"There's a pair in the cabin. Let's go on deck."

They helped Louis to the poop and stood there handing the glasses back and forth. The brown smudge had spread for several miles across the horizon and in a short time the black object vanished entirely.

"He's below the horizon," Louis said.

"Or sunk," Merryweather said. "In our Navy this calls for a drink."

"Yeah," Hank said wearily. "I got some grog called Old Granddad."

17

It was an easy walk from the naval attaché's office to the Peak Tramway. Leaning forward against the incline of Garden Road, Hank passed St. John's Cathedral and crossed the street to the tramway station. All around him in the evening there was no evidence of China. For in this small part of Hong Kong the lawns were a soft green and the buildings were elderly. There was a broad parade ground and a cricket field behind him and fat pigeons waddled in front of the cathedral. Mustachioed young British officers, their shoulders held stiffly in a guardsman's brace, strode out smartly en route to their sundowners. The stone walls along the sidewalks of Garden Road were shadowed green with moss, for the British had made this part of Hong Kong a bit of England. There was smugness. There was stability. And there was peace.

Hank bought a ticket and boarded the immaculate cable car. He took off his hat and linen coat and loosened his tie. As the tram rose quietly on the almost vertical tracks, passing between palms and ferns and overhanging tropical plants, the air became cooler and he breathed gratefully of it. It had been a long time since he had made this quiet journey—not so long in days, perhaps, but a lifetime otherwise. He sat back against the wooden seat, his big hands still in his lap, and he thought how long it had been. Now a new life was beginning as surely as it did the night in Balabac Strait. He wanted time to think about it.

The tram stopped briefly at four way stations, in the course of its steep ascent. The late shoppers dismounted. Their market bags were heavy and they ignored the view. Nor did Hank look behind him. He wanted to save the view, as he had done so often before, taking it in all at once, standing on the Peak in the cool breeze which had never failed him there, and thinking of this new life. Looking back on an old life wasn't very often possible. Usually it would be lost in a haze of associations, both angry and affectionate, but here it would be spread out like a detailed map.

By the time the tram reached the last station at the Peak, Hank was the only passenger. He walked slowly up the short incline which led from the station to Victoria Gap. Here, as if he stood in the basket of a balloon, he could see all of the old life. He leaned against a stone wall and looked toward the open sea. And from this altitude he could see the fingers of the wind as it ruffled the water before the islands of Aplichau, Lamma and even distant Lo Chau. He saw the smooth calms in the lee of the islands and he saw the microscopic specks which were the fishing junks bound in for Aberdeen Bay. And beyond, where the East China Sea met the sky, the horizon was already streaked with purple. He thought, That life is done and I am sorry in a way.

He turned and, placing his arms on the wall, looked almost straight down at the city. Here, on the Peak, there was wind, yet, below, the cooking fires of Wanchai and Lascar Road rose straight up and, meeting cooler air, spread out in a thin flat coverlet over the two extremes of the city. Stoker was down there, sweating. And he was going to lose weight. The food was simple in a British jail. Exposing him was better than kicking him in the belly.

There were the ships loading in the harbor, their funnels shining in the last of the sun, and they were no longer desirable. The Lee Empire died in infancy, Hank thought, and I am not sorry. Now there would not be a great stone building frowning over the harbor. There would never be a brass plate, or a bank, or a teak-paneled office where an old man could count his money and tell himself he was a great man, and maybe once in a while think about his sins. All of these had become sour things—now that the exile was almost over. If the world belonged to the leaders and being a leader meant fighting twenty-four hours a day, then the leaders could have it. Henry Lee was going home.

Plans? There weren't any final plans—only ideas, and that should be enough for a man who could stand alone and broke in this same place and, after less than ten years, conquer such a city. Joe and Lucy and Billy were the plans . . . they were the Empire. They would know what it was like to make their own way, once they had an education, and if the boys had to begin with a gravel truck, that would be all right, too. Hank smiled. They were over there on the other side of the harbor now, in Kowloon— eating their supper and talking about what they would do when they got to the States—as they had done for a week. Billy had the best idea. Live in the Southwest—Arizona or New Mexico, where there might be a cowboy or an Indian. Why not—even if the Indian drove a Cadillac and the cowboy couldn't sing? There was still enough money left to buy a ranch— a small one, which might some day be made bigger. With a lot of hard work. But not too big. A different kind of empire. Where a man could wake up in the morning and worry about the weather instead of other men. The mountains in the distance would be blue there, too, turning black at this time of day—but they wouldn't be the angry, tired, old mountains of China. Hank Lee could start living and maybe some of the loneliness would go away. Work . . . read books to get smart . . . and forget what it was like to be a roughneck, which was sometimes another name for a leader.

He was looking at Kowloon and the gray mass of the Peninsula Hotel when he heard a voice behind him.

"If there were a door . . . I'd knock."

He turned to see Jane. She was standing uncertainly on the path which led from the tram station, and for a moment he could only think how the red twilight revealed new freckles he had never seen before.

"Hello."

It had been almost a week since he had seen her. Now, as the breeze ruffled her short hair, he wanted more than anything else to reach out and touch it. "I thought you'd gone home," he said.

"I started. I packed my bags and at least I made the airport. But I just couldn't get on the airplane. I turned around and came back like a bad penny. That's what I called myself anyway, while I sat in the hotel and tried to figure out what's wrong with me. Among other things, I discovered I can't pretend. I never have been able to." She looked down at the city. "Louis said he was glad I didn't try."

"Where is he?"

"He got on the airplane. He said he was going to climb a mountain and that he'd write and tell me where it was, and if it was very high, and if the view was good. I hate to admit it, but when we finally kissed each other good-by . . . I think we were both relieved. Louis is a wonderful person. I hope he finds what he wants on his mountains. He's not sure just what it is, although he does have a name for it . . . his sweet beyond."

"It's none of my business, but I'm sort of curious to know if you still love him." Waiting for her answer he instinctively pulled a cigar from his shirt pocket. He held it a moment, rolling it between his big fingers. I will light it, he thought, if she says anything I can't believe.

"Yes. I'll always love Louis. Unfortunately, there's a difference between loving someone and being in love. I've found out there's quite a difference."

She was not looking at him as he deliberately flipped the cigar into the depths below. Instead she seemed lost in the view. "It's beautiful up here," she said in a voice that became almost a whisper. "I thought I was tired of thinking. But here you can see so many things."

"Yeah. You can. That's why I come. I wish you had let me know you were still in Hong Kong."

"I wasn't ever going to let you know. But this afternoon I had a talk with Maxine . . . girl talk, I suppose you'd call it. She said I should try to find you up here. She's more generous than I would have been."

"I'll have to thank her."

Then they were silent for a long time—much longer than Hank thought could have been possible. But as they leaned on the wall, their silence said many things. And they watched the lights of the city grow stronger in the dusk.

"See that aircraft carrier?" he said finally. "She's here for crew rest and recreation, along with those two cruisers. They're part of the Seventh Fleet. I saw the admiral yesterday and he happens to be a very understanding guy. He restored me to duty for one day . . . the day we brought Louis back. It makes things a lot easier."

"How?"

"I can stand court-martial under Article 85. It seems we did something the Navy or the State Department couldn't do and that helps my case. The trial takes place in Yokosuka next month. If everything works out all right, I'll have a passport again."

"Isn't that against your principles?"

"Not now. It will be good to belong somewhere again. I'm a little late, but I finally got through my thick head what it's like to have a real home."

"You're going back to the Navy?"

"No. The Navy doesn't want forty-five-year-olds these days. So I'll probably get a straight discharge."

"Then what?"

"I want to build something in my own country . . . maybe pay back a little of what I stole when I was thinking in a different way. You know anything about ranching?"

"An uncle of mine once had a cow."

"Was it an American cow?"

"Of course."

"That's the kind I'm going to have. Only they're going to be steers. . . ." He turned to look at her and his hand moved along the wall until he touched hers. "I got plenty to learn, Jane . . . and a lot of changes to make inside. It won't be easy and it's going to take a long time. I'm sort of wondering if you'd be interested in looking after Billy and Lucy while I'm trying to straighten things out. Maybe after a while, if you wanted . . . the job could be permanent."

She accepted his hand and held it a moment, still looking down at the city. "I didn't seek you out on the rebound, Hank. Because what Louis and I had really wasn't killed by either one of us. It lived much longer than it had any honest right to live. It died suddenly, but quite peacefully. That's why both of us will always cherish the memories of what we had. Lots of people try to save a marriage by pumping false vitality into something which is already dead. They pretend. Louis calls such arrangements "marriage Munichs," and I think he's right. That way, what must have been at least affection and respect in the beginning, can so easily become hatred . . . and then even the memories are poisoned. We didn't want it that way and it isn't that way. Do you understand what I'm trying to say?"

"I sure do. I guess it isn't easy for anyone to change their life completely. But I'm going to give it a try, even though I'll need a lot of help. I never have liked to ask for help, but how about my employment offer? Will you think it over?"

"How much time do I have?"

"Take a couple of years if you feel like it. The job will keep . . . and so will I."

"I told you I couldn't pretend, so I don't think it will take that long, Hank."

Standing together, their shoulders touching, they watched the night envelop the city. And below them, indifferent to their closeness, the British troops drank lukewarm beer in their NAAFI and the officers put their feet on wicker stools in their club and stared at their bony knees and drank whisky. And they did not speak of China or of the Chinese who were all around them, pressing on their sanctuaries. They spoke of home, which was England, and they listened to the tolling of the news from London on the wireless, and they had another whisky and another beer before they messed. And above them in the houses along the cliffs, the old China hands, the Pukka-sahibs and the new rich civilians of every nation sometimes looked down from their verandas and, breathing the cool air, pitied the city. And below, beneath the smoke, on Central Street and on Lascar Road, and in the deep crevasses of the inclined lesser streets, the night softened all ugliness. But there was light, all colors of light to stimulate the eyes, and there were the noises of a thousand things mixing with the babel of Cantonese and Pekingese, and Shanghai lilt and Indian. In Wanchai and near the Star Ferries, American sailors in whites moved like snowflakes through the streets, seeking out the darker ones because they were young, and walking straighter when they saw the shore patrols.

Across the harbor in Kowloon, Marty Gates entered the Peninsula Hotel through the back way and surveyed the prospects in the lobby. He poised like a hunter beside the telephone desk, studying all those he knew and did not know who sat in the lobby, because his brief case was empty. And because he was thirsty. He saw Madame Dupree, whose hair was strawberry, and he saw Icky, whose hair was white. He saw Major Leith-Phipps sitting beside a pillar, and he knew instinctively that he, too, was hunting. And he saw Maxine Chan. She was wearing a green dress which nearly matched the palm beside her and her face was alone. He went to her carrying his brief case, and stood before her, asking with his eyes. And when she smiled he sat down, carefully placing his empty brief case on the edge of the table where it could easily be seen. And she bought him a drink.

In Tweedie's Place, Gunner and Big Matt sat at the long table toying with their beers. And their faces were mournful. For Icky was dead as far as they were concerned—without benediction. His loss was disgraceful, for he was a victim of woman, and the long table was quiet and forlorn. Tweedie sat at the end of the table, massaging his long neck, and there were unpredictable groups of minutes when he stared at the ceiling rather than acknowledge Icky's empty chair. Big Matt started to hum a few bars of "Mandalay," but his voice faltered and the long table was quiet again.

In the Princess Ballroom the band played music as low as the lights, and Merryweather held the Chinese girl very closely as he glided across the polished floor. Potts was in reliable health and his chief, abandoning all reserve, had said two words—"Well done." And so when in his circle of the floor, he passed Rodman standing watchfully in the half-light, he pressed his long nose against the girl's hair and smiled.

And in the temple by the market of Pei Ho Street, Dak Lai sat at her lacquer table and listened to the rhythmic beating of the gongs which were so familiar to her, and breathed of the joss sticks, and thoughtfully examined the thing which was not familiar to her. It was a flat board covered with puzzling characters and with this present from Brother Predominant had come a heart-shaped board on three legs. And the writing across both of them said "ouija," and she could make no sense of it. So finally she set it aside and listened to the gongs and permitted her cigarette to burn out. She closed her ancient eyes and her neck retracted into her gown in the manner of a turtle. And in this position, motionless, she listened to her memories.